Performing Opposition

Modern Theater and the Scandalized Audience

NEIL BLACKADDER

Westport, Connecticut
London

Library of Congress Cataloging-in-Publication Data

Blackadder, Neil Martin, 1963–
   Performing opposition : modern theater and the scandalized audience / Neil
Blackadder.
     p. cm.
   Includes bibliographical references and index.
   ISBN 0–275–98056–1 (alk. paper)
     1. European drama—20th century—History and criticism. 2. European drama—19th
century—History and criticism. 3. Experimental theater—Europe—History—20th
century. 4. Experimental theater—Europe—History—19th century. 5. Theater
audiences—Europe—History—20th century. 6. Theater audiences—Europe—History—
19th century. I. Title.
   PN1851.B59   2003
   809.2′04—dc21   2002044967

British Library Cataloguing in Publication Data is available.

Library of Congress Catalog Card Number: 2002044967
ISBN: 0–275–98056–1

First published in 2003

Praeger Publishers, 88 Post Road West, Westport, CT 06881
An imprint of Greenwood Publishing Group, Inc.
www.praeger.com

Printed in the United States of America

The paper used in this book complies with the
Permanent Paper Standard issued by the National
Information Standards Organization (Z39.48–1984).

10 9 8 7 6 5 4 3 2 1

Copyright Acknowledgments

The author and publisher gratefully acknowledge permission to reprint excerpts from the
following:

Joseph Holloway's *Abbey Theatre: A Selection from his Unpublished Journal, "Impressions of a
Dublin Playgoer,"* ed. Robert Hogan and Michael O'Neil. © 1967 by Southern Illinois
University Press.
Lady Augusta Gregory's *Our Irish Theatre.* 1913. Oxford UP, 1977.

For Natania

Contents

Acknowledgments

A version of the Introduction appeared in *Theatre History Studies* 20 (2000), and I gratefully acknowledge permission to incorporate that material in the present work. Thanks also to the editors of *New Theatre Quarterly* who published an article based on chapter 1. Dagmar Kicherer of the Baden-Baden Stadtarchiv assisted me greatly by carrying out some crucial research and xeroxing on my behalf. I presented a good deal of the research for *Performing Opposition* at conferences of the American Society for Theatre Research, the International Federation for Theatre Research, and the Modern Language Association of America, and am grateful for all the helpful comments I received.

I also wish to thank John Clum and Michael Goldman for several years of engaged and valuable mentoring, and the many colleagues and friends who have contributed to my thinking about audience protests, including Steve Fineberg, Penny Gold, Vicki Mahaffey, Richard Riddell, Anjie Rosga, Kirsten Shepherd-Barr, Helen Solterer, and Reid Smith.

The person I've talked with the most about the topic of this book is Natania Rosenfeld, whom I thank with all my heart for that and so much more.

Preface

In a review of the tumultuous premiere of Bertolt Brecht and Kurt Weill's *The Rise and Fall of the City of Mahagonny* at the Leipzig Opera House in 1930, critic Alfred Polgar mused about such incidents with both humor and acuity:

Theater scandals are tremendously stimulating. It's good to see people ready to come to blows over the theoretical questions which art brings up—or throws down—and getting so worked up that they're beside themselves. There's nothing to be won in such battles in the theater (battles which . . . remind one of religious wars) other than the upper hand, and yet they're fought with venomous effort, as if prizes were up for grabs. . . .

And the festive character that goes along with every gathering of paying theatergoers all at once reveals surprisingly malicious traits. Perfectly healthy people are overcome by a shouting-fever, and it's contagious; they turn red in the face and whistling comes out of them; suddenly, innocuous souls conceive and admit to an opinion, instead of calmly waiting for one to be delivered to them in the morning paper.[1]

The following study grows out of my own interest in the same striking features of theater scandals that fascinated Polgar. On such occasions, those spectators who take exception to the work do not wait until after its presentation to complain about it—they perform their opposition then and there. In this book I examine the counter-performances of affronted spectators against several European plays of the late nineteenth and early twentieth centuries.

These counter-performances by opponents almost always induce other spectators who disagree with them to give vent to their contrary views, resulting in the battles Polgar compares to religious wars. Polgar wonders at the contradiction between theatergoers' intense engagement in battle and the insubstantiality of the spoils. Certainly neither side stands to win anything tangible, but often there is more at stake than merely which group will dominate during the encounter. Those who protest against a new play feel strongly that such work ought not to be produced, because, for instance, they consider its subject matter or language inappropriate for the stage, or they believe the ideas it expresses pose a threat to social order, or they regard the piece as disrespectful toward some members of their society. The questions raised by *Mahagonny* are not simply theoretical, but moral and above all political, and while neither the opponents nor the supporters of Brecht and Weill's work could score a concrete victory in the political realm by demonstrating during opening night, the confrontation between them revealed prevailing attitudes about far more than just theater. Polgar does capture well the key differences between a regular performance and one that turns into a scandal: in the former, a sociable mood among calm, orderly spectators; in the latter, acrimony and unruliness among impassioned demonstrators.

When Polgar used the term "theater scandal" in German (*Theaterskandal*), he followed common practice in that language. I choose to employ "theater scandal" with the same meaning, even though that usage is less well established in English. (Martin Esslin, for one, has used the English term in this way in describing the premiere of *Mahagonny* as "a first-class scandal, one of the most memorable in the history of the German theatre."[2]) One of the Oxford English Dictionary's definitions of scandal is "Offence to moral feeling or sense of decency." The plays I examine did cause, or give, scandal in that sense, but I apply the term to the incident itself—to the clash between a performance on the one hand, and a group of spectators protesting against that performance on the other. Thus the scandal consists not just of the fact that a certain number of people were scandalized by the performance—the OED's most pertinent definition of the verb scandalize reads "To horrify or shock by some supposed violation of morality or propriety"—but also of their enactment of opposition to the supposed violation. "Scandal" used in this way suggests at once cause and effects. And as Polgar's remarks emphasize, very often the primary conflict is augmented by the actions of other spectators who—sometimes in concert with the actors—defend the performance by opposing the protesters' protests. Many others before and after Polgar likened theater scandals to battles. A theater scandal thus entails a perceived affront that provokes a demonstration of opposition that itself generates a counterdemonstration.

I propose that theater scandals represent a distinct category of event, one that is less self-evident than it appears. A collective demonstration during a theater production seemingly manifests with force and clarity the unfavorable reaction of a group of spectators. But an auditorium protest against an on-stage performance can never altogether position itself as antagonistic to the spectacle it aims to deprecate, because the counter-performance becomes part of the performance. And much of the oppositional behavior I examine reveals itself as qualified and ambiguous. Many of the protests were premeditated rather than spontaneous. When scandalized spectators had to fight an auditorium battle against other audience members, they often exaggerated their indignation. Also, evidence abounds of the protesters' complicity in the uproar: clearly many of them wished to participate in a theater scandal, and enjoyed doing so.

The incidents I explore—triggered by first productions of plays by Gerhart Hauptmann, Alfred Jarry, J. M. Synge, Sean O'Casey, and Brecht—all took place between the 1880s and the 1930s, during a key transitional phase in the evolution of normative audience response in the theater. In the Introduction, I outline the significance of that phase in the context of theater history. During the nineteenth century, the behavior of audiences in the western non-musical theater grew increasingly subdued, and for the better part of the twentieth century, spectators sat quietly in the dark, not applauding, let alone speaking or shouting, until the end of the performance. Thus when what we call modern theater began in the 1880s, norms of behavior were shifting toward, but did not yet dictate, unprecedented restraint. The scandals I examine stood out as exceptional occurrences, when spectators overstepped the prevailing bounds of seemly behavior in order to express their outrage. The period I focus on represents the heyday of the theater scandal, when circumstances best lent themselves to such clashes. For the most part, in western theater's prior history, demonstrative expression of disapproval or approval by theater audiences was customary; and in the post-war era, scandals comparable to those I study occurred quite rarely, for reasons I suggest in the Afterword. That is the historical framework within which I investigate modern theater scandals. I argue that protests against new plays of the late nineteenth and early twentieth centuries constituted acts of resistance to the—ultimately inexorable—transition toward a more passive form of spectatorship.

The label usually attached to the incidents I explore is "riot," but as Marc Baer remarks in his study of the Old Price Riots in London in 1809, "The term *riot* has often been over-used by theatre historians in much the same way social and political historians have equated crowd with riot."[3] The Old Price Riots led to considerable property damage, and during another well-known incident, the Astor Place riot in New York in 1849, over twenty people died, so that in both those instances riot accurately describes the intensity of the disorder. Applying the same term to the uproar accompanying the first performances of *Mahagonny*, or to the 1907 protests against Synge's *The Playboy of the Western World* in Dublin—

routinely referred to as "The Playboy riots"—misrepresents the nature of those events. By describing virtually any protest in a theater auditorium as a riot, theater historians depict spectators' oppositional practices as primarily disorderly. But the theatergoers who registered their disapproval of a new play did not simply create a disturbance; they devised and enacted resistance through verbal rejoinders, physical gestures, and organized group demonstrations, in addition to making noises by shouting, stamping, and playing instruments. The theatergoers whose actions I explore were driven not simply by antipathetic, but also by creative energies. Theater artists as well as theater scholars have often dismissed hostile audience reactions as self-evident displays of philistinism; I contend that a conflict between a modern play and an affronted audience illuminates both that specific instance of reception and the basic configuration of the theatrical event—the complex interaction between the cultural institution of theater and its socially and historically constituted audience.

My goal in writing this study was not to present a comprehensive survey of modern theater scandals, but rather to investigate a significant phenomenon in the history of western theater by way of a selection of representative examples—a series of encounters between specific plays and specific audiences. I examine those scandals for which the documentary material is most extensive—productions in Germany, France, Ireland, and the U.S.—and pay special attention to Brecht's work. Chapters 1 through 4 each treat the first production of one play. Those four cases provide a considerable range of dates, style, and contexts, allowing me to deal with pronounced anti-naturalism as well as Naturalism, plays which allude directly to political circumstances and others which do not, and theatergoers with diverse habits of auditorium behavior. Having thus identified and discussed many of the characteristics of modern theater scandals, I then broaden my focus in chapter 5 to further explore the practical and theoretical ramifications of adverse audience response. Brecht's early career during the Weimar Republic serves my purpose for several reasons: productions of his plays and operas in the 1920s and early 1930s provoked many scandals, and just as the work varied enormously, so did the grounds for and nature of spectators' protests; the interwar period marks both the high point and the end of the sequence of theater scandals that began during the 1880s; and in Weimar Germany especially, the frequency of theater scandals and increased consciousness of the scandal as a mode of reception altered their significance, throwing the authenticity of protests into doubt. The Weimar Republic also interests me as a society in which the stakes in all conflicts were exceedingly high. Essentially, if the political parties on the left in Germany had responded differently and above all with greater cooperation to the rise of National Socialism, Hitler's seizure of power might have been averted, along with the war and genocide that ensued. It is partially in this light that I consider the hostile reception of many of Brecht's works and his often dismissive response to it. I do not contend that Brecht any more than any other individual could have saved the republic; but because, throughout his life, he very deliberately pursued the goal of altering and enhancing theater spectators' intellectual and political receptivity, his practical and theoretical work throws into sharp relief the question of how productive or counterproductive theater scandals have been and could be.

My research is based on examination of all available accounts of the protests and of the productions that prompted them—in newspapers and memoirs, in interviews, and in records of court proceedings. I explore the social, cultural, and political contexts in which each protest occurred, and strive to identify as accurately as possible the makeup of particular audiences with respect to class, gender, ethnicity, and political sympathies. Throughout, I will present a number of arguments that necessarily depend on universalizing and thus questionable conceptions such as "modern theater" and "the audience": clearly there are important differences among the various countries whose theater history I consider, and—increasingly during the nineteenth century—theatrical performance existed in many forms catering to distinct audiences. Yet in spite of such diversity, a fundamental transformation of the norms of audience behavior in the western theater indisputably took place between the mid-nineteenth and mid-twentieth centuries. Although most of the work that gave rise to scandals was produced by small theaters catering to a distinct audience, those incidents illuminate broader changes in standards of behavior in the auditorium, since even the most experimental productions are influenced by and in turn influence the evolving production and reception of more popular work.

Recent scholarship on theater audiences has developed and employed a variety of theoretical models to analyze production and reception, yet typically those models assume a basically passive, well-disposed audience. Little attention has been paid to the complication posed by spectators who actively resist performances. For instance, one of the most thorough examinations of the spectators' role was carried out by Susan Bennett in *Theatre Audiences*. While Bennett makes clear throughout that she is most interested in the "productive and emancipated audiences" of non-traditional theater since the 1960s, she does aim to establish "the productive role of *any* theatre audience." Drawing on reception theory and other studies of reading and viewing, Bennett proposes the following model, consisting of two frames:

the outer frame contains all those cultural elements which create and inform the theatrical event. The inner frame contains the dramatic production in a particular playing space. The audience's role is carried out within these two frames and, perhaps most importantly, at their points of intersection. It is the interactive relations between audience and stage, spectator and spectator which constitute production and reception, and which cause the inner and outer frames to converge for the creation of a particular experience.[4]

Certainly this seems a valid way of conceptualizing the process whereby an audience obligingly receives, understands, and interprets a performance; but what of spectators who fail, or decline, to play the role assigned to them in Bennett's model? In the terms of this theory, when scandalized audience members protest against a performance, the interactive relations in which they participate do not bring about a convergence at all but instead a discrepancy, a non-intersection between the two frames. So Bennett's model can be made to encompass the hostile spectators, but only by adapting it to cover a possibility she appears not to have taken into account.

Marvin Carlson also underlines the significance of the role played by the spectators in an essay advocating the use of reception theory in theater studies: "much theatre theory still regards the theatre performance as something created and set before an essentially passive audience. . . . Little is said about how that audience learns to respond . . . or what demands and contributions it brings to the event." Both critics make a strong case for regarding the audience as an active participant in theater—yet neither of them devotes much attention to forms of active participation which aim to disrupt a performance. Carlson does briefly discuss the "many examples of audiences that have not at all responded to a performed work in the expected manner," from occasions when an audience laughed at a work intended to be serious to demonstrations against plays such as Jarry's *Ubu Roi*. Yet the terms in which he describes such instances illustrate the limitations and drawbacks of applying to the theater reception theory developed for studying individuals' reading of prose and poetry: "the frequency of such disjunctures demonstrates clearly that the community of readers assembled for a theatre event may be applying very different strategies from those of the model readers assumed by the performance." While it seems to me valid to conceive of a theater audience as a "community of readers," in many cases the creators of a performance will not assume that their audience will consist only of "model readers." They may very well hope that some of the spectators will in fact differ significantly from the "model readers" who are likely to respond favorably to the performance; and when such disjunctures do occur it may be due to various factors, and not only to a discrepancy in "strategies" of reading. Whereas written works are received by individuals whose response one can only try to imagine or reconstruct, stage productions take place before real people. As Carlson mentions, "a frustrated reader may simply put the book aside and turn to something else. The theatre, as a social event, encourages more active resistance." It would be difficult, perhaps absurd, to attempt to study instances where individual readers of novels or poems have become so put off by the text that they have angrily thrown the book across the room; but one can investigate occasions when a group of theater spectators were induced to protest against a performance. By doing so I aim both to shed new light on the particular incidents I examine, and to contribute to the development of something which—as Carlson quite rightly points out—reception research has yet to provide: "A clearer understanding of how spectators today and at other historical periods have learned and applied the rules of the game they play with the performance event in the theatre."[5]

One concept derived from reception theory that does inform my analyses of modern theater scandals is the horizon of expectations, which came to prominence through—though it did not originate in—the work of Hans Robert Jauss. In his early work on the relationship between reception and literary history, Jauss deals to some extent with the connection, and possible conflict, between work and audience. He is, however, more interested in how we might make use of this relationship for classifying and judging the work than in the details of the relationship:

The way in which a literary work, at the historical moment of its appearance, satisfies, surpasses, disappoints, or refutes the expectations of its first audience, obviously provides a criterion for the determination of its aesthetic value. The distance between the horizon of expectations and the work, between the familiarity of previous aesthetic experience and the "horizonal change" demanded by the reception of the new work, determines the artistic character of a literary work.

He goes on to say that the smaller that distance is, "the closer the work comes to the sphere of 'culinary' or entertainment art."[6] For Jauss, then, the angry protestations of theatergoers at the first performance of a new play illuminate that work's place in literary history, helping us to decide how innovative or conventional, in effect how good the play was. Jauss shows little interest in how actual audiences responded to works that did not correspond with the prevailing horizon of expectations, or in what that response might suggest about those audiences. This and numerous other shortcomings in Jauss's notion of the horizon of expectations have been pointed out, and he himself later posited a more nuanced model of two horizons—one literary, the other social. Nevertheless, the horizon of expectations does provide a valuable way to conceive of the standard against which the audiences I examine measured the plays.

My ideas about evolving norms of behavior in the theater are informed by Norbert Elias's theorization of changes in behavior in *The Civilizing Process*. Elias demonstrates how, during the Middle Ages and Renaissance, the threshold of shame and repugnance shifted: "the fear of transgression of social prohibitions takes on more clearly the character of shame the more completely external constraints have been turned into self-restraints by the structure of society."[7] In the late nineteenth and early twentieth centuries the same process was still under way, as people's conception of the boundary between appropriate and unseemly conduct in the theater was affected by external constraints that they had internalized as self-restraint. The scandals I examine stand out because on those occasions new plays that went beyond the dominant horizon of expectations—of which there were plenty during the period from the 1880s to the 1930s—provoked some spectators into behaving in a manner that violated the prevailing threshold of shame and embarrassment.

Music historian James H. Johnson also draws on Elias in his recent study *Listening in Paris*, which explores 1750–1850 in order to answer the question "Why did French audiences become silent?" I have found stimulating Johnson's remarks about what he calls "available behavior": "Public expression, although freely chosen, is drawn from a finite number of behaviors and styles of discourse shaped by the culture." He asserts, for instance, that fighting during the 1913 premiere of Stravinsky's *Le Sacre du printemps* "was one of several possible responses expressing extreme divergence in taste."[8] In some cases I reach the same conclusion about the means of protest adopted by affronted spectators—that they were taken from an available repertoire; in others, however, these events constitute scandals precisely because the audience's behavior was exceptional, beyond the normal range of possible response.

My investigation of premieres which incited audiences to unusual behavior is animated by my own relationship to theater as an art form, as a cultural practice, and as a realm of experience. These incidents appeal to me because on each occasion a performance on stage moved many spectators to give expression to a strongly felt response. Rarely before or since has theater's effect on its audience manifested itself so vividly. My own attitude to theater is characterized by a kind of exacting ambivalence: there is nothing I find more powerful and inspiring than a production that for whatever combination of reasons speaks to and excites me. Yet by the same token, there is nothing I find more dispiriting than an uninspired production which leaves me cold. I am far from alone in feeling that way, and probably nobody has expressed such standards more emphatically and intensely than Antonin Artaud, who told Anaïs Nin in 1933, "I wanted a theatre that would be like a shock treatment, galvanize, shock people into feeling."[9] Artaud's longing to reach the audience on the deepest level—"directly affecting the organism"[10]—though generally recognized to be unrealizable, strikes a chord with me as it has with many other theater practitioners and scholars. While the late-nineteenth- and early-twentieth-century productions that generated exceptional audience behavior may not have touched spectators as Artaud and others have aspired to do, they did spark a fervent response—they shocked many audience members into feelings of a strength they were unaccustomed to experiencing in the theater, and thus into displaying otherwise concealed attitudes, beliefs, and fears. Such multifaceted and colorful intersections of conflicting positions seem unlikely to occur in the present-day theater, most of which is either a form of high culture struggling with the obligation to compromise with market forces, or a fringe activity attracting mostly like-minded spectators.

In discussing each scandal, I proceed by recounting the course of events, basing my narration on careful consideration of all available accounts, and in particular first-hand accounts written at the time—though even those often depict the same occurrences quite differently. Many of the individual incidents that made up these scandals strike us today not only as revealing and instructive, but also as fascinating, and in some cases quite amusing. I endeavor to tell these stories in a manner that conveys their entertaining quality even as I draw out their resonance. Yet I also approach the scandals with as much objectivity as I can, which in part means resisting the temptation to take the play's side and to dismiss those audience members who protested as philistine prigs. Certainly the reactions of those spectators often strike me as off-puttingly conservative and closed-minded, but then I was not placed in the position they were—confronted by productions far more bold and challenging than I was accustomed to, at a time when I was expected to behave in the auditorium with greater restraint than ever before.

Introduction: Modern Theater Scandals and the Evolution of the Theatrical Event

Out of respect for our readers, we would not even speak about *Ubu Roi*, had yesterday's performance not been marked by scandal. Never, in a long time, had uproar like this been heard in a Parisian house. The audience protested with uncustomary violence on hearing this succession of phrases in which obscenity vied with incoherence.

—Le Petit Parisien[1]

Yesterday, at the Oeuvre, the audience did not set an example of reserve and of good conduct. It is true that the play had started. But is not the most natural protest, and above all the most dignified, to get up and leave?

It is always aggravating to witness spectacles like those which took place yesterday on the stage and especially in the house.

—La Presse[2]

Several of the writers who published reactions to the tumultuous first performances of Alfred Jarry's *Ubu Roi* in December 1896 remarked on the audiences' response. For *Le Petit Parisien*, the evening demanded to be reported because the spectators' behavior deviated conspicuously from the prevailing norms: the scandal thus resided less in the work itself than in the exceptional display of vehement opposition prompted by the performance. For *La Presse* on the other hand, the audience's conduct was not merely more newsworthy than the play, it was actually more disturbing. And together the two writers situate the first production of *Ubu Roi* within the historical evolution of audience behavior: *Le Petit Parisien* indicates that, while such protests are exceptional in 1896, they did occur in the past; and *La Presse*, by writing of setting an example, ascribes to the audience a responsibility, not simply to respect certain already-established standards of behavior, but to determine those standards for the future. The most striking illustration of late-nineteenth-century conceptions of seemly audience conduct is the rhetorical question asked by *La Presse*, that proposed the theatergoers' primary concern should be to retain their dignity—clearly associated with the reserve that this audience failed to practice—and that doing so by walking out would be the most "natural" form of dissent.

To theater spectators in most contexts prior to the late 1800s, walking out of a performance would probably have appeared the least, not the most, obvious means of expressing opposition. For most of western theater's history, playgoers have routinely talked during performances, often shouted, and quite frequently responded in an even more forthright manner, particularly if they were displeased. Yet the point of view represented by *La Presse* in 1896 was in the ascendant: beginning in the mid-nineteenth century, subdued norms of audience conduct—for music and opera performances as well as for theater—gradually but very firmly established themselves. In the closing decades of the century, that movement toward greater restraint in the auditorium coincided with a regeneration of dramatic writing. Beginning around 1880, an art form that for decades had offered little more than light entertainment became a vehicle for radical and complex ideas; yet already by the early 1900s, the production of new plays came to be associated with shock and sensation, which necessarily made resounding displays of outrage less likely. So no sooner had the theater revitalized itself than its provocative charge began to wane, even as theatergoers were embracing a more passive role. By the middle of the twentieth century, the standard pattern of behavior for theater spectators entailed keeping silent, except for laughing and whispering, until interval or final curtain. Tumultuous confrontations during performances virtually ceased to occur after the 1930s; certainly numerous postwar productions have aroused controversy, but it has rarely manifested itself in the auditorium. The several decades between the 1880s and World War II thus stand out not only as a time of great fertility and change in western theater, but as a period punctuated by a certain kind of encounter—between works which directly challenged their audiences, and spectators who defied predominant norms of behavior in order to express their opinion of those works. By examining several of those encounters, I aim to illuminate the unprecedented, short-lived and probably unrepeatable circumstances of production and reception which accompanied the first half-century of modern theater.

The scandals I analyze in this book took place between 1889 and 1931, in Germany, France, Ireland, and the U.S. Although the social and historical contexts of those incidents varied enormously, taken together they can nonetheless be regarded as indicative of a distinct phase in the evolution of the theatrical event. In this first chapter, I lay out the salient features of normative behavior in the theater in the west from ancient Greece to the present, in order to situate the period from the 1880s to the 1930s within a historical development.

Broadly speaking, theater audiences were much more unruly and noisy before, and much less so after the half-century I focus on. Marc Baer comments that "Until the twentieth century, dramatic performances and disorder must have seemed to many a single phenomenon."[3] Some of the best historical evidence of typical auditorium behavior is provided by efforts to regulate it, such as a French police ordinance from 1780 which made it illegal "to shout or make any noise before the performance begins, and in the course of the play to blow whistles or boo, to put one's hat on one's head or interrupt the actors in any fashion and no matter on what pretext."[4] Clearly such legislation would not have been considered necessary unless interruptions and interventions of this kind occurred repeatedly. And while putting one's hat on might strike us today as a comically unthreatening form of misconduct, evidence abounds of more hazardous customs. Theater audiences in many contexts have routinely thrown a variety of objects at the stage and at each other. A 1640 prologue by John Tatham ends with the plea "Onely wee would request you to forbeare / Your wonted custome, banding *Tyle,* or Peare, / Against our *curtaines,* to allure *us* forth," vividly evoking the readiness of playgoers in the Renaissance amphitheaters to express themselves physically as well as verbally.[5] And in his 1808 description of the Amsterdam Schouwburg, A. L. Barbaz explains why he called the pit "the spittoon of the gods: indeed! spittle, chewed-up tobacco, apples and pear skins, nutshells, hats, bottles, pieces of glass, etc. cascade into it like a shower of rain or hail."[6] Even allowing for a measure of exaggeration, this sketch captures that chaotic atmosphere which for centuries went along with the majority of theatrical performances.

In the mid-eighteenth century, the Parisian authorities responded to this close association of theater and disorder by stationing guards in the auditorium. To Diderot, these "insolent fusileers" had a detrimental effect on the atmosphere in the house, as he illustrated by contrasting the theaters of 1758 with those of the 1740s:

Fifteen years ago our theaters were tumultuous places. The coldest heads became heated on entering, and sensible men more or less shared the transports of madmen. . . . There was movement, bustle, and pushing; the soul was beside itself. . . . the actor and the actress aroused enthusiasm. The infatuation spread from the pit to the amphitheater, and from the amphitheater to the boxes. People had arrived heatedly, they went away in a state of drunkenness . . . Today, they arrive coldly, they listen coldly, they leave coldly.[7]

From this one can deduce several components of a fulfilling theatrical experience for Diderot: the transport as an individual audience member, conveyed especially via the contrast of hot and cold; the excitement engendered by sharing a space, and an experience, with others who are similarly moved; the openness to being emotionally affected by the actors' performances; and the communication of that response among spectators, almost as if by contagion. Yet the whole is greater than the sum of the parts, and clearly for Diderot all these components depend upon and feed off each other. Feeling moved in the company of others who are undergoing the same experience—that is what Diderot resents the guards for disrupting. And the unruliness of audiences for most of theater's history (for, Diderot's lament notwithstanding, it required far more than a few guards to subdue theatergoers) relates directly to this fundamental idea that the spectators collectively participate in the theatrical performance, that the audience has a role to play.

One aspect of that role has always, with significant variations, entailed passing judgment on the performance. Plato describes how the public in the theater in ancient Greece, "with a great deal of noise and a great lack of moderation, shout and clap their approval or disapproval of whatever is proposed or done, till the rocks and the whole place re-echo, and redouble the noise of their boos and applause."[8] Given the competitive form of production in Greece, the spectators Plato depicts were not merely expressing their own "approval or disapproval," they were also doing their best to influence the judges. In later centuries when theater no longer revolved around organized contests, audiences often possessed even more power to determine the success or failure of plays and playwrights. In the Georgian theater in England, for instance, a premiere would end with the announcement of the scheduled date for a second performance, and the spectators would make it known whether or not this plan was to their liking. Horace Walpole both depicts and practices this kind of audience judgment in a 1761 letter about the first night of Bentley's *The Wishes:* "It was given out for tonight with more claps than hisses, but I think will not do unless they reduce it to three acts."[9] And in a famous prologue from 1747, Samuel Johnson neatly captured and gently lamented the implications for the writer of the audience's instrumental evaluative role:

> Ah! let not Censure term our Fate our Choice,
> The Stage but echoes back the publick Voice,
> The Drama's Laws the Drama's Patrons give,
> For we that live to please, must please to live.[10]

Another prologue from later in the century also underlines the extent to which "fate" was inextricably linked to the audience's judgment:

> Well fare the bard, whose fortitude, sedate,
> Stands, unappall'd, before impending fate;

When cat-call-pipers, groaners, whistlers, grinners,
Assembled, fit to judge of SCRIBBLING SINNERS!
What mortal mind can keep its terrors under
When gods sit arm'd, with awful-wooden thunder?
What heart, so brave, can check its palpitation
Before the grave dispensers of damnation?[11]

Thomas Holcroft's lines convey in more vivid language than Johnson's—albeit not without irony—the playwrights' subjugation to, even fear of, the audience.

While both writers on the face of it imply that "the publick Voice" somehow communicated a fair representation of the spectators' impartial response to the new work, in fact audiences' reactions have often been premeditated and falsified. Holcroft alludes to the practice of "damning" a play, when some members of a first-night audience would do their utmost, by means of the kind of positively frightening noise-making he depicts, to ensure that the new work was only performed once. Even more consequential than damning in England was the institution of the claque in late-eighteenth and nineteenth-century France: groups of spectators would regularly be paid to applaud a new play, and in some instances would instead hiss the work of a playwright who had refused to pay them. Such corruption of audience reaction did not, however, preclude unmistakably genuine expression of enthusiasm for a play or an actor's performance. On occasion in eighteenth-century England the vigor of an audience's approval even led to a performance being stopped before its completion, in a striking demonstration of the power wielded by the spectators: "Nothing can exceed the applause Mrs. H—most deservedly received," writes William Smith to Garrick, "The curtain ordered down, and repeated proofs of the approbation of the audience."[12] The very possibility that the audience could "order" anything to be carried out in the theater indicates a vastly different audience role from that prevailing in the twentieth century.

Another reflection of the stage's subservience to the audience, and from the contemporary perspective another form of unruliness, is the selective attentiveness of many theatergoers in the past. According to one Frenchman's description of the pit in the English Restoration theater, "Men of Quality, particularly the younger Sort, some Ladies of Reputation and Vertue, and abundance of Damsels that hunt for Prey, sit all together in this Place, Higgledy-piggledy, chatter, toy, play, hear, hear not."[13] This impression that attending the theater was a social practice prompted and facilitated by the performance but by no means necessitating engagement with that performance, is confirmed, indeed furthered in Washington Irving's account of a visit to New York's Park Theatre around 1800, where the beaux "no more regard the merits of a play, or of the actors, than my cane. They even *strive* to appear inattentive."[14] Theater has often provided a forum and outlet for social interaction, and those participating in that interaction were in no way obliged to pay attention to the performance.

At times this inattentiveness has transformed into true exhibitionism. Much evidence of this is provided by playwrights who have often satirized the behavior especially of the wealthier patrons of the theater, who habitually competed with the presentation on stage by drawing attention to themselves. In Molière's *Le Misanthrope*, when one of the "petits marquis" lists his own numerous desirable qualities, he includes his proven ability when in the theater to "cause a fracas / At all the beautiful passages which warrant ahhs" ("faire du fracas / A tous les beaux endroits qui méritent des ahs").[15] Similarly, in Fielding's *Miss Lucy in Town* (1742), when Tawdry is explaining how "fine ladies" occupy themselves, she proudly reveals that they deliberately arrive late at the theater, "make curtsies to their acquaintance, and then talk and laugh as loud as they are able."[16] Such actions were generally carried out not as any kind of protest against the play, but rather as a rival spectacle. So while they cannot be interpreted as oppositional, they do convey, perhaps more clearly than anything else, the conception of theater which obtained for centuries: that the experience was a social, participatory one, of which the performance itself made up only one part.

Certainly there were many occasions when the routine clamor and inattentiveness turned into more focused demonstrations against a performance. Sometimes such disruptions by spectators constituted the expression of political opinions, often borne of patriotic fervor. For instance, in London in 1755, shortly before the outbreak of the Seven Years War, many spectators protested violently against Garrick's *The Chinese Festival* because the cast included French performers. And a comparable but inverted case occurred in Paris in 1822, when performances of Shakespeare and Sheridan by an English troupe had to be abandoned because the actors were endangered by the audiences' demonstrations. Besides politics, the other most prominent causes of audience protests were admission and pricing policies (as in the Old Price Riots in 1809, among many others), and personal rivalry, usually between actors—as in the 1849 Astor Place riot in New York. What sets these incidents off from modern theater scandals is the relationship of such protests to customary, unexceptional behavior. Particularly fervent, in some cases violent opposition to certain productions prior to the late nineteenth century amounted to an intensification of normative audience response which was noisy and boisterous, and which was undergoing at most gradual change. Protests during and after the 1880s, by contrast, constituted marked departures from prevailing norms of auditorium behavior, and ran counter to a pervasive current of change in the direction of greater restraint.

That important difference between earlier tumultuous performances and modern theater scandals applies even to the single most famous incident prior to the late nineteenth century: the "battle of *Hernani*" accompanying the first run of Victor Hugo's drama in 1830. The forty-five nights of "continual cross fire between dignified old gentlemen and the young stalwarts upstairs" stand out among cases of stormy reception, and in some respects prefigure the scandals of the modern era.[17] The two foes in the battle were the young Romantics who supported Hugo's iconoclastic dramaturgy and his deliberate flouting of the rules which governed playwriting, and the older adherents of Classicism who vehemently opposed such change. To some extent this conflict is comparable with turn-of-the-century clashes between advocates and opponents of Naturalism or anti-realism. Yet the context of the battle of *Hernani* was substantially different: audience behavior in the French theater in 1830 still typically involved much talking and coming and going, often augmented by the sounds of applause and of jeering, even in the absence of a claque. Hugo refused to pay a claque, but did mobilize scores of young supporters to cheer for the Romantic cause; his opponents also drafted people to shout for their cause. The coordination of these troops during the seven-week run (as one critic wrote in the play's centenary year, "Battle? It would be more correct to talk of the campaign of *Hernani*"[18]) was certainly exceptional, yet it required organizing groups of Parisians to act in the auditorium as some of them were used to acting as individuals. And in the turbulent climate surrounding the already years-long struggle between Romanticism and Classicism—to which, as is often pointed out, *Hernani* constituted a culmination rather than a beginning—there was no significant social pressure promoting more subdued audience response. Modern theater scandals are frequently compared with the battle of *Hernani* in order to convey just how much they stood out from the usual audience reactions, yet in fact they were more anomalous in relation to standard audience reactions than were the clashes at the Comédie Française in 1830.

The relationship between performance and audience in the theater is often conceived of as a contract, or more specifically as a social contract—as formulated by Elaine Scarry, "an agreement similar to that in which members of the larger society give up a measure of freedom in order to form a government for their mutual benefit."[19] In most contexts in Europe and America prior to the mid-nineteenth century, that contract allowed for a good deal of active participation by the spectators; some of that participation reflected their acknowledged right to protest against the performance, some the status of the theater as a forum for social display and interaction. Overall, the "measure of freedom" which theatergoers in earlier centuries gave up was relatively small, while those who created the performances almost always faced the risk that the audience would not only respond to but react emphatically against the work.

The behavior of western theater audiences has varied considerably among different periods; Michael Booth has argued, for instance, that the typical English auditorium was quite peaceful in the second half of the eighteenth century, "the scene of much coarseness, vulgarity and tumult" in the early nineteenth, and then became calmer again until by 1880 "theatres were reasonably quiet and well-mannered places."[20] Norms of behavior also vary among different countries: prior to the modern era, the history of the theater in Germany and northern Europe features far fewer accounts of uproar in the auditorium than that of England, or France. The reasons for such divergences over time and geography are numerous and complex, yet in spite of all the variation, an overall development may be discerned between the Renaissance and the end of the nineteenth century—between the "humming, hawking, whistling, hissing," "stamping," "knocking" and "clapping of hands" in Shakespeare's London, and the "sovereign indifference, that banal, soft-spoken politeness which has superseded the fine tumults of yesteryear" in turn-of-the-century Paris.[21] Gradually, as a result of the efforts of reformers, developments in theater architecture, changes in audience composition, and innovations in theatrical practice, the unruly audience was tamed.

For probably as long as theater has existed, the predominantly disorderly behavior of spectators has frustrated not only some observers but also many practitioners; indeed, as my own selection of examples has already shown, some of the best evidence of audience conduct is provided by playwrights. Peter Stallybrass and Allon White examine Dryden's 1692 prologue to *Cleomenes*, which begins

> I think or hope, at least, the Coast is clear,
> That none but Men of Wit and Sence are here:
> That our Bear-Garden Friends are all away,
> Who bounce with Hands and Feet, and cry Play, Play.

As they demonstrate, this speech "endeavours to coax and shame the unruly audience of aristocratic Beaux and vulgar groundlings into *keeping still* and *keeping quiet*, transforming them, precisely, into a deferential and receptive bourgeois audience." Playwrights may have been complaining about audience behavior for centuries, but Stallybrass and White argue convincingly that the precise nature of such complaints changed significantly beginning in the late seventeenth century, reflecting the emergence of what has been termed the "bourgeois public sphere." Dryden was only one of many Restoration writers who "took up the task of transforming the mixed and unruly public body inherited from the Renaissance into attentive citizens." The prologue includes the lines "Arise true Judges in your own defence, / Controul those Foplings, and declare for Sence," revealing Dryden's intent, as teased out by Stallybrass and White, to "make the audience reform and discipline itself."[22] This proved, however, far more easily said than done. It would take around two centuries for the theatergoing public to be transformed as Dryden wished them to be, and the audience did not carry out the alteration altogether of its own accord, but rather contributed to a gradual and multifaceted evolution of the theatrical event.

In the course of the eighteenth century in various European countries, architects strove, as Iain Mackintosh characterizes it, "to force the actor back behind the proscenium arch to create a picture frame of illusion appropriate to Romantic sensibilities and to the staging of spectacle."[23] At first this effort was restricted to the realm of theory, but by the 1790s the ideas which had been set out in numerous treatises began to be put into practice. George Saunders's 1790 *Treatise on Theatres* articulates many of the central arguments of those who would radically change the shape of the theater, and the physical relationship of audience to actor. Regarding the use of space, Saunders declares that "A division is necessary between the theatre and the stage, and should be so characterised as to assist the idea of there being two separate and distinct places . . . The great advance of the floor of some stages into the body of the theatre is too absurd, I imagine, ever to be again practised." He thus emphatically rejects one of the most vital elements of theatrical tradition, in particular in England, as embodied in the practice of Shakespeare's time and of much of the intervening two centuries. Elsewhere Saunders approvingly quotes the Italian theoretician Algarotti, who in 1767 had argued that "The actors, instead of being so brought forwards, ought to be thrown back at a certain distance from the spectator's eye and stand within the scenery of the stage, in order to make a part of that pleasing illusion for which all dramatic exhibitions are calculated."[24] This passage is resoundingly emblematic: Algarotti treats the actors as if they were virtually inanimate objects; he highlights the audience's visual experience; and he writes about theater as if it were not a live medium at all, but rather a static one, the result of carefully computed engineering.

While the architects were developing this kind of vision of the theatrical experience, the producers who wished to make theater a profitable venture requested ever larger buildings, and advances in technology around the turn of the century made huge auditoriums possible. In his 1806 memoirs, playwright Richard Cumberland reflected on the repercussions of the recent unprecedented enlargements of Drury Lane and Covent Garden, where, understandably, productions relied increasingly on the contributions of artists other than playwrights and actors: "The splendor of the scenes, the ingenuity of the machinist, and the rich display of dresses, aided by the captivating charms of the music, now in a great degree supersede the labors of the poet. There can be nothing very gratifying in watching the movements of an actor's lips, when we cannot hear the words that proceed from them." Cumberland also encapsulated a devel-

opment which was to prove hugely influential for the relationship of audience to stage, in writing that these two London theaters "have been so
enlarged in their dimensions as to be henceforward theatres for spectators
rather than playhouses for hearers": one of the most important transfor-
mations in theatrical practice in the nineteenth century was its shift from
a primarily aural to a predominantly visual medium.[25] A similar but more
widespread indication of the same tendency is provided by the decline of
the word "auditor." Colley Cibber, for instance, writing in 1740, used it
more or less interchangeably with "spectator," but in the course of the
next century the more optically oriented term takes over almost entirely,
even if the collective noun "audience" endures.[26] In a recent study of
nineteenth-century American theater, Faye E. Dudden mentions one nice
illustration of the older aural conception of theater: a New York mayor
"laying the cornerstone of a new theatre in 1826, anticipated delights in
store for 'the enchanted Ear'." Yet within a few years Americans were no
longer expecting that kind of enjoyment from the stage, and Dudden
quotes several examples from the 1830s of writers commenting on the
change, such as a journalist's reflection that "the pleasures of the stage
had 'migrated from the ears almost entirely'."[27] By mid-century in England
the primacy of the visual had become for at least one critic not merely a
tendency but an obligation: "All must be made palpable to sight."[28]

Giving precedence to the visual image over the spoken word necessarily
brings with it a decline in the intellectual substance of the performance—
an emphasis on entertainment rather than on the communication of ideas.
One of Maurice Descotes's generalizations in his study of three centuries
of French theater audiences via the most successful plays of different eras
is that "For the vast majority of spectators, the image, more than the word,
creates the illusion, and a truly popular theater is first of all a visual theater."[29] Descotes emphasized throughout that most popular does not by
any means correspond to most admirable or interesting. In the nineteenth
century more than ever before, that mass appeal of visual imagery influenced theatrical production, so that elaborate spectacle often dominated
over drama involving actors. This trend manifested itself in the auditorium as well as on the stage, as theater architecture became more and
more ostentatious. Charles Garnier's Paris Opéra, opened in 1875, represents the apogee of huge, ornate theater design, reflecting the architect's
own statement that the building's "sole purpose was to command a 'silent
awe'."[30]

While Garnier operated on a vast scale in order to create an imposing
edifice that constituted a spectacle in itself, in general it was commercial
interests that motivated ever larger, more elaborate and less intimate theater design. The bigger and bigger auditoriums built in the nineteenth
century, along with the greater expenses incurred by the more visually
oriented productions suited to such houses, heightened and compli-

cated the conflict between economic and artistic rationales. An article from England in 1880 reflects the prevailing trends by the latter part of the century: Frederick Wegmore, responding to the Bancrofts' reduction of the size of the pit at the Haymarket, regretfully acknowledges that "a theatre, as Mr Bancroft said, is a place of business; and a manager may, in a business sense, be entitled to the utmost profit he can contrive to secure." Wegmore then wonders why exactly the pit has become unprofitable, asking rhetorically, "Is it that the exaggerated luxury of appointments and accessories absorbs so formidable a sum that the old revenues of the theatre are no longer sufficing?"[31] The ornate grandeur that Garnier strove for in the Opéra was echoed on a more modest level in many theaters, as managers' priorities shifted more and more toward creating a refined environment for predominantly bourgeois patrons.

Besides scale, configuration and decoration of the auditorium, another factor which clearly affects theatergoers' experience is how well they can see each other. The gradual introduction of gaslight in the 1810s, then limelight and eventually in the 1880s electric light, made it possible to dim the house lights. At the same time other technological developments also contributed to the subduing of the audience. Increases in the range of on-stage lighting effects fostered spectacle-oriented production which promoted a passive audience stance, and improved lighting of actors made them less reluctant to perform behind the picture frame of the proscenium arch, but also weakened the bond between actor and audience. While Garnier's Opéra provides one of the best examples of ostentatious late-nineteenth-century theater architecture, another opera house, Wagner's Bayreuth Festspielhaus, encapsulates the extreme consequences of auditorium design and lighting aimed at presenting to spectators as individuals a visually arresting performance. As Mackintosh explains, "Wagner is venerated as the first to remove all of the distractions inherent in the multitier auditorium with the aim of concentrating attention on the stage picture contained within the proscenium arch. The stage pictures which Wagner created behind a heavy black frame were naturalistic in style and were seen in a darkened auditorium as images on a cinema screen were viewed half a century later."[32] And Richard Sennett discusses both Bayreuth and the Opéra in illustrating what he terms "a new idea of spectatorship" in the nineteenth century, wherein "the role of the audience is to see, not to respond."[33] No matter how extreme those two buildings were, they embodied a general and virtually inexorable trend in theater design and the evolution of the audience's relationship to the stage.

Of course, however elaborate and spectacular productions and their surroundings became, and however commercially motivated, theater still entailed actors on stage performing to an audience. Yet if the basic facts of that situation had not changed, the nature of the relationship, of the contractual agreement between the two parties, had. The sentimental theater of eighteenth-century England provides a particularly clear example of a context in which the agreement established between actor and audience incorporated a definite role for the spectators to play. In W. B. Worthen's analysis of acting in the era of Garrick, he compares the different responses of modern and eighteenth-century audiences: "Unlike the modern spectator's deferred applause, the eighteenth-century spectator's sudden, public reaction to the events on the stage confirmed both his engagement with the dramatic action and his active participation in the theatrical community." The contract in the Garrick era called for an illuminated house in which the spectators as well as the actors performed, responding to the representation on stage with "tears or laughter, applause or abuse."[34] Whereas those eighteenth-century theatergoers could throw themselves into playing their allotted part in a social event, by the late nineteenth century audiences were increasingly discouraged, in effect prohibited, from responding except in certain circumscribed ways.

In 1880, the fundamental transformation of audience response in the theater was under way though far from completed. An English article from that year demonstrates the process whereby the threshold between acceptable and unseemly auditorium behavior shifted: external norms changed and became internalized. Lady Pollock complains about a breed of theatergoer who comment on the performance with expressions like "'Very bad this! These fellows can't speak!' or 'What a shocking lot!' Meanwhile they are torturing some honest neighbor with no wish to hear them and a strong one to hear the play." So in 1880, spectators were still talking during performances, as they had to some extent for centuries; but the remarks Pollock gives as examples are addressed from one audience-member to another, rather than to the stage—these spectators are not engaged in damning, but rather in comparing notes with their companions. Both Pollock and the theatergoers she is complaining about emphasize the audibility of the performance, which points backward to the aural conception of theater; at the same time, the implied assertion that each individual audience member, each "honest neighbor," has the right to listen to the play unimpeded by other spectators points forward to the later decades of the twentieth century when convention forbad any talking louder than a whisper. Pollock goes on to reflect that "I don't know how such annoyances can be effectually checked, but it has sometimes occurred to me that the actors should have fair play, and be allowed to admonish their audiences."[35] This wish that actors might have the option of actively responding to the audience, that the relationship between stage and audience might in effect be more equitable, further situates this passage within the evolution of behavioral norms, since in earlier periods actors could and did respond to comments and interruptions by spectators. To the modern sensibility, doing so would amount to breaking the illusion by failing to remain in character; but for a long time theatergoers did not bring such expectations to the performance.

The conduct of theater audiences also changed because the composition of those audiences changed. The nineteenth century saw the rise in power and influence of the bourgeoisie in the theater as in so many other contexts, and the increasingly restrained behavior of spectators in the theater—especially from mid-century on—is intimately connected to what Michael Booth, writing about England but echoing many comments about other countries, characterizes as the "middle-class takeover of the theatre."[36] Visiting from France in the 1860s, Hippolyte Taine observed that "Good society does not patronize the theatre in England"—but that situation was actually in the process of significant and fairly rapid change, so that even by the close of the following decade such a generalization would no longer be valid.[37] Thus in 1886 an Englishman observed that "men and women are found in the Lyceum to-day who, a few years ago, would have been shocked at the thought of being seen in a theatre."[38] Theater underwent a transformation from a place frequented by hardly any bourgeois patrons to one in which almost all the patrons came from the middle or upper classes. As urban populations grew, so did the proportion of that population who achieved or aspired to membership in the middle classes, and to a considerable extent the tendency of theater producers to think and operate commercially went along with a decided effort to woo middle-class patrons. So the developments in theater architecture also entailed greater comfort, systems for reserving seats, and eventually separate entrances for wealthier audience members. The theater became one of the primary realms in which the middle classes could distinguish themselves from the masses, and this segmentation was reflected not only in increased class-based separation within individual theater auditoriums, but also in an almost unprecedented stratification of the very medium of theater. By the latter third of the century in England, for instance, "legitimate" theater had largely become the preserve of the middle and upper classes, while—some overlap notwithstanding—the audience for music hall was drawn from the lower classes. And norms of audience behavior also varied according to the predominant social class of the spectators: the unruliness that had gradually been eliminated from the bourgeois theater continued for considerably longer in the music hall.

The single most important historical change in spectators' experience of theater, the change most intimately connected with and influential for norms of audience behavior, has been the shift from theatergoing as participation to theatergoing as observation—from active involvement in the event to passive witnessing of a spectacle. In identifying the new attitude to the audience captured in Dryden's *Cleomenes* prologue, Stallybrass and White highlight the speech's attempt "to homogenize the audience by refining and domesticating its energy, sublimating its diverse physical

pleasures into a purely contemplative force, replacing a dispersed, het-
erodox, noisy participation in the *event* of theatre by a silent specular intensity."[39] In this respect as in others, Dryden's prologue stands as an early
declaration of principles—principles which would not be fulfilled in practice for about two centuries.

By the final decades of the nineteenth century, audience behavior at the
leading theaters in Europe and North America was more often than not
quite restrained. A satirical portrait of well-to-do English theatergoers in
1877 generalizes that "dress-circle gentility is not critical," and that the
patrons in the balcony "if they do not show much mind exhibit a vast
stock of patience."[40] A Russian journalist describes the typical house for
a premiere at Moscow's Maly theater in the 1880s as "A cautious audience,
commercially wary, anxious not to applaud out of turn."[41] It was against
the background of such norms of behavior that the scandals of the decades
before and after the turn of the century took place: each of these events
caused a stir at the time, and left its mark on theater history, because such
occurrences were the exception and not the rule. The spectators who protested in effect reverted to older, no longer current modes of audience
behavior.

For the most part, the transformation both of normative behavior and
of theatergoers' internalized conception of appropriate conduct took place
remarkably smoothly. Indeed, some of the most revealing indications of
late-nineteenth-century norms of behavior take the form of complaints
about the passivity of the average audience. For instance, an 1883 article
in the English magazine *Theatre* complained, "It is a melancholy but un-
doubted fact that an ordinary, every-day theatrical audience is chiefly
composed of a very dull set of people, stupid, yet captious, who only ask
to be amused, and object to being emotionally excited."[42] The new works
which incited spectators to overstep the prevailing bounds of behavior all
confronted the audience with depictions of human and social relations,
and approaches to theatrical representation, which forcefully challenged
conventional thinking. Descotes writes of Dumas *fils*, one of the most em-
blematically successful playwrights of the second half of the nineteenth
century, "Dumas shocks and reassures at the same time; but he reassures
far more than he shocks."[43] The same could not be said of Ibsen or of his
key contemporaries and successors. The most innovative modern playwrights did not temper their assaults on the public's values; indeed in
many cases they strove to affront the spectators as forcefully as circumstances would allow. In contexts other than theater auditoriums—in drawing rooms, in letters and newspaper articles—considerable resistance was
expressed to theater's new confrontational stance, as illustrated in particular by the controversy surrounding the very name of Ibsen in many
European countries in the late 1880s. At the same time, changes in the

physical configuration and lighting of theater space had maneuvered the spectators into a position from which they could only look at, but not contribute to the theatrical event. An audience rendered unprecedentedly passive found itself confronted with unprecedentedly challenging theater—and the famous scandals of modern theater constitute the most violent consequences of that clash.

Thus while the protests against modern theater might resemble the more customary unruliness of earlier audiences, they were actually for the most part differently, and more deeply motivated. Any opposition expressed in response to a theater performance must stem from a discrepancy between what is presented on stage and what the spectators consider acceptable; but the criteria, the standards of measurement, can and do vary substantially. If we compare, for instance, a Londoner in the 1700s throwing fruit at the actors on stage and a late-nineteenth-century theatergoer shouting in enraged response to a naturalistic play, the contrast in psychological and cultural content is considerable. Above all, in the latter case there is, or the spectator feels that there is, far more at stake. For much of theater history, when audience members have voiced their dissatisfaction about a performance, that negative response has amounted to "This is not good" and/or "I don't like this"; they have felt cheated, deprived of the pleasure they had expected to experience. The frequent adverse response of modern audiences, on the other hand, has signified "This is wrong" and "Watching this disturbs me," because these spectators have felt personally affronted. Marvin Carlson briefly discusses one cause of spectator protests: "theatre history abounds in instances of audiences bitterly protesting a popular actor unexpectedly appearing in a role out of harmony with a previously established persona."[44] However bitter such demonstrations may have been, they cannot have entailed the same pitch of intensity and personal engagement as the outraged response to the productions I examine in the following chapters. The audiences Carlson describes expressed displeasure because they didn't get exactly what they expected; the spectators whose behavior I study performed their opposition because they got something they would never have expected.

CHAPTER 1

"Are We in a Brothel Here, or a Theater?": Resisting Naturalism

Hauptmann's *Before Sunrise*

In a single performance at Berlin's Lessingtheater on Sunday October 20, 1889, the recently formed theater organization Verein Freie Bühne mounted the second production of its opening season: *Vor Sonnenaufgang* (*Before Sunrise*), a new play by a young German author. The Freie Bühne was Germany's first independent theater society, established in order to present before a members-only audience plays whose staging by regular theaters was not possible for legal or commercial reasons; Gerhart Hauptmann's *Before Sunrise* is generally recognized as the first German Naturalist play to have been produced. The premiere thus brought a new kind of audience formation up against a new kind of play, and that clash provoked the spectators into a tumult of exceptional behavior. This is how one reviewer described the audience's response: "The battles between enthusiasm and disapproval, bravos and boos, hissing and clapping, the heckling, the demonstrations, the unrest, the excitement, all of which followed each act, indeed burst in on the action, transformed the theater into a meeting place filled with a passionate, heaving mob."[1]

During the 1880s, theater in Germany had been thriving as a business but stagnating as an art form. The introduction of freedom of trade under Bismarck in 1869 lifted restrictions on the number of theaters, which tripled between 1870 and 1896.[2] Especially in Berlin, attendance at the principal non-musical theaters was central to the cultural life of those who could afford it: the nobility and the more affluent sectors of the bourgeoisie. Yet the productions which the wealthy few paid to watch offered little more than formulaic entertainment.

As the novelist and theater critic Theodor Fontane remarked in 1890, a significant portion of the Berlin theatergoing public "knew ahead of time what plays must look like for all eternity."[3] Plays which did conform to such people's expectations had dominated the German stage for many years, and it looked as if they might very well continue to do so indefinitely. The main Berlin theaters presented almost exclusively the plays of a few tried and tested German and French authors and their lackluster imitators. The repertoire relied heavily on the society dramas of Dumas *fils* and Lindau and on comedies by writers such as Sardou and Schönthan. The works of Schiller epigones like Ernst von Wildenbruch were performed more often than those of Schiller himself or other classics, and the more recent serious drama of writers like Hebbel rarely found its way on to the stage. The style of the productions was just as lacking in innovation as the choice of plays: much of the acting was very poor and under-rehearsed, since the works were conceived of primarily as vehicles for the performance of one star actor, and various showy effects were employed to highlight the "virtuoso" and to ensure a suitably diverting spectacle. The success or failure of a production could depend entirely on its reception by the audience and the critics at the premiere, so that often the quality declined even further after the first performance. And circumstances did not lend themselves to any change in this situation. The Prussian authorities practiced strict censorship: as a result of an 1851 law, no play could be performed without the express permission of the police. In addition, self-censorship was carried out by the theaters, since the highly competitive market led managers to back assured successes rather than taking any risks.

Conditions which all but ruled out innovation were exacerbated by a public which, judging by the plays which found success in the 1880s, felt little dissatisfaction with such predictable theater. Most of the well-to-do theatergoers were content to give themselves over to Wildenbruch's patriotic rewritings of German history or to the simple pleasure of an insubstantial comedy. In addition to functioning as a source of escapist entertainment, the theater served to present the bourgeoisie with a reassuring vision of its world and values. In examining the German public's predilection for French drama, Michael Hays has concluded that it was above all "the solid principles of middle class morality and stability underlying Dumas's and Sardou's plays that satisfied the needs of a somewhat more slowly developing German middle class."[4] The Berlin theatergoing public either wished to be temporarily transported away from their environment or, if they were to look in any kind of mirror, they wanted it to be a flattering one.

Some members of the educated classes (*Bildungsbürger*) were, however, frustrated by the dearth of variety and innovation in the drama and other literature of the 1880s. Naturalism in Germany grew out of the desire of a few mostly liberal-minded intellectuals to reinvigorate contemporary writing. (Not until the end of the decade did they themselves readily adopt the term Naturalism, which was first employed pejoratively by the movement's opponents.) As early as 1882, the Hart brothers demanded a radical change in the function of the theater: "We need to dispel the disastrous delusion that the stage is nothing more than an institution of pleasure ... We need to turn the theater back into a reflection of the times."[5] The Harts and other advocates of a new direction for literature wanted to see the dominant form of drama based on conventions and artifice replaced with a theater of "truthfulness" and "representation of life." But for most of the decade the Naturalist vision of a new drama remained a vision, articulated in numerous theoretical and polemical statements—many of them holding up Zola or Ibsen as models to be emulated—and in plays which in the prevailing conditions stood little chance of being performed. Not only were those dramas almost bound to be banned or drastically cut by the censor, but the public had also been led, by conservative writers' responses to the Naturalists' manifestos, to look unfavorably upon the movement. In an 1891 essay, Otto Brahm—a key figure in the production of *Before Sunrise*—discussed the conflict between the established drama of the 1880s and the new movement, and focused on the French society drama as the epitome of all that the Naturalists opposed: the "society drama is the enemy of Naturalism in content and form. It fabricates a world which does not exist: in which one loves and does not starve."[6] But in the late 1880s the vast majority of theatergoers expected and wanted to see characters loving and not starving. To them, Naturalism was a movement of extremists who aimed to fill the theaters with depressing plays about the vice and depravity of the proletariat, and it seemed unlikely that the bourgeois public would ever have cause to revise this view through experiencing first-hand one of the new plays. If the *Jüngstdeutschen*, the would-be literary revolutionaries, were to change the state of German theater, they had to circumvent a situation which rendered innovation virtually impossible. The Verein Freie Bühne finally provided a means of doing so.

In 1887 in Paris, André Antoine had founded the Théâtre Libre, a subscription theater society which, because its performances were open only to members, was not subject to censorship. Antoine thus virtually invented the independent theater, creating a model that was soon imitated by others in France and beyond. The group of ten Berliners who founded the Verein Freie Bühne endeavored to learn from the shortcomings as well as the success of Antoine's venture. According to the announcement sent out to prospective members in June 1889, the organization's purpose was "independently of the operations of the existing theaters, and without entering into competition with them, to found a STAGE which will be FREE of the considerations of censorship and profit-making."[7] The Freie Bühne placed its productions beyond the reach of the censor and the market by setting itself up as a registered, non-commercial organization. The Théâtre Libre had struggled financially during its early years; the Freie Bühne planned carefully so as to ensure fiscal stability, including among its original board, in addition to writers and theater critics, a lawyer, a publisher, and a theatrical agent. The founders also aimed for higher production standards: Antoine had to rely on amateur actors, but the Freie Bühne planned to perform on Sunday afternoons, making it possible to cast professionals.

One consequence of the founders' financially prudent approach was that the only Berliners who could afford to join the Freie Bühne were already regular theatergoers. According to the most thorough analysis of the membership, many theater practitioners and most of the critics subscribed, along with a handful of nobles and military officers and two members of parliament. The rest appear to have been educated professionals, the vast majority of them Jews—whose patronage was essential to Berlin's cultural life during this period.[8] Julius Bab characterized the majority of the members of the Freie Bühne as "followers of the theater who had been attracted by their curiosity, but who in their hearts were thoroughly old-fashioned."[9] An article in the *Berliner Presse* was more cynical, claiming that 90 percent of the members were people "who merely want to be included in the lists of members and seen at the performances."[10] Far from creating a new audience of Berliners ready to embrace innovation, for the most part the Freie Bühne inevitably drew members who regarded the younger generation's call for change with skepticism, if not downright hostility. That stance caused the members to conceive of the contract they had entered into with the Freie Bühne in an unusual way: unlike with any other theater, they anticipated responding unfavorably to the performances they saw, and believed they would be within their rights in expressing their objections.

The new organization did not present itself as a Naturalist project, and of the founders only a couple explicitly associated themselves with the movement. But just as Naturalism needed the Freie Bühne to break through into the mainstream of German drama, the Freie Bühne needed a German Naturalist play to make a real impression on the state of theater in Berlin. For the opening production, the board chose Ibsen's *Ghosts*, which had been staged once in Berlin in January 1887 and banned ever since, even though other German cities had permitted public performances. *Ghosts* was too familiar by 1889 to arouse much excitement, and the September 29 production was successful but uneventful. While *Ghosts* was in rehearsal, the board considered and agreed to a proposal by chairman Otto Brahm—a theater critic in his mid-twenties—that the program for the opening season be altered and that they next produce Hauptmann's *Before Sunrise*.

Gerhart Hauptmann was only twenty-six in 1889. He had been living in Berlin for five years, during which time he had come into contact with several of the writers associated with Naturalism, and had published some poetry and two novellas. Hauptmann's friends included Arno Holz and Johannes Schlaf, who together had written and published *Papa Hamlet* under the pseudonym Bjarne P. Holmsen. In these prose pieces, Holz and Schlaf experimented in innovative and influential ways with representation of and through language. Hauptmann would acknowledge his debt to them by dedicating his own play, entitled *Before Sunrise* at Holz's suggestion, to Holmsen. The five-act "social drama" is set in rural Silesia, where would-be social reformer Loth looks up Hoffmann, a friend from university, who has become a nouveau riche by marrying into a landowning family, the Krauses, and mercilessly takes advantage of the local peasants and miners. Frau Krause, stepmother to Hoffmann's wife Martha and to Helene, is having an affair with Kahl—her nephew and Helene's fiancé. Krause is "always the last guest to leave the inn," and his whole family and circle are depicted as alcoholics, except Helene, who falls in love with the visitor Loth, a proselytizing teetotaler.[11] Loth returns Helene's love, until Dr. Schimmelpfennig enlightens him about the alcoholism in her family. This information disqualifies Helene as a potential wife for the principled Loth, since any children Helene bore would probably suffer the same fate as those of Martha, whose son died at age three and who gives birth to a second stillborn child during the final act. Loth decides to flee, leaving Helene a hastily written note; when she finds it, she exits and commits suicide.

Before Sunrise was published in mid-August 1889, and Hauptmann and his publisher Paul Ackermann embarked on a publicity drive which succeeded in bringing the play to the attention of a considerable segment of Berlin society. Hauptmann sent copies to eighty people: not just to family and friends, but also to other writers and to influential critics and theater directors, including Brahm. Ackermann sent the script to Theodor Fontane who wrote to Hauptmann in mid-September to tell him how impressed he was, and word of his high opinion of Hauptmann's play spread rapidly. Fontane also recommended the play to Brahm, who around the same time published an enthusiastic review in *Die Nation*. *Before Sunrise* became the talk of the town: Paul Schlenther—another of the theater critics among the Freie Bühne's founders—estimated that "Within a fortnight half of Berlin had read the play."[12]

This publicity guaranteed Hauptmann's play a large readership, but not an impartial one. In Bab's words, *Before Sunrise* was surrounded by a "wild whirlpool of persistent rumors."[13] While the approval of such a respected authority as Fontane made people take an interest in the work, the majority of them were far less open-minded than the seventy-year-old Fontane toward Hauptmann's bold originality. Because of the argument of Brahm's review—headed "A German Naturalist"—and the circles

Hauptmann was known to frequent, people assumed that the play embodied the new approach to literature that the Naturalists had been advocating. In this instance, the readers' horizon of expectations was determined not only by their familiarity with other drama, but also by the conception they had developed of Naturalism and by others' characterizations of work most of them had not themselves read. As Schlenther put it, "It was not the literary merit of the book which provoked people to read it, but its Naturalistic content": many of those who read *Before Sunrise* found in it just the sort of crude excess they expected from a Naturalist work.[14]

Brahm and his colleagues on the board of the Freie Bühne soon decided to produce *Before Sunrise;* they would not, however, stage the script quite as Hauptmann had written it. In the letter in which Brahm informed Hauptmann that his play had been accepted, he already expressed the wish that the young author should agree to "a few minor changes"; in fact, Brahm and the director Hans Meery had made a great number of significant cuts. According to Schlenther's account, they did so in order to tone down those parts of the text that they felt departed too radically from the prevailing norms, through either the political ideas they expressed or the dramaturgical techniques they employed. Apparently Hauptmann was convinced by their arguments and gave his approval to the cuts. Meanwhile Meery prepared his actors, who themselves were drawn into the mounting storm when they began to receive outraged and threatening anonymous letters. Those responsible for the production approached it fully expecting a hostile response; on the day before the premiere, Brahm wrote to Hauptmann, "I trust that you are facing these battle hours with the same feeling as I am: that now only the audience can disgrace themselves, not you nor us."[15]

The premiere of *Before Sunrise* began at noon on Sunday October 20, before a house of around 1,000. As Curt Baake wrote in a sympathetic review in the *Berliner Volksblatt,* "It was for the most part Berlin's old first-night audience, made up of brokers, lawyers, civil servants, roués, and women of the bourgeoisie and the demi-monde, who applaud smutty farces at the Residenz-Theater and venerable classics at the Schauspielhaus with the same pleasure."[16] Such were the people who had joined the Freie Bühne, many of them motivated less by an interest in new artistic endeavors than by a desire to be au courant, and, especially where *Before Sunrise* was concerned, to witness what promised to be a sensational event. The influential conservative critic Karl Frenzel complained in his review that he saw many people "whose names are not to be found on the printed list of members, some ... who cannot afford the luxury of membership."[17] He was probably correct; unsold tickets may well have been sold cheaply or even given away to the minority of young spectators seated in the upper circles, described by Baake as "students, writers, painters and actors: supporters of the new artistic movement, some of whom understood, some who did not."[18] Many descriptions of that afternoon, like this one written some years later by Adalbert von Hanstein, compare it to a battle, as two sides faced off: "The excited 'Jüngstdeutschen' came into the theater as if they were going into battle. For them it was now a matter of using hands and feet to clap and stamp victory for the Naturalist view of art. But the opponents' troops were ready to fight too."[19] Schlenther focused less on the drawing up of sides beforehand, and more on the effects of several weeks of controversy and anticipation: "Everyone brought an opinion with them, everyone was expecting something unusual."[20] It is not the case, however, that most of the spectators came to the Lessingtheater with the intention of "fighting" for one side or the other; had they done so, the reactions to Hauptmann's play would have been partisan and predictable, and far less revealing.

By the late 1880s, the customary behavior of audiences in the non-musical theater in Germany was less subdued than it would become in the twentieth century, but more restrained than in earlier decades. House lights remained illuminated after performances began, and it was still common and acceptable for spectators to talk, to come and go, and to applaud during as well as at the end of acts. While many contemporary accounts remarked that audiences in Berlin were especially lively, none disputed that the premiere of *Before Sunrise* was exceptional; several compared it with the "battle of *Hernani*." Some of the less thorough accounts of the audience response give the impression that the audience in the Lessingtheater reacted with a frenzy of hissing and clapping throughout the five acts, but the more detailed reports indicate that the predominant disposition of the spectators toward Hauptmann's play underwent a series of distinct and telling changes. Brahm gave a fairly accurate summary when he wrote that, beginning in the second act, "there arose a battle of lungs and hands, of hissing and clapping, that was waged with quite unusual intensity and which for a long time raged indecisively back and forth until a big love scene in the fourth act elicited applause even from the play's opponents."[21] Had Brahm extended his description to include the final act, he would have had to mention that the tide then turned back the other way with a renewed intensification of hostile reaction.

The trajectory of the audience's response began at a surprisingly subdued level: as Hanstein put it, "To general disappointment, the first act passed quite peacefully." The language and themes of the primarily expository opening act do differ from those of the works to which the audience members were accustomed—several characters speak in dialect, and much of the conversation revolves around alcohol and alcoholism—yet such departures did not constitute the sensation many had been looking forward to. But the end of the act gave the spectators an opportunity to express themselves, and it was at this point that the battle was joined.

It seems that Hauptmann's supporters determined to proclaim their approval through loud applause even though there had as yet been no expression of disapproval. And eventually their "clapping joke" provoked a response: as Hanstein described it, "The opponents remained silent and allowed the author to appear three times before his clapping supporters. But that was not enough for the supporters who then continued to make noise until they had aroused opposition."[22] Not surprisingly, others perceived the contest the other way around: "It is no wonder that the opponents' hissing and shouts of 'Boo!' and 'Enough!' made the play's friends wild too, and that there was no shortage of exaggerated cheering."[23] Yet the supporters of Hauptmann and the Freie Bühne certainly had the most reason to provoke an altercation: given the build-up to the premiere of *Before Sunrise*, the *Jüngstdeutschen* knew that this performance gave their movement its big chance, and it was vital for them that the play should provoke some reaction, adverse or otherwise. It would have been disastrous if the production by the Freie Bühne of a brand new German drama had failed to make a loud and lasting impression on the Berlin theater scene, so they contrived to ensure that the members of the new organization were provoked by other audience members even if not by the work. As in other theater scandals, the response to *Before Sunrise* consisted not simply of an audience protesting against a play, but of a complex conflict involving the performance and a crowd of spectators with widely varying individual reactions, many of whom participated in the "battle" between approval and disapproval, enthusiasm and rejection.

While Act I consists almost entirely of conversations between bourgeois or would-be bourgeois characters, much of Act II focuses on the less privileged characters. Most significantly, in the second act more than any other of Hauptmann's play, sexuality is fundamental to the action. In the complete text, Krause, in a drunken stupor, gropes his own daughter Helene; Kahl emerges half-dressed from Frau Krause's room and pays the farmhand Beibst not to tell anyone he has seen him; Frau Krause fires Marie, a maid who has been sleeping with one of the other servants; and Helene warns her stepmother that if she does send Marie away she will tell everyone that Frau Krause is sleeping with Kahl. Although the Freie Bühne production omitted the scene between Helene and her father, and toned down the rest of this sequence, what remained was still bold and explicit enough to provoke a strong hostile reaction. The conservative critic Isidor Landau wrote that "Already during the second act, the audience's distaste hissed its expressions of disgust and repugnance."[24] That hissing prompted the play's supporters to respond, so that Act II saw some of the most intensive exchanges, described by Heinrich Hart as "On one side raging and hissing, angry shouts of dismay and indignation, on the other a thunder of applause, a jubilant screaming somehow elemental in nature."[25] While Hart maintains that the noise made by Hauptmann's supporters expressed a deep-seated reaction, his description of "jubilant

screaming" suggests rather that they were very much aware of their behavior, and were even taking some enjoyment from it. When the two sides
in a conflict of this kind incite each other to ever more insistent demonstrations, their noise-making is liable to become decreasingly genuine;
certainly displays of support often appear performative in the same way
as those of opposition.

Landau declared the final scene—the confrontation between Helene and
Frau Krause—"the nastiest [häßlichste] . . . for which a German stage has
ever been used."[26] At some point during or right after that dialog, Isidor
Kastan, a Berliner described by one contemporary as "a doctor and journalist, very well known here and always 'outraged' at something or
other," made the first of a series of protests against Before Sunrise.[27] Kastan
shouted the rhetorical question "Sind wir hier in einem Bordell oder in einem
Theater?" meaning, "Are we in a brothel here, or a theater?" Kastan's
outburst instantly changed the focus of the uproar from the stage to the
auditorium, and brought about a reversal which further complicated the
three-way conflict: those who had previously hissed at the actors now
applauded Kastan, while those who had applauded the action on stage
hissed at him.

The next act brought with it a further change in the mood of the play
and a corresponding shift in the audience response. As Landau characterized it, "In the third act, scorn seemed to take over the control that up
until then been held first by excited curiosity and then by indignation."[28]
Act III consists entirely of conversations among Hoffmann, Schimmelpfennig, Helene, and Loth, and since nothing depicted or uttered on stage
immediately gave offense, the spectators began to distinguish between
the positions of the different characters, and to become engaged in the
performance by identifying with certain characters more than others.

The longest conversation in Act III, and the one to which the audience
was to respond most vocally, involves Loth and Hoffmann. In the preceding acts, these two characters have contrasted vividly with each other, not
just in what they have said but also in how they have said it. Loth, when
talking about his life and his ideas, repeatedly plays down the personal,
emotional side in favor of abstract principles. Hoffmann, on the other
hand, greets his old school friend with energetic hospitality and a light-
hearted manner. As Landau described it, "the tirades of the shallow starry-
eyed idealist Loth . . . were followed by scornful laughter."[29] It is hardly
surprising that Landau should thus dismiss Loth and his ideas, but even
the principal apologist for the Freie Bühne, Schlenther, characterized Loth
as a "pedantic and unworldly fanatic who sees himself as God's gift to
humanity."[30] The dialog between Hoffmann and Loth reaches its climax
when Loth makes it clear that he fully intends to continue with his study
of the local miners despite the potential harm this could do to his friend
and host. Hoffmann gives vent to his anger, both railing in general against

"demagogues" ("Volksverführer") like Loth, and criticizing the entire conduct of his life: "Why don't you get a job instead? Stop all this crazy
drivel!—*Do* something! *Get* somewhere! *I* don't have to crawl to anyone
to mooch 200 marks."[31] Schlenther reported that when the actor playing
Hoffmann left the stage "he was followed in mid-scene by such tumultuous and long-lasting applause that he might have been a party-leader
in parliament."[32]

Act IV centers on a lengthy love scene between Loth and Helene, which
Landau called "the pearl of the play," a view that virtually all the critics
shared.[33] Dr. Kastan made a second apparently premeditated attempt to
disrupt the performance, by emitting a "heartless burst of laughter" contrived to induce the spectators to join him in protesting against the frequent hugs and kisses.[34] In doing so, he was employing a form of
expression that figured quite prominently in the audience's response to
Before Sunrise: as Fontane noted, the various noises heard off and on
throughout the performance included "an approving laugh here, a mocking laugh there."[35] But such was the impact of the moving scene between
the two lovers that Kastan found no support: "in a trice the laugher was
made to shut up."[36]

Landau wrote that the applause at the close of Act IV "was the most
heartfelt, undivided and undisputed . . . Hence the best mood was prepared for the final act."[37] But the favorable climate was not to last long,
primarily because Act V dwells on the impending birth upstairs of Hoffmann and Martha's second child. Landau was mistaken in referring to
"the woman giving birth, whom one could definitely hear sighing in her
labor pains off stage," a detail in the script that was omitted from the Freie
Bühne's production.[38] Yet throughout the series of dialogs among Loth,
Hoffmann, Schimmelpfennig, and Helene, the audience is never permitted to forget the matter of childbirth, as the expectant father, his sister-in-
law, and the doctor exit and re-enter to check and then report on the
progress of Martha's labor. The audience's increasingly apparent aversion
to this insistent focus on childbirth was once again expressed most forcefully by Dr. Kastan. At some point, possibly at the moment when the script
calls for Martha's moaning to be heard, Kastan stood up, removed from
his jacket—or perhaps from inside a newspaper—a large pair of forceps,
and held them up as if to offer them to the doctor on stage. Since Kastan
was sitting in the stalls, the majority of the spectators noticed this sup-
plement to the action on stage. (According to one memoir, for some time
afterwards people in Berlin referred to obstetrical forceps as *Kastanietten.*[39])

It appears that the protests accompanying and following Kastan's
third disruptive action were the most intense of the whole performance.
Between them, the contemporary accounts convey quite a full picture of
the form those protests took. One reviewer recorded some of the verbal
utterances: "'Outrageous!' they shouted, 'What a nerve! Disgusting!'"[40];

another describes the audience members' physical behavior: "People exchanged angry looks, jumped up from their seats and shook their fists at each other."[41] Brahm later objected to the protestors' tactics in relation to the actors, criticizing those spectators who tried "to put them off through making noises at them, jeering them, and all the first-nighters' familiar, ill-mannered tricks."[42] He suggests that this disruption was an extreme manifestation of a common form of protest—one drawn from an established repertoire, and not an innovation of any kind. Landau also expressed sympathy for the performers: "again more than once people hissed crudely right at the unfortunate actors," and described the noise in the auditorium following the end of the play as a "passionate, long-lasting battle between applause and whistling, between cries of 'Bravo!' and wild shouts of 'Nonsense!' and 'Disgusting!'—a battle for whose finish we did not stay around."[43]

While a large proportion of the audience at the premiere of *Before Sunrise* expressed their displeasure, Dr. Kastan made the most marked individual performance of opposition to the play. Undoubtedly the gesture with the forceps, and probably the cry of "Are we in a brothel?" were premeditated, scripted by Kastan; even his vain attempt to protest against the love scene may well have been planned. He seized on three passages in the text and mounted one-man demonstrations against them, casting himself in the role of spokesman for the spectators, who will not allow reprehensible use of the stage to pass unchallenged. The scenes which Kastan disrupted most successfully highlight sexuality and childbirth—topics which according to prevailing mores ought to be kept confined within strict boundaries.

The difference of opinion between Kastan and the Freie Bühne lasted beyond the premiere and his several attempts to disrupt it. Little more than a week after the performance, the board of the Freie Bühne sent an announcement to the members of the society, informing them that "in response to complaints received by the board, as well as our own observations, we have expelled a gentleman who with the preconceived intention of disturbing the peace during the second performance by the organization, provoked the outrage of those in his immediate and distant vicinity through offensive words and behavior."[44] To Kastan himself, the Freie Bühne sent a sum of money equivalent to his membership dues, along with the request that he return his membership card. When Kastan refused to accept his expulsion, returning the letter unopened, the Freie Bühne instituted legal proceedings against him, and a Berlin court duly ruled on the case that winter.

While the statement by the board draws no distinction between Kastan's two principal disruptions of the performance, the decision handed down by the court discusses and rules on them separately (the court did not consider Kastan's thwarted attempt to interrupt Act IV). With regard

to the cry "Are we in a brothel?" the court judged this "an utterance that
did not go beyond the right of defense." They reached this conclusion
through considering the particular situation of a performance by an independent theater society, that is, a production that does not require a license
because it is open only to the paying members of the organization. The
court points out that utterances during the performance by Kastan or by
any other members of the Freie Bühne "cannot be judged according to what
is permitted at ordinary theatrical performances, because in those cases the
audience is protected by the authorities against attacks on its views of propriety and morals, whereas here it must protect itself."[45] The court was in
effect commenting from a legal standpoint on the renegotiated contract
between performance and audience that necessarily went along with the
advent of the independent theater. The fact that Kastan supplanted the play
and made himself the center of attention was a direct consequence of the
very mode of existence of the Freie Bühne: the counterpart to an independent theater society's circumvention of censorship was that it had to accept
greater freedom of self-expression on the part of its audience.

What the court does not address in judging Kastan's disruption of
Act II is the form of his protest. After all, he did not simply yell "This is
disgusting!" or "Shouldn't be allowed!" as plenty of other spectators did.
Instead he staged a small performance of his own, shouting "Are we in a
brothel here or a theater?" not because he sought an answer to his question
but in order to draw attention to the discrepancy between *Before Sunrise*
and theater as usually practiced. Kastan reminded his fellow spectators
that the only place one would expect to encounter lewd sexuality and
adultery was the brothel, yet one might argue that in doing so he underlined and exacerbated the alleged offensiveness of the play. The court did
not read it this way, but focused on Kastan's right, as a member of an
independent theater society, to protest against what he considered a mis-
use of the theatrical medium. The court's judgment of Kastan's interjection
suggests that according to their model of attack and defense, or offense
and defense, whereby spectators had to protect themselves against assaults by an uncensored performance, any tactics were justifiable.

The court's decision does indicate why *Before Sunrise* would have been
perceived as an "attack on the audience's views." Kastan's assessment of
Act II is endorsed by the court when they mention, as if this were an
indisputable feature of the script, the play's "crude offensiveness." And
the decision refers to a law which "makes impossible the public performance of a play in which situations such as precede or follow sexual
intercourse are concretely brought into view, because according to our
morals such representations cause offence."[46] (This paraphrase of the law
conspicuously doesn't cover the depiction of intercourse itself, presumably because the court took for granted that simulating actual sex was so
far out of bounds as to be unimaginable.)

For the authorities in Wilhelmine Germany, and for those well-to-do citizens whose interests coincided with those of the authorities, certain subjects were suitable for dramatic representation before the public, and others were not. Act II of *Before Sunrise* actually includes two unmistakably post-coital scenes, and all the accounts of the premiere make clear that the majority of the audience felt and expressed growing revulsion as the act proceeded. The overwhelmingly negative response to Act II reveals much about the interplay between prevailing aesthetic standards and the actual process of reception. Rather than considering what point Hauptmann might have been trying to make in foregrounding sexuality, the spectators took offense at the mere fact that he did so. The last episode of Act II demonstrates that Helene's social consciousness has been raised by Loth, as she makes a bold and principled stand on behalf of the unfortunate Marie and against the hypocrisy of her stepmother. The spectators might have considered the positions of the characters involved, and have come either to approve Helene's gesture or to side with Frau Krause; instead many of them reacted only to the subject matter of the dispute. The response of taking offense usually involves this kind of shutting down, whereby the instinctive repulsion felt by the offended party forestalls openness to other possible interpretations of the work—the initial offense generates a closed attitude of defense. Explicit references to characters sleeping with each other was just the sort of obscenity they knew they could expect from a Naturalist play, and here as elsewhere they resisted looking beyond their immediate aversion. Landau described the final scene of Act II as "häßlich," which can apply to aesthetics, connoting ugliness, or to morals, connoting meanness, or to both. For Landau and for those who shared his reaction, the moral aspect probably dominated—to them, it was low and insulting of Hauptmann and the Freie Bühne to force their audience to face the verbal and visual representation of an adulterous woman.

Kastan's objections to the love scene in Act IV were not shared by the majority of his fellow spectators, but his vividly expressed disgust at the final act was. Whereas the court sanctioned Kastan's first verbal outburst during Act II, they indicted him for the second, purely physical gesture with the forceps during Act V. In explaining their opinion of Kastan's disruption of the final act, the court wrote that "he brought what was only being talked about on stage into *actual* view in the auditorium, and in doing so he even outdid what was taking place on the stage and transplanted the offensiveness—if one wishes to regard the events on stage as offensive—right into the auditorium. But this involves crudeness for which the author of the play cannot be held responsible."[47] The court posits a hierarchy of causes of offense, according to which the discussion of a potentially offensive subject is necessarily less reprehensible than the actual representation of that subject; and a dramatic representation on the stage is less likely to give offense than presentation in the immediate vicinity of the spectators. Act II of *Before Sunrise* involves not just discussion but on-stage representation of drunkenness and of characters who have recently been engaged in sex, and moreover extramarital sex; therefore, to the court, Kastan was perfectly within his rights in protesting verbally against such a spectacle. But the final act of Hauptmann's play, as performed at the premiere—without the moaning of the woman in labor—did not go beyond the first of these three levels, that is, beyond talking about, until Kastan's gesture took the event from the first level to the third, from discussion to enactment in the auditorium. Whereas the court's ruling on Kastan's first interruption implied that they regarded any form of protest as justifiable, their response to his conduct during Act V suggests that they did not consider all defensive tactics legitimate.

The court's judgment of Kastan's two actions presents some telling inconsistencies, in that several of their objections to the gesture with the forceps might also be raised against the shout of "Are we in a brothel?" The primary measure applied by the court to determine whether or not the Freie Bühne was justified in expelling Kastan was the extent to which his behavior had contravened the purpose of the organization. They ruled that Kastan's holding up the forceps "went directly against the purpose of the organization, viz. presenting dramatic performances to other people, because these other people had come to see the play, but not the defendant's forceps."[48] The other members of the Freie Bühne did not attend the performance to see Kastan's forceps, but neither did they do so to hear him shout out rhetorical questions. And if holding up the forceps "transplanted the offensiveness right into the auditorium," did Kastan's outburst not do the same? The court even maintains that a demonstration like Kastan's with the forceps could have prevented the performance from continuing; why would a gesture incite a disturbance so much more readily than a shout?

One reason for the court's divergent judgment of the two incidents is that, to them, discussion of or allusions to childbirth are not in themselves offensive, whereas references to sexual relations are. While the decision flatly states that Act II contains "disgusting things," it emphasizes that Act V would only give offense "if one wishes to regard the events on stage as offensive," that is, any repugnance depends on the individual's subjective view. For the court, the substance of *Before Sunrise* warranted Kastan's protest against Act II, but not his protest against Act V. However, if the members of the court found nothing exceptionable in talk about childbirth, clearly they felt differently about the sight of a pair of obstetrical forceps. It seems that for the men who made up the court, forceps in the theater constituted (to borrow Mary Douglas's definition of dirt) "matter out of place," and one detects beneath that conviction a broader fear of things female entering too fully into the bourgeois public sphere.[49]

Overall, however, the court's response to *Before Sunrise* was somewhat less conservative and more discriminating than that of Kastan and many of the spectators at the premiere. Act V appears to have offended the majority of the audience just as much as Act II did. In analyzing the spectators' opposition to the final act of Hauptmann's play, Landau wrote that "the discussion of matters having to do with the delivery of children . . . was felt to be crude"—an apt formulation, in that the spectators witnessing the performance *felt*, on an instinctive level (as distinct from the considered one on which the members of the court were able to operate), that the repeated mention of childbirth was crude.[50] It also seems that the audience reacted against the play's unremitting focus—beginning in a brief dialog at the very end of Act IV—on childbirth. Unaccustomed as they were to encountering any true-to-life representations at all on stage, many of the Berlin theatergoers must have felt that *Before Sunrise* was administering them with an overdose of reality. The members of the court probably agreed that drama should not aim to reproduce reality, but unlike many of the spectators they distinguished among both different aspects of reality and different means of depicting reality. Considering the court's judgment of *Before Sunrise* along with the audience's draws attention to the complexity of aesthetic and other standards prevailing in a given social and historical context, which are often conceived of and represented as commonly held and unified.

Above all, the court objected to the manner of Kastan's gesture with the forceps because it failed to function as a clear protest *against* the performance. Both Kastan's disruptive actions were scripted, but whereas "Are we in a brothel?" sets an alternative text against that being acted out on stage, by holding up the forceps, Kastan was on the face of it not so much protecting himself against the performance as offering it his help. The court condones verbal, but not physically enacted self-defense by the members of an independent theater society; presumably if during the final act Kastan had shouted "Are we in a delivery room or a theater?", the court would have declared his actions justified throughout.

Yet the court's task was not to evaluate Hauptmann's play, but to judge Dr. Kastan's conduct. They pronounced Kastan's behavior innocent in one instance, culpable in the other. That suggests that the contest was tied, but in fact Kastan won on points: the court ruled that, since the law requires "persistent violation," and the defendant had thus far committed only a single offense, the Freie Bühne was not justified in immediately expelling Kastan. Having achieved this victory, Kastan chose to withdraw after all, and returned his membership card to the Freie Bühne. Apparently for him there was above all a principle at stake in the case, that of the members' right to express their objections to the works being performed by the new organization. Kastan was making a stand against the revised contract between performance and audience introduced by the independent theater.

Once his protests against *Before Sunrise* had been vindicated by the court, Kastan presumably felt that the best form of further opposition was to boycott the Freie Bühne by ceasing to patronize their subsequent productions. (Though he must have come to revise this dismissive view: in a memoir about Berlin published in 1919, Kastan devotes only a few lines to the Freie Bühne, but does express considerable respect for the founders' motivation: "the non-material impetus of this organization cannot and shall not be disputed, even here."[51]) Kastan also found other means of continuing to express his objections to the Freie Bühne's selection of scripts. When the board refunded his membership dues, he declined the money and requested that it be donated instead to an organization for the reform of habitual drinkers. Kastan's refusal to accept the money presumably went along with the principled stand he felt he had made throughout the conflict. And by requesting the donation, he once more enacted a typical response to Naturalism, implying that the theater ought not to preoccupy itself with the depravity of such people as alcoholics, who would benefit far more from being "reformed" than from misguided efforts to dignify their wretched lives in works of dramatic art.

In the circular originally sent out by the board of the Freie Bühne announcing Kastan's expulsion, they justify their action by arguing that they need to "ensure that everybody in the audience for Freie Bühne theater performances observes those social proprieties which are customary in the company of educated persons."[52] It is striking that the men who ran this progressive theater society, whose raison d'être was to produce work which fell outside the parameters of current theatrical practice, did not expect their members to react in anything other than the usual and "proper" manner. They wanted it both ways: freedom to experiment and innovate in their selection of plays, along with freedom from any active resistance by the spectators. In his book about the reception of *Before Sunrise*, Schlenther twice describes Kastan's actions during the premiere as "unanständig," meaning "indecent."[53] He thus criticized Kastan in the very terms frequently applied to Naturalist works by their opponents, invoking a supposedly stable boundary between acceptable and unacceptable. Yet the "social proprieties which are customary" are not stable, but rather currently prevailing, historically determined norms of conduct. By rebelling against this reduction of his right to self-expression, Dr. Kastan forged a link between himself and the disorderly audiences of the past, returning to behavior which had all but ceased to be available to theater spectators.

In addition to the antics of Dr. Kastan, the premiere of *Before Sunrise* featured some revealing receptions of particular scenes. The Act III dialog between Hoffmann and Loth provoked a striking instance of performing opposition through enthusiasm rather than hostility. Landau remarked that the spectators "began dangerously to play along: by applauding those passages which run counter to the bias of the writer and his play, they determinedly placed themselves in opposition to the work."[54] Indeed, it was only when they were able to cheer on Hoffmann against Loth that those audience members countered what they perceived as Hauptmann's position. There is no record of any hostile reaction to the radical social critique articulated by Loth in Act II. Even once his speeches had been extensively edited—for instance, his sweeping criticism of the army and the church was undoubtedly deemed too inflammatory to be retained in performance—the general idea which Loth expounds to Helene, about "the wrongness of our circumstances" ("die Verkehrtheit unserer Verhält-nisse") (41), constituted an indictment of contemporary society's structure and standards. Yet it seems that the depravity depicted at the start of Act II distanced the spectators from the play and led them to evaluate it only in terms of what was being represented; from that perspective, a conversation between Helene and Loth about society was preferable to a conversation between Kahl and Beibst about adultery, regardless of what Loth might actually have been saying.

The Act III encounter between Hoffmann and Loth is preceded, and in an important way set up, by a shorter conversation between Hoffmann and Helene. When Hoffmann declares to his sister-in-law that Loth is "an exceedingly dangerous fanatic . . . endowed with the gift for confusing the minds not only of women, but even of sensible people" (51), his warning to Helene functioned also as a warning to the doctors and lawyers in the auditorium. Hoffmann's remark provided the "sensible people" in the audience with an explanation as to why they were not more scandalized by the radical ideas Loth had expounded to Helene in the previous act: he had managed to confuse even them. Moreover, Helene has difficulty repeating what she learned from Loth with any clarity and conviction. She thus confirmed the view held by Hoffmann and by the predominantly male spectators that women are not "sensible," and gave those spectators even more reason to take Hoffmann's side. This conversation ends with Hoffmann "assuring" Helene that "to go around in today's world with opinions like his is far worse and, above all, far more dangerous than stealing" (52). One can easily imagine the bourgeois spectators enthusiastically greeting this aphoristic declaration. Holding Loth's opinions in Germany at this time was indeed dangerous—for anyone who expressed them, and who could be imprisoned for doing so; but the danger about which Hoffmann holds forth is the danger such ideas represented for respectable society. When Loth reappeared, the audience was primed to perceive and respond to his speeches as confirmation of Hoffmann's warnings.

The highly partisan response to the conversation between Hoffmann and Loth was unwittingly encouraged by Hauptmann's heavy-handed characterization of Loth, which made it all too simple for the majority of the audience to take sides against the character whom they assumed to be the mouthpiece for the playwright's own views. And while Loth is portrayed as a virtual caricature of the joylessly principled activist, Hoffmann probably appealed to the members of the Freie Bühne all the more because he did not represent in equally extreme terms the other end of the political spectrum. In Act I, Hoffmann claims that he still shares Loth's commitment to a more democratic society, but he has a different conception of how best to achieve it: "I'd be the last man short on sympathy for the common folk, but if anything is going to be made to happen, it must be made to happen from above" (13). Such a view, which allows the well-to-do to pay lip service to the social question without actually having to do anything about it, was probably shared by many of the bourgeois spectators. During the Act III dialog, the more opportunity Loth has to express his ideas, the more he risks alienating most of the audience. It is easy to understand if they failed to warm to a character who declares that "the bulk of my productive energy belongs to my work . . . It doesn't belong to *me* any more" (56). The impression Loth gives of cold rigidity is underlined by the counterimage of Hoffmann and his criticism of Loth's principles, such as "Some people seem to behave as if they'd cornered the market on all the good deeds that need to be done in this world" (57). Here too, siding with Hoffmann gave the bourgeois spectators an explanation for not effecting any "good deeds" at all.

While Hauptmann made it all too easy for the audience to feel antipathy toward Loth, he also gave Hoffmann plenty of dislikable traits. In Act I the audience learns via Loth how Hoffmann exploited the locals to take advantage of the coal, and in Act III, Hoffmann is shown to be manipulative, patronizing, and egocentric in his interaction with Helene, and hypocritical in his conversation with Loth. Yet all these discreditable characteristics seem to have been forgiven or conveniently overlooked in most of the spectators' eagerness to support Hoffmann. Even Hoffmann's self-abasement at the beginning of Act IV apparently did not dent the audience's allegiance to their kindred spirit. The act opens with Hoffmann retracting what he said to Loth in the previous act: "Name any way at all, and I'm ready to do it! . . . I really regret all that. I'm deeply sorry" (64). The character who only moments before had been hailed for putting the socialist intruder in his place now prostrates himself in front of him. One might expect that the audience would have seen this as a betrayal on Hoffmann's part and booed him as loudly as they had cheered him; but again it appears that they ignored anything that disrupted their identification with Hoffmann as the potential victim of and noble fighter against left-leaning activism. The extremely selective perception of *Before Sunrise*'s two principal male characters by the majority of the audience is a symptom of the strong resistance to and fear of socialism in the German Empire. Socialism was outlawed from 1878 to 1890, and the upper classes often assumed that Naturalism, along with virtually all other new movements in this period, was based on socialist ideas. The bourgeois spectators expected Hauptmann's controversial new play to have a socialist bias, and they unhesitatingly regarded Loth as the mouthpiece for that anti-establishment message. Thus however questionable some of Hoffmann's behavior may have been, he remained preferable by far to a threatening socialist like Loth.

Preconceived notions about Naturalism also played into the reception of other scenes in *Before Sunrise*. Many critics of Hauptmann's drama and of Naturalist work in general reproached the writers for dwelling on unpleasant aspects of life—on alcoholism and other illnesses, and on poverty, degradation, and vice. Treating the Naturalists' choice of subject matter as a reflection of the dramatists' unnatural preoccupations was a way of refusing to confront the writers' real aims: "The Naturalists' intentions of criticizing society were thus denounced as a mere joy in wallowing in 'filth'."[55] For the Naturalists, the key criterion was of course not filth, but truth. In the 1880s, the notion that art should aspire to truthfulness was restricted to the mostly young would-be innovators such as Hauptmann and the founders of the Freie Bühne. The dominant conception of drama corresponded to the ideas set out by Gustav Freytag in 1863 in an influential playwriting manual called *The Technique of Drama*, where he wrote, for instance, "The most important thing for the poet is the aesthetic effect of his own invention, for the sake of which he plays around with and changes the real facts however it suits him."[56] That the action of *Before Sunrise* constitutes a plausible depiction of life in this setting would therefore have been virtually irrelevant to most of the spectators.

Freytag also declared that people from the lower classes, "whose chief ability is not that of creatively transposing feelings and thoughts into speech" could not be the heroes of drama, and the audience response to the parts of *Before Sunrise* featuring poor characters demonstrates how unaccustomed the theatergoers of the 1880s were to taking such figures seriously.[57] In Act I, most of the audience reacted to the passages in Silesian dialect with laughter, less because the dialog is humorous than because they expected any lower-class character to be a comic character. As one critic put it, the majority's "judgment was prejudiced by the conventional use of such figures in popular theater."[58] In Act II, it was far less easy for the spectators to dismiss the dialect as comic, since much of it referred to the various sexual liaisons. One scene which does not foreground sexuality, when the farmhand Beibst converses intelligently with Loth about the latter's work, nevertheless contravened prevailing standards. That Beibst spoke in dialect but did not make the audience laugh probably struck most of the spectators not only as wrong, as unconventional and therefore bad dramatic writing, but also—albeit on an unconscious level—as threatening. One of the principal goals, and eventually one of the significant accomplishments of Naturalism was the democratization of literature. At a time when the bourgeoisie felt increasingly insecure about its hard-won place in the more privileged sector of society, Beibst's conversation with Loth set a disturbing precedent.

Received ideas about writing for the stage also affected the first-night audience's response to the love story in Hauptmann's Naturalist play. The failure of Dr. Kastan's mocking laugh during Act IV's love scene to instigate a demonstration of opposition emblematizes the audience's receptivity to that aspect of *Before Sunrise* which most resembled the plays they were accustomed to watching. It became evident as early as the first act that the strand of the plot involving the relationship between Loth and Helene held considerable power to affect the audience. Act I closes with Helene alone on stage, "with tear-stained eyes, holding her handkerchief in front of her mouth," listening for signs of Loth and pleading "Oh, don't go, don't go away!" (31–32), and Hanstein reported that this ending clearly moved many of the spectators.[59] In Act III, the long conversation between Hoffmann and Loth is followed by a short scene between Loth and Helene, culminating in her fainting into his arms. Landau wrote that this closing dialog met with virtually unanimous approval: "the spectators were disarmed, captured by the spell of the play and of the actors. A tumultuous, sincere, and very weakly disputed round of applause followed the third act."[60] Moments earlier, most of the audience had rapturously applauded Hoffmann on his exit, but Helene, struggling to express her alarm over the possibility that Loth might leave, proved to have as much if not more power to move. And the spectators' emotional involvement in Helene's fate provides more evidence that their antipathy toward Loth only emerged in relation to his foil Hoffmann. Already by the end of Act I, Loth's ideas have influenced Helene—she joins him in declining to drink during the meal—yet apparently the spectators, rather than worrying that Loth is leading the young innocent astray, empathized with her sudden attachment to him as a light in her dark world. Even once Loth's unappealing personality and radical political views had been demonstrated to the full, and many of the spectators had gleefully opposed him in the Act III confrontation with Hoffmann, the audience as a whole became caught up in the progress of Helene and Loth's budding romance, which blossomed in Act IV.

The spectators and even more so the critics who voiced their disapproval of *Before Sunrise* had to somehow reconcile their opposition to Naturalism as a whole with their near-unanimous acclaim for Act IV's long love scene. The most common and most significant solution was to treat the love scene as an aberration. This is what a number of critics argued, as Ernst von Wolzogen complained: "They all curse with the strongest repugnance about Naturalism's assassination of beauty, and how it sees truth only in what's filthy; and then when they're offered the finest, lightest poetry via the means of Naturalist representation, they scornfully say

'Ha, see how you betray your principles? Now that's a fine kind of Naturalism!'"[61] Loth and Helene's conversation does not differ substantially from a dialog in the kind of plays the audience was used to: they speak high German, not dialect; they talk about emotions, not about social issues; and the scene highlights a wholesome rather than a potentially offensive aspect of human relations—love, not sex. It seems quite plausible that the play's opponents in the audience thought to themselves: "I have to admit I think this scene is beautiful and moving—but that's because it isn't Naturalist." Susan Bennett writes that for theater audiences, "The horizon of expectations constructed in the period leading up to the opening frame of the performance" is subject to "substantiation, revision, or negation."[62] It appears that many in the audience for *Before Sunrise* refused to carry out such modification of the expectations they had brought to the performance, opting instead to measure the parts of the play which moved them in relation to a different horizon of expectations. Rather than adjusting their image of Naturalism as a movement devoted to the depiction of illness and degradation, audience and critics alike chose to regard this affecting scene as a failure on Hauptmann's part to remain consistent to the principles which they were convinced ruled out anything touching or uplifting.

The reception of *Before Sunrise* thus exposed various inconsistencies within the sensibilities of the Berlin theatergoing public of the late 1880s. Just as those spectators who opposed Hauptmann's play put aside their horizon of expectations for a Naturalist play when it came to the love scenes, so their reaction to the putative crudity of *Before Sunrise* illustrates the extent to which they approached other kinds of theater with quite different criteria. Heinrich Hart, among others, pointed to the double standard in the public's reaction to Hauptmann's play and to more popular fare: "And it was typical that the same spectators who applaud the dirty jokes and nudity that are the usual thing in *The Clemenceau Case*, in *Fifi*, in *The Roudinot Firm*, were outraged at a drama which admittedly depicts vulgarity with unvarnished German words, but which also indicts it from the highest moral standpoint."[63] The crucial difference between the indecency in those mildly titillating popular entertainments and that in *Before Sunrise* was the far more serious purpose of Hauptmann's play. Protesting spectators and hostile critics focused their opposition on those parts of *Before Sunrise* which defied prevailing aesthetic standards, as if the moral and political implications of those dramaturgical innovations were immaterial; but references to, for instance, adulterous sex would not have given offense in a different kind of play. Unconsciously perhaps, the spectators did recognize the implications of Hauptmann's departures from conventional playwriting. As another critic recalled it with a metaphor some years later, "It was more of a dull feeling, like the fine sense of smell of a hunting-dog, a feeling that an enemy is nearby."[64] The enemy as embodied by the socialist Loth was easy for the audience to see and therefore to defend themselves against—they simply cheered for Hoffmann. Their response to the enemy of which they caught a vague scent in the rest of the play was mediated by their attachment to conventional writing for the stage. The spectators who hissed during Acts II and V may have believed they did so because the subject matter of those passages struck them as obscene and not because they constituted a critique of their society, but they were almost certainly repelled all the more because those passages flew in the face of their society's inequitable structure.

The negative reaction to *Before Sunrise* by many members of the Freie Bühne is emblematic not only for what they protested against, but also for what they approved of. The fluctuations in their response to Hauptmann's play reveal almost as strong a desire to get caught up in a love story as they do a determination to resist anything which might resemble socialist propaganda. There can be little doubt that the audience unconsciously detected the threatening political implications of Hauptmann's taboo-breaking play; at the same time they appear to have been unconsciously attracted to its fresh approach. Close examination of the premiere of *Before Sunrise* reveals signs of this more open-minded attitude even amid all the fervent protests. Those audience members who hushed Kastan during the love scene of Act IV were probably more receptive to new material and approaches than was Kastan, and perhaps more so than they themselves realized. With the benefit of hindsight it is possible to argue that the Berlin audience was itself bored with the stale fare offered by the theaters in the 1880s, that the bourgeoisie was eager to be stimulated by the shock of the new, and found Naturalism "a welcome change."[65] Looking back in 1890 on the Freie Bühne's opening season, Fontane pointed to an element of ambivalence in the audience's attitude, lamenting the fact that some of them "wanted both the unfamiliar and the familiar, the thrill of the latest novelty and the stable serenity of the classics."[66] And subsequent developments bore out Fontane's observation, for Kastan's spirited resistance to Naturalist theater proved ineffective. The single performance of *Before Sunrise* represented a vital breakthrough for the new movement, and the climate for and nature of theatrical practice in Berlin and beyond were soon transformed. Theater came to be associated not with the expected and derivative but with the sensational. In April 1890, a member of the Prussian parliament called the modern theater an "intellectual brothel"; while that comment, like Kastan's shout, exaggerates for rhetorical effect, undoubtedly the German public's criteria and tastes did undergo a gradual yet far-reaching alteration.[67] The fact that *Before Sunrise* had caused such widespread controversy and such passionate expressions of support and opposition meant that subsequent potentially scandalous productions seemed tame by comparison. Playwrights such as Hermann Sudermann found success in the early 1890s with works which, while considerably less strictly Naturalist in theme and composition than *Before Sunrise*, would not even have reached the stage in the previous decade.

Dr. Kastan was quite a well-known figure in the cultural life of Berlin, described by one contemporary as "a character of the most comical sort and a furious enemy of the 'new movement'."[68] In keeping with that attitude, Kastan's protests against *Before Sunrise* have usually been depicted as eccentric and amusing. Yet it would be wrong simply to dismiss Kastan as a reactionary who resisted Naturalism in general and Hauptmann's play in particular out of a self-serving interest in preserving the status quo of patriarchy and class inequality. All that is no doubt true, yet it is equally true that he showed greater energy and imagination in protesting against the premiere of *Before Sunrise* than those responsible for the production showed in responding to his actions. Brahm and his colleagues wished by means of Hauptmann's and other plays to shake up a theatrical climate which made innovation virtually impossible, but not to have anyone perform opposition to their productions. The three-sided encounter between Dr. Kastan, the Freie Bühne, and the Berlin court emblematizes key changes in the history of theater and audience: Kastan's stunts point backwards to an earlier form of the theatrical event; the court's judgment reflects the transitional nature of the period by endorsing his right to protest, but only with substantial qualification; and the stance of the Freie Bühne points forward to twentieth-century norms of audience behavior, which were to become more and more restrained.

CHAPTER 2

"Down with Lugné Chamber Pot!": Playing with the Taboo

Jarry's *Ubu Roi*

The uproarious 1889 premiere of Hauptmann's *Before Sunrise* was only the second production by Germany's first independent theater. By 1896, when Alfred Jarry's play *Ubu Roi* caused a similar scandal, the existence in Paris of alternative "fringe" theaters alongside the established houses had been a feature of the French theater for almost a decade. Initially these companies had, like the Freie Bühne, aimed to create a forum for the presentation of new drama which no commercial theater would ever stage. Antoine's Théâtre Libre lasted from 1887 until 1894, presenting a great variety of work yet primarily associated with Naturalism. As early as 1890, the reaction against stage realism had found expression in a group that expressly set out to produce Symbolist work, the Théâtre d'Art, led by Paul Fort. Like the Théâtre Libre, Fort's company presented programs of several short plays for two or three performances. Fort was unable to sustain his organization for as long as Antoine did the Théâtre Libre, but soon after the Théâtre d'Art folded in 1892, Aurélien Lugné-Poe founded the Théâtre de l'Œuvre. And in 1896, the twenty-three-year-old Jarry cajoled Lugné-Poe into producing *Ubu Roi*, a work which corresponded neither to the Naturalist nor the Symbolist aesthetic, and which by the time Lugné-Poe came to write his memoirs in the 1930s had become the most celebrated play performed by his company. *Ubu Roi* famously prompted one of theater history's greatest scandals, but the audience's response was considerably more complex than is suggested by the established narrative according to which the play's taboo-breaking opening word *merdre* functioned as a bombshell, and provoked virtually the entire audience into shocked and outraged protest.

Henry Fouquier, one of the most prominent and influential drama critics in turn-of-the-century Paris, took his review of *Ubu Roi* in *Le Figaro* as an opportunity to reflect on the role of the *théâtres à côté*, the fringe theaters in Paris: "It would have been extremely regrettable had we not kept the public informed of all the efforts of the 'fringe' theater. This fringe theater has produced a good dozen artists whose talent, which is today being confirmed on the regular stages, is unquestionable. . . . Moreover, authors have emerged from these fringe theaters whose works, however debated and debatable they may still be, are of high quality."[1] A few months prior to the production of *Ubu Roi*, Jarry had outlined his own view of the significance of the fringe theaters, in responding to a questionnaire sent out by a literary journal: "The role played by the 'fringe theaters' is not finished, but as they have been running for several years now, people have stopped finding them crazy, and they are the regular theaters for a minority. In a few more years . . . these theaters will have become regular in the worst sense of the word if they do not remember that their essence is not to be but to become."[2] Fouquier and Jarry conceived of the role of the fringe theaters quite differently, yet in certain respects their views overlapped. For Fouquier, the fringe theaters form a desirable counterpart to the regular theaters, a kind of research and development laboratory in which experiments can be carried out. The most successful experiments provide new actors, directors, and playwrights for the established mainstream theaters; production on those regular stages constitutes the sole true test of a new work's quality. While Jarry did not consider the purpose of the fringe theaters as being to supply the regular theater, like Fouquier he did believe in a fundamental distinction between the two realms. For Jarry, it was vital that the work of the fringe theaters continued to be radically different from work performed on mainstream stages—that it strike the public as "crazy"—and he was afraid that the distinction had become blurred.

Almost a decade after Antoine founded the Théâtre Libre, the fringe theaters had indeed necessarily become an established part of the Parisian theatrical landscape. By the mid-1890s, the most prominent noncommercial companies were supplemented by a wide range of other producing entities, including amateur groups, authors paying to have their own work staged, and numerous societies formed by young actors. Productions by the Théâtre d'Art and later by the Théâtre de l'Œuvre for the most part drew, as Jarry remarked, a minority audience. That subgrouping of the Paris theatergoing public consisted of people interested in the latest developments in writing for the stage, by French and foreign authors. There were plenty of divisions within that audience, in particular between supporters of Naturalism and Symbolism, and also among proponents of different political views. Also, during the 1890s those divisions had found expression in a number of scandals at productions of plays by Maeterlinck, Ibsen, Villiers, and others, featuring booing and hissing, mocking laughter, and shouting matches between opposing sides. The climate in which the first performances of *Ubu Roi* took place thus differed significantly from that in which *Before Sunrise* premiered. Paris in 1896 had far less in common with Berlin in 1889 than with later circumstances during the turbulent early decades of the twentieth century in Europe, when Futurists, Dadaists, and others would mount their assaults on the audience. Nevertheless, the scandal generated by *Ubu Roi* cannot be regarded as simply one more uproarious production by a company for which such incidents occurred frequently: contemporary accounts make clear that the first performances of Jarry's play were exceptional. Fouquier wrote that the first night "seems to me to have considerable symptomatic importance." In this evening he saw "the victory of enlightened and progressive common sense over vulgar idiocy and of true art over the caricature of art." The fringe theater audience had for years shown great receptivity to all kinds of new work, but those responsible for this production "demanded too much of the public's indulgence and counted too much on their docility. They got angry and it was not without some pleasure that I witnessed the revolt."[3] He was appalled by *Ubu Roi* because he considered it a pretentious hoax, when for him the purpose of the fringe theater was to present serious work which might enrich the regular stage. For Jarry, meanwhile, the fringe theaters' "essence is not to be but to become"—to continually reinvent theater and expose the public to the unexpected. Reinvesting the fringe theater with that quality is in large part what Jarry set out to accomplish with *Ubu Roi,* and in the end he as well as Fouquier would be pleased and amused by the reception of his play.

Jarry arrived in Paris in 1891 at the age of seventeen, and immediately stood out among the students at the Lycée Henri IV with his unusual clothes—at first a stovepipe hat and a long hooded cape, later cycling gear—eccentric manner, and erudite wit. Within a couple of years Jarry had all but given up on his studies, having thrown himself into the literary scene in Paris: he soon won the support of writers associated with the important journals *Mercure de France* and *L'Echo de Paris,* and attended Mallarmé's Tuesday soirées. He won prizes for prose and poetry published in 1893, and his first book appeared in 1894. Jarry's involvement with the theater began only a year or so before the performance of *Ubu Roi.* Writings which have survived from his schoolboy years demonstrate an interest in drama and in the possibilities of the medium, but his adult work focused less on theater for live actors than on Guignol puppet theater. He had, however, supported the Théâtre de l'Œuvre from its inception in 1893. At the end of 1895, after a year of military service at Laval, Jarry returned to Paris and soon became more closely acquainted with Lugné-Poe, eventually being taken on by him as *secrétaire-régisseur* in May 1896. From the beginning of this association, Jarry had a personal goal in mind: to have *Ubu Roi* staged. While he approved of Lugné-Poe's efforts at the Œuvre, it was above all through his own creation that he wished to put into practice his ideas about how theater should function.

Lugné-Poe was only four years older than Jarry, and had also made his mark on the artistic scene in Paris with considerable success, first as an actor then as a director. But Lugné-Poe lacked the boldness and originality which were so integral both to Jarry's personality and to his literary output, and Lugné-Poe was far more comfortable with Jarry's administrative work for the company than with the bizarre play that the younger man wanted the Œuvre to produce. *Ubu Roi* depicts the rise and fall of Père Ubu, an obese, foul-mouthed buffoon who leads a plot to kill the Polish king, usurps the throne, and briefly rules with an uncompromising and frequently cruel devotion to enriching and gratifying himself. The king's son and heir returns—with the help of Bordure, one of Ubu's co-conspirators whom he had promptly betrayed—defeats Ubu in battle and takes back the throne, but Ubu's cowardice enables him to survive and escape into exile. Jarry's five-act play unfolds through a series of short scenes of seldom plausible, often funny, and more often crude dialog. This cartoon-like parody of *Macbeth* bore little resemblance either to the earnest treatment of social issues in realistic drama, or the static, elusive would-be poetry of symbolist drama. In his memoirs, Lugné-Poe recalls reading *Ubu Roi*, "which I didn't know how on earth to go about presenting on stage."[4] So Jarry had to make producing his play appear worthwhile and attractive to Lugné-Poe, and he did so in part by highlighting the likely reception by the Œuvre's audience.

In a January 1896 letter, Jarry described his ideas for a possible production of *Ubu Roi*, telling Lugné-Poe that the result would have "a definite comic effect," and maintaining that his play "has the advantage of being accessible to the majority of the public."[5] Jarry thus tried to sell his project to Lugné-Poe as an amusing entertainment that would be sufficiently out of the ordinary to strike the Œuvre's audience as experimental, without being so unusual as to perplex them. The closer Jarry came to the realization of his planned production of *Ubu Roi*, the more he revealed to Lugné-Poe about his real motivation. During the summer—when Jarry was taking care of the Œuvre's business and regularly corresponding with Lugné-Poe while he was away from Paris—he proposed casting in the role of the young prince Bougrelas a teenage boy rather than a young woman, as conventional practice would dictate. Jarry argued that this "might be a highlight for *Ubu*, it would excite old ladies and would cause an outcry from some of them; in any case, it would make people pay attention; and also it's never been seen, and I think the Œuvre has to monopolize all the innovations."[6] By this point Jarry had progressed from pushing *Ubu Roi* as simply a potentially entertaining spectacle to one that could radically differ from anything that had previously been done on stage, and therefore would provoke some of the audience members. Yet

Jarry still cunningly justified his ideas with arguments he knew would appeal to Lugné-Poe: the Théâtre de l'Œuvre needed to command people's attention, and to be considered at the forefront of innovation. In explaining why casting a boy as Bougrelas might be a highlight, Jarry only mentions the possibility of scandalizing certain elderly women, that is, only a minority of the audience. He knows Lugné-Poe would be reluctant to risk causing a major controversy, but that he would look favorably upon a production which by offending a few people would lead many others to talk about his theater's work.

Jarry in his letters to Lugné-Poe may have represented the patrons of the Œuvre as for the most part open to his play, but other writings dating from autumn 1896 revealed a far less optimistic view of the capacity of the Paris public to appreciate demanding theater. Jarry drew an important distinction between the masses—la foule—and a smaller, more intelligent audience. In the article "On the uselessness of theater in the theater," published in September in the Mercure de France, Jarry wrote of the masses who go to see the classics at the Comédie Française that it is "quite certain that their substance escapes them," and he regretted the fact that "The theater has not yet acquired the freedom forcibly to expel anyone who doesn't understand." Jarry believed that the correct understanding of new and original theater must be imposed on the audience, "the masses not understanding by themselves, but when they are told how to."[7] The other segment of the public, the "small number of intelligent people," by contrast, do not need such instruction.[8] Jarry refered to that group as a "public of artists" because of their participation in the theatrical experience: their theater "is neither a festival for its audience, nor a lesson, nor relaxation, but action; the elite participates in the actualization of the creation of one of its own."[9] The masses prefer "spectacle plays . . . that offer above all relaxation, a bit of a lesson perhaps, because the memory of it lasts, but a lesson of false sentimentality and false aesthetics, which are the only true ones to those for whom the theater of the minority appears incomprehensible boredom."[10]

Jarry's division of the audience into the masses and a minority of intelligent artists can to some extent be related to the regular and fringe theaters. René Peter, surveying the period several decades later, took Maeterlinck's symbolist tragedy Pelléas et Mélisande and Miss Helyett, a long-running operetta, as examples to typify the attitude of the majority toward the two kinds of theater: "the public doesn't want . . . to be offered the spectacle of people about whom they understand nothing, like the heroes of Pelléas et Mélisande. They don't like making the effort. Miss Helyett responds exactly to all their wishes. There they take pleasure in joys that are easily attained; they let their minds be gently tickled and don't ask for anything else, for they are happy."[11] Jarry looked with contempt upon this kind of resistance to making an effort, yet accepted as inevitable that the vast majority of the public felt such resistance. He saw the fringe theater as the only forum that might allow the smaller portion of the public to participate actively in a production, and hoped with *Ubu Roi* to create such an opportunity. His drive to bring his play to the stage was thus motivated both by a wish to reinvigorate the fringe theater and by an interest in putting into practice certain ideas about theater's involvement of the audience.

In mid-November 1896, the Œuvre produced Ibsen's *Peer Gynt* to some acclaim, a success to which Jarry contributed a great deal as translator/adaptor, co-director, and actor. Yet Jarry had still not altogether won over Lugné-Poe, who was "overcome by a vague apprehension about the impact of *Ubu*." It required a letter from Rachilde—an important friend, supporter, and eventually biographer of Jarry, herself a novelist and the wife of Alfred Vallette, the director of the *Mercure de France*—to convince Lugné-Poe to commit himself once and for all to the staging of *Ubu Roi*. She told him that it would be wicked of him not to keep his word to Jarry, and that the production would "marvelously prove your eclecticism." Her arguments also gave an early indication of the excitement that soon came to surround the production of *Ubu Roi* in Parisian artistic circles: "I keep hearing people at our place saying that the whole young generation, including a few of the good old folks who like a joke, is looking forward to this performance."[12] By the time *Ubu Roi* reached the stage in the second week of December, the text had been published three times in various forms and Jarry had mounted a successful publicity campaign, so that everyone in literary and artistic circles was eager to see the much talked-about new play. At the very last moment, for instance, the writer Colette anxiously told the Vallettes "I implore you to give me some means of getting in this evening, even if it's up in the gods."[13]

If a theatergoer in 1896 knew only one detail about *Ubu Roi*, that detail was its opening and most prominent word: *merdre*. Jarry's playful and provocative modification of *merde* became the primary focus of his supporters' expectations before the performances, and of his opponents' outrage during and after them. As Géroy put it in his recollections of salon conversation in 1896: "everyone was waiting with curiosity to see what effect would be produced first by the work and second by the 'word,' the famous word enriched with a sixth roaring and sonorous letter."[14] The very distinction between the play as a whole and this single word is a dubious one: there was no way for *Ubu Roi* to have an effect without *merdre* doing so. Then as now, the word *merde* was used, with varying degrees of frequency and openness, by French people of high as well as low social rank—as reflected by the euphemism "le mot de Cambronne," which alludes to one of Napoleon's generals who reportedly exclaimed "Merde!" during the defeat at Waterloo. Émile Zola, in an 1891 article, captured both the widespread usage and the force of the word in advising young writers to "dire merde au siècle" ("say shit to the century").[15] Yet it was one thing to write this widely used though transgressive word, another to utter it in public. It was still virtually inconceivable that what Laurent Tailhade dubbed "the essential word of French parlance" might be spoken in a play performed by one of Paris' respectable theaters.[16] It is a striking illustration of the radical nature of Jarry's decision to highlight this word that even half a century later Géroy repeatedly refered to it as "le mot," and avoided spelling it out. A more recent critic explained that in the 1890s the stage was still regarded as a "privileged site for the conservation of fine language, which has always been above common practice," so that Jarry's act of writing *Ubu Roi* amounted to "the devastation of theatrical language."[17]

In addition to flouting standards for distinguishing theatrical language from everyday speech, Jarry's inclusion of *merdre* in *Ubu Roi* ran counter to more recently developed notions regarding filth and its place in the private and public spheres. While the significance and status of the word *merde* may have remained largely unaltered in the course of the nineteenth century, by the 1890s important changes were under way regarding the treatment of and attitudes toward human and other waste in French society. As cities rapidly grew, the inadequacy of existing waste management systems became increasingly apparent, and greater efforts were made to improve sanitation. At the same time, a new preoccupation with cleanliness developed, reflecting the realization that improved sanitation would help minimize the spread of disease, but also coinciding with a parallel shift in attitudes toward personal hygiene. In the 1890s, it was still the case that few French people even among the wealthiest washed with any frequency, and all of them smelled bad. The gradual yet marked change of attitude toward both smells and the lack of cleanliness signaled by those smells represented a clear-cut "rise of the shame threshold," as explored by Norbert Elias in *The Civilizing Process:* "The standard of what is socially demanded and prohibited changes; in conjunction with this, the threshold of socially instilled displeasure and fear moves."[18] At the time of *Ubu Roi*'s first performances, the threshold of such displeasure and fear concerning filth, and not least human excrement, was shifting quite rapidly.

The aspirations of the middle and upper classes to an unaccustomed degree of fresh-smelling cleanliness also composed part of a broader effort to distinguish and distance themselves from the dirty, foul-smelling poor. As Stallybrass and White demonstrate in their examination of changes in the city during the nineteenth century, the new preoccupation with cleanliness appeared as doubly self-serving: "Disgust was inseparable from refinement: whilst it designated the 'depraved' domain of the poor, it simultaneously established the purified domain of the bourgeoisie."[19] This process of differentiation manifested itself in multiple forms in the public sphere, for instance through the stratification of theater: increasingly, the middle- and upper-class Parisians who patronized the established houses and the fringe theaters disdained and decried the spectacles presented on the popular stages. Jarry's forceful highlighting of bodily functions in *Ubu Roi* thus clashed at once with the bourgeoisie's efforts to embrace new standards of cleanliness and their wish to regard such standards as setting them apart. Jarry brought into the public arena of the respectable theater an aspect of life which the bourgeois citizens who formed the audience were in the process of trying to make more private than ever before.

In breaking the taboo surrounding the use of *merde*, Jarry chose not to preserve the word in its established form, but to add an extra "r." The neologism *merdre* was one of the many features of *Ubu Roi* that Jarry drew directly from the schoolboy pranks in which his play originated: at the *lycée* Jarry attended in Rennes, pupils had for some years devised mock epics ridiculing a fat, incompetent physics teacher called Hébert. The hero became *le père Heb* or *Ébé*, and a range of invented and altered words developed, including *merdre*. The additional "r," far from diminishing the force of *merde*, makes the obscenity both more effective and more complex. Most simply, the extra letter augments the acoustic effect of the word. The two syllables of *merde* sound like only one because the second is a mute "e"; the addition of the extra "r" makes the second syllable more distinct. This elongates the word and the obscenity, and provides the speaker with greater scope for enunciating "merd-re" in an expressive and aggressive manner. Furthermore, by modifying *merde*, Jarry accentuated the offensiveness of the word. If the extra letter ostensibly changes and thereby disguises *merde*, it does this so ineffectually that the addition actually serves to underline rather than camouflage the obscenity. A word that has been disguised but remains absolutely recognizable draws attention to itself. The non-camouflaging camouflage also potentially insults in another way, by suggesting that the audience is not smart enough to recognize the *merde* in *merdre*. Finally, in retaining the schoolboys' idea of adding the extra "r," Jarry made the word *merdre* the keystone of Père Ubu's inventive, idiosyncratic, and easily recognizable vocabulary (whose many resonant neologisms include "rastron" and "cornegidouille"). Thus part of the effect of the supplementary letter was to make Jarry's assault on the audience via Père Ubu more direct and personal: just as *merdre* simultaneously is not and yet is *merde*, so *merdre* is a word which only Père Ubu uses and one which everyone uses.

Jacques Lacan, commenting in passing on the extra "r," regards its inclusion as a playful move which serves to get at the truth:

one letter sufficed to give to the most vulgar of French jaculations the joculatory value, verging on the sublime, of the place it occupies in the epic of Ubu: that of the Word from before the beginning.

. . .

the fool is the one, oh Shakespeare, in life as in literature, for whom the destiny was reserved of keeping available through the centuries the place of truth which Freud was to bring into the light.[20]

Lacan brings out particularly well the way in which the conversion of *merde* into *merdre*—like Jarry's play as a whole—is at once simple and resonant. In keeping with the ages-old technique of pointing to the truth via irreverent humor, the modification creatively brings to the fore a deeper meaning behind the obscenity, shedding light on human beings' fraught relationship with their physical selves. *Merdre* is just one example of the creation and re-creation of language in *Ubu Roi* which contributed to the notoriety author and play acquired before and after the Œuvre's production. In her biography of Jarry, for instance, Rachilde recalls "carters who, from time to time, added the *r* to accentuate the swear-word!"[21]

Jarry did not simply include the modified obscenity in his play, he gave it pride of place. In the first act alone, Père Ubu says the word ten times, Mère Ubu six; by the end of the complete text, *merdre* has been pronounced thirty-three times. Not only would the patrons of the Œuvre be confronted with the unremitting use of a term they did not normally expect to hear at all, but more often than not *merdre* is employed in a very aggressive manner. The play begins in medias res: Père Ubu says "Merdre," and since there is no indication of what he could be responding to, the curse might well appear to be directed at the spectators. Mère Ubu's reply is "Oh! well that's very nice, Père Ubu, you great big lout," which, rather than clarifying the situation and Père Ubu's motivation for saying *merdre*, reinforces the impression that her husband had aimed the word outward and therefore into the auditorium.[22] Many spectators would have been astonished by the mere fact of hearing the word *merdre*, and even those who knew to expect it would probably not have foreseen such a forceful first utterance.

Some accounts indicate that those Parisians who were aware that Jarry had dared to include in *Ubu Roi* a form of the vulgar word *merde* looked forward to the imminent production with far more than mere curiosity. According to Jehan Adès, an actor who witnessed events from the wings, "the audience was informed, and well disposed. People expected obscenities and desired them. And even the ladies were not about to take offense."[23] Thus in some instances the horizon of expectations shifts not due to the influence of new work but, already before reception, through deliberate adjustment based on prior knowledge. It seems that advance warning about the taboo-breaking language and themes of Jarry's play not only permitted some Parisian theatergoers to brace themselves against a spectacle which might otherwise have given offense, but actually brought to light a distinct appetite for obscenity and for the prohibited. The reactions of some spectators during the performances would provide further evidence of such an appetite.

A fascinating commentary on the excited anticipation surrounding *Ubu Roi* was written by Rachilde, half a year after the performances. She reflected on the apparently contradictory situation which Jarry had contrived through his highlighting of the word *merdre*, that is: "A full house, the elite of humanity, of journalism, come to hear *that* like flies go you know where."[24] Those were the unprecedented circumstances Jarry had succeeded in bringing about: a large number of the more privileged members of society flocked to witness a work of art whose language placed the most unsavory bodily functions in the foreground. This was, of course, the era of decadence, when in fashionable circles, as Eugen Weber points out, "Perversion was à la mode"; the examples of dissipated behavior he gives even include coprophagy—though he maintains that "it was probably the idea of coprophagy—as of much else—that was in fashion."[25] For Rachilde, the public's expectations went as far as imagining that the stage debut of *merdre* would bring out and even transform "all the red hatreds of the old towards the young, of the young towards the old, of the young towards the young, all the kinds of sexes, newly discovered, hoping to set themselves up thanks to a dawn of more direct obscenities." She also employs the vocabulary of desire paradoxically coupled with fear to capture the mood in the auditorium, recalling the spectators' "concupiscent terror of finally hearing *the word*" and describing the finely dressed female audience members as "divine clay shivering with voluptuousness in expectation of *the magic word*."[26] Adès characterized women's attitude as the most telling measure of the audience's expectations, and so does Rachilde in a rather different light, depicting the female spectators as those most excited by the possibility that the utterance of *merdre* might function as a catalyst for social change. The idea that women were particularly engaged by the idea of liberation via Jarry's play is supported by the action of the female audience member who, according to one first-hand account, assailed the prominent conservative critic Francisque Sarcey by shouting at him: "Vieux c. [i.e., *con*]" ("Bloody old fool").[27]

Jarry's taboo-breaking use of the word *merdre* was, however, far from the only unusual and challenging feature of *Ubu Roi* as first staged at the Œuvre. Even during a period of considerable experimentation, Jarry's script had little in common with the work produced by any other theater and its uniqueness was augmented by the style of the production. In the January 1896 letter which marked the beginning of Jarry's determined effort to convince Lugné-Poe to take on *Ubu Roi*, he proposed half a dozen ideas for staging his play, most of which were carried through into the production. He wanted the actor playing Père Ubu to wear a mask; the first Ubu, Firmin Gémier, did perform the role in a pear-shaped mask, along with an oversized belly made out of cardboard. Jarry also suggested that when a scene called for Ubu to ride a horse, the actor should employ "A cardboard horse's head which he would hang around his neck."[28] In a letter written just before the opening, Jarry tells Lugné-Poe about arrangements for the life-size horse prop that they had to create because Gémier "is asking for a whole horse." The costume list from the Œuvre's production suggests that cardboard horses' heads were used for other characters such as the two cavalrymen who represented the Russian troops.[29] That diminutive army would have fulfilled another of Jarry's proposals: "Elimination of crowds, which often look bad on stage and impede understanding. Thus a single soldier in the review scene, only one in the scramble where Ubu says 'What a mob, what a retreat, etc.'"[30] The production also seems to have followed Jarry's suggestion that the costumes be "as lacking in local color or historical accuracy as possible . . . modern, preferably." One account says the actors performed "in everyday clothes, apart from a few who dressed slightly differently, for instance by rolling their pants up to their thighs," and the costume list gives for Ubu a steel-gray suit, and a suitcase in the closing scene.[31]

For the overall stage picture, Jarry recommended "Adoption of a single set or, even better, of a plain backdrop, doing away with the raising and lowering of the curtain during the single act. A character in evening dress would come, as in the Guignols, and hang up a placard indicating the scene of the action."[32] In the end, the Œuvre's production featured a backdrop that was anything but plain. This is how one critic described the set, in a tone that captured his dismay:

On the left one notices a bed draped with yellow curtains that do not conceal a certain quite intimate prop. Onto this bed is falling a storm of snow . . . A gallows, in open country, supports the skeleton of a hanged man and, opposite it, a gigantic boa snake winds itself round a palm tree. At the back, a window mounted by a few owls is outlined above some undulating hills. Right in the middle a chimney is represented, its mantelpiece ornaments of fake zinc, but what's unusual about this chimney is that it opens in the middle and serves as a door . . . [33]

Another reviewer chose to evoke the backdrop through a list of items, including the one about which his colleague was so vague: "an owl, an elephant, a bat, a boa, some palm trees, a dog, a bed and a chamber pot."[34] While the program credited only Sérusier and Jarry himself with the painting, Lugné-Poe plausibly maintained that a much larger, and quite impressive group of artists collaborated on the set: Bonnard, Vuillard, Toulouse-Lautrec, and Ranson. As Jarry had desired, placards indicated where each scene took place. An old man with a long white beard changed the signs, on which words were often misspelled—on purpose, one assumes.

Finally, Jarry proposed "Adoption of an 'accent,' or even better of a special 'voice' for the main character."[35] In this respect, Jarry's unconventional ideas for staging his play made the performance easier rather than more difficult for the actor: Gémier was struggling with the role until Lugné-Poe instructed him to "Imitate Jarry's way of talking, with two notes, that will be funny, don't be afraid to really push it—articulate like he does, with the exaggeration of the gentleman who's sure of his facts."[36] That is how Gémier delivered Père Ubu's lines, and reviews indicate that the other actors spoke in a variety of ways—Mère Ubu in a patois, Bordure with an English accent, others with Belgian, Auvergnat, and Alsatian accents—and that Jarry directed not only Gémier but also the other actors to modify their voices as well as their accents. And the same concertedly non-naturalistic style was applied to the actors' movements. Arthur Symons described Jarry's overall directorial approach as "setting human beings to play the part of marionettes, hiding their faces behind cardboard masks, tuning their voices to the howl and squeak which tradition has considerately assigned to the voices of that wooden world, and mimicking the rigid inflexibility and spasmodic life of puppets by a hopping and reeling gait."[37]

Jarry did not mention music in the January letter, though in a November letter to his friend André-Ferdinand Hérold (who was responsible for the lighting) he wrote: "Ubu will have an orchestra of 16 musicians, with timpani and trombones dominating so as to drown out the whistling."[38] It proved impossible to assemble such an orchestra during the remaining few weeks before opening, but the incidental music that Claude Terrasse had written for Jarry was performed by the composer on a piano and various percussion instruments. One review included this description of the music: "zing, zing, badazing, boum, boum!"[39]

Following standard practice for productions by the Œuvre, Jarry gave a short speech before the performance of *Ubu Roi* began. As an effort to communicate with the audience, Jarry's introduction failed almost completely; this reviewer's account is corroborated by almost all others: "A beardless young man with black hair stuck down on either side of his forehead comes out and sits at a table placed in front of the prompter's box and covered with rough packing-cloth. He reads, in a colorless voice, an announcement of which only a few phrases at intervals reach the ears of the audience."[40] Jarry was trying to let the spectators know that in certain respects the performance they were about to see fell short of his intentions: the masks were only approximations of those he had planned, time had run out for assembling the orchestra, and he had been obliged to make some cuts in the script. But Jarry's regrets about certain details notwithstanding, the first production of *Ubu Roi* did constitute a realization of the unorthodox and provocative spectacle the young author had contrived.

In her biography of Jarry written three decades after the production at the Œuvre, Rachilde maintained that *Ubu Roi* was performed once only, and that as soon as Gémier pronounced the opening *merdre*, "Such a tumult ensued that Gémier had to remain silent for a quarter of an hour."[41] This version of events is confirmed by no contemporary accounts, yet it has been treated as trustworthy and recounted many times since, forming in effect the legend of *Ubu Roi*'s scandalizing power. In fact, *Ubu Roi* was performed twice in December 1896: the *répétition générale*, the public dress rehearsal, took place on Wednesday, December 9, the premiere the following evening. Both performances prompted considerable uproar: as Symons wrote shortly afterwards, Jarry's play "has been given, twice over, before a crowded house, howling but dominated, a house buffeted into sheer bewilderment by the wooden lath of a gross, undiscriminating, infantile Philosopher-Pantaloon."[42] Although discrepancies exist between the various descriptions of the two performances, the consensus gives us a fairly reliable record of how the audience's response at the premiere differed from that at the *générale*. In responding to the questionnaire, Jarry writes: "*Répétitions générales* have the advantage of providing theater without charge for a few artists and friends of the author, where for one evening the boors are just about expurgated," but Jarry appeared not to have got, nor desired such a uniformly like-minded audience.[43] According to some accounts, Jarry had prepared a claque to make sure that a scandal occurred at the *générale*, but if so this proved to be unnecessary, as the initially animated but amused reactions of the spectators gradually gave way to more ardent protestations which eventually necessitated an interruption of the performance. The majority of contemporary descriptions probably describe the *générale*; reviews and memoirs provide a less detailed picture of the premiere, though it seems that on the second evening the reactions were more consistently negative, but less intense and less varied. The audience at the *générale* included far more spectators who were already familiar with the play (one review mentions people loudly demanding the scenes involving the bear, which were among those Jarry had cut[44]), and many came to the first performance predisposed either for or against *Ubu Roi*. At the premiere, the composition of the audience was less diverse and factionalized, and more spectators must have been taken by surprise when the play began. Many critics and other observers of the two evenings commented that the performance in the auditorium supplanted the one on stage: "the performance was the auditorium itself."[45]

The theater in which the Œuvre presented *Ubu Roi*, the Nouveau Théâtre on Rue Blanche, held around one thousand spectators, and the house was close to full for both performances. Laurent Tailhade—himself a prominent figure in the vibrant artistic environment of turn-of-the-century Paris—compared the conflict over *Ubu Roi* with its famous precursor from 1830: "a battle of *Hernani* between the young schools, decadent, symbolist, and the bourgeois critics."[46] Tailhade's account, written in 1920, misrepresented some details of the events in December 1896, but his evocation of the composition and disposition of the audience—probably at the *générale*—appears to be quite accurate. Certainly the division between mostly young artists and their associates on the one hand, and the older representatives of established cultural values on the other, underlay the pandemonium, especially at the first performance. Yet both houses also included, between those two poles, many Parisians who took an active interest in the productions of the fringe theaters, without necessarily either identifying with or looking askance upon their artistic experimentation. And however much the audiences may have varied in age and aesthetic orientation, almost all the spectators belonged to quite a limited cross-section of the Paris population. By the final decades of the century, the lower classes in Paris generally frequented the suburban theaters that catered to their tastes and their limited resources. Few if any working-class Parisians were likely to attend the occasional performances of fringe theaters like the Œuvre, and the same appeared to be true for members of the aristocracy. Although Tailhade characterized only the critics as bourgeois, most members of the two audiences brought to *Ubu Roi* the expectations and values of the bourgeoisie.

Tailhade goes on to describe at greater length some of the groups within the principal division: "Long-haired poets, grimy and grandiloquent aesthetes, every last representative of the new literature was arguing, gesticulating, scandal mongering and gossiping like porters. The editors of the *Mercure de France*, the whole lot of them, brought to this hubbub an elegant and more discreet bearing. . . . Then came the plebeians, poets and journalists, without counting the inevitable Jews, to whom theater seems to belong."[47] In 1890s Paris as in 1880s Berlin, Jews made up a significant proportion of the public for literature and the arts; as Tailhade's malicious comment reflects, Jews' success in numerous realms of French life in the final two decades of the century led to increasingly pervasive anti-Semitism, including unfounded allegations of Jewish control of theater, the press, and publishing. Tailhade erroneously implies that the Jewish spectators formed a distinct group, when in fact there would have been some Jews in several of the different parts of this quite diverse audience.

In an important 1974 study, Noël Arnaud attempted, rather more carefully than Tailhade had done, to break those 1,000 audience members down into groups; his remarks also no doubt apply more to the *générale* than to the premiere of *Ubu Roi*. Apparently, at this and all productions by the Œuvre, the 600 spectators in the circles entered without paying: "friends of the authors and the set painters and the stagehands and the caretaker, students, painters, anarchist fellow travelers, suppliers who were being compensated in this way for old unpaid debts, girlfriends of the friends of all these people, a noisy, yelling crowd, applauding in the wrong places, pouring jibes and insults on to the reactionary journalists sitting in the stalls." The audience members who were subjected to such treatment consisted of around 300 invited guests seated in the balcony and orchestra: the critics "accompanied by their own guests, the famous little botticellian women."[48] Finally there were around 100 paying subscribers, whom Arnaud characterized as the spectators who felt the least in common with the spirit of the Œuvre. Thus, as with the Freie Bühne, this specialist theater attracted members predisposed against, as well as those sympathetic to, its artistic orientation. The examples Arnaud mentions include Victorien Sardou, the highly successful commercial playwright who perhaps more than any other embodied the work opposed by the fringe theaters, and Zola, who had been instrumental in the rise of realistic theater in the 1880s.

Arnaud also quotes some contemporary statements which convey the animosity felt by more conservative audience members toward the spectators most closely associated with the Œuvre. Romain Rolland called this "a disgusting audience of tarts and spivs." André Suarès fulminated at greater length against those who supported Lugné-Poe's productions: "faces plastered with make-up; shiny white cheeks; young men with dead eyes, like the eyes of fish out of water; old men with lustful eyes and glowing cheeks; bloodless lips, or swollen mouths, bleeding with mucous; not men, but vices in masks; diseases in clothes." Naturally the same unconventionality that repelled conservatives was celebrated by those who, like critic Henry Bauer, sympathized with and supported the predominantly young avant-garde contingent: "A unique gathering populated by a crowd different from other crowds in their cerebral capacity and in the shape of their beards and in the cut of their clothes. . . . An audience with intelligence, concentration, perceptiveness and daring."[49] The less extreme conservative critics actually shared something of this view that the Œuvre's audience was a special one. In *La Paix*, for instance, Georges Vanor complained that Lugné-Poe should never have expected the "fervent and loyal admirers of the Œuvre" to take such a spectacle seriously.[50] Yet Vanor simplified matters in suggesting that those admirers made up a unified group; the audience for productions at the Œuvre had very often been factionalized, and given the heightened anticipation surrounding *Ubu Roi*, the audience for this production was even more divided, even more primed for battle than usual.

Ubu Roi prompted an exceptionally energetic and varied response from this mixed audience. One reviewer summed up the pandemonium this way: "People booed and hissed, meowed, barked, played whistles, all of this with enough sincerity and persistence that . . . I find that I've come away having understood no more than fragments of *Roi Ubu*."[51] Some of those verbs might seem to indicate exaggeration on the reviewer's part, yet several other observers described the noises made by the spectators in the same terms. Many of the contemporary accounts emphasize the fact that the audience members who wished to show support for Jarry's play demonstrated with just as much vigor as his opponents; for example,

"And tomorrow opinion will be divided just as the house itself was yesterday evening: turbulent, very combative, curious, bursting into applause and protests, laughter and whistling mixed in with the bravos."[52] Another critic depicts this conflict between those for and those against the performance through a succinct sampling of utterances: "'Bravo!' 'It's disgraceful!' 'It's superb!' 'It's idiotic!' 'You wouldn't understand Shakespeare!' etc."[53] However, while some represent this skirmish as quite good-natured, others suggest that the degree of tension in the auditorium was much higher: "From the middle of the first act one senses that things are going to turn nasty."[54] Catulle Mendès adopts a mode of description which highlights the range of reaction prompted by *Ubu Roi:* "Whistling and hissing? yes; yells of rage and groans of malicious laughter? yes; seats ready to fly on to the stage? yes; occupants of boxes screaming and shaking their fists? yes; and in a word a whole throng, furious at being the victims of a hoax, jumping with a start towards the stage."[55] This list demonstrates the various behaviors which were available to and therefore employed by the protesting spectators, and the location of the threshold beyond which they did not go—that is, though seats may have been "ready to fly on to the stage" and angry spectators may have been "jumping with a start toward the stage," no objects were thrown and no one actually invaded the stage.

Many of the contemporary critics who regarded *Ubu Roi* as an elaborate and tasteless practical joke reported with satisfaction the manner of the audience's response: "beginning in the second act, the evening was nothing but a series of jibes in the auditorium, the least witty of which was without question less inept, and above all less disgusting than what was being said on stage."[56] Fouquier recorded a contribution to the debate over the merits of new versus old drama: "one spectator shouted out 'Long live Monsieur Scribe!'"—a reference to Eugène Scribe, the prolific and enormously successful playwright who dominated the mid-nineteenth century.[57] As one description quoted above indicated, the supporters of Jarry and of the avant-garde adopted a similar strategy: "Someone, among the hubbub of booing, shouted out: 'You wouldn't understand Shakespeare any better!'"[58] (One of the most famous and most often quoted witnesses of Père Ubu's debut, W. B. Yeats, was disadvantaged through understanding little French; he noted simply that "The audience shake their fists at one another."[59]) Jules Renard, in a brief entry in his diary, described some further protests against the protests, in this instance attributed to two individuals close to Jarry: "Vallette says 'It's funny,' and one can hear Rachilde shouting 'Enough!' at those who are hissing."[60] Rachilde herself characterized the verbal exchanges among spectators thus: "People were shouting at each other from one box to the next, hurling abuse." She also maintains that Willy—Colette's husband—offered a kind of encouragement to the shouting spectators: "Willy, waving his famous hat with the flat rim, of legendary renown, ended up yelling to the audience: 'Let's keep it going!' as if he considered that the only important scene was the one in the house."[61] Indeed, the majority of recorded shouts have been attributed to some known figure from the Parisian artistic scene, and many of them to more than one person. Jules Lemaître, himself a successful playwright as well as a leading critic, supposedly asked out loud, "This is a joke, isn't it?"; and Lugné-Poe describes the participation of another playwright associated with the Théâtre Libre: "Courteline, standing up on a foldaway seat, shouted: 'Don't you see that the author's taking us for idiots!'"[62] The protests and counterprotests during the *Ubu Roi* scandal were almost all verbal: with the exception of some shaking of fists and other gesticulating, no one mounted a performance of opposition of the kind Dr. Kastan had devised against *Before Sunrise*. In comparison to the response to Hauptmann's play, the uproar during *Ubu Roi* also consisted far more of utterances aimed by one audience member at others, rather than being contrived as direct protests against the performance. At the *générale* in particular, many of these spectators were participating in an ongoing contest between different positions regarding theater—in some instances with genuine anger and hostility, in others with good humor and enjoyment.

As Gémier himself recalled it some years later, for the first two acts at the *générale*, "Everyone was laughing. Some of the laughter came in response to the lines, some of it functioned like applause, but the important thing was that they were laughing." But the mood deteriorated quite abruptly during Act III, scene v, which takes place in the dungeon where Père Ubu has imprisoned Bordure. Ubu goes to see him there and, as Gémier recounts it,

To take the place of the prison door, an actor stood on stage with his left hand held out. I put the key in his hand as if in a lock. I made the noise of the bolt, "crrreak," and I moved the arm as if I was opening a door. At that moment the audience, who no doubt felt that the joke had gone on long enough, began to yell, to rant and rave; cries burst out from every corner, insults, a volley of whistling accompanied by a whole variety of noises.[63]

This seems to have been the first point during the *générale* at which the actors were compelled to suspend the performance. And they weren't able to resume until Gémier had found a rather surprising means of changing the mood once again. Another eyewitness, Valentin Mandelstamm, recalled how Gémier "began, by way of an outlet, to dance a frantic jig. This spectacle looked so comical that people started to laugh. He was able to continue his performance, and complete it more or less without further disruption."[64] According to Gémier, at some point during the remaining scenes he sat on the edge of the stage, which prompted someone to shout

out "This way to the exit!"—a remark which several others attribute to
André Antoine, though one can't help but regard with some skepticism
such a perfect moment of conflict between the realistic and anti-realistic
tendencies.[65] For the premiere, Gémier equipped himself with a tramway
horn with which to silence the audience: "every time people remonstrated
a bit too much, he blew on the horn and that calmed the murmurs in a
burst of gaiety."[66] Gémier maintained that "I only had to use it at a couple
of points. The audience at the premiere was, as always, less impassioned
than the one at the *générale*."[67]

The performance in the auditorium revealed much about prevailing
attitudes toward filth by adopting and adapting the play's most striking
word. According to Henri de Régnier, *merdre* played a starring role
(though almost forty years later he still declined to spell out the term): "It
was 'the word' which, greeted by the spectators with laughs or whistles,
with applause and boos, had the honor of the evening. It fluttered about
from the stalls to the circle, and was exchanged from seat to seat."[68] While
Régnier's colorful memoir should perhaps be taken with a grain of salt,
one of the contemporary reviews confirms his basic contention: "the first
word of the play recurs all the time; the audience gets angry and sends it
back."[69] Two of the most noteworthy verbal protests during the *générale*
entailed emulation of the play's crude language and themes, the first
through a pun combining Lugné-Poe's name with *pot de chambre*, the
French term for a chamber pot: "when in the midst of the uproar one
interrupter was heard to exclaim, 'A bas [Down with] Lugné-Poe . . . de
Chambre,' the approbation was virtually unanimous."[70] And at another
point, an audience member shouted a wordplay devised even more in the
spirit of the play: "At the cry of 'Merdre,' someone replies 'Mangre!'"[71]
Presumably the wordplay "A bas Lugné-Poe de Chambre!" was intended
as a protest against the director of the Œuvre for having sanctioned the
performance of *Ubu Roi*; but in imitating the play's vocabulary of excretion
the pun actually served to underline how much that audience member
and his supporters had in common with the foul-mouthed and ill-
mannered Père Ubu. The cry of "Mangre!" is more extreme than the play
on Lugné-Poe's name, since it amounts to telling those responsible for the
production to "eat shit." Both interventions seem to have been received
by the other spectators with approving amusement, suggesting that most
audience members regarded them as playful acts of resistance to the performance; but clearly the effectiveness of both as opposition was severely
compromised by their own scatology.

While *Ubu Roi* and its key word *merdre* did not, in the event, inaugurate
a new era of uninhibited openness as some Parisians, according to Rachilde, hoped it might, Jarry's forceful use of the term did prompt in the
auditorium an extraordinary display of unrestrained behavior. The theatergoers who repeated the forbidden word were, of course, assisted by the

fact that *merdre* at once is and is not *merde*, so that they could experience the thrill of transgression and yet feel that they were not actually violating a prohibition. And clearly many of those who did shout "Merdre!" enjoyed doing so. The spectators' conflicting responses to *merdre*—their revulsion at hearing it on the one hand, their pleasure at getting to utter it themselves on the other—reflect adults' ambivalent attitude toward the basic physical functions that Jarry's play brought to the fore. Freud theorized that the coprophilic instincts of the child become suppressed in the adult, but that they occasionally reveal themselves: "Certain forms of mental activity such as joking are still able to make the obstructed source of pleasure accessible for a brief moment, and thus show how much of the esteem in which human beings once held their faeces still remains preserved in the unconscious."[72] Those spectators who repeated Jarry's scatology or invented their own evidently took childish enjoyment from uttering and even playing with the taboo term. Considered in the light of Freud's theories, the word *merdre* substituted for the thing itself, and that displacement into language afforded the spectators a rare opportunity to relive their childhood connection to their own excrement.

Other critics have examined the processes whereby cultures attempt to deny any positive feelings associated with bodily products by banishing them from social discourse. That exclusion never succeeds altogether; as Dominique Laporte states in his *History of Shit*, "Civilization does not distance itself unequivocally from waste but betrays its fundamental ambivalence in act after act."[73] Stallybrass and White demonstrate how efforts by the dominant culture to reject and thus separate itself from the 'low' ultimately fail: "The bourgeois subject continuously defined and redefined itself through the exclusion of what it marked out as 'low' . . . But disgust always bears the imprint of desire. These low domains, apparently expelled as 'Other', return as the object of nostalgia, longing and fascination."[74] The spectators at the Œuvre were confronted by insistent verbal and other references to excrement, that is, to an element of human existence from which they customarily dissociated themselves, as part of the bourgeoisie's broader project of distinguishing themselves as cleaner and superior. The audience's fervent performance of opposition to *merdre* might appear simply consistent with that exclusion of the 'low', were it not undermined by the kind of indications of desire which Stallybrass and White repeatedly identify: the eager anticipation of many of the informed spectators beforehand, and especially the eager participation of many audience members in uttering, indeed in playing with the taboo term during the performances.

If the shout of "Mangre!" was designed to protest against *Ubu Roi* by outdoing its obscenity, then strictly speaking it could not succeed, since Jarry had already brought together *merdre* and eating in the third scene of the play, where the final item on the dinner menu Mère Ubu announces, and which the Ubus and their guests proceed to eat, is "choux-fleurs [cau-liflower] à la merdre." And Père Ubu augments that element of the meal by throwing on to the table a "balai innommable [unnamable brush]"—a lavatory brush—from which he tells his guests to take a taste.[75] One critic focused on this scene as an example of how repugnant the play's dialog is: "You will have an idea of what was dared when you know that King Ubu, at table with his guests, has them served an ordinary dinner of ex-crement. And the meal takes place on the stage!"[76] But Jarry's reasons for including this detail were not as primitively offensive as such reactions presume. "Choux-fleurs à la merdre," rather than simply representing the extreme of Jarry's desire gratuitously to force his audience into contact with bodily functions, is the most explicit illustration of Père Ubu's ele-mental nature. At the start of scene iv, Ubu and Bordure compare notes on the meal:

Père Ubu: Well, Captain, did you enjoy your dinner?

Capitaine Bordure: Very much, monsieur, apart from the merdre.

Père Ubu: Eh! the merdre wasn't bad.

In a different context, it might seem as if Ubu's intention was to provoke his guest, to put him in the position of having either to lie about the dinner or to be honest and risk insulting his hosts. But in fact Père Ubu is perfectly sincere when he claims to have enjoyed the "choux-fleurs à la merdre." For him, unlike for Bordure or for the others who "fall down poisoned" after tasting from the brush, consumption and excretion are two sides of the same, basic, life-sustaining process, so that eating faeces symbolically brings the two together.[77]

The 1896 reviews suggest that many audience members misconstrued Jarry's intentions in presenting *Ubu Roi*. More than one critic interpreted the preponderance of *merdre* in the script as indicating the author's fa-vorable attitude toward filthy matter. One called the play a "scatophile insanity,"[78] another observed that "the attitude of a good number of my fellow guests showed me that I am not the only one who does not at all appreciate the charm of filth."[79] Both apparently assumed that Jarry wished to celebrate filth, to sing the praises of *merdre*. Now it may be justifiable to accuse Père Ubu of being a "scatophile," but it by no means follows that the same is true of Jarry. Yet it is clear that many critics and presumably many other spectators identified the author with the play's central character, apparently not considering the possibility that Jarry cre-ated Père Ubu in order to expose and indict certain attitudes and behavior. Another recurring motif in the reviews was the satisfied declaration (fre-quently expressed via the writer's own rather ponderous puns, such as "It was in vain that Mr Jarry put in *r* [air]—it did not smell good"[80]) that the audience proved themselves to be wittier than Jarry. For example, "wit has not lost its rights among the spectators. Lord knows, it was certainly necessary to make up for what was absent from the stage."[81] This response is also based on the conflation of Père Ubu and Jarry: because Père Ubu said stupid things, people concluded that the play and its author were stupid. On the basis of such misguided interpretation, the scatological verbal interventions were legitimized through being conceived of and perceived as protests against the performance. But while the spectator who shouted "A bas Lugné-Poe de Chambre!" may have done so to demonstrate that he or she was just as witty as Jarry, all this audience member really showed was that he or she was just as dim-witted as Père Ubu.

A couple of writers who wrote first-hand accounts of the *générale* reflected on the shout of "Mangre!" and the reaction it prompted, and both regard the incident as representative of a good-natured mood in the auditorium. Henry Bauer, one of the established critics who wrote most favorably about *Ubu Roi* before as well as after the performances, suggested that more than one audience member shouted "Mangre," and remarked that, "It does not displease me that some jokers collaborated with the protagonists on stage, and, when the latter added an R to the Cambronne illustration, felt obliged to reply 'Mangre' to the Poles. What was taking place on the boards was only a suggestive appearance and theme for those who approached it with goodwill."[82] And Francis Jourdain, recalling the "epic" first performance of *Ubu Roi* many years later, wrote that "The first few 'Merdre!'s from Monsieuye Ubu and his spouse made the spectators less indignant than the more unexpected riposte from one of them, 'Mangre!', made them laugh."[83] So the famously rancorous response to the first production of *Ubu Roi* did in fact include a substantial element of light-heartedness, and the shouts of "A bas Lugné-Poe de Chambre!" and of "Mangre!" capture particularly vividly the unusual combination of opposition and enjoyment.

The enthusiasm with which some audience members shouted *merdre* at each other, and their attempts to outdo the primitive humor of the play, remind one more of the uninhibited uproar of the nursery than the supposedly civilized, decorum-bound environment of the auditorium. This is ironic given that one of the most common criticisms leveled at Jarry's play was that it was childish. If *Ubu Roi* was an "enfantillage," was not the spectacle in the auditorium also? Jarry would no doubt have agreed that his play, and certainly its main character, were in some respects childish; the spectators, by contrast, would probably have denied any significant resemblance between their behavior and the events on stage. In the later play *Ubu enchaîné*, Père Ubu remarks that "what makes little children laugh risks frightening the grown-ups," and the members of *Ubu Roi*'s first audiences reacted at once like little children, laughing at and making jokes against the performance in an often puerile manner, and as adults unsettled by a work they suspected of deriding them and their values.[84]

This is one of the many ways in which Jarry's carefully planned assault on the standards and expectations of the public forced the spectators, in spite of themselves, to react in a different and more revealing way than they normally did in the theater.

The eruption of protests in response to the prison scene about halfway through the *générale* also provides insights into the audience's theatrical tastes, aversions, and expectations. Contemporary reviews and other accounts indicate that the spectators believed they understood what Jarry was trying to achieve with *merdre* and with the play's obscenity, and expressed approval or disapproval of that tactic. The production's unconventional approach to onstage representation posed much more of a challenge, since it surpassed by some distance many audience members' horizon of expectations. Several accounts suggest that the prison scene marked the turning point at the *générale* from an audience that was for the most part enjoying the occasion to one that was predominantly angry. It seems that while to begin with the unfamiliar puppet-like style struck most spectators as at least intriguing, by the mid-point in the text that novelty had worn off and given way to rising impatience. The depiction of a door by an actor's arm was the straw that broke the camel's back, probably because it was regarded as an abuse of the human body. The representational short-hand involved in using a single, far from realistic backdrop accompanied by placards, the use of one actor to stand for a crowd—such techniques did not threaten the integrity of the body as the prison scene did. Like the audience at the premiere of Brecht's *Lehrstück* over thirty years later, this audience was deeply troubled by a representation that appeared to make light of the human body. The protest which erupted in Act III can be seen as a collective cry of "Is this a theater or a Punch and Judy show?!" Jarry in effect designed the performance to be both, and exposed within the public a resistance to representations of human beings which dehumanize them.

As in the case of *Before Sunrise*, it is instructive to consider which parts of *Ubu Roi* met with a positive response as well as which parts provoked protests. The placards indicating where each scene takes place aroused no opposition; according to one review, the actor who played the old man who changed the placards even won some acclaim.[85] Unlike the use of an actor's arm as a door, the unconventional stylistic device of the placards, rather than throwing over standard modes of onstage representation, added an element to the production, and moreover one which supplied the audience with helpful information. The uproar over the prison scene also led to a revealing instance of favorable reaction when Gémier succeeded in restoring calm by dancing his comical jig. Like the spectators for *Before Sunrise* who abandoned all their animosity toward Loth and the play once they got carried away by a love scene, the audience for *Ubu Roi* stopped yelling and began to laugh when the disturbing use of an arm as a door was supplanted by Gémier's clown-like dance. Both instances suggest that an audience confronted with work which goes beyond their horizon of expectations will eagerly seize opportunities to respond as if the work actually remained within that horizon, in an unconscious denial of strong, unfamiliar feelings.

Many of the critics regarded Jarry's well-publicized production as a tasteless hoax, and ardently demonstrated that they had not been taken in. Sarcey devoted only two short paragraphs to *Ubu Roi*, dismissing it as "a filthy fraud which deserves nothing but the silence of contempt."[86] In Sarcey's view, the vulgarity was employed exclusively in the service of a hoax to which he was not about to fall prey. While Sarcey concluded that Jarry was trying to con his audience into taking his play seriously, other critics assumed that the idea behind *Ubu Roi* was above all to provoke. Thus Robert Vallier wrote: "The imagination in it is slight and laborious, in its filthy truculence. Everything, or nearly everything, seemed to me even more puerile and pretentious than smutty and shocking."[87] The implication of the parenthetical "or nearly everything" is that Vallier was in fact somewhat shocked and disgusted, but because he is convinced that provocation was Jarry's aim, he strives to deny it.

Several of the journalists who reviewed the performances of *Ubu Roi* expressed their pleasure at the way the audience had resisted Jarry's attack. For example, Sarcey wrote: "I noted with pleasure that the audience (this nonetheless very special audience one finds at performances by the Œuvre) eventually rebelled against this excess of ineptitude and obscenity."[88] It is significant, however, that the spectators did not immediately protest against the play. Sarcey's explanation for this appears to be that these were not typical spectators, but the exceptional patrons of the Œuvre, who are prepared to tolerate more than the average audience. But part of the reason is that, for much of the *générale* at least, *Ubu Roi* entertained many in the audience for some time before it offended them. And if some critics were pleased with the way the audience responded, that satisfaction is mitigated by others who point out that the spectators could have expressed themselves in a still more emphatic manner, for instance by walking out. As I discussed at the beginning of this book, one critic in effect spoke on behalf of norms of behavior which would establish themselves in the next century by suggesting that the spectators ought to have left in order to retain their dignity. Perhaps hardly any patrons of the Œuvre did get up and leave because most of them were enjoying themselves. Another critic lamented that "In the old days the performance would not have been allowed to finish. Perhaps our fathers were right, and perhaps they also had more energy than we do."[89] The spectators for *Ubu Roi* did not create such a ruckus that the performance had to be abandoned, let alone start a riot, but they did briefly return this late-nineteenth-century auditorium to conditions reminiscent of "the old days," and in doing so displayed considerable energy, though not all of it directed against the performance.

One of the more thoughtful unfavorable reviews, by Henry Céard, included a perceptive analysis of the audience response, probably at the *générale.* Céard pointed to a "triple conflict" within the audience (and predicted, quite correctly, that "Yesterday evening will remain legendary in the annals of disorderly performances"). The first group he singled out was the subscribers of the Œuvre, who, "always in search of symbols and thoroughly convinced that, in this theater, there's nothing to be understood that isn't sublime, looked in this practical joke for a deep meaning and a philosophical authority which the author didn't delude himself he was giving them. After a few moments of patience, they got annoyed at finding nothing, since everything was missing, and they fiercely showed their disappointment." He contrasted those spectators with another group who pretended to understand the work: "Laboring to admire and applying themselves to uncovering a beauty that was absent, they considered themselves offended by the protests of their neighbors. They in turn protested, in the name of great Art in peril." In Céard's view, the final third of the audience "took enormous pleasure from this manner of restoring the violent parades of the fairground theater."[90] Céard regarded *Ubu Roi* as nothing more than a hoax in which no one could find any meaning, but that does not invalidate his assessment of the scandal, since very few spectators did comprehend Jarry's play. A large proportion of the audience for productions by the Théâtre de l'Œuvre comprised people who expected to respond favorably to the work, and who therefore approached *Ubu Roi* hoping to enjoy and appreciate it. When the performance turned out to diverge by some distance from their horizon of expectations, some of these audience members voiced their objections, while others, perhaps motivated more by a desire to defend the work on principle than by any conviction of the work's value, opposed the others with counterprotests. Considered in this light, the *Ubu Roi* scandal consisted less in animated reactions to a new play than in reactions to that play's thwarting of any familiar form of audience engagement. As Céard points out, many in the audience did not appear to mind if the performance afforded them no enjoyment, since the uproar in the house provided plenty.

Not surprisingly, most of Jarry's supporters were in the end disappointed by the evening. According to Tailhade, before the performance began, "the atmosphere was heavy, a certain uneasiness troubled this expectant and tumultuous throng," and he attributed this to the ambivalence felt by Jarry's fellow writers, who did not want the production to prove too great a success.[91] Above all, it appears that the overly high expectations of the progressive writers and sympathizers led to their disappointment. It was almost impossible for the performances of *Ubu Roi* to meet those expectations. As Romain Coolus wrote only a few weeks afterwards, "*Ubu*

Roi constituted an unusual spectacle which the public greeted in rather a stupid manner. People were generally disappointed, as if Jarry had promised the world the gospel of future art."[92] Jourdain recalled that "the text, which we knew by heart, seemed to us to have lost a lot of its accent, and we had trouble defending right up to the end this play whose truculence seemed less funny to us, and its cruelty a little heavy."[93] Yet the range of reactions shows that for audience members who had little or no prior knowledge of the text, *Ubu Roi* seemed very truculent indeed. Camille Mauclair wrote that Jarry's play "disappointed. It bored people: nothing is fatal like a failed explosive charge . . . it lasted too long. People laughed for ten minutes, yawned at the end of the first half-hour, and at the end of the first hour people whistled."[94] This summary also depicts the reception of *Ubu Roi* very much from the viewpoint of those who had hoped for something more significant than the pandemonium that did occur. Rachilde wrote the most evocative account of certain Parisians' unreasonably high expectations, and her description of the disappointment many felt afterwards indicates that in the end *Ubu Roi* was not as deliciously dirty as some had hoped. In her view, "People whistled above all at the lack of real filth. They had thought that this Punch of an Ubu would function sexually."[95] What she and others do not seem to have realized is that Jarry took advantage of the backing of those who supported the fringe theater in order to affront not only the less open-minded bourgeois, but also those who believed they could understand and appreciate experimental art. So while many of Jarry's sympathizers felt let down by the performances of *Ubu Roi*, the author himself was pleased with the scandal he had created (the scrapbook of reviews he put together does not include the few favorable notices).

Jarry's objective had been to present the spectators with an unvarnished, authentic image of themselves, as he explained in an essay he published after the performances, "Questions de théâtre": "I wanted the scene that the audience would find themselves in front of when the curtain went up to be like that mirror in the stories of Madame Leprince de Beaumont, in which the depraved see themselves with bulls' horns, or a dragon's body, each according to the exaggeration of their vice; and it's not surprising that the public should have been aghast at the sight of their ignoble double." He finds it entirely understandable that the audience should have been taken aback by this unprecedentedly direct representation of human baseness, but at the same time he is frustrated that their habitual way of perceiving and understanding drama impeded their readiness to recognize in Père Ubu their "ignoble double." Jarry believed that many spectators treated *Ubu Roi* as if it did fall within their horizon of expectations, as if it were supposed to be a conventional, witty comedy, but as he explained, "Really, there's no reason to expect an amusing play. . . . And above all no one understood . . . that Ubu was not meant to utter witticisms, as various little ubuists demanded of him, but stupid remarks, with all the authority of the Ape." And in reference to theater's relationship with the public in general, Jarry wrote: "It is because the public [*la foule*] are an inert and obtuse and passive mass that they need to be shaken up from time to time so that we can tell from their bear-like grunts where they are—and where they stand."[96] Whatever one may think of Jarry's at times contemptuous opinion of the majority of the public, there can be little question that he succeeded in inducing the spectators at the two performances to a revealing display of their own makeup, including their ambivalent attitude toward the bodily functions which his play highlighted.

The importance of *merdre* in *Ubu Roi* carries over into Jarry's writings about the play; indeed his reflections feature quite a nuanced conception of filth. Writing on the eve of the premiere about the character of Père Ubu, Jarry clarified that: "*He is not* exactly Monsieur Thiers, nor the bourgeois, nor the boor: he is rather the perfect anarchist, with that which prevents *us* from ever becoming the perfect anarchist, that he is a man, whence cowardice, filthiness [*saleté*], ugliness, etc."[97] Jarry was trying to forestall the efforts of critics and others to regard Ubu as a satirical portrayal of a particular kind of person, emphasizing instead how much Ubu has in common with all people—and through the pronoun "us" he includes himself. The "not exactly" acknowledges that Ubu possesses something of the bourgeois, just as he does something of its opposite, the anarchist; for Jarry it is fundamental to being human that one cannot actually make the transition from conformist bourgeois to lawless anarchist. The three properties Jarry names as characteristic of human beings each represent the opposite of how we like to think of ourselves—as brave, clean, and beautiful. Yet the second term, "filthiness," is the least expected and most provocative, and best reflects Jarry's desire to confront the public with a representation of their "ignoble double." Elsewhere too, Jarry made clear the connection between Ubu's baseness and the fundamental nature of our species. In the program, for instance, he wrote: "M. Ubu is an ignoble being, which is why he resembles (from underneath) all of us."[98] So it would appear that Jarry is referring to a kind of natural filthiness, an unavoidable engagement with the body and its products that it is customary yet absurd to deny. For Jarry, that kind of "filth" characterizes not only Père Ubu, but humans in general.

In "Questions de théâtre," Jarry again employed the term "sale," but to make another, complementary point. Reflecting on the audience's response, Jarry wrote: "It would have been easy to fit *Ubu* to the taste of the Paris public by making the following minor modifications: the opening word would have been Zut (or Zutre), the unspeakable brush a pretty girl going to bed, the army uniforms would have been First Empire style, Ubu would have formally embraced the Czar, and various people would have been cuckolded—but that would have been filthier [*mais ç'aurait été plus sale*]."[99] Jarry may well have been responding to the frequent use of the term *sale* in spoken and written objections to his play, such as this complaint which encapsulates the common dual charge of offensiveness and pointlessness: "It is not only that it is filthy [*sale*], but it takes up space."[100] Whereas for most of the public, filth connoted vulgar language and the bodily functions to which it referred, for Jarry, filth in this context would consist of presenting the audience with precisely what they expected and wanted: inoffensive language, erotic titillation, mild satire, a happy ending, and plenty of adultery. (Jarry's reference to the "coucher de petite femme," may well have been an allusion to a curious genre of entertainment which evolved following the 1894 success of *Le Coucher d'Yvette*, shows which, as Weber writes, "turned around the actions of a young woman undressing to go to bed or else rising from bed to dress."[101])

In his reflections following the production, Jarry bemoanes the very limited capacity of most people to understand theater and literature of any substance, listing several examples including Ibsen, Baudelaire, and Mallarmé. To him, the response to productions by fringe theaters has proven emblematic and disheartening: "We know this from observing the audience for the four years of the Œuvre: if you are absolutely determined to give the masses an inkling of something you must explain it to them beforehand." But later in the same essay, Jarry suggests that explaining a work to the audience beforehand is not the only possible way to ensure that they comprehend it. *Ubu Roi* demonstrates the other way of going about it: "Since art and the comprehension of the masses are so incompatible, we may well have been mistaken in attacking the masses directly in *Ubu Roi;* they got angry because they understood only too well, whatever they may say."[102] Jarry is being ironic when he writes of his direct attack on the public as a mistake: it would only have been a mistake if angering them was a result he wished to avoid. He implies that *Ubu Roi* is not a work of art, since the masses were able to understand it. It seems that for its author, *Ubu Roi* represents an alternative both to predictable theater which can be understood but is uninspiring and unmemorable, and to real art that inevitably will not be appreciated by most of the public. This alternative involves forcefully confronting the audience with a performance that cannot fail to stimulate a reaction. And such a reaction will bring with it both anger and denial: Jarry believes that the spectators at the Œuvre took offense at his play because they did recognize themselves in Père Ubu, even if on the face of it they were offended by the language or by the style of the production.

The development of theater in France from 1896 on supports the notion that *Ubu Roi* constituted an artistic form unto itself, so distinctly did it stand apart from other productions. In stark contrast to *Before Sunrise*, Jarry's play made no immediate impact on theatrical repertoire or prac-

tice. It was not until the 1920s—long after Jarry's early death in 1907—
that many people began to consider *Ubu Roi* anything other than a
historical curiosity. In the course of the twentieth century, Jarry came to
be widely regarded as a noteworthy precursor of key developments in
literature, and in particular as a pioneer of a deliberately provocative approach to theater. Yet unlike some later practitioners of confrontational
art, Jarry did not present his work as the last word; instead, he saw himself
as part of an ongoing and valuable process. At the very end of "Questions de théâtre," he wrote: "And new young people will come along,
who will find us quite outdated, and will compose ballads to express
their loathing of us, and there is no reason for this to end."[103] Jarry suggests that those young successors will in turn stimulate theater spectators into fervently opposing new work in the auditorium. He would
perhaps have been surprised at the subsequent decline of scandals like
the one generated by *Ubu Roi*.

CHAPTER 3

"This Is Not Irish Life!":
Defending National Identity

Synge's *The Playboy of the Western World*

For one week at the end of January 1907, the Irish National Theatre Society (INTS) presented J. M. Synge's *The Playboy of the Western World* at the Abbey Theatre in Dublin. It became and remains the most tempestuous week in Irish theater history. During several of the eight performances the actors could not be heard, so intense and sustained were the shouting and stamping. Often the performance was temporarily abandoned so that order might be restored, and many people were arrested for their participation in the protests. Where the scandal kindled by *Before Sunrise* entailed a single performance and *Ubu Roi* provoked distinct responses from two separate audiences, the row over Synge's play might be considered one weeklong scandal, in the course of which the spectators' reactions ebbed and flowed just as they did during those earlier one- or two-night scandals. The Dubliners who participated in the so-called *Playboy* riots are typically represented as narrow-minded nationalists; but to consider them philistines is to disregard both the broad political context and the specific conditions in which Synge's play was forced upon them.

By 1907, the INTS had existed for five years, and since 1904 had occupied the converted building that became world famous as the Abbey Theatre. But the fact that those premises were purchased for the self-proclaimed national theater by a wealthy Englishwoman emblematizes the Abbey's unavoidably disputed position in pre-independence Ireland. Around the turn of the century, the key criterion according to which many Irish assessed any new organization was whether or not its activity served the nationalist cause. Like the Irish Literary Theatre out of which it grew, the INTS was founded and for the most part run by people of Anglo-Irish descent, who did not associate themselves with, and in some cases even distanced themselves from, nationalism.

Early in 1899 W. B. Yeats—by then in his mid-thirties, and already a successful and widely admired poet—joined forces with two wealthy patrons of the arts and would-be writers, Lady Augusta Gregory and Edward Martyn, to establish the Irish Literary Theatre. The stated purpose of the new theater in some respects echoed that of the Freie Bühne ten years earlier. In the letter sent to various writers, academics, and politicians soliciting support, the founders emphasized their hope of being granted "that freedom of experiment which is not found in theatres in England, and without which no new movement in art and literature can succeed." Whereas the Freie Bühne and the Théâtre Libre presented themselves above all as non-commercial theaters, the Irish Literary Theatre characterized itself primarily as "not English." The founding of the new theater, like that of the Gaelic League devoted to reviving the Irish language, and of the *United Irishman* newspaper, reflected a broad movement during the 1890s to assert Ireland's identity independent of England. The Irish Literary Theatre aligned itself with those other organizations, but also took up the position that some years later would make the Abbey's production of *The Playboy* so inflammatory: "We will show that Ireland is not the home of buffoonery and of easy sentiment, as it has been represented, but the home of an ancient idealism. We are confident of the support of all Irish people, who are weary of misrepresentation, in carrying out a work that is outside all the political questions that divide us."[1] These declared aims of the new theater became the standard against which its productions and those of its successor, the INTS, would be measured. The misrepresentation the letter alludes to is the centuries-old stereotype of the Stage Irishman, which was particularly prominent on the nineteenth-century British stage—a figure described by George Bernard Shaw as "generous, drunken, thriftless, with a joke always on his lips and a sentimental tear always in his eye."[2] The Irish Literary Theatre strove to displace that demeaning portrayal of the Irish, but the danger existed that the public would want the alternative version always to reflect "ancient idealism," and would be quick to respond adversely to depictions which did not patronize but also did not glorify the Irish. The confidence the letter expresses in winning wide public support would only have been warranted if the theater had committed itself to presenting Dubliners with nothing but flattering representations of themselves. A similar underestimation of complexity is apparent in the writers' supposed belief that a theater could actively engage in the struggle over how the Irish are represented yet remain "outside all the political questions that divide us." At the turn of the century, just what kind of representation of the Irish should be set up in place of the longstanding misrepresentation was itself a political question. Many acrimonious episodes in the Abbey's early history would revolve around divisions over that political question, and none more so than the controversy over *The Playboy.*

The Irish Literary Theatre presented seven plays before it effectively dissolved in the autumn of 1901. Its occasional performances had attracted a good deal of attention, and generated both considerable enthusiasm and some controversy. One focus of criticism was the use of English actors, whose accents and inability to correctly pronounce Irish names marred the productions for many spectators, as well as appearing to contradict the organization's mission. In a letter in the summer of 1902, Yeats wrote that "the Irish Literary Theatre has given place to a company of Irish actors."[3] The nucleus of that company was two brothers, William and Frank Fay, experienced amateur and sometimes professional performers, who in April 1902 produced a double bill including a new play written by Yeats with Lady Gregory: *Cathleen Ni Houlihan.* This patriotic drama, with the militant nationalist and feminist Maud Gonne in the title role, was very well received, and moreover served to affirm Yeats's nationalism—a demonstration he would have cause to remind people of in later years. Over the next several months, culminating in an inaugural meeting in August 1902, the Fays' National Dramatic Company was turned into the Irish National Theatre Society.

The new organization continually changed in the subsequent years as Yeats, Lady Gregory, and others sought the best means to remain true to their artistic principles while building an audience. They performed in London, where their work was often more highly regarded than in Dublin, and toured the British Isles. In 1904 the English heiress Annie Horniman, a friend and admirer of Yeats, who had already helped fund the Irish Literary Theatre, paid for the modest building on Lower Abbey Street that became the company's home. The following year, again with Horniman's financial assistance, the organization became the Irish National Theatre Society Limited, and began paying the actors but excluding them from the process of selecting plays. In the course of these changes, the INTS lost the support of some members, including many prominent nationalists, notably two of its first vice presidents—Douglas Hyde, founder of the Gaelic League, and Maud Gonne. Soon after that rupture, the company appeared to further compromise its claim to be a national theater by accepting so much aid from Horniman, who not only was English, but contemptuously opposed to Irish nationalism. In June 1906, the conversion into a limited company funded by Horniman even drove various seceding members to form a rival company, the Theatre of Ireland.

J. M. Synge met Yeats in Paris in 1896, and through him got to know Lady Gregory. He shared with them an Anglo-Irish background and ambitions as a writer. He had seen and reviewed the Irish Literary Theatre's final production in 1901, and in August 1902 became one of the original members of the INTS. By September 1905 he was so prominently involved in the organization that he along with Yeats and Lady Gregory was named a director of the newly professionalized company. And he had also already become the society's most controversial playwright. It was primarily over his *In the Shadow of the Glen*, produced in October 1903, that Gonne and Hyde resigned from the INTS. The one-act play, which unflinchingly depicts adultery and greed among Irish peasants, also prompted some actors to resign. Even before the production, Arthur Griffith, editor of the *United Irishman*, had begun a protracted debate in the press over its perceived slander of the Irish. When another one-act play by Synge, *Riders to the Sea*, was staged six months later, it too fared poorly with the critics, though they could not accuse this evocative tragedy of undermining nationalism, especially since the production clearly moved most of the spectators. February 1905 saw the first premiere of a work by Synge at the Abbey, *The Well of the Saints*, which depicts two blind tramps whose sight is restored by holy water, but who prefer their illusions to reality. Not surprisingly, the three-act play, described by Joseph Holloway—the devoted observer of Dublin theater, whose journal provides a valuable record of the Abbey's evolution—as "Mr. Synge's harsh, irreverent, sensual representation of Irish peasant life, with its strange mixture of lyric and dirt." Again Synge was made the target of a good deal of criticism from the nationalist press. In a later entry where Holloway contrasts Synge's work with that of William Boyle, he captures the preconception most Dubliners would bring to future productions of Synge's plays: he acknowledges that Synge's are superior to Boyle's "as literature," but emphasizes that "nevertheless, there is no denying that much of his work rings so false to Irish ears, that a red rag to a bull is the only way to describe its effect."[4]

During its first years at the Abbey, the INTS often played to meager houses, particularly at the second and subsequent performances of a new production. Probably the most regular audience member was Holloway, who commented on the Abbey's relationship with its audience in his entry about the December 1906 premiere of Lady Gregory's *The White Cockade*: "A goodly crop of the usual first-nighters, but very few of the ordinary public put in an appearance. Yeats, as the mouthpiece of the Society, is forever saying in print that they don't want them, and certainly the public caters strictly to the Society's wish in the matter by remaining away."[5] The Abbey did draw sizeable houses of "ordinary" Dubliners for productions of more conventional drama, especially Boyle's uncomplicated realistic plays. But only a limited portion of the Dublin public appeared to be interested in work which better reflected Yeats's and Lady Gregory's wish to practice and foster innovation. And far from refuting people's suspicion that the supposedly national theater aimed to attract only a minority of the potential theatergoing public, public statements by Yeats continually reinforced that perception. In 1904, for instance, in a speech at the opening of the Abbey, Yeats told the audience, "as our salary list and our expenses are very small, we shall be able to ask ourselves when we put on a play, first, 'Does it please us?' and then 'Does it please you?'"[6] Another policy that alienated much of the Dublin public was Miss Horniman's stipulation that the theater she funded must not sell sixpenny seats as the other Dublin theaters did—a pronounced act of exclusion that naturally drew much criticism from nationalists. Nevertheless, after appointing a secretary who introduced various effective changes, and making some concessions, most significantly on ticket prices, the INTS seemed by the autumn of 1906 to have turned a corner. On October 20, following the opening night of a double-bill by Lady Gregory and Boyle, Holloway wrote: "Has the era of success dawned at last for the National Theatre Society? To judge by the crowded house to-night at the Abbey, one would be inclined to say so!"[7]

Nothing could provide a better measure of just how much goodwill the INTS had managed to build up by the end of 1906 than the premiere of another play by Synge. Those involved in the production realized from the outset that *The Playboy of the Western World* risked causing more outcry even than his earlier work. Willie Fay claims that Synge, resentful over the hostile reception of *The Well of the Saints* two years earlier, told him "the next play I write I will make sure will annoy them."[8] While it is difficult to assess how much the desire for revenge really did motivate Synge, he certainly did little to lessen the provocative potential of *The Playboy*. Yeats and Lady Gregory along with Fay had feared another major conflict from the point when Synge read them parts of the script in November. But in response to the appeals of his colleagues to temper the boldness of his new play, Synge consented to only a few alterations. And the directors of the INTS did not need to take possible censorship into account, since this was one respect in which Britain's rule in Ireland was restricted: the Lord Chamberlain's authority to license plays did not apply. So the company rehearsed the play largely as Synge had written it in an atmosphere of considerable apprehension. According to one memoir, "reports spread through Dublin that there were improprieties in the play and that the womanhood of Ireland was being slandered."[9]

Like Synge's previous plays, *The Playboy of the Western World* depicted life in rural Ireland, yet went even further than *In the Shadow of the Glen* and *The Well of the Saints* in seeming to suggest that the peasants were degenerate and immoral. A diffident young man called Christy Mahon turns up in a shebeen in a Mayo village and reveals that he is on the run because a little over a week ago he murdered his father. Almost all the villagers who learn about his deed react not with horror but with admiration, and Christy quickly blossoms into a confident and eloquent "playboy," who defeats all comers in the village games and wins the heart of Pegeen, the publican's daughter. But when Christy's father appears, invalidating the story on which Christy's success depends, the peasants turn against him for having lied to them. Even when Christy attacks and this time seemingly does kill Old Mahon, he cannot regain the villagers' favor. They plan to either hand Christy over to the police or hang him themselves, but just when they are about to take him away, his father re-enters. When Christy leaves at the end, he defiantly declares that this experience has transformed him into a stronger man, but the villagers, and especially Pegeen, are left with nothing but regrets. In the course of the three acts, most of the peasants show the same lack of respect for the Church as they do for the law. The Abbey's audience knew to approach the production of a play by Synge with different presumptions from those appropriate to any other author, yet The Playboy surpassed even that modified horizon of expectations.

The auditorium of the Abbey held around five hundred and fifty people, most of them seated either in the stalls immediately in front of the stage or in the pit which took up the rear part of the house, with the remainder in the narrow horseshoe-shaped balcony. As in other contexts, the different parts of the auditorium were generally occupied by, and therefore associated with, distinct social groups. One memoirist enthused that the audience at the Abbey was responsive "whether they were students or workingmen in the pit, or the bourgeoisie or aristocracy in the stalls."[10] Some of the stalls spectators at INTS productions must have been from the protestant Ascendancy, while many in the pit would have been sympathetic to, or even actively involved in, nationalist movements. Normative audience behavior at the Abbey reflected the prevailing values and standards of the wealthier spectators. Dubliners who watched from the pit did not feel at liberty to respond as they customarily did during performances of patriotic melodramas at the Queen's Theatre, where "the audience regularly hissed the villain, cheered the hero, yelled advice to the characters, and sang patriotic songs."[11] Just as Yeats and Lady Gregory wanted their enterprise to be taken seriously—as seriously as comparable ventures in several other European countries—so they wanted their audiences to practice the kind of restrained receptivity that by this time was conventional at performances of most non-musical theater. Opening nights at the Abbey usually attracted a more distinguished audience than other performances, including prominent figures in Dublin's cultural and political life. There was a full house for the premiere of The Playboy, so that, in contrast to later performances, the audience was not dominated by the kind of Dubliners likely to object to perceived attacks on the nationalist cause, and used to expressing their response in the theater in a performative manner.

As Donna Gerstenberger aptly noted, "In an inflated gesture appropriate to the linguistic exaggerations of The Playboy itself, the disorderly conduct of the Abbey Theatre audiences has gone into stage history under the title of the Playboy Riots."[12] The word "riot" rarely if ever appears in the press coverage of, and commentary on, the production that provides the most immediate accounts of the events. The opening night in particular has frequently been depicted as far more tumultuous than it in fact was, as one witness pointedly complains:

I was present at the much misrepresented first performance of *The Playboy of the Western World* and find the reaction of the audience still grossly distorted. So late as 28 January 1963 I find a special correspondent of *The Times* reporting an interview with one of the surviving actors, Mr J. M. Kerrigan, and putting into his mouth the statement that he "remembers Synge on the stage as the bottles and garbage flew . . ."[13]

In fact the response of the audience on Saturday, January 26 was tame compared with the uproar during the performances at the start of the following week. Lady Gregory's summary of the shifts in mood during the first night is largely corroborated by other witnesses: "The first act got its applause and the second, though one felt the audience were a little puzzled, a little shocked at the wild language. Near the end of the third act there was some hissing."[14] Yet "some hissing" almost certainly understates the degree of hostility expressed during the closing scenes of the play, just as the most damning first-night review probably overstates it. According to the *Freeman's Journal*, the protests intensified from the point near the end of the third act where the villagers tie Christy up with a rope: "Now angry groans, growls, hisses, and noise broke out while the pinioning of Mahon went on. It was not possible—thank goodness—to follow the dialogue for a time."[15] The complexity of Synge's play endows this particular hostile audience response with a greater richness than the earlier examples. The spectators at the Abbey were in part protesting against the maltreatment of a character with whom they most likely had found themselves sympathizing even though they believed he was a murderer.

The *Freeman's Journal* reviewer goes on to write, in connection with the subsequent confrontation between Christy and his father, "A brutal riotous scene takes place. The groans, hisses, and counter cheers of the audience drowned the words."[16] This suggests that once the objections against the performance grew into something more than just "some hissing," those spectators who did not approve of the protests responded by voicing their support for the play. The resulting contest between opponents and supporters of *The Playboy* became an integral part of this as of other modern theater scandals. And at the Abbey, more noticeably than at many of the other theaters which witnessed similar uproar during this period, the physical separation of stalls and pit largely divided pro and con. As Maire Nic Shiubhlaigh—an important Abbey actress who was also one of the founding members of the INTS—recalled, "People in front leaned over the back of seats and demanded quiet—a lot of people seemed to be doing this—and those at the back responded by shouting and hissing loudly."[17] And Holloway's account of the first night in his diary includes the remark, "'This is not Irish life!' said one of the voices from the pit"[18]— the charge that *The Playboy* did not accurately depict the reality of rural life in Ireland was among the most frequently expressed, and probably the most representative, of the protesters' objections to Synge's play.

Accounts of Saturday's performance suggest that prior to the play's closing scenes, the audience was more taken aback than offended by *The Playboy*; it was not until the denouement that insistent protests occurred. In the final moments, real physical violence is enacted on stage in contrast to the potentially comic character of the action when Christy "*runs at old* MAHON *with the loy, chases him out of the door, followed by* CROWD *and* WIDOW QUIN"; the villagers now put a rope around Christy, pull it tight on his arms, then drag him on to the floor.[19] This is followed by Christy biting Shawn's leg, and having his own leg scorched with a lighted sod by Pegeen. The spectators' repulsion at the bodily harm depicted in this episode was compounded and complicated by uncertainty over where their sympathy did and ought to lie. When it appears that Christy has committed parricide after all, the villagers declare that they will lynch him, and demonstrate their readiness to follow through on this threat by treating him like an animal. So a play that seems all along to have suggested Irish peasants glorify violence, but has done so within an apparently comic mode, now vividly shows those peasants unhesitatingly engaging in violence themselves. If Synge just had Old Mahon turn up, thus exposing his son as a fraud, and then go off with Christy, *The Playboy* would still on the face of it imply that villagers in rural Ireland are overly credulous and inclined to admire violent crimes, but the force of that critique would be attenuated by the simple comic resolution. Instead, Synge added a phase during which the villagers believe that the man whom they had adulated on the grounds that he had killed his father, then despised because he had lied to them, did just murder his father, and in response they reveal their own capacity for vengeful, immoral aggression—so rather than mitigating the criticism suggested by the rest of the play, the ending expands it. The final twist, whereby Old Mahon returns from the dead a second time, thus making the hanging unnecessary and allowing father and son to leave together, comes too late to alter the apparently disparaging representation of the villagers—and besides, may well have been barely audible for many even on the first night.

Throughout the week, the daily *Freeman's Journal* strongly criticized Synge's play and the Abbey's decision to produce it, so that there is good reason to regard its arguments as indicative of the views of the protesters. In the political realm the *Freeman's Journal* was quite moderate in its support for independence, a stance which appealed to the Catholic middle class but often exasperated more radically inclined nationalists. The Abbey's production of *The Playboy* prompted, or allowed, the editors decisively to defend nationalist interests for once. While all the daily newspapers indicted Synge and the INTS, only the *Freeman's Journal* attacked so unreservedly. The *Irish Independent*, also identified with Catholics and nationalism, was more restrained in its criticism, as were the titles generally read by the Anglo-Irish—the *Irish Times, Daily Express*, and *Evening Mail*. But toward the end of the run when the weekly journals appeared, the Abbey was the target of further vehement attacks, above all from Arthur Griffith's *Sinn Féin* (the successor to his *United Irishman*), and from *The Leader*, founded by another ardent nationalist, D. P. Moran.

For the second performance on Monday, January 28, the house was many times smaller than on opening night: as few as eighty audience-members, to judge from the box office receipts, with far more spectators in pit and gallery than in the stalls.[20] As on Saturday, Synge's *Riders to the Sea* opened the program, and was well received throughout the auditorium, as would continue to be the case for the whole run. But on Monday, the receptive atmosphere prevailing during *Riders* soon degenerated once *The Playboy* began. According to the report in the *Freeman's Journal*, what provoked the audience was first the villagers' admiring and hospitable response to Christy's revelation that "I killed my poor father, Tuesday was a week" (16), and second the decision reached by Pegeen and her father, Michael James, that Christy should stay the night even though Michael would be away.

Now, the uproar assumed gigantic dimensions, stamping, booing, vociferations in Gaelic, and the striking of seats with sticks were universal in the gallery and pit. Amidst this Babel of sounds the refrain of 'God Save Ireland' was predominant.

Loud shouts were also raised of "We won't have this," "It is not good enough for Dublin," and "What would not be tolerated in America will not be allowed here."[21]

Again the *Freeman's Journal* probably overstated the magnitude and the pervasiveness of these protests, but without question the opposition took on a different character from the first night.

Unlike Hauptmann's *Before Sunrise*, Synge's play was not published before being staged, so the first-night reception was in large part a spontaneous reaction to an unknown quantity. By the second performance on Monday, at least the basic contours of Synge's play were no doubt known to many in Dublin, and in particular to acquaintances of the first-night audience members who had groaned and hissed their disapproval. Evidently some of those who attended Saturday's performance returned on Monday. So the circumstances were much changed for the second night: a small house dominated by pit and gallery, including some spectators who had already seen the play, and probably many others who had been told about it. The timing of the earliest protests on Monday suggests that those in the audience primed or predisposed to take offense at the action on stage were scrutinizing each moment in search of any discernible insulting implication. They thus seized on the representation of the villagers as immoral, first in welcoming a parricide, then in allowing an unmarried woman to remain overnight unaccompanied in the same house as a young man.

"The striking of seats with sticks" during Monday's performance described by the *Freeman's Journal*, like the "belabouring of seats and walls with sturdy sticks" mentioned later in the same report, constitutes a quite different form of protest from the purely verbal shouting, booing and hissing, and makes the stamping of feet appear restrained by comparison.[22] The arresting notion of spectators coming to the second performance of *The Playboy* equipped with instruments which would inflict damage on the Abbey as well as creating noise must be discounted as perhaps the most blatant instance of that newspaper's partisan exaggeration. Such premeditated and violent behavior would hardly have gone unremarked, yet no other account of any performance bears out the *Freeman's Journal*. (Nic Shiubhlaigh described members of Tuesday night's audience hitting their seats, but indicated that they used only their fists.[23]) Footstamping is, however, reported by other witnesses too, and even that reflects a contrast with the scandals provoked by *Before Sunrise* and *Ubu Roi*—though in neither of those cases did the production ever face spectators who had formed an opinion of it based on previous performances. Partly because the Dublin theatergoers had the opportunity to disrupt further performances after the premiere, partly also because the work was considered offensive to an entire people, the protests against *The Playboy*, more than those against Hauptmann's or Jarry's plays, entailed collective acts by a group. While stamping after the end of a performance can signal acclaim—as it does today—stamping during a performance offers a kind of disapprobatory equivalent of applause since, like clapping, it can be carried out in unison by many people at once. Booing, hissing, and whistling do not lend themselves as well to sustained or rhythmic performance. By stamping their feet, the protesters in the Abbey also put their whole selves into it, and they did in effect perceive the play as an affront to their whole selves. The collective nature of the protests against *The Playboy* is also captured in the *Freeman's Journal*'s account of shouts from the auditorium early in Act I on Monday. When a member of this audience shouted "We won't have this," he was speaking for a large group of like-minded people in a way that does not hold true for Dr. Kastan. The other comments likewise object to Synge's play from the perspective of a constituency acutely conscious of and sensitive to representations of their compatriots within and beyond Ireland itself.

According to the report on Monday night's performance in the *Daily Express*—which depicted the uproar as noticeably less "gigantic" than the

Freeman's Journal did—"the disturbance became so loud that it was impossible for those in the front seats to hear a word said on the stage, the mingled boohs, groans, and hisses turning the play into a dumb show."[24] It is worth bearing in mind that this drowning-out of the actors in a relatively small theater was accomplished by probably only fifty or so people. Yet there was little point in continuing, so the performance was suspended after about two thirds of the first act. Willie Fay—who played Christy and directed—then came to the footlights and engaged the audience in the first of several verbal exchanges:

When a sort of comparative calm had been obtained,
    Mr. Fay said—Now, as you are all tired, I suppose I may speak (boos, and yells of 'We won't have it.')
    Mr. Fay—There are people here who have paid to see the piece. Anyone who does not like the play can have his money returned.
    Cries of 'Irishmen do not harbour murderers'.
    A Voice—'We respect Irish virtue.
    . . .
    Cries were then raised of 'Where is the author? Bring him out, and we will deal with him.'
    Mr. Fay—What do you want the author for? You can have your money back.
    Hundreds of Voices—We don't want the money.[25]

This was the first public discussion of an issue that would be central to the controversy surrounding *The Playboy*: the clash within the auditorium between the right of one group of spectators to hear and see the play and the right of another group to voice their objections to that play. Fay's effort to resolve the conflict by reimbursing the shouting spectators was well-intentioned but doomed to failure, since it was not a matter of liking or disliking the play, but rather a matter of principle. The protesters felt obliged to demonstratively register their disapproval of a work they believed slandered the Irish and their values, and for them that feeling that overrode the competing principle that other audience members should be allowed to take in the performance. The shout ostensibly threatening Synge was not the only one to suggest that the protesters' commitment to their cause might manifest itself through physical aggression, though in the end what little fighting did occur during the week of "riots" took place among spectators rather than being directed at the author, directors, or actors.

Fay withdrew, and the curtain was closed. The orchestra played for a while, but instead of succeeding in subduing the hecklers, the music induced them to perform their opposition in a new way: "the singing of verses in Irish, and also the enthusiastic rendering of 'Hurrah for the Men of the West'."[26] Then a new element was introduced into the conflict, one which would play an important role in the days to come: several policemen entered the auditorium, apparently called in by Lady Gregory in consultation with Synge. But the mere presence of the police made no impact on the protesters, and when the actors resumed the performance their words again could not be heard. At this point then, the opponents of *The Playboy* had the upper hand, having defied not only the theater's attempts to force Synge's play on the public, but also resisted the effort to intimidate them by bringing in the police. Fay later wrote that he instructed the cast to embrace this unusual performance situation: "As it was impossible for any of us to be heard, I arranged with the cast that we should simply walk through the play, not speaking a word aloud, but changing positions and going through all the motions, so to speak. The noise was terrific, but we finished the play."[27] This presents a wonderful image of the encounter between a dissenting audience and a production that refuses to yield to interference: on one side, a group of spectators doing their utmost to prevent the performance reaching the audience, on the other a group of actors determinedly defying the protest by completing the visual spectacle even if the aural one is rendered meaningless.

On Monday more than at any other performance, the vast majority of the audience joined in protesting against *The Playboy*, and clearly they relished this predominance. The interruption of Act I had prompted "triumphant cheers," which were of course repeated when the police—perhaps in response to a request from Lady Gregory and Synge[28]—left the auditorium:

Needless is it to state that the victorious occupants of the pit and gallery signalised their success by triumphant yells, shouts, tramping of feet, and the belabouring of seats and walls with sturdy sticks, mingled with the singing of "The West's Awake," "A Nation Once Again," and such like well-known patriotic compositions, in which nearly all the audience joined.

And once the dumb show on stage had come to an end, the protesters lingered to relish this victory: "Those who had objected to the entertainment gave effect to their elation in energetic outbursts in both Irish and English on the success they had achieved, and energetically declared that they would adopt a similar attitude on every occasion the play would be produced."[29] In fact, this second performance would constitute the high point of the protesters' campaign against *The Playboy*, and according to another report, there were already signs on Monday night of the more factious audience response of subsequent evenings: "The falling of the curtain at the end was the signal for a renewal of the demonstration, besides the groans and shouting there also being loud applause from those who seemed to wish to disassociate themselves from the disorder."[30]

The final interaction between stage and auditorium again involved Willie Fay: "Mr. Fay came before the footlights and said, 'Those who hissed to-night will go away and say they saw the play.' This was greeted by a retort from the gallery, 'We saw it on Saturday,' and loud cheering followed."[31] This suggests, as do other accounts, that the protests against the play on Monday were carried out by a portion of those who had taken offense on Saturday; at the second performance, these opponents of *The Playboy* not only came prepared to express their outrage, but the make-up of the far smaller house lent itself to an exuberant and almost unopposed demonstration. The question of just how organized the protests were featured prominently in the debate surrounding the Abbey's production of *The Playboy*. Some newspapers made declarations such as "we are opposed to organised demonstrations of the kind that took place last night,"[32] while later in the week the directors of the INTS sent to the press an announcement appealing to readers to "Support Abbey Theatre Against Organised Opposition."[33] It seems very unlikely that the protests against Synge's play were organized to quite the extent Yeats and others claimed. Rather, *The Playboy* quickly became a rallying point for a large group of already organized nationalists who did not need much persuading through newspaper and word-of-mouth reports to go to the Abbey and demonstrate their opposition to the production.

A house of over two hundred watched the third performance of *The Playboy* on Tuesday evening, including more protesters than at Monday's performance, but also more spectators ready to express their support for Synge's play. And at least some of the latter did constitute an organized group—almost certainly more organized, in fact, than those who opposed the production. This claque was encouraged by the directors of the Abbey: the *Freeman's Journal* reported that twenty or so young men "were admitted to the stalls, without the formality of purchasing tickets," and Lady Gregory explains how they came to be there:

I had asked a nephew at TC to come and bring a few fellow athletes, that we might be sure of some able-bodied helpers in case of an attack on the stage. But, alas! the very sight of them was as a match to the resin of the pit, and a roar of defiance was flung back,—townsman against gownsman, hereditary enemies challenging each other as they are used to do when party or political processions march before the railings on College Green. But no iron railings divided pit and stalls, some scuffles added to the excitement, and it was one of our defenders at the last who was carried out bodily.[34]

Tension between the two sections of the main floor characterized this performance more than any other, and Gregory's account usefully situates that tension in the broader context of the Dublin of the 1900s, though perhaps rather overstates it for dramatic effect. If the enmity between the two factions was as constant and intense as she suggests, surely she would have foreseen that she was putting match to resin? Not surprisingly, her description also reflects her bias, first in suggesting that it was the townsmen in the pit who initiated the mutual provocation, second in focusing on one supporter who was ejected at the expense of the many opponents who got arrested.

Yeats was out of the country when *The Playboy* opened, and did not return to Dublin until the Tuesday, when the controversy was already in full swing. Particular importance had been attached in the press to the decision taken by the Abbey's directors to continue the run of Synge's play in spite of widespread objections. As an editorial in the *Irish Independent* put it on Thursday, "we think that the verdict of the first-night audience—as sympathetic a house as actors ever played to—should have been accepted, and the play withdrawn."[35] On Tuesday, Yeats took a stance on this issue before the performance even began. While the audience was still applauding *Riders to the Sea*, he appeared on stage and gave a short speech inviting anyone who "wished to discuss the merits of the play, or their right to produce it" to participate in a debate the following Monday evening. He ended his speech by declaring, "We have put this play before you to be heard and judged. Every man has a right to hear and condemn it if he pleases, but no man has a right to interfere with another man who wants to hear the play. We shall play on and on, and I assure you our patience will last longer than their patience (applause and groans)."[36] Yeats' prediction about the eventual triumph of *The Playboy* was to prove accurate—yet by the time it came about, the directors of the Abbey had asserted their authority through rather more than just patience.

The curtain rose on *The Playboy,* and at first the audience responded only with some laughter to the opening dialogue between Pegeen and Shawn; but very soon—sooner than during Monday's performance—the shouting began. Just how intense the uproar became is unclear: the *Freeman's Journal* subheading "a scene of the greatest disorder" may be a typical overstatement, yet the shouting against the play, and the calls for "Order" and "The play" certainly grew so loud that the actors "resigned themselves to the inevitable and abandoned even the dumb performance they had been carrying on."[37] Yeats came on stage again

and asked the audience to remain seated and to listen to the play of a man who, at any rate, was a most distinguished fellow-countryman of theirs (applause, groans, and hisses). Mr. Synge deserved to be heard. If his play was bad, it would die without their help; and if it was good, their hindrances could not impair it either (applause and hisses); but they could impair very greatly the reputation of this country for courtesy and intelligence.

These comments were even less likely than Yeats's opening speech to promote calm or to persuade the play's opponents to desist from their protests. He was asking the audience to accept that Synge's Irishness mitigated the attack on the Irish that many of them perceived in his play;

his appeal to them to trust Synge on the grounds that he is "distinguished" fell on deaf ears since it was by the overly Anglo-Irish INTS that he had been distinguished, in part for earlier plays which many Catholics believed disparaged his countrymen and -women; whereas Yeats' earlier speech had ostensibly granted to all the spectators the right to judge the play, he now cast their opinion of it as immaterial; and finally, sounding decidedly reminiscent of a schoolteacher chastising children, Yeats saw fit to tell the audience that their opposition to a perceived attack on their country would actually do harm to the very country they were defending. Small wonder that, as the *Freeman's Journal* report described it, "Mr. Yeats then left the stage, amidst renewed cheers, groans, and hisses, above which could be heard bugle notes."[38]

Those bugle notes represent one unusual feature of the audience response to *The Playboy*, especially it seems during Tuesday's and Wednesday's performances. The *Daily Express* reported that once the play had restarted, "gradually a din arose, created by tin trumpets and stamping in the gallery, and soon it was impossible to hear the dialogue."[39] Puzzlingly, in all the discussion of the protests against Synge's play—in the press, in court, and in the public debate the following week—little attention was paid to this noteworthy form of dissent. Assuming that Dubliners at the turn of the century did not routinely carry trumpets around with them (Joyce, for one, gave no indication that either Leopold Bloom or anyone he encounters in the course of *Ulysses'* twenty-four hours in 1904 did so), the bugle notes resulted from a preconceived and considered decision to interfere in the performance of *The Playboy*. In Dublin—unlike in the U.S. some years later—nothing was thrown at the stage during the one-week run at the Abbey. It appears that, for the most part, the protesters' objective was to make the performance of Synge's play unreceivable by mounting their own, primarily aural, counter-performance.

Following some consultation between Lady Gregory and Yeats, and probably Synge, several policemen filed into the theater. In contrast to their inaction during the previous performance, which left the play's opponents triumphant and its supporters indignant, on Tuesday the police played a very active role in the events. The division between stalls and pit took on a new form: some audience members in the more expensive seats, along with Yeats, pointed to certain individuals in the pit and demanded their arrest. Holloway wrote afterward that Yeats "was busy just now as a spy aiding the police in picking out persons disapproving of the glorification of murder on the stage."[40] Eventually the actors resumed their performance and completed it without further cessation, though according to the *Freeman's Journal's* summary, by the end, "not half a dozen consecutive sentences had been heard by the audience."[41] The presence of the police, whose numbers were soon augmented, served not to suppress the shouting but only to broaden its focus, as the protesters continually booed both the actors on the stage and the constables who were removing spectators, always from the pit.

Lines in the script which presented in concentrated form Synge's purported slanderous depiction of rural Ireland instantly provoked opposition. The *Daily Express* reported that when Act II began on Tuesday, "There was not much noise until the point in the play where Peggy asks Christy Mahon was he the man who killed his father. On his replying in the affirmative Peggy exclaims, 'Then a thousand welcomes to you.' This drew forth a perfect Bedlam of yells, and various cries, such as 'That is not the West; I defy you to prove it,' 'Travesty,' etc." As well as turning Pegeen's name into Peggy, this writer attributes to her a line actually spoken by Sara before Pegeen has entered; but the force of the line does not depend on the speaker, and the error—committed by others too—reflects the focus of attention on Pegeen as the single character who most eagerly enters into an intimate relationship with the supposed murderer. The bedlam prompted by Sara's line is fully understandable given the literal reading to which opponents of *The Playboy* subjected the work. Synge was alleging that if a self-confessed parricide turned up in a village in the west of Ireland, he would be welcomed with open arms. On Tuesday, "The most frequent exclamation was 'That's not the West'"; on other evenings it appears to have been "That's not Irish life!" In addition to continually seeming to imply that Irish peasants embrace criminality, Synge knowingly incorporated into his play other elements likely to provoke angry objections to his representation of western life. For instance, the scene in which Pegeen's drunken father blesses her engagement to Christy suggests a lack of respect for the Church in rural communities, and aroused loud demonstrations on Tuesday. The *Daily Express* reporter judged that "The point which caused the most offence was where Peggy finds that Christy has only wounded and not killed his father, and exclaims, 'You let on you had him slitted, and now you are nothing at all'."[42] Presumably this line proved so inflammatory because in it Pegeen so explicitly and unrepentantly expresses her wish for Christy to be the violent criminal she took him for. Perhaps if, on discovering that Christy did not in fact murder his father, the villagers realized the error of their ways, then the spectators might have accepted *The Playboy* as a cautionary tale; instead, they heard Pegeen state more clearly than ever her view—and by implication the view of the other villagers, and of all people in rural Ireland—that only a man who has brutally slain his father is worthy of admiration.

In the row over *The Playboy*, as in the earlier scandals, the battles in the auditorium soon became three- rather than just two-sided, a feature that was particularly pronounced on Tuesday because of Lady Gregory's nephew and his friends. When certain lines triggered protests from the play's opponents, those protests in turn prompted demonstrations of support from the other side: "At every hiss and booh the young fellows in the stalls clapped and cheered, which called forth the remark, 'The boys all got a free seat to come and clap'."[43] That retort does seem justified, and for those who found Synge's play offensive, the student claque, like the use of the police, must have exacerbated the sense of affront. Holloway wrote in his diary entry on Tuesday's performance that "At the end chaos seemed to have entered the Abbey, and the college youths clambered onto the seats and began the English national anthem, while those in the body of the hall sang something else of home growth."[44] This singing battle continued outside after the police had cleared the building, and more arrests were made when fighting briefly broke out between the two groups.

Wednesday's performance drew the largest house since opening night. Box office receipts suggest that over a hundred seats remained empty, yet the *Freeman's Journal* wrote that the Abbey was "thronged to excess." The discrepancy might result from the free admittance of some spectators, as on Tuesday. Certainly, the overall response to this the fourth performance was more evenly divided between positive and negative. This time the police positioned themselves in the auditorium after *Riders to the Sea*, and once the curtain rose on *The Playboy*, "At last the tug-of-war began." Yet the tussle did not altogether follow the pattern of previous evenings: "Shouts of 'Get out' were hurled from all directions, whilst cat-calls, strident bugle notes, and fierce denunciations added to the terrific din. But, on the other hand, there were shouts of 'Order', and 'Fair Play'."[45] The discord between stalls and pit took a new form during the interval between Acts II and III, when a young apparently English spectator in the stalls challenged another young man from the pit to fight him, and the bout took place in the theater's vestibule; there is no record of which man prevailed.

Undoubtedly a larger proportion of the play was audible on Wednesday than on the two previous evenings. A telling moment during Act III indicates a significant change in the predominant response to *The Playboy*: "Almost at its commencement one of the characters declares, 'There will be right sport before nightfall'. This was so very apropos to the exciting situation that all parties in the theatre joined in an outburst of hearty laughter."[46] The audience response to Philly's line recalls a significant phenomenon in the French theater of the late eighteenth and early nineteenth centuries: as F. W. J. Hemmings explains, spectators in the pit developed the habit "of *making applications*, that is to say, seizing on a line or a couplet in a well-known play and drawing attention, by shouts and clapping, to its applicability to some current crisis."[47] Whereas the Parisian theatergoers made connections between a script and the political situation outside the theater, the Dublin spectators laughed at the relevance of Philly's line only to recent and current events in that auditorium; but in both instances shared knowledge and associations directly influence the response of a significant portion of the audience. This incident also resembles the episode during the *générale* of *Ubu Roi* when Gémier altered the mood in the auditorium through his comical jig, to the extent that in both cases opponents as well as supporters of the performance found humor in the same thing, and the tension between them was thus somewhat diminished. The noise continued during the rest of Act III, and the police again ejected and arrested some spectators; but this moment when supporters and opponents of the production were united by their amusement marks a turning point in the weeklong run.

The *Playboy* drew sizeable houses again for Thursday and Friday's performances, yet anyone who went to the Abbey in order to witness the uproar firsthand might have been disappointed, as the gradual ebbing of the protests' intensity, perceptible on Wednesday night, continued. A few audience members were arrested on Thursday evening, only one on Friday. The *Evening Mail* reported about Thursday's performance that

Again there was a large and mixed audience, again there was a strong body of police stationed inside and outside the building, and again boohing, hissing, stamping, and applauding occurred throughout the course of the play; but, for the first time, the piece was accorded a fair hearing . . . the words spoken on the stage were never drowned for any length of time, and some portions of the act were enthusiastically received even in the pit.[48]

Willie Fay claimed that those involved in the production "had taken the precaution to pad the floor with felt, which frustrated the rhythmic stamping that had been the opposition's most effective device."[49] A number of more recent accounts of the first production of *The Playboy* accept the rather appealing idea that the protesters against Synge's play were foiled in this cunning way, yet no evidence exists to support Fay's tale, and he is never the most reliable source (claiming, for instance, that no police were present in the auditorium until Thursday night). The *Evening Mail* report also describes an incident similar to the one on Wednesday: "Good humour was restored when the expression 'Jim would get drunk on the smell of a pint' was made use of, and someone in the pit called out, 'That's not Western life'."[50] The line in question actually refers not to Jimmy but to Christy, and is spoken by Old Mahon when he tells Widow Quin about his son's prior reputation as a cowardly idler. Yet it seems unlikely that the person who shouted the comment truly felt indignant at the implication that any young men in the west of Ireland cannot hold their drink. This spectator must have been ironically mocking the way that audience members at the previous performances of *The Playboy* had judged each line against some standard of accuracy. The fact that most of Thursday night's audience saw the humor in this raillery indicates the shift in the balance of power away from the most ardent opponents of Synge's play.

Friday evening featured an affirmative form of opposition to *The Playboy*: during and after the performance, many in that night's audience loudly cheered Mr. Wall, a magistrate who had shown himself quite sympathetic toward the arrested protesters who appeared before him in court. But the performance of approval for Wall remained a peaceful demonstration. The one-week run of Synge's play ended with two performances on Saturday, which according to the *Daily Express* "were characterised by an extraordinary change of feeling on the part of the audience": the play's opponents "would seem to have had all the courage taken out of them by the determined front displayed by the management, as well as of the players themselves."[51] The house was probably about half full for the matinee, close to full in the evening. Holloway tried to dismiss the predominantly positive response by noting that the afternoon audience "was not very large and mostly ladies," while "the evening audience looked as though the music halls had 'emptied themselves out into the pit and balcony'."[52] Other accounts, however, indicate no such pronounced change in the composition of the audience at the Abbey. Yeats's prediction on Tuesday that "our patience will last longer than their patience" had been borne out, and the directors of the INTS had good reason to be satisfied with their decision to complete the weeklong run. Nonetheless, the opposition was only defeated if one regards the week's events as a battle over the Abbey's capability to mount all the scheduled eight performances of *The Playboy*; if the protesters' goal was rather to forcefully register their outrage in public, then they too fulfilled their aim. As one of them stated in court, simply and unrepentantly, "I have made my protest. I consider every true Irishman would act in the same way."[53]

Language in general and one word in particular were central to the controversy over *The Playboy*. Immediately after the first performance on Saturday, Lady Gregory sent the absent Yeats a telegram which read "Audience broke up in disorder at the word 'shift'."[54] In Willie Fay's account of the first night, he wrote that the response to the first two acts was largely positive, but that early in the third "the audience began to show signs of restlessness," then

when we came to my line about "all bloody fools," the trouble began in earnest, with hisses and cat-calls and all the other indications that the audience are not in love with you. . . . Yet the queer thing was that what turned the audience into a veritable mob of howling devils was not this vulgar expletive, but as irreproachable a word as there is in the English dictionary—the decent old-fashioned "shift" for the traditional under-garment of a woman.[55]

It is indeed rather a "queer thing" that the single most provocative component of a play decried, in a *Freeman's Journal* editorial, as a "squalid and repulsive travesty," should have been such an essentially inoffensive word.[56] A note in a widely used edition of *The Playboy* refers to the word "shifts" as "the notorious obscene word to which Dublin objected" (79)—but as Fay emphasizes, the word itself was not vulgar. More than a decade after the outcry over Jarry's *merdre* in Paris, the Dubliners rose up against a term which was not scatological, yet was regarded as equally unspeakable.

On Friday, by which point the protests in the Abbey had diminished significantly, an interviewer asked Lady Gregory, "Has not the play been considerably pruned, and have not some of the expressions to which the greatest objection was made been deleted?"[57] Certainly the question is an important one: the eventual success of *The Playboy* looks less like a victory for the INTS if it necessitated watering down Synge's text. Because of inconsistencies among different documents, it is impossible now to establish just how extensively the script was cut before and during the run. Judging from contemporary accounts, it does appear that the "bloody" mentioned by Fay, in Christy's Act II line "And to think I'm long years hearing women talking that talk, to all bloody fools, and this the first time I've heard the like of your voice talking sweetly for my own delight" (69) was not repeated after the first performance. One review of the first night complained that "Everything is a b——y this or a——y that," which is hardly true—but the exaggeration captures an undoubtedly common perception of the language as unremittingly crude.[58]

There is no question that the vocabulary of *The Playboy* represented a challenge to prevailing expectations about speech on stage. When Synge first read the text to Yeats and Lady Gregory they both felt that "there was far too much 'bad language,' there were too many violent oaths," and "It was agreed that it should be cut in rehearsal."[59] Even after the cuts Synge would agree to, the language of *The Playboy* shocked many in the first audiences, though in this respect as in others different newspapers suggest quite different standards. In an editorial in *Sinn Féin* near the end of the play's run, for instance, Synge's play was condemned as "a vile and inhuman story told in the foulest language we have ever listened to from a public platform." Yet the initial *Evening Mail* review had faulted the playwright only for "occasional indelicacy in the dialogue."[60] One frequently used word which probably captures well the typical contemporary perception of the language of *The Playboy* is "coarse"—a step down from "obscene," but conspicuously more vulgar than the scripts of most plays performed at the Abbey.

In answer to the interviewer's question in 1907, Lady Gregory said, "'Very little change has been made. It is true that a few adjectives have been taken out, as have been most of the invocations of the Holy Name, but curiously enough the words and phrases to which most objection has been raised have not been interfered with'"; but in her 1913 autobiography she recalls that "the play was never acted as it is printed . . . after the first public performance, we, the players and I, went through it and struck out any expressions that had given offence, and which were not necessary to the idea."[61] The discrepancy between these two statements suggests that in 1907, in the midst of a conflict which she later characterized as "a definite fight for freedom from mob censorship," Gregory deliberately and strategically played down the extent of the cuts.[62] Other evidence indicates that the revisions carried out by Lady Gregory and the actors in fact made little difference. One editorial after Wednesday's performance remarked that "Last night many of the offensive phrases were cut, but the pruning did not make the play one whit more presentable." When journalists mentioned deletions, invariably the writer did not find the play any less objectionable because of them, and presumably many other members of the public felt the same way.[63] Such reactions corroborate Lady Gregory's observation that the words she and the actors expunged did not in fact bear the greatest power to offend.

However many other words and phrases may have been cut from *The Playboy*, that word "shift" was without question preserved throughout the run. The curious potency of "shift," its capacity—like a reverse talisman—to bring down the wrath of Dublin on to Synge's head, makes all the tinkering with the rest of the play's language appear virtually irrelevant. From the beginning, the term "shift" stood out in the response of spectators, critics, and the writers of editorials and letters to newspapers. While Fay and others involved in the production were surprised by this reaction, in most instances the offensiveness of the word appears so self-evident to those writing about the play that—often in addition to declining to repeat it, as was the case with *merdre*—they do not bother to clarify why exactly this was the case. Thus one not especially critical review of the first night reported that in the third act "there is a sentence, spoken by the hero, which gave rise to an emphatic expression of dissent from the gallery, and which nobody could say was not justified."[64]

Yeats, of course, had something to say about Synge's use of "shift": in an interview after Thursday's performance, "Mr. Yeats pointed out that the word . . . appeared in Longfellow, and was a word commonly used in the West of Ireland. No peasant hesitated for a moment about using it. 'It is a good old English word,' he declared."[65] Given the importance to the row over *The Playboy* of nationalists' resentment about the unflattering depiction of rural Ireland in a theater run largely by Anglo-Irish intellectuals, Yeats's defense probably exacerbated rather than attenuating public hostility: the more English the word was, the more suspect. The fact that a famous non-Irish poet had used it made it no better; since "shift" was perceived as crude, Yeats insulted the peasants by asserting that they habitually uttered it, and Yeats's implication that he and Synge were more familiar with the linguistic habits of peasants than the nationalist opponents of the play no doubt appeared condescending at best.

Synge used the word "shift" three times in the text of *The Playboy*. All three passages involve Widow Quin, another woman in the village somewhat older than Pegeen who tries to win Christy for herself. In Act II, Pegeen returns to the shebeen to find the widow and the village girls cavorting with Christy, and makes to send the woman away:

PEGEEN: . . . (*To the WIDOW QUIN, with more elaborate scorn*) And what is it you're wanting, Widow Quin?

WIDOW QUIN: (*insolently*) A penn'orth of starch.

PEGEEN: (*breaking out*) And you without a white shift or shirt in your whole family since the drying of the flood. I've no starch for the like of you, and let you walk on now to Killamuck. (39)

One report on Tuesday evening describes what would appear to be this moment of the performance: "The next point of offence in the play is where one of the characters refers to an undergarment in a way which it is unusual to reproduce on the stage. There were loud boohs, and cries of 'Oh, oh'."[66] In attempting to account for the hostile response, this writer suggests that while people did employ the word shift, they did not expect nor want that usage to be duplicated in the theater. Such an argument represents the issue as primarily one of theatrical propriety—but the intensity of the subsequent adverse reaction to "shift" indicates that far more was involved.

Later in Act II, Widow Quin herself uses the word, telling Christy about the life she leads, of "darning a stocking or stitching a shift" (54). This occurence goes unmentioned in all but one description of the audience response to the Abbey production. The lack of attention paid to this moment may reflect the general antipathy felt toward the character of Widow Quin. Fay observed that the first-night audience "couldn't abide her," and one account of Wednesday's performance reports that "The wooing by Widow Quin of 'The Playboy' gave rise to a demonstration of marked hostility."[67] The widespread repugnance at the widow's efforts to lure Christy away from Pegeen sheds light on the more important question of how the audiences' feelings toward the two principal characters evolved. One can plausibly conjecture that the audience did not object to hearing Widow Quin pronounce the word shift because that was just the sort of detestable conduct they would expect from such a person. Yet the spectators would not have so emphatically repudiated the widow without feeling drawn to Christy and Pegeen—and the problem was that those more appealing characters were ostensibly a parricide and the would-be wife of a parricide.

The sole contemporary statement about the offensiveness of Widow Quin's utterance of shift is unusually revealing. In a letter to the *Freeman's Journal* after the first performance, a correspondent signing herself "A Western Girl" considered the implications of the play's sordidness for the actress playing the widow: "Miss Allgood (one of the most charming actresses I have ever seen) is forced, before the most fashionable audience in Dublin, to use a word indicating an essential item of female attire, which the lady would probably never utter in ordinary circumstances, even to herself."[68] The idea that there are words so awful that one would not even expose one's own ears to them may strike us today as comical, but suggests a good deal about prevailing conceptions of propriety and language usage. The Western Girl declines to write the actual word in her letter; she implies that what makes the word improper is the fact that it refers to a garment that is fundamental to female dress, as if a crucial distinction exists between those items of clothing which are visible, and can be named, and those which are hidden and functional but should not be referred to, even by women themselves (one assumes that she did not take exception to Allgood's having to say "stocking"); and she also conceives of theatrical production as a process in which actresses lack agency and risk being compelled to behave and speak as they would never do in their own lives. Like the hostile response two decades earlier to the discussion of childbirth in the final act of *Before Sunrise,* the Western Girl's indignation indicates unquestioned notions about what subject matter and words ought to be considered out of bounds for the stage.

The third occurrence of "shift" comes in a speech by Christy to Widow Quin toward the end of the play. She wants to save him from the angry crowd—"Come on, or you'll be hanged, indeed" (78)—but Christy refuses to leave Pegeen. When the widow tells him that there are plenty more women like Pegeen, Christy responds: "It's Pegeen I'm seeking only, and what'd I care if you brought me a drift of chosen females, standing in their shifts itself, maybe, from this place to the Eastern World?" (79). Holloway described Christy's line as "an unusually brutally coarse remark," then added in a note that it "was made more crudely brutal on the first night by W. G. Fay. 'Mayo girls' was substituted for 'chosen females'."[69] That change renders the line more "brutal" to the extent that Christy thus refers more specifically, and less poetically to young women from the county in which *The Playboy* takes place. Whether or not the substitution did take place is uncertain, since neither Fay himself nor anyone else other than Holloway mentions it; the interest of this detail lies in the fact that, if Fay did change the line, it appears to have made little difference. Even without such heightening of the line's offensiveness, this passage possessed the power to infuriate a large portion of the Abbey audience. The evidence indicates that what gave most offence was not the name applied to the hypothetical women, nor the notion that they might be gathered in a herd ("drift"), but the reference to their underwear.

Christy's use of the word "shift" differs from the two earlier lines in various significant ways. Both Pegeen and Widow Quin referred to a shift as one example of those items of clothing which, no differently from the shirts and stockings they also name, need to be laundered and occasionally repaired—household tasks associated in the text with women in general and Widow Quin in particular. When Christy talks of women "standing in their shifts," not only does a male character violate the boundary between male and female realms by pronouncing a word that is automatically and intimately related to women's physical as well as economic existence, but he also does so in the context of an imaginary situation of extreme sexual license. However much antipathy Widow Quin may have aroused in the spectators, they would not have expected the character to present Christy with a selection of women to choose from. Christy's fantasy would in itself have been potentially quite provocative, but Synge exacerbated the line's capacity to shock by making Christy specify that the imagined women who made themselves available to him would wear only their undergarments. The "Playboy's" point, of course, is to underline his absolute devotion to Pegeen by maintaining that he would reject even the realization of such a harem fantasy in favor of her. Christy doesn't argue that women in the West of Ireland might be expected collectively to offer themselves to men like him, but many of the spectators must have read such an insinuation into the speech. Interpreted in that way, Christy's line constituted an intensification of the whole play's slanderous implication that loose morals were characteristic of Irish women. The Western Girl made quite clear that she believed Synge was maintaining that Irish women in the west would act as the villagers in The Playboy do: "Is it necessary for me to say that in no part of Ireland are the women so wanting in modesty as to make advances to a total stranger, much less to a criminal?"[70]

The position of Christy's use of "shift" during the play's closing scenes no doubt further contributed to the concentration of so much attention on this single moment. Padraic Colum, a fellow playwright of Synge, wrote in his memoir of the first night that the hissing provoked by Christy's line, "was a signal for a riot in the Theatre. They had been disconcerted and impatient before this, but the audience, I think, would not have made any interruption if this line had not been spoken."[71] And it is striking that the individual lines highlighted in the furor over The Playboy related not to the implied appeal of a murderer, but to the female body. The fact that the play's central character supposedly "slayed his da" upset the Abbey's patrons less than his voicing his devotion to Pegeen through an image of unchaste female behavior. In a play which cunningly toys with the audience's involvement in the action, Christy's Act III line probably provided a welcome focus for the gathering outrage of the Abbey's patrons. The single suggestive reference to the female body offered a more concentrated and therefore expedient focal point for opposition than did the play's comic and ironic suggestion that a self-confessed murderer might be celebrated rather than condemned.

In a letter written a couple of months after the *Playboy* row, Synge told this amusing and pertinent anecdote:

I wonder did you hear that Dublin and the Freeman were chiefly outraged because I used the word "shift," instead of "chemise" for an article of fine linen or perhaps named it at all. Lady G. asked our charwoman—the Theatre charwoman—what she thought of it. The charwoman said she wouldn't mention the garment at all if it could be helped, but if she did she hoped she would always say "chemise," even if she was alone! Then she went down on the stage and met the stage carpenter. "Ah," *says she*, "isn't Mr. Synge a bloody old snot to write such a play!" There's Dublin delicacy![72]

The charwoman reinforces both the Western Girl's idea of coarse language's capacity to offend even oneself, and Fay's observation about the surprising hierarchy of obscenity whereby "shift" apparently outdoes even "bloody." Apparently, whereas "bloody" was so widely used that any connection it might seem to have with the body had been forgotten, the association between "shift" and the body it was designed to cover was so unmistakable that for many Dubliners it was to all intents and purposes as obscene as *merdre*.

Other witnesses suggested that the style of the first production of *The Playboy*, especially as concerns physical violence, scandalized the Abbey audience more even than did the play's language. Colum made the following observation about the audience on opening night: "they had been growing hostile to the play from the point where Christy's father enters. That scene was too representational. There stood a man with horribly-bloodied bandage upon his head, making a figure that took the whole thing out of the atmosphere of high comedy."[73] It seems unlikely that the first half of Synge's play had struck many of those in the Abbey on Saturday as "high comedy" exactly, but certainly any production's interpretation of the stage direction for Old Mahon "*He takes off a big hat, and shows his head in a mass of bandages and plaster, with some pride*" (49) could either harmonize or clash with the predominantly light-hearted mood of the preceding action. Colum's view is supported by AE (George Russell, a writer actively involved in the early years of the INTS), who wrote that "If in this first performance the father of the Playboy had been acted more fantastically and less realistically, I am convinced that there would have been no row of any kind."[74] Others believed that this aspect of the reception of *The Playboy* was especially important in the play's denouement: the Fays tried to persuade Synge "to take out the torture scene in the last act where the peasants burn Christy with the lit turf," but it was not omitted, and for one observer, "it was the unrelenting realism of the production in its last scene . . . that threw the audience into final revolt."[75] Certainly a less naturalistic approach might have kept the opening night free of disruption, but it would not have altered the primary grounds for the protests during later performances. However comically or fantastically the scenes revolving around the appearance of Old Mahon had been played, for those who found *The Playboy* slanderous, the work's latter half would still have aggravated the already offensive implications of its first half.

The protesters against *The Playboy* performed their opposition primarily, and most revealingly, by shouting retorts. In a couple of instances, those exclamations promoted violence as a response to the offensive action on stage. During Tuesday's performance, "A gentleman stood up in the pit and shouted—'They should be beaten off the stage.' (Prolonged applause.)"; another newspaper recorded the cry as "The little travesty should be beaten off the stage."[76] There have been plenty of occasions in theater history when indignation over a performance has manifested itself as physical threats or even assaults on actors; but nothing suggests such an intention in this case. Hostility aroused by *The Playboy* was directed far more at Synge and the other directors of the INTS than at the actors. It was against the characters that this gentleman proposed taking such extreme measures—against these fictional figures, in whom Synge seemed to be suggesting that the audience would recognize themselves. Either way, this remark and the support it received indicate the intensity of many Dubliners' reaction to *The Playboy*. Another retort shouted during Monday's performance reveals that intensity more clearly still: "The final act was then proceeded with, but no one in the house heard a word of it owing to the din created by the audience, many of whom cried—'Sinn Fein'; 'Sinn Fein Amhain'—and 'Kill the Author'."[77] This exclamation—yelled by more than just one spectator—theoretically incited a far more severe act of violence than those depicted at the close of Synge's play. The *Playboy* "riots" involved no encounters more serious than some scuffles between audience members, yet the cry of "Kill the Author" signals the full depth of the animosity felt toward those responsible for this production, first and foremost Synge.

Many of the less extreme comments interjected by spectators during the performances responded to specific lines, and invariably they prompted clear indications of agreement from other audience members. On Tuesday, for instance, "Referring to the murder of old Mahon by his son, the publican said, 'It is a hard story,' whereupon a number of the audience aptly remarked, 'It is a rotten story,' a remark which was loudly applauded."[78] When the tide turned in midweek in favor of those Dubliners who wished to hear *The Playboy*, some protesters responded by devising novel, nonverbal forms of opposition: during Act II on Thursday, "a new form of interruption was invented. Everybody in the pit seemed to be attacked by a violent fit of coughing and sneezing, which lasted for a couple of minutes." And during Act III, "a number of young men walked ostentatiously

out from the pit shouting as they went—'Rotten'."[79] The performance of
opposition to *The Playboy* as in other scandals had two distinct though
overlapping aims. The initial objective of the play's opponents was to
compel the Abbey to cancel the rest of the run, which they tried to accomplish by rendering the performances inaudible; the directors' and the
company's determination to continue as scheduled, supported by the intervention of the police, prevented them from succeeding. But the protesters also set out to register their objections to Synge's play through
shouting and singing, which they forcefully and effectively carried out,
especially on the second to fourth nights. The group performances on the
fifth night constituted an imaginative means of ensuring that opposition
continued to be perceived and recorded even once vociferation had become an established and predictable element of audience response to *The
Playboy*.

One telling comment responded to a scene rather than to a particular
line: on Tuesday, during the scene in Act I where Pegeen listens to
Christy's account of how he killed his father, "a voice shouted 'Why not
get the police to arrest him.'"[80] On the stage, the police were conspicuous
by their absence, indeed it is Christy's question to Michael, "Is it often the
polis do be coming into this place, master of the house?" (13) that first
excites the villagers' curiosity, and the play appeared to suggest that all
Irish peasants would likewise embrace lawlessness. In the auditorium,
meanwhile, the police were manifestly present, and by this point had
begun arresting occupants of the pit whose crimes were negligible and
debatable. The involvement of the police in the Abbey's production in-
censed the opponents of *The Playboy*, ultimately perhaps more than did
the play itself. As the *Freeman's Journal* commented after Monday's performance, "It was a curious spectacle: an Irish National Theatre persisting
under police protection in outraging an Irish audience."[81] At this time the
police in Ireland was of course still a British force, governed from London
via Dublin Castle, and increasingly the focus of nationalist resentment, if
not yet the target of violence.

In a letter published in the *Evening Telegraph* after the end of the run,
Horniman wrote that "The directors are in a position of trust in regard to
my property, and when there was a threat to pull down the curtain it
became their duty to call in the police."[82] That certainly makes the decision
to bring in the police appear entirely understandable, but no other account
or document mentions any such threat; in fact the justification first for the
introduction of the police and second for the arrests they eventually made
was very much open to interpretation, and hotly disputed. After Monday's performance, during which the police entered the auditorium but
remained inactive and thus did nothing to quell the uproar, the *Irish Times*
represented that restraint as understandable since audience protests "can
only be stopped on a complaint either of the members of the audience

who desire to hear the play or of the manager of the theatre."[83] But clearly many spectators had objected to the noisy opposition, including one who wrote the next day to disagree with the reporter's assessment of the situation: "I was under the impression that everyone in the stalls protested audibly, and many, like myself, were astonished that no use was made by the management of the able-bodied policemen who lined the walls of the pit."[84]

That the police did not make arrests on Monday but did on Tuesday resulted not so much from a greater degree of disorder at the later performance as from a greater determination on the part of the theater's directors to suppress the protests. And when Yeats and some occupants of the stalls began to single out protesters, the police officers were at first reluctant actually to arrest them: "The constables still seemed doubtful, and intended only to warn the men pointed to, who seemed disposed to be quiet."[85] But before long the police acceded to the demands of the audience members in the stalls, prominent among them Lady Gregory's nephew Hugh Lane, an art dealer and a key figure in Dublin's cultural life. Gregory mentions that "A caricature of the time shows him in evening dress with unruffled shirt cuffs, leading out disturbers of the peace."[86] What outraged the opponents of the Abbey was therefore not simply that the police protected the production, but that the all too influential directors had been able to call in the police, and moreover that the officers were so much in the thrall of these people of standing that they had in effect followed their instructions in arresting spectators. The *Freeman's Journal* underlined the class implications of the stalls/pit division in the wording of sentences like this one: "A gentleman pointed out a young man to the police as causing disorder, and the man was immediately ejected"— clearly the gentlemen of the stalls had a distinct advantage over the men of the pit. That report further suggests that the gentlemen threw themselves with relish into their self-assigned task of pointing out culprits to the police: "Mr. Yeats and some of his supporters employed themselves watching people who were making noise, with the object of drawing the attention of the police to them and getting them ejected. They succeeded in getting a number of young men pulled out amidst a terrific uproar, and shouts of 'Where are the militia?'"[87] One can certainly understand the resentment of the protesters, and their sense that the contest was unevenly balanced. And the shouts of 'Where are the militia?' underline the fact that the conflict reverberated far beyond the production of one play at the Abbey. No element of the row over *The Playboy* emblematizes more succinctly its prefiguring of the approaching violent struggle for independence than this episode which saw officers of a British police force arresting Irishmen on spurious grounds, in response to which the Irishmen invoked armed resistance to British rule.

The protests against *The Playboy* differed from those against *Before Sun-*

rise and *Ubu Roi* as regards the relationship between the affronted spectators and the theater company responsible for the production. That relationship is conveyed particularly well by an article about Tuesday's events in the *Freeman's Journal* headed "The Scene at the Theatre. By one of the Ejected." The author writes in a sober, sad tone, rather than with the anger and resentment that one might expect: "I am not one of those who take a mean delight in the degradation of things that once promised nobly; and I, who welcomed and supported the Abbey Theatre while it followed the counsel of wisdom feel nothing but pity for the contemptible bedraggled position which it occupies to-day." This man was not the only protester against *The Playboy* to have been all the more outraged by the play for having been a supporter of the INTS. The demonstrations against Synge's play, far more than those against the productions by the Freie Bühne and the Théâtre de l'Œuvre, were intensified by the genuine political, psychological, even emotional investment by many of the play's opponents in the society as an enterprise. Predictably this writer indicts the directors, especially Yeats, for the deployment of police, but he also focuses on the drafting of students: "What a spectacle for gods and men, the champion of a free Irish theatre calling in the police, and admitting drunken anti-Irish rowdies to the stalls free for the purpose of supporting what those rowdies welcomed with delight as giving an unfavourable picture of their countrymen." And he underlines the contrast in behavior and motivation between the play's supporters and its opponents: "I saw seated facing the stage a number of respectable young men who were certainly not making as much noise as the supporters of the play, who were quite sober, and who, I am absolutely satisfied (for I was among them) were not an 'organised gang'."[88] One detects partisan exaggeration in much of the press coverage of the row over *The Playboy*, not least in the pages of the *Freeman's Journal*, yet this unusually restrained testimony seems very credible. The slander which many Dubliners read into Synge's play was compounded by the contrived counterprotests of privileged, drunken youths, as well as by the heavy-handed actions of the police.

The free admission of a claque to defend the play is also unfortunate in that it interfered with the genuine difference of opinion between two distinct groups in the auditorium, two sides which at some points entered into something of a debate. On Tuesday evening, according to the *Daily Express*, the continuing uproar following Yeats's second speech included the following exchange:

a gentleman in the stalls mounted his seat, and said—. . . "The management are responsible to me for having brought me here." (A Voice—"And to us also.") "They are responsible for giving me something, and they are not allowed to do so. You also have made a contract, and want something for your money, to see this play. Have you seen the play?" (Loud shouts of "Yes.") "I say you have not, and you have no right to judge it until you have."[89]

The *Freeman's Journal* gives a briefer and slightly different account:

"The men who brought me here," he said "are responsible to me, and must give
me value for my money."
   A Voice—This is more than a matter of money (loud applause followed by
further uproar).[90]

This gentleman and his respondents highlighted very succinctly the issues
of rights and responsibilities raised by all theater scandals. Audiences
have the right to see the performance they have paid to see; but spectators
also have the right to express their opposition to that performance—and
as we shall see, the law in 1907 granted theatergoers that right. This exchange also underlines the two ways in which the production of *The Playboy* pushed the nature of the performance-audience contract to an extreme:
the play so offended a large segment of the public that they believed they
were within their rights in disrupting the performance; and the fact that
some of them were protesting against a play they had already seen un-
dermines their claim to be fairly judging Synge's work.
   The arrests during Tuesday's and Wednesday's performances led to
court cases in which magistrates judged the conduct of individual spectators, and also took up varying positions about the legitimacy of audience
protests in the theater. The first defendant in connection with Tuesday's
performance was charged with "being guilty of offensive behaviour in the
pit of the Abbey Theatre . . . by shouting, hissing, and booing and stamping his feet, and with, when spoken to by the constables, using obscene
language to the annoyance of the audience." Yeats appeared in court, and
argued that "there was an obviously organised attempt to prevent the
play being heard. . . . The section that caused the disturbance was not part
of the regular audience. The conduct of the section was riotous and offensive, and disturbed and annoyed the audience."[91] To obtain a conviction,
Yeats shrewdly recycled the terms of the charge, but he also exaggerated
some key aspects of the evening's events: the protest was perhaps partially, but not "obviously" organized, and a good proportion of the protesters did regularly attend the Abbey. The implied distinction between
the Abbey's regular audience and these intruders who marred the regular
audience's experience reflects Yeats's belief from the outset that a theater
producing new and experimental work would almost inevitably, and not
regrettably, draw only a small audience. As he wrote in connection with
founding of the Irish Literary Theatre, the theater he imagined would play
to "that limited public which gives understanding and not to that unlimited public which gives wealth."[92]
   The newspaper reports on the trial do not tell us how the first defendant
responded to the charges, but the second one took advantage of the opportunity to make a public statement about his conduct and motivation.

Like the contributor to the *Freeman's Journal* who called himself "One of
the Ejected," this defendant identifies himself as a regular supporter of
the Abbey, and vehemently denies having acted as part of an organized
group. His tone, however, is far less temperate: he tells the court that "his
blood boiled at the attempt to coerce public opinion." Yeats had pointed
him out to a constable when he, along with many others, booed at a "particularly objectionable expression." Face to face with Yeats in the courtroom, he insists that "no threats or penalties would deter him from
objecting to what he considered an outrage on the Irish people," even
when Yeats agrees to the magistrate's proposal of a mild penalty in exchange for "an undertaking that he would not take any part in these
disturbances in the theatre again." The magistrate, Mr. Mahony, tells the
defendant, "You were determined to stop the play," but the reply is "I
was not your worship. I particularly objected to a thing I heard." No doubt
Mahony was trying to make his own decision easier, in that attempting
to force the cessation of a performance would be a more clear-cut offense
than merely causing disturbance to other audience members. The defendant did not allow him that option, and Mahony found both defendants
guilty and set the penalty at forty shillings or one month's imprisonment.
In one exchange with the second defendant, the magistrate told him: "You
are entitled to indulge in legitimate criticism, and also in a reasonable
form of disapproval, but you are not entitled to be guilty of such behaviour as would be offensive to other persons in the play and prevent their
performance."[93] Of course, the crucial issue is exactly where the dividing-
line falls between acceptable and unacceptable audience protest. In the
Dublin of even a few decades earlier, or in other theaters in 1907, "a reasonable form of disapproval" would probably have included some booing
and hissing, and that behavior would have been unlikely to offend other
spectators. In giving priority to the interests of the quiet and attentive
audience members—and one assumes that those are the spectators he
casts as the owners when he speaks of "their performance"—ahead of the
objections of the protesters, Mahony represents the norms of his times.

Another magistrate, Mr. Wall, indicated early in the trial of a student
arrested on Wednesday evening that his own views would figure much
more in the courtroom than did Mahony's. As he went about establishing
just where the defendant and the policemen were positioned during the
performance, he remarked: "All this will advertise it well in London. The
vile Irish will be well exposed up there." Unlike Mahony, Wall questioned
the witnesses extensively himself, focusing particular attention on exactly
which words spoken on the stage incited the protest, and on the behavior
of spectators other than the defendant. Wall then entered into a debate
with the prosecutor Mr. Tobias over the charge. Tobias had charged the
defendant with offensive behavior in the knowledge that a magistrate
could rule on such cases if they were isolated, but not if together with

other offenses they constituted a riot. "Mr. Wall said as he understood it
the people in the pit were of one way of thinking and the people in the
stalls of another, and there was so much shouting going on that the audience could not hear the play. Was not that a riot?"[94] For Wall, the conduct
of the audience as a whole was riotous, but the conduct of the defendant
was not. Wall prefaced his verdict by referring at some length to earlier
decisions on similar cases, particularly one by former Lord Chief Justice
Bushe, who in an 1823 case said that theater audiences

might cry down a play which they disliked, or hiss and booh the actors who
depended for their positions on the good-will of audiences, but they must not act
in such a manner as had a tendency to excite uproar or disturbance. Their censure
or approbation, though they might be noisy in expressing it, must not be riotous,
and must be the expression of the feeling of the moment. If premeditated by a
number of persons combined beforehand to cry down a performance or an actor
it became criminal.[95]

This view allows audiences far more assertive expressions of opinion than
does the standard adopted at the previous trial by Mr. Mahony, and the
key criterion for determining when a protest exceeded the permitted intensity is different: rather than focusing on whether or not some spectators
are offending other audience members, Bushe highlights the threat of civil
disorder. The contrast between the positions represented by Bushe and
Mahony, separated by eighty years, emblematizes the nineteenth-century
shift in conceptions of normative audience behavior. For Mahony, the right
of spectators to watch a play undisturbed by fellow audience members
took precedence over the right of an audience uninhibitedly to express its
feelings about a performance. Although Wall inclined far more toward
Bushe's view than Mahony's, he did find this and other defendants guilty,
on the grounds that their protests were not "the expression of the feeling
of the moment," but made clear his misgivings, and fined the men only
a quarter of the penalty imposed by Mahony. As he said in another case,
"I am afraid, however, that the defendant went to the theatre with a preconceived intention."[96]

Wall repeatedly questioned the arbitrary nature of the few arrests: "It
seemed a strange thing that this man was singled out and arrested, while
the people all around were either boohing or hissing."[97] More significantly
still, Wall firmly argued not only that the supporters of the play were just
as guilty as its opponents—"He did not think the defendant's conduct
was any worse than the conduct of the others, who differed from him"—
but also that there was greater justification for prosecuting the directors
of the Abbey:

it might be well to consider on the part of the Crown whether those who persisted
in bringing forward theatrical procedure of such a character as to excite popular

odium and opposition, and which could not be tolerated, at all events, in Ireland, where, practically, there were two worlds, one wishing to be at the throat of the other, and one wishing to avoid what the other wished to intrude—whether those who were responsible for that should not themselves be brought forward.[98]

No wonder Magistrate Wall became something of a hero to the opponents of *The Playboy*. In another trial, Wall admitted that "I know nothing about the play," and his conservative position excludes any consideration of the artistic merits of the work.[99] For him, in view of the unavoidably divisive climate in Ireland, the mere fact that Synge's play had given offense to many people made it a bad play which should not have been performed. He characterizes the theater in Ireland as having historically been "the resort of people who sought interest and culture and instruction"—clearly for Wall, theater should not confront the public or compel them to ask difficult questions about themselves.[100] In this respect, as in regard to the permissible behavior of audiences, Wall stands for centuries-old notions which by 1907 had been under attack for several decades.

The open discussion which Yeats had promised before Tuesday's performance duly took place on Monday, February 4. The Abbey was full for the debate, whose two topics were announced as "the Freedom of the Theatre" and *The Playboy of the Western World*. Yeats spoke first, followed by a series of speakers opposed to the production, then later a few who defended the play and the Abbey, and the meeting ended after three hours with a final speech by Yeats. Throughout all these speeches the audience cheered, hissed, groaned and shouted. The next day Lady Gregory wrote to Synge, who was not present, to tell him "The meeting last night was dreadful, and I congratulate you on not having been at it." She felt this way partly because "No one came to support us," but she goes on to admit that "it didn't much matter for the disturbances were so great they wouldn't even let their own speakers be well heard."[101] The *Daily Express* characterized the evening as "not so much tinged with rowdyism as with boisterous foolery," though the people who cared most about the issues under discussion were clearly irked by the disorder.[102] Gregory wrote that "Many of our opponents called for order and fair play and I think must have been disgusted with their allies." Nevertheless, those who spoke did receive and take an opportunity to make a range of serious points about the play and the events of the previous week. Lady Gregory concluded, "I think it was spirited and showed we were not repenting or apologizing."[103] The Dubliners who protested against *The Playboy* had ample reason to feel the same way.

While the directors of the INTS could feel satisfied with their principled stand over *The Playboy of the Western World*, the controversy dealt a serious blow to the company's finances. Attendances, and thus box office receipts, fell precipitously. Willie Fay wrote of the consequences for the actors: "For

weeks on end we had to play to five or ten shillings a night—a full programme to half a dozen people scattered all over the house. I used to
invite them all into the stalls to sit together."[104] Fortunately, touring England and Scotland offered both a fresh public and a source of revenue.
In May and June the company performed in several cities, declining to
include *The Playboy* in the repertoire in those where trouble could be anticipated—Glasgow and Birmingham—but producing Synge's play to
critical acclaim in London. The performances at the Great Queen Street
Theatre did provoke some demonstrations against the play from Irish
residents of London, especially on the second night: "in the last act from
all parts of the house came frequent storms of groans, cries of 'Shame,'
counter-cries of 'Geese' from some spectators who wanted to follow the
play, and forcible remarks to the players from at least one man in the
stalls."[105] Yet the efforts of a few protesters were insufficient to whip up a
controversy comparable to that in Dublin. Fay attributes the contrast to
the difference in refinement between the two cities' theatergoing populations, describing the London performances as "the first time we had an
opportunity of putting the play before a sophisticated audience that simply judged it as a play."[106] But if it came more easily to Londoners than
to Dubliners to respond to *The Playboy* without taking offense at the play's
apparently damning depiction of the Irish, this probably indicated less
about the spectators' sophistication than about their nationality. The proportion of Irish spectators in London must have been considerably smaller
than it had been in Dublin, so that those who wanted to shout down the
play were unable to prevail against those who wished to hear it.

When *The Playboy* was revived at the Abbey in 1909—a few months
after Synge's death at the age of thirty-seven—the first-night hissing and
negative press did not gather sufficient force to bring about a repetition
of the 1907 uproar. But further intense confrontation with outraged spectators did lie ahead in the United States, where the Abbey company toured
for the first time from September 1911 to March 1912. By then *The Playboy*
and other plays in the Abbey repertoire were quite well known in America, some having even been taught in universities. Lady Gregory claimed
that the Boston public was so familiar with the scripts "that we were now
and again reproved by some one in the audience if a line or passage were
left out, by design or forgetfulness."[107] Often widespread public knowledge of a work, especially if combined with the passage of a considerable
period of time, renders it far less likely to shock, but during the four-and-
a-half years between the Dublin premiere and the American tour, the Irish-
American community's determination to protest against Synge's play had
not diminished at all. An article in the *Gaelic American* declared that "Mr.
Yeats, Lady Gregory and the players themselves must be taught the lesson
that the Irish in America cannot be insulted with impunity. . . . *The Playboy*
must be suppressed, and it will be suppressed."[108]

The conflicts between *The Playboy* and its opponents in Dublin and the U.S. differed in a number of respects. The Abbey company did not tour America under the name of the Irish National Theatre Society, but as the Irish Players, "to distinguish it financially and so avoid the charge of diverting the resources of a national theater for the entertainment of other nationals," as John P. Harrington explains.[109] So it was out of sensitivity about the Irish rather than the Irish-American public that the directors chose to adopt the alternative name; but the change probably also contributed to the relative unimportance in the U.S. of the company's claim to represent the Irish nation. The intensive focus in 1907 on the script's language also was not repeated in the U.S., partly because "most of the passages in Synge's play which, in Dublin, had caused offence, had been eliminated."[110] That may not account for all that much, however, since in general opponents of *The Playboy* in American cities expressed their objections—in print and in the auditorium—to the overall image of the Irish suggested by the play, rather than to the details which made up that representation. In addition, protests against Synge's play tended to target single performances, rather than persisting through a series of performances, so there was no comparable development of response, or individual reactions to particular lines.

A clear indication that the opposition to *The Playboy* might prove even more vehement in the U.S. than in Dublin came when a Boston newspaper attacked two other plays in the repertoire—Murray's *Birthright* and Gregory's *Hyacinth Halvey*—neither of which had caused any trouble in Ireland. It is easy to understand why Irish emigrants, and especially those trying to build a life in the fractious melting pot of the United States, would be even more sensitive to perceived attacks on their national character than Dubliners. Lady Gregory recalls a conversation with a New England journalist who explained to her that immigrants of other nationalities showed similar sensitivity: "The Swedes had a play taken off that represented some Swedish women drinking. The French Canadians, he says, are as touchy as the Irish."[111] In the multiethnic context of the U.S., it was necessarily far more difficult for opponents of Synge's play to win support than it had been for their predecessors in Dublin. Partly because of this, they argued their position in the most extreme terms, and such overstatement may well have diminished rather than increased others' sympathy with their cause. The theater possessed special power to offend expatriate Irish because of the Stage Irishman stereotype. Irish-Americans had been waging a campaign against the Stage Irishman for some years. In 1903 in New York, for instance, they drove the actors in a musical review entitled *McFadden's Row of Flats* from the stage with a carefully planned bombardment of eggs and vegetables. In Dublin, the indignation aroused by *The Playboy* and Synge's earlier plays was exceptional, and all the more intense because they were staged by an institution which called itself the national theater, and which had developed considerable support including among nationalists. In the U.S., by contrast, the Irish Players' opponents treated *The Playboy* as the latest in a series of plays which they felt compelled to demonstrate against. Thus in October 1911, the United Irish Societies of New York resolved to "drive the vile thing from the stage, as we drove *McFadden's Row of Flats*."[112]

Shaw, interviewed during the tour by a New York newspaper, cuttingly analyzed the response of these "American pseudo-Irish," people who "call Ireland the Old Country": "Their notion of patriotism is to listen jealously for the slightest hint that Ireland is not the home of every virtue and the martyr of every oppression, and thereupon to brawl and bully or to whine and protest, according to their popularity with the bystanders."[113] Shaw's damning interpretation seems fully borne out by the most vehemently expressed Irish-American reading of *The Playboy*, which was less subtle still than that of the angriest Dublin letter writers. That reading inferred not only that in Synge's view all Irish people love a good parricide, but also that the text unequivocally misrepresented Irish customs regarding marriage. According to an article in the *Gaelic American*, the offensiveness of Christy's "what'd I care if you brought me a drift of chosen females, standing in their shifts itself" "was in the plain intimation that in making matrimonial matches it is common to line up practically naked women for a suitor to choose from."[114] On the whole the Abbey's U.S. tour was a success, but the six months were punctuated by a variety of protests staged by those who found in Synge's play "a brutal misrepresentation of the Irish race."[115]

By the time the company first performed *The Playboy*, in Boston on October 16, the actors were quite apprehensive, having been condemned in various publications, and warned that protests in the auditorium were quite likely. As it turned out, the opposition in the Plymouth Theatre amounted to little more than some booing and hissing that never developed into anything more, partly because a contingent of Harvard students drowned out the dissent with cheering, partly because would-be troublemakers were swiftly ejected. While in Dublin in 1907 the same means of protecting the play against opposition had seemed to many an unfair suppression of legitimate objections, clearly in Boston the protesters represented only a small minority, as the success of the rest of the run bore out. Nic Shiubhlaigh, who was in the cast, recalled that "To our relief all further attempts to make trouble in Boston fell flat."[116] The audience on the first night in Boston included the Mayor's secretary, assigned to report on the supposedly offensive plays presented by the Irish Players. He wrote: "If obscenity is to be found on the stage in Boston, it must be sought elsewhere and not at the Plymouth Theatre," an opinion shared by the police censor. This pattern was repeated in other American cities: the mayors of New York and Chicago responded to written protests against

The Playboy by considering what justification there might be for forbidding its performance, only to conclude that there was none. The closest the Irish Players' opponents came to a sympathetic hearing was in Chicago, where the Mayor declared, "I do not see how the performance can be stopped. I have read part of it and its chief characteristic seems to be stupidity rather than immorality."[117] Whereas the expatriate Irish who believed Synge's play should not be performed were caught up in the struggle to adapt to life in the U.S. on the one hand and nostalgia for the island they had left behind on the other, the men who occupied positions of authority in early-twentieth-century America were settled enough to recognize—even when they could not see the artistic merit of the piece—that *The Playboy* did not constitute an attack on the Irish people. In Dublin, the directors of the Abbey had recourse to the police in order to quell dissent, and that augmented the outrage and the protests; in the U.S., local authorities repeatedly sided with the company, which took wind out of their opponents' already flimsy sails.

When the New York performances of *The Playboy* began on Monday, November 27, the threat of violent protest was even greater than it had been in Boston. The *Gaelic American* had continued to wage a virulent campaign against the Irish Players, declaring right before the first night that "The New York Irish will send the Anti-Players back to Dublin like whipped curs with their tails between their legs"; and Lady Gregory was told of a priest who had "advised his people from the altar if they did come, to bring eggs to throw."[118] And the actors certainly did have to contend with far more than they had in Boston. At first the dissenting spectators expressed themselves through the familiar means of hissing, shouting and stamping. But soon the demonstration took on a different form:

A potato swept through the air from the gallery and smashed against the wings. Then came a shower of vegetables that rattled against the scenery and made the actors duck their heads and fly behind the stage setting for shelter.

A potato struck Miss Magee, and she, Irish like, drew herself up and glared defiance. Men were rising in the gallery and balcony and crying out to stop the performance. In the orchestra several men stood up and shook their fists.[119]

The protesters had designed their assault to unsettle the audience as well as the actors: their weapons included pepper and asafoetida. The actors carried on with the performance, until the houselights were turned on, and a good number of policemen entered the auditorium and began ejecting and arresting the troublemakers. One of the actors announced that they would begin the play again from the beginning, which they duly did, and completed the performance with no further serious disruption. During the second performance the following evening, according to Lady

Gregory's account, "There was a scuffle now and then during *The Playboy* but nothing violent and always great clapping when the offender was thrown out."[120] The audience included former President Roosevelt, whose unreserved support for the company and for the play helped the company to complete an ultimately very successful run. The Irish Players' opponents seem to have focused all their energy on disrupting the premiere, and once the company had survived that, they could enjoy the very receptive New York audiences.

But having conquered New York did not insure the Abbey tour against further protests; in each of the major cities they visited, they encountered some form of organized opposition. In Philadelphia in January, the offensives against *The Playboy* ranged from the curious to the cunning. The first night followed the pattern of the New York premiere, though in less extreme form: gradually intensifying shouted protests, some missiles (Lady Gregory comments dismissively on the Philadelphians' unimpressive barrage: "Nothing was thrown but a slice of currant cake, which hit Sinclair, and two or three eggs, which missed him—he says they were fresh ones"[121]), then ejection of the troublemakers by the police. The actors were only rendered inaudible for a few minutes, so this time the company did not feel it necessary to restart the play. On the second night the play's opponents adopted a form of protest employed in Dublin four years earlier: "two whole rows of the auditors were seized with a desire to cough or clear their throats. That caused a momentary lull in the play." Lady Gregory claims that turning on the houselights suppressed this bizarre chorus, and certainly the lighting, along with a good number of mostly plainclothes policemen, helped to quell disorder. But the most determined protesters refused to be silenced:

The disorder approached the dignity of serious rioting, in the second and third acts of the piece, and at the last a man from Connemara rose in the body of the house, whipped a speech from his coat pocket, and proceeded to interrupt the players with a harangue against the morality of the play.

His philippics were short-lived. Sixteen cops in plain clothes reached him at the same time, and the red man from Connemara disappeared, while the play was being brought to a close.[122]

In wryly remarking that the disturbances during the latter part of the performance were of higher quality than those during Act I, this reporter criticized the protesters' coughing chorus, presumably because he (or she, though probably not) felt that any demonstration ought to make clear just what objections it was articulating. And the existing documentation suggests that opponents of *The Playboy* in the U.S. did not succeed in winning the sympathy of anything like as large a portion of the public as did their predecessors in Dublin. Judging by this and other newspaper reports, the protests against Synge's play in America were generally regarded as the quite amusing but also rather irksome antics of a minority of extremists.

It was a Philadelphia liquor dealer who resorted to the classic American tactic of taking legal action, in an effort to prevent further performances. Under a recently passed law forbidding "the production in the city of any stage play that might be deemed immodest . . . any citizen was entitled to bring a charge of indecency against theatrical companies appearing within the city boundaries."[123] Shortly before curtain on the fourth night of The Playboy, the entire cast was placed technically under arrest. However, the performance went ahead as planned, because the Chief of Police turned out to be one of the many American public officials who supported the Abbey's tour, and he refused to let his officers actually arrest the actors. The company did have to appear in court the next day, but they came off well in the trial. The accuser presented a flimsy case, having sat through only the first part of the play on opening night. The Irish Players were expertly defended by New York lawyer John Quinn, and the Philadelphia Director of Public Safety testified that "he had attended the theatre with his wife and that neither of them was 'shocked'; on the contrary, distinctly pleased."[124] It was almost a week before the judge dismissed the case, but as Nic Shiubhlaigh recalled, "the trial had happy results for us. People came to see us who had never even known we existed and, liking what they saw, came back for more."[125]

The contours of Irish-American opposition to the Irish Players and to The Playboy were very similar in other cities: forthright vows to disrupt performances beforehand (and in Chicago even a threatening letter sent to Lady Gregory, telling her "Your doom is sealed"[126]) followed by demonstrations in the auditorium during the first few performances, although these became increasingly halfhearted as the tour proceeded further west. And in most instances the primary effect of the opposition was to provide the company with publicity and so to contribute to their success. American opponents of the Abbey did not concede defeat. Tours in 1913 and 1914 encountered similar outbursts of hostility. But overall the protests against The Playboy in the U.S. amounted to little more than the demagoguery of a small extremist minority.

The scandals caused by The Playboy of the Western World in 1907 and 1912 present an intriguing contrast. In Dublin, for the better part of a week, a significant proportion of those who attended a performance expressed their objections to Synge's play, so that the row over The Playboy became a major event, debated at length in various public forums. In the U.S., the vast majority of the audience members in several different cities responded positively to the Irish Players' production, and the fervent protests of a minority took on the quality of an entertaining sideshow, a topic lending itself to ironic journalism. Yet theatergoers in both countries saw essentially the same play. The contrast cannot be accounted for simply by the differences between the sensibilities of Irish nationalists and Irish-Americans at the start of the twentieth century. Taken as a whole, the early reception of *The Playboy* illustrates the multiplicity of factors contributing to the reaction of any group of spectators. The protests against Synge's play provide less evidence of immediate audience response to a previously unknown work than did *Before Sunrise* and *Ubu Roi*. But they provide perhaps more evidence than any other modern play of all the performative means an affronted audience can adopt in order to make a clear public statement of its opposition.

CHAPTER 4

"A Slander on the Citizen Army!": Vindicating Fallen Heroes

O'Casey's *The Plough and the Stars*

The Irish National Theatre Society might well have ceased to exist during the years following the row over *The Playboy of the Western World* without the revenue provided by tours outside Ireland. Attendance at performances in Dublin declined significantly beginning in February 1907, and that summer Horniman turned her attention to another theater venture in England, letting Yeats know that she would provide no more support to the Abbey once her initial commitment ended in 1910. Through a campaign during 1910, Yeats and Lady Gregory managed to raise some funds through subscriptions, and the theater's finances were also improved by a new emphasis on plays of rural realism which proved quite popular. But a low point was reached in 1914 when even an American tour resulted in a financial loss. The years before and after the first world war were generally difficult for the INTS, until the advent of the Free State brought with it the possibility of something Yeats had hoped for as early as the 1890s: state support for a theater in Ireland. He and Lady Gregory first petitioned for such support in 1922, but even once the Civil War ended in May 1923, it was some years until the government granted the request—years during which the theater produced more plays in Irish than before, partly in order to strengthen their case for being officially recognized as the National Theatre of Ireland. A government subsidy was finally granted in August 1925. But that state support brought with it a new potential threat to the artistic freedom that mattered so much to Yeats and Lady Gregory: a government representative—George O'Brien, an economics professor at University College—was appointed to the Abbey, though the extent of his authority was not clearly determined.

Only a few months into the Abbey's new relationship with the government, the implications of the subsidy were tested by Sean O'Casey's latest
play, *The Plough and the Stars*. This four-act tragedy is set during the Easter
Rising, the 1916 rebellion in which around 1,500 Irish nationalists held out
for a week in various Dublin buildings against the might of the British army.
The rebels had no chance of winning, and the fighting left hundreds of
civilians dead and much of the city in ruins, but the nationalists ultimately
scored a significant victory for their cause when the British injudiciously
arrested thousands of Irish and executed fifteen of the rising's leaders. The
one-week opening run of O'Casey's play in February 1926 aroused protests
which were immediately compared to those incited by Synge's play two
decades earlier. A recent book on the history of the Abbey maintains that
"the protests against *The Plough* were basically the same as those against
The Playboy," but such an argument overlooks many significant differences
between the nature of the two plays, the motivation for and character of
the protests against them, and the historical circumstances in which the
opening runs of Synge's and O'Casey's plays took place.[1]

The first two acts of *The Plough and the Stars* take place in November 1915,
six months before the Rising. All of the play's central characters are residents of the same Dublin tenement, but represent a range of different
attitudes toward Ireland's efforts to achieve independence. Jack Clitheroe
is a young bricklayer active in the Irish Citizen Army (ICA)—an armed
militia with origins in a labor union, formed in 1913. Jack's wife Nora
fervently wishes he would devote less time to the ICA and more to her.
Near the end of the act, when Captain Brennan brings him a dispatch
from General Connolly—James Connolly, the commander-in-chief of the
ICA, and of all the insurgents during the Rising—Jack finds out that Nora
burned the letter informing him of his promotion to Commandant. Two
relatives live with the Clitheroes and are constantly quarrelling: Nora's
uncle Peter Flynn, and Jack's cousin the Covey. Peter is a committed member of the Irish National Foresters, a fraternal organization whose elaborate uniform he likes to wear and the Covey likes to mock; the Covey
himself is a Communist and shows contempt for all the nationalist groups.
Their neighbor Fluther Good is not involved with any organization, but
holds and expresses strong if changeable opinions. Upstairs lives Bessie
Burgess, an outspoken loyalist who continually clashes with another res-
ident Mrs. Gogan, mother of the consumptive teenager Mollser. By the
end of Act I, most of these characters have gone off to a demonstration
involving various paramilitary and other nationalist groups, of a kind that
did quite regularly occur in Dublin during these years. Act II takes place
in a pub outside which a speaker, who is periodically seen and heard, is
addressing the marchers. Although O'Casey gives him no name, his words
are drawn from the speeches and writings of Padraic Pearse, one of the

founders of the Irish Volunteers and the leader of the Easter Rising. The barman and Rosie Redmond, a prostitute, are joined at various times by the characters introduced in Act I. As the speaker exhorts the crowd to take up arms and fight for Ireland, even at the cost of bloodshed, first Mrs. Gogan and Bessie, then Fluther and Peter vehemently argue, and virtually come to blows. Clitheroe comes into the pub with two fellow nationalists, Brennan carrying the banner of the ICA—the plough and the stars of the play's title—Langon, a member of the Irish Volunteers, a Republican tricolor.

Act III and IV occur during the Rising in April 1916. In Act III, set outside the tenement, O'Casey combines through the characters' words and actions several incidents from the early days of Easter Week: the occupation of the General Post Office; Pearse's reading a proclamation of an Irish republic; the British counterattacks, including the charge of British Lancers down O'Connell Street and the shelling from the gunboat *Helga;* and the widespread looting. In the midst of such events, Nora has been racing around trying desperately to find Jack. Fluther in turn pursued her and now brings her back. When Jack comes, Nora implores him to stay with her, but he won't desert and goes off with Brennan to find help for the wounded Langon. Nora collapses then lets out screams which the two older women recognize as signaling premature labor. Act IV is set in Bessie's attic apartment at the end of the week, when the might of the British military was finally overcoming the poorly armed rebels. Bessie is looking after Nora, whose baby was stillborn, and who has lost her sanity. Mollser has also died. Brennan, no longer in uniform, comes to tell the residents of the tenement gathered in Bessie's apartment that Jack has died during the ICA's last stand at the Imperial Hotel. British soldiers oversee the removal of Mollser's coffin, and then take the men off to be held in a church—as happened to O'Casey himself in 1916. Nora in her crazed state goes to the window and shouts for Jack, and when Bessie tries to pull her back, she herself is mistaken for a sniper and shot dead—a fate which nearly befell the playwright's mother. The play ends with two British soldiers drinking tea and singing "Keep the Home Fires Burning" as the sounds of fighting continue outside, the British army's artillery now audible along with rifle shots and machine-gun fire.

Sean O'Casey, born in 1884, had served as secretary of the Irish Citizen Army for several months in 1914. He resigned because the labor-based organization allied itself with the Irish Volunteers, whose membership and orientation was more middle class. During Easter Week O'Casey was twice briefly imprisoned along with other non-participants. His involvement with the ICA continued in a different form: in 1919 he wrote *The Story of the Irish Citizen Army.* But playwriting was his principal interest, and by 1926, O'Casey had seen four of his plays staged at the Abbey. The two most important ones both, like *The Plough and the Stars,* deal with episodes from Ireland's recent history. *The Shadow of a Gunman* takes place during the Anglo-Irish War, only a couple of years before the play premiered in April 1923; a year later the Abbey produced *Juno and the Paycock*, set during the Civil War which followed the Free State Treaty of 1921/22. The Dublin public received *Shadow* with great enthusiasm, and *Juno* broke attendance records. When *Shadow* was revived in August 1924, Holloway wrote of O'Casey in his diary: "he has written the two most popular plays ever seen at the Abbey, and they both are backgrounded by the terrible times we have just passed through, but his characters are so true to life and humorous that all swallow the bitter pill of fact that underlies both pieces."[2] Holloway's comment probably captures the expectations most of the Abbey's audience brought to O'Casey's third full-length play—that they would once again be presented with a thought-provoking but well-grounded treatment of recent Irish history, leavened with comic touches.

The Plough and the Stars first prompted an adverse response from people who worked in various capacities for the Abbey. In some respects their objections prefigured the reactions of the spectators, but in others the Abbey employees appear to have been more sensitive than their audience. O'Casey showed his play to the board and artistic staff in August 1925, and in early September Abbey manager Michael Dolan and George O'Brien wrote to Lady Gregory and Yeats respectively, expressing similar concerns about the script. Both men found fault with the play's language, which Dolan described as "beyond the beyonds," while O'Brien gave some examples of words which "would certainly give offence," including "Jesus" and "Christ" used as expletives, "bitch," and "lice." O'Brien objected most strongly to Act II, in which "the introduction of the prostitute is quite unnecessary to the action," mentioning Rosie Redmond's bawdy song which closes the act as an example of the many "phrases to which I take exception" and which "I think could not possibly be allowed to stand." Dolan also condemned the song as "unpardonable."[3]

Dolan and O'Brien also gave similar grounds for their reluctance to see the Abbey produce such a potentially offensive script. Dolan respectfully reminded Lady Gregory that "we cannot afford to take risks especially at the present moment. The theatre is booming at the present and unfortunately there are too many people who are sorry that such is the case. We don't want to give them anything to grasp at."[4] In the light of the sharp decline in attendance at the Abbey following the row over *The Playboy*, Dolan's worry seems justified, though the fact that he and O'Casey had not long before argued violently in the Green Room over Dolan's direction of Shaw's *Man and Superman* detracted from his impartiality. Once O'Brien had received a reply from Yeats, he wrote back to make more explicit his concern about "the possibility that the play might offend any section of public opinion so seriously as to provoke an attack on the theatre of a kind that could endanger the continuance of the subsidy." O'Brien's position of cautious pragmatism, "based altogether on my desire to be of service to the theatre," ran counter to the inclinations of Yeats and Lady Gregory.[5] Of the already controversial second act, the poet wrote to O'Brien: "To eliminate any part of it on grounds that have nothing to do with dramatic literature would be to deny all our traditions"; and when Gregory was told of O'Brien's objections, "I said at once, 'Our position is clear. If we have to choose between the subsidy and our freedom, it is our freedom we choose.'"[6] Nevertheless, something approaching the compromise O'Brien had hoped for was eventually reached, through a process whereby those who admired the play agreed to changes of less important elements in order to preserve more important ones. O'Casey, for instance, said about the omission of the song from Act II, "Yes, it's a pity. It would offend thousands. But it ought to be there."[7]

Next it was the reactions of several actors to O'Casey's play that caused strife. Gabriel Fallon, who played Captain Brennan in the first production and later wrote a memoir about his friendship with the playwright, recalled that "Rehearsals of *The Plough* began in an atmosphere of tension, suspicion and distrust."[8] Eileen Crowe, who was due to play Mrs. Gogan, felt uncomfortable with that character's Act II speech responding to Bessie Burgess' questioning of her marital status: "any kid, livin' or dead, that Jinnie Gogan's had since, was got between th' bordhers of th' Ten Commandments!"[9] After consulting her priest, the actress refused to say this line. O'Casey pointed out in a letter to Lennox Robinson—who was directing—that Crowe's misgivings were inconsistent with her readiness to speak more problematic lines in his *Nannie's Night Out*, produced a year earlier; no doubt the actress' increased concern over the later play reflects the greater public attention being paid to *The Plough and the Stars*.[10] Crowe agreed to switch parts with May Craig who had been cast in the minor part of the Woman from Rathmines who appears briefly in Act III. The second actor who made a stand against the language of O'Casey's script was Crowe's husband, F. J. McCormick, the first Jack Clitheroe. He objected to this line in Jack's Act I dialogue with Nora: "Oh, well, if we're goin' to be snotty!" to which Nora replies: "It's lookin' like as if it was you that was goin' to be . . . snotty!" (154). As O'Casey wrote, "Snotty is simply an expression for sarcastic or jeering," but his efforts to convince McCormick of this made no difference.[11] A month before the production was due to open, the playwright was so frustrated by the actors' recalcitrance that he wrote to Robinson to withdraw the play. But shortly afterward another compromise solution was agreed upon—even though dramaturgically it made little sense—whereby McCormick substituted "nosey" for "snotty," though Shelah Richards who was playing Nora retained "snotty." Perhaps because they each approached the script very much focused on their own part, it seems that few of the Abbey actors objected to O'Casey's play for the reasons some in the audience would. The actors were most concerned about individual lines and words, but the public would take exception rather to scenes and to the implications of the play as a whole.

In O'Casey's letter to Robinson, he argues that if "canonical pruning" of his work was permitted by a "Vigilance Committee of Actors," then "impudent fear would dominate the place of quiet courage." As an example of another member of the company who might conceivably request further changes he mentions Ria Mooney, cast as the prostitute Rosie Redmond, but although she had "complained to me about the horror of her part," she for one showed the kind of quiet courage O'Casey wished to see.[12] Mooney was certainly the member of the company with most reason to worry about the potential ramifications of playing her role in *The Plough*. As O'Casey described it with a typical flourish in his autobiography, Mooney was "bombarded with barbed beseeching to rise out of the part; for, if she didn't, she might no longer be thought respectable, and might risk her future in this world and even the next."[13] Mooney herself more soberly recounted that "some of the company tried to frighten me out of playing the part. I need hardly say that it was some of the women who tried to put me off, because they felt that they would be besmirched by the fact of one among them playing such a role." The female company members extend their argument even further than did the Western Girl who in 1907 expressed her compassion for the actress in *The Playboy* who had to say "shift," but did not suggest that the rest of the cast had been affected. The pressure exerted on Mooney was based on the principle that she ought to show solidarity with her fellow actresses by refusing to contaminate them by playing the prostitute. Yet, as she herself dimly yet instinctively realized, in doing so she would have failed to show solidarity with her fellow women. Mooney carried out research for the part by observing the young prostitutes in the lane behind the Abbey, though as she admits "I had reached twenty-three years of age without knowing precisely what was meant by a 'prostitute'. . . . Without knowing exactly why, however, I felt very sorry for these young girls I had seen in the lane." By contrast, various accounts report that opponents of O'Casey's play insisted prostitutes did not exist in Ireland. Mooney explains that she believes her performance as Rosie was much stronger because of her "total sympathy with the character," and O'Casey apparently felt the same way, telling her after the first performance, "Thank you for saving my play."[14] The conflict of positions between Mooney and other female members of the company anticipates a key aspect of the clash between O'Casey's actual motivation in composing *The Plough and the Stars*, and the perception of his aims by opponents of the play. The playwright wished through his depiction of a variety of characters from the tenement world, including Rosie Redmond, to arouse sympathy for those Irish whose lives had not been improved by the supposedly glorious Easter Rising; but it seemed to many—and particularly women—that by dignifying the lives of such characters he was defaming those who fought during Easter Week.

Word got out of the conflicts within the Abbey over O'Casey's play, so that in the weeks leading up to opening night, "Dublin was seething with rumours . . . that the Abbey was about to stage one of the most 'immoral' plays in its history."[15] As with *The Playboy*, such rumors affected the expectations some spectators brought to the new play, and in O'Casey's case such adjustment was more significant than in Synge's, since the public was generally well-disposed to rather than mistrustful of the playwright. In the event, in 1926 as in 1907, the first night proved relatively uneventful, and serious protests did not occur until a few performances into the one-week opening run. The premiere took place on Monday February 8 amid tense anticipation and before a packed house. Many Dubliners queued in vain for the unreserved places in the pit, and some of those who were admitted "were content to stand two and three deep along the walls."[16] Holloway recorded some disapproving comments by individuals— "Monty [Irish film censor James Montgomery] said after Act II, 'I am glad I am off duty.' . . . Mr. Reddin after Act III said, 'The play leaves a bad taste in the mouth'."[17] But the collective audience response on the first night was unquestionably enthusiastic: "at the final curtain no one in the stalls or pit moved; those on the balcony were standing; and amid the continual clapping and cries of 'author' Mr. O'Casey himself appeared to receive an ovation."[18]

Lennox Robinson wrote to Lady Gregory after the opening night, in a tone suggesting pleasant surprise, "I heard of no one being shocked!"[19] But the audiences at subsequent performances would not prove so impassive. During the second performance, "there was a scene in the back pit, when six women sitting together tried by voice and foot to prevent the hearing of the concluding part of the second act."[20] A similar though even more fleeting protest occurred on Wednesday night, as Holloway noted afterwards: "A sort of moaning sound was to be heard to-night from the pit during the 'Rosie Redmond' episode and when the Volunteers brought in the flags to the pub."[21]

It was the fourth performance of *The Plough and the Stars* that provoked a protest of such severity as to prompt comparisons to the uproar over *The Playboy*. As the *Irish Times* reported, "From the start of the play there were minor incidents, such as stamping of feet, hissing and shouting. Those came mostly from the pit. When the curtain went up for the second act there began a pandemonium which continued until the curtain fell."[22] The *Irish Independent* provided the most detailed account of that pandemonium:

The interrupters began to keep up a continuous shouting, and the players could not be heard, even in the front row of the stalls.

Then a man in the pit shouted: "Send out O'Casey—O'Casey, the coward!" There were cries of "Put them out," and similar exclamations from other members of the audience.

In the gallery, Mrs. Sheehy Skeffington, with whom were a number of young women and men, endeavoured to make a speech.

Amongst remarks that were heard from her were: "The Free State Government is subsidising the Abbey to malign Pearse and Connolly. We have not come here as rowdies. We came here to make a protest against the defamation of the men of Easter Week."

While Hanna Sheehy-Skeffington—widow of Francis, one of the casualties of the Easter Rising—was the most prominent protester against *The Plough* during and after Thursday night's performance, other spectators also tried to make themselves heard, men as well as women. The barely audible speech of one young man in the pit articulated the same objection as his female counterparts: "'We fought in Easter Week, and we don't want any more of that play. It is a slander on the Citizen Army.'"[23] Just as the protesters against *The Playboy* had judged the truthfulness of each part of that play according to their own conception of life in rural Ireland and repeatedly found Synge guilty of defamation, some in this audience reacted to each element of O'Casey's play according to how positively it represented the Rising.

Ria Mooney's commitment to her character in O'Casey's play was now subjected to a far more intensive test than her fellow actresses had managed: "Shocking epithets were hurled at Miss Ria Mooney while she played Rosie Redmond in pantomime."[24] According to her own account—written over forty years later and thus not altogether trustworthy—"lumps of coal were thrown at me, and pennies fell noisily beside me on the stage. There were shouts from members of the audience, urging me to 'get off,' which only made me more determined to stay on."[25] O'Casey had compounded the provocative potential of Act II by not simply including a prostitute, but keeping her on stage from beginning to end. As with Hauptmann's insistent focus on childbirth in the final act of *Before Sunrise*, the constant presence of Rosie Redmond amounted to an overdose of something Dublin theatergoers did not generally expect, let alone wish, to see at all.

The closing of the curtain for the transition to the third act calmed the audience a little, though not entirely: some spectators even took exception to the orchestra: "The cry of 'Stop that music' was taken up."[26] Then the most spectacular protest against *The Plough and the Stars* occurred early in Act III, when Nora returns to the tenement house from her frustrated efforts to find Jack amidst the fighting, and declares: "there's no woman gives a son or a husband to be killed—if they say it, they're lyin', lyin', against God, Nature, an' against themselves!" in a speech which ends "I was pushed down th' street, an' I cursed them—cursed the rebel ruffians an' Volunteers that had dhragged me ravin' mad into th' sthreets to seek me husband!" (184–85). In the subsequent dialogue with Peter, the Covey, Fluther and Mrs. Gogan, Nora goes further still in her embittered analysis of Jack's motivation and that of his comrades: "An' he stands wherever he is because he's brave? [*Vehemently*] No, but because he's a coward, a coward, a coward! . . . [*with denunciatory anger*] I tell you they're afraid to say they're afraid!" (185). This is how Richards, the first Nora, later described the response to this scene: "I suddenly noticed as I sat on the steps, relieved that the house was quiet for this difficult speech, several female figures climbing up from the auditorium onto the stage, and trying to set fire to the front-of-house curtains. With a scream, I dashed to the side of the stage, followed by the other players, and a hand-to-hand battle took place!"[27]

Inevitably, there are considerable discrepancies among the various accounts of this protest. Richards's memoir, like Mooney's, is probably more useful as a chronicle of how she experienced the evening's events than as a record of exactly what happened, yet it corresponds with other accounts in its description of the protest's principal features. It is unclear just how many spectators invaded the stage, but they were at least a dozen, almost all of them women who must have made their way down from the gallery and forward through the pit and stalls. While Richards and Mooney both recall an attempt to set fire to the curtains, others suggest only that the protesters tried to pull them down. It seems that one young man who joined with the women was instrumental in this effort. Richards does not appear to have exaggerated what one newspaper called the "fistic encounter" between the insurgents and the actors.[28] It seems there were two such incidents, and the high point—described with slight variations by several witnesses—starred the actor playing Fluther Good. According to the account in the *Irish Times*, "One young man succeeded in getting on to the stage along with the women. He deliberately struck Miss Maureen Delany [Bessie Burgess] in the face, and then aimed a blow at Miss May Craig [Mrs. Gogan]. In a moment Mr. Barry Fitzgerald ("Fluther Good") with one blow sent him sprawling to the wings."[29] That particular tussle was followed up the next day, as Lady Gregory recounts in her journal:

The papers said Miss Delany had been struck on the face by a young man. But the actors said he came next morning, very indignant at the accusation, said he had thrown something at Seaghan Barlow [the Abbey's set designer and chief stage-hand] and it had accidentally hit Miss Craig. Miss Richards says she herself threw a shoe at one of the intruders and it missed its aim and one of them took it up and threw it at Yeats, but it then also missed its aim.[30]

Richards's own account adds to the accidentally comic impression one gains from reading about this skirmish: "I had already been struck on the head by a shoe which I recognised as belonging to a friend of mine who was in the audience. When, some days later, I charged her with this act of disloyalty, she assured me it had not been meant for me, but for one of our attackers."[31]

It made no sense for the actors to proceed with Act III so long as the theater was in a state of uproar. F. J. McCormick, the actor playing Jack Clitheroe, tried to reason with the audience, and eventually was granted a hearing. He appealed to the spectators to "differentiate between the players and the author," and asked of them "Don't mob us. We have our rights as human beings and as players." He received a mixed response:

A voice—"Ask O'Casey to remove that scene and we will willingly look at the play. It is a disgrace in a Catholic country."

"I am only speaking for the players," Mr. McCormick reminded him. There were further shouts of "Carry on the play." "It is a scandal," cried another voice.[32]

One wonders just which scene the first protester had in mind, given the reference to Ireland's denominational orientation: Nora's provocative Act III speech indicts nationalists' motivation rather than Catholics' sensibilities, but if it was the scene with the prostitute the speaker wanted omitted, that would have entailed reducing the play by one full act, Act II. Either way, this spectator in effect admits to a mode of reception discernible also in the case of *Before Sunrise*: the inclusion in a play of passages which prompt immediate repulsion will tend to preclude any readiness to "look at" the rest of the work. The audience for Hauptmann's play did make an exception for the love scenes which resembled the drama they were accustomed to. O'Casey did not include in *The Plough and the Stars* any comparably accessible passages.

McCormick's belief that the spectators should not hold the actors responsible for O'Casey's play was not shared by the entire cast: as Richards writes, "We, the pro-O'Caseyites, felt that this was a betrayal. We were involved, and we were prepared to fight, literally, for Sean O'Casey and his play. So we pro-O'Caseyites brought the curtain down on McCormick."[33] This division among the actors rendered the multifaceted conflict over *The Plough and the Stars* more complicated than the one generated by *The Playboy*, whose cast unanimously and determinedly proceeded with their performances even when they could not be heard. In the 1907 scandal, the actors seem to have regarded themselves as the instruments for the performance of a play that deserved a fair hearing, as if their work was indivisible from Synge's. McCormick attempted to position the cast of O'Casey's play as a distinct party whose interests the audience ought to bear in mind separately from those of the author, but only some of the cast sided with him. Fallon argued later that McCormick figured in the scandal surrounding *The Plough* in another way too, simply through having been cast as Clitheroe: "He was a sensitive soul and rather highly strung and this accompanied by all the pother which preceded the play tended in performance to make Jack Clitheroe appear to be an arrant coward. And this outcome helped in no little way to increase the anger of the protesters."[34] So the actor who attempted to disclaim any responsibility for the provocative play actually unwittingly increased its capacity to give offense. Fallon's observation recalls Colum and others' that the realistic mode in which *The Playboy* was presented served to intensify protests against Synge's play.

Following McCormick's exchange with the audience there was a short-lived effort to resume the performance, apparently interrupted by a second invasion of the stage—which may well be when Fitzgerald administered his much-admired punch. According to newspaper reports, "During the next few minutes matters looked so ugly that several people hurried out of the theater. The footlights were again switched on, and all the players reappeared"; "Scuffles, wordy and otherwise, went on in all corners of the audience, and Mrs. S. continued to orate."[35] Of all the scandals I examine in this book, the audience response to the fourth performance of *The Plough and the Stars* most approached a riot: people did come to blows, certainly on the stage and very probably briefly in the auditorium. At the high point of the uproar, Yeats decided to address the house. As O'Casey himself described it, "The whole place became a mass of moving, roaring people, and Yeats roared louder than any of them."[36] Transcriptions of what the poet said vary somewhat, which is understandable given that "his words were inaudible to a large section, who could merely see his lips moving, and his hand waving dramatically."[37] The following version is a distillation from two contemporary accounts:

I thought you had got tired of this. You have disgraced yourselves again. Is this to be an ever-recurring celebration of the arrival of Irish genius? Synge first, and then O'Casey! The news of the happenings of the last few minutes here will flash from country to country. Dublin has once more rocked the cradle of a reputation. From such a scene in this theatre went forth the fame of Synge. Equally the fame of O'Casey is born here tonight. This is his apotheosis.[38]

One can understand Yeats's frustration over a recurrence of hostile reception likely to embarrass his theater, though on examination, the terms in which he expressed himself appear problematic. When Yeats twice addressed the audience during the third performance of *The Playboy* in 1907, he objected to the protests above all on the grounds of rights. The Abbey had the right to produce Synge's play, the public had the right to listen to it in order fairly to judge it, and no one had the right to prevent others from hearing it. Only at the end of his second intervention during *The*

Playboy did Yeats express hostility toward the protesters, disparaging their critical judgment and condescendingly berating them for harming Ireland's reputation. When he spoke to the audience in 1926, Yeats began where he left off. In a patronizing tone, he treats those Dubliners who disrupted the performance of O'Casey's play as philistines whose repeated failure to recognize true talent in their own writers would lead others outside Ireland to associate the country with ignorant resistance to outstanding new work. In overstating his point, Yeats contradicts himself: the partially scandalized reception of first Synge's then O'Casey's plays did not determine their renown outside Ireland as much as he suggests. Besides, if true genius had manifested itself, how could the objections of a few Dubliners stand in its way? In neither case did the protests erupt in response to the work of a previously unknown playwright; O'Casey especially had earned success and admiration for his earlier plays. Yeats's grandiose final point suggests what can happen when anger is filtered through a poet's sensibility, as O'Casey himself gently mocked: "he conjured up a vision for them of O'Casey on a cloud, with Fluther on his right hand and Rosie Redmond on his left, rising upwards to Olympus to get from the waiting gods and goddesses a triumphant apotheosis for a work well done in the name of Ireland and of art."[39]

Baz Kershaw discusses the confrontation between Yeats and the spectators at the fourth performance of *The Plough and the Stars* in a recent article about the growing importance of applause and the decline of unruly audience behavior in Western theater. For Kershaw, Yeats's speech emblematizes the way theater aims for a "disempowerment of the audience," while the spectators' response provides an unusually clear example of resistance to that aim: "In denying *The Plough and the Stars* the applause that Yeats thought was its due, the Abbey audience manufactured a refusal that exposed the role of the protocols of theatre in the structures of domination." That is, the fourth-night audience for O'Casey's play rejected the role whereby theater audiences "participate in the making of masterpieces" by applauding them. Of course, the Abbey audience did not merely deny O'Casey's play their applause, but actively performed their opposition to it. According to Kershaw's central argument, which overlaps with my own, "applause became more important to Western theatres in the second half of the twentieth century as other forms of audience engagement were reduced." The reception of *The Plough and the Stars*—like that of many of the Brecht works I shall discuss in the next chapter—demonstrates the variety of forms of audience response that still existed in the interwar period.[40]

By the time Yeats spoke, some spectators in the stalls had vacated their seats—perhaps fearing for their safety, perhaps because they did not believe the performance would be completed—and the protesters took full advantage of the opportunity to get nearer to the stage: "A number of

women swarmed from the pit into the empty chairs and kept up a din
while Dr. Yeats was speaking."[41] When he left the stage, "shouts of 'We
want the play' mingled with countercries of 'Up the Republic'," then the
women in the stalls began to sing 'The Soldier's Song'—the national anthem of the Irish republic—soon joined by others further back and in the
gallery.[42] It required the arrival of police to quell the continuing uproar.
This was a step O'Casey was reluctant to take; as he tells it in his autobiography, he found himself in a dreadful position when asked for his
consent to call for the police: "The police! Sean to agree to send for the
police—never! His Irish soul revolted from the idea; though Yeats and
others reminded him that the police were no longer in a foreign service,
but were now in Ireland's own."[43] Indeed Yeats—though by this time a
senator in the Free State government—relished the situation, according to
Fallon, who describes the poet animatedly telling him "I am sending for
the police; and *this time* it will be *their own* police!"[44] That comment, along
with his remarks to the audience, make clear that throughout, Yeats considered the protests against *The Plough* in relation to those against *The
Playboy*. But it seems the spectators may not have regarded O'Casey's play
in the same light: although much of the press coverage compared the
uproar over *The Plough* with the *Playboy* row, none of the recorded shouts
during Thursday's performance complained about this affront as a repetition of the earlier one. The Dubliners who took exception to O'Casey's
depiction of Easter Week were not thinking about the nuances of how this
scandal compared to the earlier one, but were caught up in the moment
by a deeply felt compulsion to perform their opposition.

The contingent of police that entered the Abbey seems to have consisted
of both plainclothes detectives and uniformed officers, and their presence
soon subdued much of the protest, while energizing the supporters of the
play. So when the performance of Act III was resumed, "This was hailed
with a wild outburst of enthusiasm from the general body of the audience,
in which the counterdemonstration was entirely drowned." But the
women in the front of the stalls did not desist from interrupting, and
before long the police began to forcibly eject them; "One of the women
protested against her removal as an interference with personal liberty"—
but because there were no arrests and therefore no court appearances, the
Plough scandal did not give rise to the same kind of legal debates as the
Playboy row had done.[45] When the leader of the protesters left, she made
sure that she made one final speech, delivered from back upstairs:

"We are now leaving the hall under police protection," declared Mrs. Sheehy-
Skeffington as she rose to leave the gallery . . .
    She attempted to address the audience amid cheers and jeers. Above the din
she was heard to exclaim: "I am one of the widows of Easter Week. It is no
wonder," she proceeded, "that you do not remember the men of Easter Week,
because none of you fought on either side.

"The play is going to London soon to be advertised there because it belies Ireland. . . . All you need do now is sing 'God Save the King'." She then left.[46]

The remainder of the play was performed to the accompaniment of further hissing, whistling and singing by the protesters, and cheering and applause by their opponents.

The uproar during Thursday's performance was not repeated the following evening. As Lady Gregory—who did not see the production herself until the Friday—recorded in her journal, "There was no attempt at disturbance, though one man said from the gallery, in the public-house scene, 'This is an insult to the memory of Pearse,' and walked out. Someone else cried out . . . 'Those flags were never in a public-house!'"[47] While claiming that no banners of the ICA and the Volunteers had ever been taken into a pub was less preposterous than maintaining that there were no prostitutes in Ireland, it reflects a similarly unrealistic determination to believe what one wishes to believe. One further attack against *The Plough and the Stars* mounted on Saturday morning constituted quite an original form of protest, but was let down by comically incompetent execution. Three armed youths turned up at what they believed to be the house of Barry Fitzgerald, with the intention of kidnapping him for long enough to prevent his playing Fluther in the two performances scheduled for later that day. This plan was most obviously thwarted by the fact that they had actually targeted the house where Fitzgerald's mother, sister, and brother-in-law lived. But even if the actor had been present, it is doubtful whether the young would-be kidnappers would have succeeded, since even with their revolvers they failed to intimidate Fitzgerald's relatives: "The spokesman ordered Mrs. Mortished to put her hands up, and she point blank refused. Her mother and sister then appeared on the scene, and also refused to put their hands up."[48] This episode did prompt the Abbey staff to take the precaution of keeping the actors at the theater between the afternoon and evening performances, for which they were compensated by a special recital by pianist Walter Rummel.

Saturday's matinee and evening performances had been fully booked since the start of the week, and, as had happened on opening night, the demand for unreserved seats far exceeded the number available. It appears that by the time the initial one-week run of *The Plough and the Stars* came to an end, opposition to O'Casey's play in the auditorium had all but ceased:

At the end the whole company were called back no fewer than four times. Then came the big scene of the night, started with a demand, which soon became a roar, for "Author; author." Rising above the noise there came from the pit the voice of a full-throated man, repeating over and over again, "Good ould Dublin workingman!"

At last Mr. O'Casey came on, rather was he forced on, to the stage, and the demonstration which followed lasted for a full five minutes.[49]

It is fitting to end an account of the week's events with that shout from the pit, since O'Casey's roots in and fundamental dedication to the interests of the working class motivated his recusant depiction of the Easter Rising. When the Irish Citizen Army joined forces with the Irish Volunteers to mount the rebellion, a socialist organization of mostly blue-collar Dubliners collaborated with a nationalist body with predominantly white-collar members. O'Casey's choice of the ICA's symbol for the title of his play reflects both his allegiance to that group and his belief that the Rising was by no means a glorious and productive act—that the stars, which stand for the aspirations of the movement, had taken precedence over the reality represented by the plough. O'Casey's primary commitment was to socialism rather than to nationalism. As one critic puts it, "His sympathy remained steadfastly with the slum dwellers of Dublin, whose sufferings were not to be cured by getting rid of the English."[50] By 1926, many Irish people regarded the casualties of the Easter Rising as noble martyrs who sacrificed themselves to help bring about Ireland's freedom, and not surprisingly some of those people considered *The Plough and the Stars*, in which most of the characters do not support the rebellion but merely take advantage of the chance to benefit from the looting, as both inaccurate and disrespectful. But in 1916 many Dubliners were indifferent to the progress and outcome of the Rising, and O'Casey has his characters help each other in the fight against poverty while the rebels fight a hopeless battle for their ideals. At the end of Easter Week, rebel prisoners were even pelted with rotten vegetables by other Dubliners, though by the time they were released that anger had turned into admiration, and the Rising came to be held up as a vital step on the road toward independence. Yet if the long-term effect of the rebellion was positive for nationalism, it was the opposite for socialism. As David Krause points out, ICA leader Connolly may have "believed that he could best support the cause of Irish socialism by fighting and dying for Irish nationalism," but instead "the nationalist Rising led to the eclipse of Irish socialism."[51] O'Casey recognized that fact, and while his opponents saw his play in a very different light, this audience member's repeated cry of "Good ould Dublin workingman!" on Saturday indicates that other contemporaries shared his interpretation.

Ten days after the opening run of *The Plough and the Stars*, O'Casey wrote in a letter "The play has raised something of a whirlwind in Dublin."[52] In addition to the exchange of widely divergent opinions in the letters pages of the Dublin newspapers, O'Casey probably had in mind the innumerable animated conversations about his play taking place on the streets and in living rooms and pubs. The most prominent conflict was that between the playwright and Mrs. Sheehy-Skeffington, who each wrote two letters to the *Irish Independent*, then two weeks after the final performance featured as principal speakers in a public debate. If it was ironic that O'Casey's play should be attacked above all by women, the identity of the playwright's principal opponent was more ironic still, since she was the widow of a man with whom O'Casey in fact felt much in common. Francis Sheehy-Skeffington was a well-known socialist, feminist (when he and Hanna married they agreed to each use both their surnames) and militant pacifist who opposed the Rising. In the first days of Easter Week "Skeffy" saved a British officer's life, and tried to stop the looting of shops and pubs. On Tuesday evening he was arrested and imprisoned, used as a human shield, then on Wednesday illegally executed on the orders of one Captain Bowen-Colthurst, who was later declared insane. In O'Casey's 1919 book *The Story of the Irish Citizen Army* he described Sheehy-Skeffington as "the first martyr to Irish socialism," and as "the living antithesis of the Easter insurrection."[53] So the most outspoken opponent of O'Casey's alleged denigration of the rebels was the widow of a man who had died not while leading, but while contesting the insurgency.

In her letters and speeches, Sheehy-Skeffington elaborated on what she had shouted during Thursday night's performance, and initiated an exchange with O'Casey over his artistic approach, arguing that in this work he had carried realism beyond the point at which it becomes "not art, but morbid perversity. . . . It is the realism that would paint not only the wart on Cromwell's nose, but that would add carbuncles and running sores in a reaction against idealisation."[54] O'Casey responded with his own indignation to the charge that he had misrepresented the events of Easter Week, contending that "the National tocsin of alarm was sounded because some of the tinsel of sham was shaken from the body of truth."[55] He also seized on a formulation by Sheehy-Skeffington which captured that sentimental glorification of the Rising he aimed to counter: "The Ireland that remembers with tear-dimmed eyes all that Easter Week stands for."[56] O'Casey wrote that her "heavy-hearted expression" "makes me sick. Some of the men can't get even a job. . . . Tears may be in the eyes of the navvies working on the Shannon scheme, but they are not for Ireland."[57] In the debate on March 1, the two returned to the issue of O'Casey's selection and emphasis in creating his portrait of 1915–1916; as the *Irish Independent* characterized their main arguments, for Sheehy-Skeffington, O'Casey's play "concentrated on pettiness and squalor, unrelieved by a gleam of heroism," whereas the playwright "said he was not trying, and never would try, to write about heroes. He wrote only about the life he knew and the people he knew."[58] In contrast to the largely futile attempt seriously to debate Synge's play twenty years earlier, the event at which Sheehy-Skeffington, O'Casey and several others spoke about *The Plough and the Stars* appears to have succeeded as a forum for the exchange of opinions; as Holloway noted, "It had been conducted in the most peaceful way and in the best good humour, each taking and receiving hard hits in their turn."[59]

In talking to the actors after Thursday's performance—or perhaps during his impromptu speech to the audience—Yeats declared that with *The Plough and the Stars* O'Casey had "cut very close to the bone."[60] Certainly that was true, and—in contrast to the high esteem in which *The Playboy* came to be held within a few years of its first run—O'Casey's play continued to wound his compatriots for decades beyond 1926. In 1966, for instance, when Ireland celebrated the fiftieth anniversary of the Easter Rising, the Abbey agreed not to perform *The Plough* for fear of spoiling the occasion. O'Casey had depicted a decade-old episode in Ireland's history, but in 1926 that episode was almost as much a piece of Ireland's present. As Robert Welch writes, the Rising was a "foundational event" which ten years on was "already hallowed in nationalist memory and emotion," so that "To many this play was not just an affront; it was a betrayal and a calculated insult."[61] When in their shouts from the auditorium the protesters labeled O'Casey's play "a slander on the Citizen Army" and "an insult to the memory of Pearse," they came to the defense not only of the rebels, but of themselves. And for those who considered it slanderous merely to represent the Rising as anything less than—in the words of one letter of protest from 1926—"that most glorious episode of Irish history," there was ample reason to conclude that O'Casey deliberately made his play as insulting as possible.[62] Had he simply composed a poignant tragedy suggesting that Easter Week did little to improve the wretched lives of Dublin's tenement dwellers, others might have disagreed with that position without finding the play defamatory. Instead in Act II he used Pearse's very words, referred to by the *Voice of Labour* as "sentences that were and are still part of our spiritual and national life," only to show them generating at best a comic parody of themselves.[63] For instance, the speaker outside the pub is heard to say, "we must accustom ourselves to the use of arms. . . . Bloodshed is a cleansing and sanctifying thing." Then when Fluther comes in for a drink with Peter, both of them *"hot, and full and hasty with the things they have seen and heard,"* Fluther declares, "I said to meself, 'You can die now, Fluther, for you've seen th' shadow-dhreams of th' past leppin' to life in th' bodies of livin' men that show, if we were without a titther o' courage for centuries, we're vice versa now!' Looka here. (*He stretches out his arm under* Peter's *face and rolls up his sleeve.*) The blood was BOILIN' in me veins!" (162–63). In the course of that act, as the speaker continues to urge the demonstrators to embrace war, the characters fight among themselves, and by its close Fluther's blood has stopped boiling and he turns his attention to Rosie. That small

victory by a prostitute over Pearse is compounded by the other most provocative passage in Act II, when the banners of the two armies are brought
into the pub. No doubt the spectator who shouted "Those flags were never
in a public-house!" would not have changed his opinion of the play if
presented with compelling evidence to the contrary: the real point of contention was not whether such a thing ever happened, but what O'Casey
was suggesting by making it happen in his play. Given that the Easter
Rising had taken on symbolic significance for many Irish, it is hardly
surprising that some audience members took exception to this perceived
abuse of nationalist symbols. Finally, rather than presenting Nora as one
woman who like many others suffered through losing her husband to the
noble nationalist cause, O'Casey made her an outspoken critic of the rebels
who repeatedly strives to keep her husband at home and away from the
fighting. It was thus because of O'Casey's incisive and unambiguous presentation of a heretical analysis of Easter Week that *The Plough and the
Stars* cut so close to the bone.

In the public debate which followed the run, Mrs. Sheehy-Skeffington
stated that "She thought that it was necessary that a protest should be
made to hit the Abbey directorate in the eye," and suggested that she and
others determined that accomplishing this goal would require something
beyond "the usual method of hissing and booing."[64] The most extreme
protest against *The Plough* appears to have been more organized than any
of those against *The Playboy*. Sheehy-Skeffington and her collaborators
needed to do something spectacular, needed to violate not simply the
prevailing norms of audience behavior, but also the prevailing norms of
audience protest. Booing and hissing was a familiar behavior, both in the
customary response to popular theater when spectators loudly opposed
characters they found antipathetic, and in the far less frequent outbreaks
of resistance to new plays, in particular Synge's *The Playboy*. Rather than
merely continuing to disrupt the production of O'Casey's play by drown-
ing out the actors through shouting, this group of protesters invaded the
stage in order to bring the performance to a halt. They succeeded in this,
albeit briefly, and then resumed their verbal demonstration. For a short
time, the protest against *The Plough* was decidedly riotous: the *Irish Independent* reported that "The pandemonium caused a number of the audience to become panic-stricken. They ran for the exit doors and left the
theatre."[65] And the *Irish Times* summarized the "little damage" done: "Two
of the footlight lamps were injured, and portions of the curtain were torn.
The orchestra lost a few sheets of music (which were torn) and the cover
of Mr. Fred Deane's double bass fiddle." Surprisingly, however, that report
adds, "There was no necessity for arrests as in the 'Playboy' scenes" (one
wonders whether Mr. Deane accepted the losses with the same equanim-
ity).[66] The necessity for arrests in 1907 is of course highly debatable, and
in fact the police could have arrested audience members during the fourth

performance of *The Plough* on the same grounds and with just as much, or as little, justification as they had during several performances of *The Playboy*. Perhaps if the protests in 1926 had recurred over several nights, arrests would have been made—though as Yeats delightedly remarked, by then the police were Irish (and the higher social standing of the leading protesters against O'Casey's play no doubt also made arrests less likely). That none of the participants in the invasion of the stage was detained suggests that the incident was perceived and essentially accepted as a performance. In an interview on Friday, Yeats argued that "The best thing these people could have done would be to have kept quiet."[67] Many others made this point too—even Mrs. Sheehy-Skeffington, who later wrote, "The incident will, no doubt, help to fill houses in London with audiences that come to mock at those 'foolish dead,' 'whose names will be remembered for ever'."[68] Yet she gives no indication of regretting her actions. Certainly if the primary aim of those who most forcefully objected to O'Casey's play was to prevent it from achieving international renown, they adopted a strategy that proved counterproductive. But clearly the context in which they were considering the work's significance was not the canon of contemporary dramatic literature, but evolving conceptions of recent history in newly independent Ireland.

As I mentioned in the Preface, James H. Johnson contends that protesting spectators must needs draw on "a finite number of behaviors and styles of discourse shaped by the culture"—in effect, that no audience could ever protest through behavior that was not available to them.[69] If Sheehy-Skeffington and the others chose their form of opposition from the range available to them in the culture of early-twentieth-century Ireland, then they selected it not from behavior in the theater but from action in the political arena. In order to register their condemnation of O'Casey's treatment of the Easter Rising, they performed their own Rising. Just as the insurgents occupied buildings in Dublin and proclaimed their repudiation of the foreign government, the protesters occupied the stage, however briefly, and proclaimed their repudiation of O'Casey's depiction of the events of 1915–16. The rebellion against *The Plough and the Stars* did not prove as influential in years to come as did the Easter Rising, yet the future did likewise bring confirmation that many Irish shared the protesters' point of view.

Besides the radical nature of the stage invasion during Act III, the other most striking—possibly even unique—feature of the scandal set off by *The Plough and the Stars* is the leading role played by women. Although many in that night's audience vocally expressed their hostility toward O'Casey's play, including some who had themselves participated in the Rising, it was "about twenty ardent young women and a few young men," led by Mrs. Sheehy-Skeffington, who most determinedly performed their opposition.[70] This aspect of the play's reception suggests that whatever gave offense in *The Plough* was especially insulting to women, but in fact the row over O'Casey's play revolves less around and is less revealing of prevailing attitudes to women than the row over *The Playboy*. When Sheehy-Skeffington insisted in a letter the following week that the demonstration was not aimed at "the moral aspect of the play," but "was on national grounds solely, voicing a passionate indignation against the outrage of a drama staged in a supposedly national theatre, which held up to derision and obloquy the men and women of Easter Week," this was not disingenuousness.[71] Hanna Sheehy-Skeffington was a militant suffragette, who would not have hesitated to charge O'Casey with sexism if she considered him guilty of it. In fact, ironically, his play can more justifiably be considered feminist than the protests against it. In the Act III lines which prompted the most extreme protests, O'Casey has Nora passionately, wrenchingly criticize the men's fearful and feigned bravery from a woman's point of view. Sheehy-Skeffington later objected that Nora cannot be regarded as representative of Irish women. Sheehy-Skeffington's accomplices on Thursday night, Holloway informs us, included the mother of Padraic Pearse and the widow of Tom Clarke, another of the rebels executed after the Rising. What distinguished the leaders of the protest was thus far more their direct connection to the Rising as, in Sheehy-Skeffington's term, "widows of Easter Week," than their gender in itself. Holloway quotes Dan Breen, a prominent Republican, explaining that the widows' objective was "to vindicate the manhood of 1916": in effect, they mounted their demonstration as surrogates and executors of their fallen husbands and sons.[72] Their demonstration stood out all the more because it was led by women, and it may well have appalled even some of the spectators who shared the women's antipathy toward the play. Presumably the man who shouted at Sheehy-Skeffington, "You are a disgrace to your sex," whatever his opinion of O'Casey's depiction of the events of 1916, believed that in the independent Ireland of 1926 women should not be leading others in a public disturbance.[73]

One of the most provocative elements of *The Plough* was undeniably associated with women and their status in the Ireland of the 1910s and 1920s: the character of Rosie Redmond. This role first troubled female members of the Abbey company, then aroused some indications of displeasure in Wednesday's audience and a tumult of hostility directed at Ria Mooney on Thursday. Such indignation did not result from the mere fact that this production would depict a prostitute on stage. As Mooney mentions, she herself had played a prostitute in a Shaw play that had been well received at the Abbey the previous season. O'Brien objected to Rosie as dramaturgically unjustified rather than inherently scandalous, and Mooney's fellow actresses tried to dissuade her from playing the part, but did not apparently insist that no woman be asked to do so. Rosie gave offense because of her context—center stage in a pub while Pearse's words are marginalized, in a play which had already represented nationalists in 1915 critically. The other Abbey actresses worried that by playing Rosie, Mooney would "besmirch" her fellow company members; the spectators who protested during Act II probably felt that, through a similar process of contamination, O'Casey's inclusion of Rosie besmirched the Easter Rising. And while most of the recorded comments and later written statements focus on the mere fact of Rosie's presence in the pub and on the stage, the lines Mooney delivered can only have augmented hostility: at the beginning of Act II, she complains to the Barman, "They're all in a holy mood. Th' solemn-lookin' dials on th' whole o' them an' they marchin' to th' meetin'. You'd think they were th' glorious company of th' saints, an' th' noble army of martyrs thrampin' through th' sthreets of paradise. They're all thinkin' of higher things than a girl's garthers" (161–62). Much of O'Casey's critique of the Rising and its mythologization is contained in that speech, and for anyone who vehemently rejected that critique, hearing it articulated by a prostitute must have added insult to injury.

Early in May 1926, the Abbey's production of *The Plough and the Stars* was revived for a second week, and again the play incited opposition. Yeats even heard earlier in the month that "the anti-Casey republicans are going to blow up the Abbey."[74] Mrs. Sheehy-Skeffington again organized a demonstration, this time outside the theater, where she and other women including Maud Gonne MacBride held up placards protesting against O'Casey's play. Inside the building, the distinctive feature of this second outbreak of hostility toward *The Plough and the Stars* was the explosion of stink bombs in the auditorium during several performances. This tactic presumably aimed to prevent people from watching the play by driving them out of the theater, but while it succeeded with some audience members, others devised ways to counteract the noxious smell. As Holloway described it, "Many left the balcony after the stink bombs were thrown, and others in the audience commenced smoking and stood the stink; otherwise, though, it was in keeping with much they witnessed on the stage."[75] Throughout his many diary entries on *The Plough and the Stars*, Holloway reiterates through comments like this his own antipathy toward the play, and in this case that feeling was shared not only by nationalists, but also by O'Casey's fellow writers and many critics. As he put it in his autobiography, following the debate, "the turn of intellectuals came to cheat Sean from any success he might be expecting. Sean saw another side of Ireland's enterprising malice and envy."[76] By the time of the revival in May, O'Casey had left Ireland for England, leaving his countrymen to quarrel about his representation of Easter Week without him.

The uproar generated by *The Plough and the Stars* replicates the weeklong scandal over *The Playboy* in little more than the basic grounds for opposition. Both gave offense to some Irishmen and Irishwomen who felt that the plays maligned their nation and its people. But the circumstances under which Dubliners watched these or any other depictions of Ireland were quite different in 1926 than they had been in 1907. When Synge's play was produced, the spectators attended a performance by the national theater of a nation which in effect did not yet exist, so that supporting the theater was in some respects a nationalist act. In those conditions, positive representations of the Irish on stage could serve the nationalist cause, negative ones undermine it or even set it back. The subtlety and complexity of Synge's ironic masterpiece led almost everyone at the time to conclude that its production subverted rather than contributed to the building up of Irish national consciousness and pride. And the confrontation between *The Playboy* and its first audiences was further aggravated by the Abbey's directors' drafting British police in order to complete the one-week opening run by force. By 1926, the INTS was a state-subsidized theater in an independent Ireland, so that any controversy surrounding work they produced amounted to an internal affair, rather than jeopardizing nationalists' campaign to free the country from British rule. That a much smaller proportion of the first week's audience demonstrated against O'Casey's play than had against Synge's reflects in part the Irish public's diminished sensitivity about how they were depicted. *The Plough and the Stars* is also much less elliptical than *The Playboy*, so that taking offense at it required a rather literal-minded interpretation which only a minority adopted. The protests against O'Casey's play took a more concentrated and violent form than those against Synge's, yet reverberated less, leading to no arrests and fewer disruptions of the production's run. The differences between the two scandals at the Abbey also point up the changes in norms of audience behavior during the intervening two decades. In 1926, uninhibited expression of reactions in the auditorium constituted much more of a departure from conventional conduct than it did in 1907. Whereas the opponents of *The Playboy* brought into the Abbey a heightened, more deeply felt version of behavior they routinely practiced in other kinds of theater auditoriums, the means of opposition which the protesters against *The Plough and the Stars* resorted to were, and needed to be, more radical. In the context of theater history, their invasion of the stage looks like a fervent, even desperate attempt to cling on to theater audiences' centuries-old but disappearing right to object.

CHAPTER 5

"Pfui!": Disdaining Experimentation

Brecht during the Weimar Republic: *In the Jungle, Baal, Lehrstück, Mahagonny,* and *A Man's a Man*

The scandals generated by *Before Sunrise* and *Ubu Roi* stood out within their particular cultural contexts as exceptional instances of energetic audience protest at a time when normative behavior in the non-musical, non-popular theater had become more restrained than ever before. By the time the twentieth century began, theater and other art forms had lost some of their capacity to shock, because the public associated new work with an adversarial stance. While Jarry's forceful assault on the audience's sensibilities remained for some years an anomaly, before long others were adopting a similarly confrontational approach: the performances of the Italian Futurists beginning in 1910, and later of the Dadaists in Zurich, Cologne and Paris developed the same impulse to deliberately shock the public, in particular the bourgeois public. Yet because audiences were often well aware of the performers' wish to affront them, they sometimes resisted reacting with the indignation they realized the artists aimed for, and when they did protest, accounts indicate that those demonstrations were more knowing, less authentic than was the opposition to Hauptmann's play, more comparable to the mixture of outrage and enjoyment perceptible in the case of *Ubu Roi*. The two scandals at the Abbey, while revealing of norms of behavior in the theater in the early twentieth century, stand apart somewhat from the main current of experimental theater and performance in Europe. Both *The Playboy of the Western World* and *The Plough and the Stars* provoked a portion of the Dublin public because of their relationship to Irish identity and history, rather than because of radical artistic innovation on the part of Synge or O'Casey. Dramatic, operatic, and musical works which did represent marked departures and met with considerable disapproval when first produced include Blok's *The Fair-ground Booth* in St. Petersburg in 1906, Stravinsky's *The Rites of Spring* in 1913 and Cocteau's *Parade* in 1917, both in Paris, and Pirandello's *Six Characters in Search of an Author* in Rome in 1921. During the 1910s and 1920s, two contrary developments proceeded simultaneously. Subdued behavior further established itself as the norm at most theater perfor-mances: the principle that spectatorship in the theater should entail no utterances other than laughter except at the end of acts steadily became more widely held. At the same time, work which surpassed the horizon of expectations frequently caused audiences to protest unrestrainedly, if not always convincingly.

The decade and a half of the Weimar Republic in Germany, between the end of World War I and Hitler's appointment as chancellor in 1933, pro-vides a rich context in which to examine audience response in the theater during the 1920s. Probably no period in any country has witnessed such a profusion of innovation in the theater and other arts as did the Weimar Republic, and none has given rise to such a concentration of theater scan-dals. Weimar's artistic fecundity excites and inspires when contemplated from the vantage point of later decades, but at the time it repelled and unsettled many Germans. As Klaus P. Fischer points out, "What some historians have called the first 'modern' culture was in fact a curious hy-brid of conservative tradition and creative experimentation."[1] Bertolt Brecht, whose career began in the Weimar era, was at the forefront of that experimentation, and his work incited some of the most fervent opposi-tion. Brecht's work is all the more worthy of investigation because he also achieved great success; because the plays and operas he wrote and/or directed were produced in all manner of venues; and because, increasingly in the course of the 1920s, he specifically explored, in theory and practice, the relationship between stage and spectators.

Beginning with Leopold Jessner's anti-nationalistic staging of Schiller's *William Tell* at the Staatstheater in December 1919, a few months after the establishment of the republic, productions of new and classical plays and operas in Berlin as well as in provincial cities repeatedly incited angry protests, which invariably drew equally vehement expressions of support. Before long, critics began to represent uproar in the auditorium as a com-mon rather than exceptional occurrence: for instance, one reviewer wrote that the 1922 premiere of Arnolt Bronnen's *Patricide* (*Vatermord*) prompted "one of those theater scandals which in our country are the custom at any literary experiment."[2] Such an abundance of literary experiments would not have found an audience at all without an unusual degree of openness toward innovation. State funds supported some of the groundbreaking cultural activity. Walter Panofsky, in his study of the musical theater in Germany during the 1920s, underlines "the consistency with which the cultural authorities at that time strove to promote the new in all the arts."[3]

And a critical mass of the theatergoing public in Germany's major cities seems to have thrived on productions that generated strong opinions and lively debate. Carl Zuckmayer, one of the playwrights whose work stimulated both enthusiasm and outrage, later described the stance of the Weimar-era public with some nostalgia: "The audiences, too, played a part. They loved sarcastic wit and a juicy theatrical scandal, which could enthrall them like a boxing match or a six-day bicycle race; but they also had the nerves for what was strong, potent, and new, and were prepared, after the initial cries of indignation and whistles, to let themselves be convinced, carried away, enchanted."[4] According to Walter Hinck's analysis of the Weimar climate, "the German theater's pleasure in experimentation during the 1920s . . . presupposed a mentally highly agile spectator. So there was a German public hungry for discussion"; this was a time "in which provoking and being provoked were agreed to, if not actually required, by society."[5] During the republic's most prosperous years between 1924 and 1929, the theatergoers who took in challenging new work included some of those Germans who ideologically had little or nothing in common with the work. As John Willett wrote, "The new right-wing establishment in fact was so comfortably settled-in that it could not only afford to tolerate a good measure of sharp sniping from the more uncomfortable artists . . . , but would pay good money to experience the process."[6] But before and especially after the Golden Twenties, when the republic was under the greatest threat, the public readily condemned anything that departed too far from the conventional and easily digestible. Hitler's National Socialists strove to capitalize on that reactionary inclination—actor Fritz Kortner described the audience members who disrupted *William Tell* as "the brown beast in the sheep's clothing of the artistically scandalized theatergoer"[7]—and by doing so would ultimately destroy struggling German democracy. Hence the vibrant and controversy-ridden theatrical environment vividly reflects the unparalleled mixture of creative innovation and simmering tensions that was fundamental to Weimar culture.

One of Brecht's earliest statements about audience response in the theater occurs in a diary entry from his twenty-fourth birthday, in February 1922. By then Brecht had written three plays, though none of them had been produced. He writes: "I hope that in *Baal* and *Jungle* I've avoided a great mistake of much other art: its effort to carry people away." Brecht maintains that his plays are different because "The splendid isolation of the spectators isn't touched . . . they're not reassured by being invited to feel with the characters."[8] From the very beginning, Brecht regarded deliberately entangling the receiver in the drama as an artistic error, yet throughout the Weimar era—beginning with the two works he named in the 1922 note—his plays and operas repeatedly provoked a response which might equally be considered a mistake: he caused the spectators not merely to resist becoming caught up in what was offered to them, but to turn against it.

In autumn 1922, Brecht's second play, *Drums in the Night* (*Trommeln in der Nacht*), became the first one staged, in Munich and then Berlin, to a generally very positive response from audience and critics. Reviews of the Munich production at the experimental Kammerspiele were virtually unanimous in hailing Brecht's comedy about the return of the soldier Kragler in the midst of the 1918 Spartakus uprising as a refreshing and promising change from the prevailing norms. For example, "These night-time drums drown out the for now quite impotent chatter of modern drama, victoriously cover over the manner of Expressionism, which has frozen into a gesture, and create a public for a poet. Bertolt Brecht is among the most promising of our younger playwrights."[9] What the critics appreciated in *Drums in the Night* was the fact that Brecht dealt with topical issues and concerns in a concrete way, in contrast to the often overblown pseudo-mythical representations of the Expressionist drama which had dominated German stages since the end of the war. Brecht's play was one of the earliest *Heimkehrerdramen* (Returning Soldier Dramas), produced at a time when the mood of German arts was beginning to shift from Expressionism to *Neue Sachlichkeit* (New Sobriety), and German audiences were becoming more receptive than they had been to works which treated the painful experience of the disastrous war and its consequences. But when Brecht's *In the Jungle* (*Im Dickicht*, later renamed *Im Dickicht der Städte: In the Jungle of Cities*) premiered in Munich in May 1923, it was regarded by many as emblematic of the worst excesses of new writing for the stage.

In the Jungle seems to have disappointed critics and vexed audiences because they found it all but incomprehensible. No doubt many of the spectators went to the first performance at the Residenztheater expecting to enjoy an accessible play like *Drums in the Night*; instead they were confronted with a drama lacking any discernible plot for them to follow and become engaged by. Brecht did try to warn them, by highlighting this aspect of his piece in the notes for the program: "This play offers only what has been knocked together for the theater, perhaps rather crudely, out of subject-matter which is bound to be of interest to a wider public. There are rather a lot of gaps in it."[10] But many in the audience disliked and eventually resented having to fill in these gaps themselves. While it is clear from the opening scene of *In the Jungle* that the play will center on a conflict between Garga and Shlink, the initial pretext for this disagreement is an unusual one: Shlink tries to buy Garga's opinion of a book, but Garga refuses to sell. It is difficult for the spectator to relate to the motivation behind this exchange, then to the obsessive way both characters throw themselves into the battle, and finally to the indications that Shlink and Garga regard such intense all-out warfare as an effort to overcome human beings' essential isolation from one another. Shortly after Shlink

declares that "People's never-ending loneliness makes enmity an unreach-
able goal," Garga tells him "I've understood that we are comrades."[11] The
mystifying and inaccessible quality of the events in *In the Jungle* was compounded by the setting in which those events unfolded—a dark urban
environment based on Brecht's conception of Chicago. In Horst Wolfram
Geißler's review for one of the Munich papers he described the play's
milieu through a disapproving list of examples: "Schnaps-bars. Hotels
for Chinese. Attic rooms. Alcohol. Slave trade. And again and again
alcohol."[12]

Geißler's account of the performance at once describes the audience's
gradually degenerating response, and expresses the low opinion of *In the
Jungle* shared by most of the critics: "To begin with the audience behaved
in a silent, waiting manner. But when after the interval the nonsense carried on unremittingly, the house became restless and several times was
close to exploding. At the end there was whistling and hissing, which
gave the brunette majority of those in attendance the opportunity ostentatiously to clap down the dissatisfaction."[13] Other reviewers likewise coupled criticism of the play with belittlement of its supporters: one declared,
"The fact that this Expressionist potpourri received applause was not a
sign of general appreciation"; another wrote that the end brought "applause that was more loud than genuine."[14] Especially since the Residenztheater was part of the Bavarian State Theater, which had not
previously produced experimental new work, it may well be that those
audience members who wished to see Brecht's play succeed amplified
their acclaim in some measure. Yet the differentiation by several critics of
the applauding spectators from the rest has disturbing implications. In
virtually the only favorable review of *In the Jungle,* Herbert Ihering—one
of the most prominent critics during the Weimar era, and an influential
admirer of Brecht's work—praised the theater's artistic director Carl Zeiss
for having "dared" to produce the play, and explained why: "Brecht may
well come from Augsburg, and there may well be not one single remark
in the play which could be exploited politically, but the battle which is
being waged everywhere one looks in Germany no longer has anything
much to do with political positions. It is a battle against what is uncomfortable and unconventional, against the non-philistine and the irrational
in all realms."[15] Ihering's fellow critics fought in that battle not only by
dismissing *In the Jungle* as "a great pile of rubble," the production as "a
waste of human reason," but also by disparaging those who did appreciate the work.[16]

The reactionary tendency Ihering commented on was particularly pronounced in Munich, as Brecht himself had noted in a letter to a Berlin
dramaturg in September 1922 while preparing for the production of
Drums in the Night: "If you have ever premiered a play here yourself, then
you know how unfavorable a place it is for things which are even slightly

out of the ordinary."[17] But *Drums* was far less out of the ordinary than *In the Jungle,* which soon prompted a vivid demonstration of Bavarian hostility toward such art. Thomas Mann reported on the incident in a September 1923 piece for the American magazine *The Dial:* "The popular conservatism of Munich was on its guard. It will not stand for any Bolshevist art. At the second or third performance it entered protest, and this in the form of gas bombs. Frightful fumes suddenly filled the theatre. The public wept bitterly; yet not through emotion, but because the expanding gases had a strongly sympathetic effect on their tear ducts."[18] This was almost certainly the work of National Socialists, quite probably incited by an odious review in the Nazi *Völkischer Beobachter* which maliciously attacked the audience members who applauded Brecht's play:

In the theater it smelled of *foetor judaicus,* for Munich had mustered the entire intelligentsia of its Jewish community in order, through wild applause, to deceive people about the play's total flop. At the end of the sixth scene, which marked the interval, not one hand stirred, and during the following scenes the anxious scraping, coughing and laughing did not stop. But after the final fall of the curtain, the sons and daughters of Zion applauded as if possessed.[19]

Far from being Bolshevistic in any strict sense, *In the Jungle* was actually one of the least directly political works Brecht wrote, but the production provided the right-wing extremists in Munich with a convenient vehicle for mounting a conspicuous assault on the political and cultural orientation epitomized for them by Brecht. The reviewer's claim that Brecht—who was not Jewish—wrote the dialog in Yiddish typifies the inflammatory misrepresentation habitually practiced in the pages of the *Völkischer Beobachter.* While the Hitler supporters' teargas bombs did not succeed in preventing that performance from being completed, their actions probably did contribute to the fact that *In the Jungle* received only six performances: the production was withdrawn, and the dramaturg Jakob Geis lost his job.

1923 brought the Weimar Republic's worst financial crisis, culminating by the autumn in hyperinflation that rendered German currency effectually worthless. Already in May, when *In the Jungle* opened, inflation was unprecedented: one dollar, which in July 1922 cost 500 marks, now cost over 50,000. The economic chaos eventually ruined the majority of middle-class Germans and inevitably exacerbated the political polarization characteristic of the entire Weimar period. In September, Mann evoked the altered mood in Munich—"this city which was once so jolly, but which is now saddened by the general fate of Germany and is torn by political hatreds."[20] He went on to call Munich "the city of Hitler," which would become more apt than ever in November when the leader of the NSDAP led the Beerhall Putsch. The conflicts in the auditorium of the Residenztheater over Brecht's *In the Jungle* thus reflected a social and political conflict of greater consequence even than the division over Irish identity and history that underlay the rows at the Abbey over *The Playboy* and *The Plough and the Stars*.

In December 1923, half a year after the scandal over *In the Jungle* in Munich, Brecht's earliest play *Baal* finally reached the stage at Leipzig's principal house, the Altes Theater. It is hardly surprising that *Baal* should have caused offense at its premiere, since the main character, the poet named in the title, behaves abominably by almost any standards. In the first scene Baal responds to the hospitality of a wealthy and admiring patron by getting drunk and flirting with his wife, with whom he subsequently begins an affair, only to reject and humiliate her when he tires of her. He goes on to abuse a succession of other women, including a young virgin who commits suicide after he has seduced her, and his friend Ekart's lover, whom he rapes. Baal shows no remorse over any of this, nor over the brutal and deceitful way he behaves toward everyone, including Ekart, whom he eventually stabs to death in a jealous rage. As Brecht himself put it in a later note, "The life of this figure was one of sensational immorality."[21]

Baal resembles Père Ubu in his single-minded commitment to the satisfaction of his own sensual appetites, but does not exist in the same infantile state as Jarry's boor. For Baal the drive toward pleasure goes along with an eager embrace of and creative response to nature, which he expresses through lyrical, image-laden language. Brecht wrote the first version of *Baal* in 1918, as a rejoinder to Hanns Johst's melodramatic and idealizing Expressionist play *The Lonely One* (*Der Einsame*). Johst had dramatized the final years in the life of the nineteenth-century playwright Christian Dietrich Grabbe, depicting the writer as a genius who gets repulsed by a society which fails to value and reward him. Johst's Grabbe is represented, not least by himself, as an exceptional being. In the opening speech he cries out "I am the cosmos! Without my words, without the glowing garlands of my poetry, everything falls apart!" and he is so pleased with his latest work that he declares Beethoven "the only one whose powerful voice can keep pace with my poem."[22] Brecht named his writer after a god, but a pagan fertility god, and Baal voices no aspirations toward transcendence, seeking instead to experience worldly life to the full through all his senses. Rather than being rebuffed by society, Baal turns away from it and toward the natural world. And where Johst had Grabbe speak in ecstatic exclamations, Brecht gives Baal language much like that of his own early poetry: vital and rugged, full of striking and haunting images such as "love is like letting your naked arm drift in the water of a pond with weeds between your fingers" or "You've got a face with room for plenty of wind. Concave." Brecht did retain the basic shape of the poet's life: like Johst's Grabbe, Baal dies in dismal circumstances, though unlike Grabbe, Baal is still focused on the world around him: when asked what he is thinking about, he replies "I'm still listening to the rain."[23]

Alfred Kerr—one of the leading critics of the period and a rival of Ihering—summarized the reception of *Baal* as "scandal, whistles, laughter, stamping, half an hour of playful shouts—so that next morning the representative of the most widely read paper wrote: 'I have never seen the Leipzigers so completely beside themselves.'"[24] The reviewer for one Leipzig newspaper pointedly held Brecht responsible for the shouted disruptions, writing of his "disastrously rigid obsession with originality, which from one scene to the next offered the spectators, who were growing increasingly restless, more opportunities for fatal passing comments."[25] Another Leipzig critic, Hans Georg Richter, found more to praise in Brecht's work and criticized the audience, observing that "if the spectators do not understand what is going on, then they make stupid jokes," and gave one example from the play's closing moments: in response to Baal's deathbed cry of "Mama!" a voice from the auditorium shouted "Papa!"[26] Ihering for his part contended that Brecht's "brilliant scenic ballad" was poorly served by the acting, especially by Lothar Körner in the title role. He reported this example of the Leipzig audience's reaction to Körner: "As he massacred one of the play's most splendid lyrical passages, a voice from the balcony shouted in a Saxon accent: 'Come on, explain the poem!'"[27] The curtain calls took place amidst a "clamorous battle of whistles, boos and applause."[28]

The shouts during the premiere of *Baal*, like those during any other performance, become part of the event: unlike, for instance, angry exclamations scribbled in the margins of a novel, which do not affect that work, angry shouts in the auditorium at once oppose and contribute to the performance. Leipzig critic Hans Natonek reflected on that kind of audience involvement: "This excited participation by the audience is splendid (except for the forms in which it gets expressed). A contest between different views is, after all, what an evening in the theater ought to trigger. But the audience involvement should not be fixed so exclusively on what is purely concrete; the concrete can easily be offensive even if what lies behind it is not offensive." Natonek's complaint that many in the audience took offense at what was most immediately presented to them applies also in part to the audience response to *Before Sunrise* over thirty years earlier. Dr. Kastan and others could not or would not look beyond their instinctive repulsion at Hauptmann's daring to include allusions to extramarital sex and childbirth in his dialog. In Leipzig it seems that many spectators found Baal too antipathetic to listen to his poems or give any proper thought to Brecht's play. The closed reaction to *Baal* perhaps appears less surprising than that to *Before Sunrise*, given the extreme nature of Baal's immoral behavior. But the opposition to *Baal* did surprise Natonek in light of the range of work theatergoers had been exposed to by 1923: "The public, who on this occasion went more berserk than ever, has remained quiet in response to other, no less strong material."[29] Richter wished these spectators had remained quiet, and, if they insisted on "publicly taking offense," left the theater instead of remaining and contributing to the "public nuisance" of shouting against the performance.[30] Both these critics argued for the same contract desired by the directors of the Abbey and by other playwrights and directors at this time: one that would allow new work to get a fair hearing before an audience without being impeded by the protests of those who were not open to it. Yet the nature of the opposition to *Baal* in Leipzig was significantly different from that prompted by *Before Sunrise*, *The Playboy* or *The Plough*: the impression emerging from the various accounts indicates less engagement and more dismissive, often mocking rejection. Natonek found this troubling: "Not everyone is able to feel the human side of the most dissolute. Those who are not able to do so, they shout '*Pfui*.' Baal is a bad play . . . —but it is not '*Pfui*'." The German word *Pfui* carries more weight than "phooey" or other such interjections in English; it seems that for Natonek *Pfui* characterized a disdainful attitude which even a "wild, shapeless juvenilia" like *Baal* does not deserve.[31]

That derisive response to Brecht's play is somewhat reminiscent of the reception of *Ubu Roi*, which also provoked a combination of genuine anger and lighthearted mockery. But Jarry's piece was produced in a quite different context, and no remotely comparable clash of drama and audience was to occur for many years afterward. The scandal over *Baal*, by contrast, was very much embedded in a culture of frequent conflicts between new work and protesting spectators. Although the tumult at *Baal*'s premiere was relatively tame by Weimar standards, and although the performance had ended with multiple curtain calls for the actors, director and Brecht, Leipzig's mayor intervened to remove Brecht's play from the theater's schedule after the single performance. Ihering criticized that action, which reflected a disturbing increase in the frequency of "intrusion by the authorities in the artistic freedom of the theater." He praised the director of the Altes Theater, Alwin Kronacher, for producing contemporary work and forcefully argued that "interventions against these departures from the conventional are not in the interest of development, nor even in the interest of tradition."[32] Ihering's article echoed his comments half a year earlier about the "battle against what is uncomfortable and unconventional," without being so explicit. A Leipzig newspaper pointed to more of the implications of *Baal*'s withdrawal, distinguishing between those people who liked to watch plays such as *My Cousin Edward* (*Mein Vetter Eduard*), one of that season's hits, and those who preferred to see the plays of Brecht and other young playwrights: "Are the Cousin-Edward-People to practice censorship over the friends of literature? By no means. The two parties should just go to the theater on different evenings. How peaceably we would then be able live with one another."[33] Intentionally or not, this proposal for theatergoing reflects a climate of polarization in the country at large. By December 1923, the worst of the inflation was over and the German currency stabilized, but the crisis and accompanying chaos left deep divisions. The rejection of *Baal* in Leipzig through cries of "Pfui!" was indicative of a society with many loyalties and animosities which could easily harden into more substantial hostility.

It was not until over two years after the Leipzig production that *Baal* was staged again, this time in Berlin. In February 1926 Brecht himself directed a revised version entitled *Life of the Man Baal* (*Lebenslauf des Mannes Baal*) for a single Sunday matinee performance at the Deutsches Theater. The production was mounted by the Junge Bühne, a theater group founded by Moritz Seeler in 1922 with the aim of staging new work unlikely to be accepted by the mainstream houses. Brecht had actually started out as the director of their first production, of his friend Bronnen's *Patricide,* but his domineering manner antagonized the cast of well-known Berlin actors, who were working without pay, until eventually a row erupted and Brecht was replaced for the final weeks of rehearsal. The performance of *Patricide* concluded with a noisy battle between enthusiastic applause and angry shouting, helping the new theater to make its mark. By September 1923, when the third production led to questioning of its right to public funding in the state parliament, the Junge Bühne had established itself as the leading producer of provocative drama. When Seeler invited him to direct *Baal* for the Junge Bühne, Brecht took the opportunity to reconceive the work in ways which reflected his changing ideas about both playwriting and theatrical presentation. He cut the number of scenes from more than twenty to a dozen, and eliminated much of the material relating to Baal's lyrical response to nature in favor of more evocation of the poet's environment as modern and industrial. The performance began with a prologue which informed the audience that "In this dramatic biography by Bertolt Brecht you will watch the life of the man Baal as it took place in the first part of this century."[34] In a short piece published shortly before the production, Brecht even went so far as to invent an identity for Baal's supposed model. The actor who read the prologue also announced titles for each of the scenes, for example, "Baal abandons the mother of his unborn child."[35] By presenting Baal's life story as illustrative of early-twentieth-century conditions, Brecht hoped the audience would respond to the play's action in a considered, critical manner; but in the event, the reception of *Baal* in Berlin was all too similar to that in Leipzig.

One review began with this detailed description of the shape of the audience's response:

The audience took in the first four or five scenes without excitement, but then the protest began, quietly and with warm-hearted whistling. And after the sixth scene, in which "Baal earns money for the last time," the whistling turned into a storm!—into howling, yelling and blowing on trillerpfeifen, so that it almost seemed doubtful whether the thing would be played to the end. But people calmed down again, carried on whistling, clapping and shouting, and slowly exhausted themselves. At the end the applause needed to be aroused by the whistlers, though once it was it became fervent.[36]

Other reviews confirm the principal observation of this account: that the Berlin audience's reaction to *Baal* grew quite fervent, yet also appeared at times to lack conviction. As in Leipzig, the spectators played an active role in the performance. Kerr reported that "When in the final scene someone shouted at Baal, 'Who's interested in you?' the house laughed their agreement. Someone forecasts Baal's death. In the house: Bravo." And he remarked that "The difference between the Leipzig theater scandal and the one yesterday in Berlin consists more or less in the fact that in Leipzig it was more opposition, in Berlin more calm clowning-around which dominated."[37] That comparative assessment is all the more striking because at the time Kerr himself had emphasized the mocking tone of the response in Leipzig. Other reviews confirm that the opposition to *Baal* in Berlin was more jovially participatory than genuinely outraged.

Several other critics dispiritedly contemplated the significance of the willed and inauthentic appearance of the protests against *Baal*. Julius Hart's review began: "The usual Sunday matinee theater. People do not go for the sake of art, but rather to make a ruckus and a scandal."[38] Another critic agreed that at the Junge Bühne in particular, the spectators' role had reached a questionable extreme: "in the Sunday matinees of this organization, equal rights to have one's say have gradually come about for audience and performers"; the examples he gives include a soprano voice shouting "Come on, throw the fellow out!"[39] Ernst Heilborn wrote that Brecht's play had been received "with the theater scandal that has virtually become traditional," and commented that "at the sight of these temperamental outbursts—from a public which otherwise is extremely short on temperament—one has become more and more convinced that it is a case of premeditated behavior."[40] And it was not only the critics who were inclined to question the sincerity of the protesters' demonstrations: at one point during the performance someone shouted out, "You aren't really outraged, you're just pretending you are!"[41]

The significance of the Berlin premiere of *Baal* as an indicator of prevailing attitudes toward drama and toward behavior in the theater is mitigated by certain factors including the nature of the work itself. For Hart, *Baal* "gives the impression of having been written almost deliberately for the sole sake of such Sunday-afternoon pleasures and noises," and the production suggested to him and others that Brecht and his fellow young playwrights—those "young nihilists" whose work Seeler's Junge Bühne was dedicated to staging—had nothing new with which to replace "the old form, the old spirit" they had exploded.[42] This production of *Baal* was something of an anachronism, since although Brecht had reworked the script and experimented with certain new ideas in directing, the core of the work was by 1926 almost a decade old. That anachronistic quality accounts in part for the inauthentic appearance of the audience response in Berlin: *Baal* was not a new play, and its production, rather than provoking a scandal, created the opportunity for a scandal.

Heilborn argued that it was the critics "who wrote the music to concerts like this"—that they encouraged people to go to the theater having already determined either to applaud or to protest.[43] Heilborn acknowledged that he too played that role, implying that all critics inevitably do so. Ihering, however, firmly believed that some reviewers abused their influence. Kerr's archrival was furious because he believed the unruly audience response had been deliberately provoked by the older critic:

At a matinee yesterday, Brecht's early work *Baal* gave rise not so much to a battle as to a scandal that had been prepared in advance. Indirectly encouraged by the reviews of Mr. Kerr—who in cases like this invariably fails to mention applause for the writer and work, only to point with schadenfreude to whistles and heckling—scandal-addicted theatergoers felt it their duty to unleash their fury. . . . During *Baal*, Mr. Kerr even made a few successful attempts to disrupt the performance in a very personal way through provocative laughter and talking.[44]

Ihering's charge that Kerr habitually misrepresented the balance between enthusiastic and unsympathetic audience reactions in accordance with his own point of view could of course be leveled at any critic, including Ihering himself. More often than not, observers of the same scandal reach quite different conclusions as to whether applause or whistles dominated, and that judgment tends to reflect the writer's opinion of the play. But such partisanship had greater significance in this context. Kerr's role in the *Baal* production and Ihering's complaint about it formed only the latest episode of a long-running dispute between the two critics over the quality of Brecht's work. Kerr had established himself as an important critic around the turn of the century through his support of the Naturalism of Ibsen and Hauptmann, but Ihering was calling Kerr's criteria and his style into question as early as 1911. When Brecht emerged in the early 1920s, Ihering supported him right from the start, showering the premiere of *Drums in the Night* with praise and shortly afterwards awarding Brecht the prestigious Kleist prize. It seems that the more Ihering championed Brecht, the more Kerr felt bound to disagree with his rival and to write disparagingly of Brecht's plays; and as Ihering protested in 1924, Kerr's reviews of Brecht productions often served more to attack Ihering than to evaluate the playwright's work.[45] Prominent actor Fritz Kortner illuminates the rivalry between the two critics: he contrasts the influence of Ihering's opinions on people directly involved in the theater—"We read him as one would a grammar, and learned from it"—with Kerr's influence on theatergoers—"His commentaries either encouraged or discouraged readers' interest and had a direct effect on attendance at theaters."[46] While all drama critics affect public attitudes toward the productions they review, rarely do they exercise that capacity with such unapologetic partiality as did Kerr when it came to Brecht's work. Kerr's interventions in the reception of *Baal*, before and during the first and only performance, probably heightened what would in any case have proven an uninformative example of audience response. Some of the critics—even Kerr—reacted favorably to Brecht's experiments with playwriting and staging techniques, but it was all but impossible for him to draw any conclusions from the audience's reaction.

One review of the Berlin production of *Baal* provides striking evidence of how some Germans felt about such work. Johannes W. Harnisch was so appalled by this example of contemporary art—"And just what is the art of these youngsters who are sullying German literature and dramatic art today? *To be revolting*"—that he appealed to the authorities to act against it: "Your honourable nose reflects the sovereignty of the people—so stick it in this filth for once and smell what an odor it gives off!" In a disturbing indication of the kind of divisive strategy which would prove so crucial in the years to come, Harnisch also vehemently attacks those who support modern works like Brecht's—"These snobs of the male and female sex, these meticulous literary types and hysterical would-be call-girls sixteen to sixty years old, who are aphrodisiacally tickled by the faecal smell of this literature." Harnisch's diatribe appeared not in the organ of an extreme right-wing political party, but in the journal *Der Montag*. The Leipzig reviewer of *Baal* who in 1923 imagined keeping those who appreciated work like Brecht's apart from the "Cousin-Edward-People" had done so in a spirit of live and let live. Harnisch also proposes separate spheres, but wishes to force the contemporary work underground: "*It would, however, be intolerable if filth were to triumph in full view of the public.*" This hysterical piece exemplifies the right-wing's increasing focus on the political importance of art, and their recognition of its potential for mobilizing public opinion: "This anarchy on the German stage has become altogether intolerable in the context of both national and state politics."[47] Harnisch's article constitutes the most significant performance of opposition to *Baal* in 1926.

The readiness of many Germans to agree with Harnisch's position is reflected by the public response to new work by some other playwrights during these years, especially outside Berlin. Carl Zuckmayer's hit comedy *The Merry Vineyard* (*Der fröhliche Weinberg*) began a two-and-a-half-year run in Berlin in December 1925, but ran into trouble beyond the capital because of its mockery of various aspects of rural German life; those sufficiently offended by Zuckmayer's play to protest against it included not only Nazi politicians, but also university students. Zuckmayer reflected on the significance of such protests in his 1966 memoirs:

The fuss over *The Merry Vineyard* was not simply a fools' row that one might have made fun of. It had unveiled the scowling, distorted, and irreconcilable grimace of a vengeful, hate-filled reaction which was about to cheat the German people out of their best and most hopeful period, and which was already digging the grave of their free future. All that was already under way then—camouflaged, hidden, but steadily hounding some and stirring up others.[48]

Zuckmayer wrote with the benefit of hindsight; at the time of the controversies over *The Merry Vineyard* and the Berlin production of *Baal*, when the Weimar Republic had entered its most politically and economically stable period, few people realized the full significance of the process he described. An incident involving Kortner, one among many Jews prominent in the culture of 1920s Berlin, even suggested that the "hate-filled reaction" could be resisted and defeated. In September 1929, Kortner was accused, first in the Nationalist Socialist press then in other newspapers, of having raped a young non-Jewish woman. He declined to flee the country as some recommended, and insisted on continuing to perform in—of all things—*The Merchant of Venice*. When he appeared on stage, he was greeted with a thrilling storm of applause: "The audience needed no detective's proof of my innocence, no refutation of the charge. They demonstrated on behalf of the hunted; they protested against the attempt at political extortion." Unfortunately this moving display of support for Kortner manifested only the stance of the small minority of Germans who attended the theater. In his recollections about the antagonism between Ihering and Kerr, Kortner comments ruefully on the actual import of what at the time seemed so significant: "This newspaper war also drew an astounding amount of public interest away from the political battles for power. And yet what depended on the outcome of the political struggle was the structuring of life and for many life itself. Whether and how one would be able to stay alive was forgotten in favor of the dispute over how life should be dramatized and put on stage."[49] Such disproportionate attentiveness typified the Weimar climate: the artistic radicalism which generated so much original work was constantly accompanied and eventually overwhelmed by political radicalism.

A few years after the Berlin production of *Baal* at the Junge Bühne, Brecht reflected on the experience of working with Seeler's group: "I don't regret having worked with these people . . . I was doing what all those who have too much self-confidence about the battle against reactionariness do, when they believe that they can accomplish something by entering into it; I don't regret it, because it was only through doing so that I could see what all of them can't see."[50] This statement typifies the combination of acuity and shortsightedness which marked Brecht's overly confident assessment of the Weimar-era production of his work. At first he did not spend much time pondering the repeated angry rejection of his plays; it seems that his inclination was to move on and not to dwell on the various scandals and controversies he left in his wake—well aware, of course, of what effective publicity they afforded. Scandals also provided Brecht with concrete, clear-cut examples of audience response, and no doubt he drew more insights from those performances than he admitted in writing. When he reflected at all in published texts on the uproar over *In the Jungle* and *Baal,* he tended to dismiss it as inevitable, given the constitution of the theatergoing public, and as evidence that theater as an institution was in need of radical change. Sometimes he wrote of retraining those who were offended by his plays. At other times, and increasingly, he dismissed them as in any case not the people—in particular not the social class—that he wished to reach. What he only gradually began to take into account was the possibility that *his* writing and direction might have contributed to the rejection of his work in performance, and impeded the response he wished to generate.

In the year and a half after the Berlin production of *Baal,* two new factors changed the nature of Brecht's writing for the stage. It was in the summer of 1926 that he first began to read and study Marx, whose influence from then on increasingly informed his thinking and practice. The following spring brought a significant change in Brecht's use of music. Up until that time, all of his plays had featured songs, with deliberately unsophisticated music devised, or borrowed, by Brecht himself. Now Brecht was approached by Kurt Weill, who wished to use poems from Brecht's recently published collection *Manual of Piety* (*Hauspostille*) as text for a chamber opera, and Weill became the first of many composers with whom Brecht worked closely. They called the product of that first collaboration *Mahagonny Songspiel,* deliberately altering the German term *Singspiel* by incorporating the English word "song." This short piece, consisting of six songs interspersed with orchestral interludes, was first performed at a chamber music festival in Baden-Baden in July 1927. That festival, founded by a group of young musicians in Donaueschingen in 1921, typified the prevailing climate of artistic experimentation, about which John Willett aptly observed, "the Weimar period was remarkable for its freedom from those distinctions between 'high' and 'low' culture."[51] Composers of music for small and large ensembles, and for theater, opera and film, rejected the styles inherited from the nineteenth century in favor of *Neue Musik,* which strove to make serious work accessible to a broader audience, and embraced popular forms previously dismissed as trivial, most notably jazz. *Mahagonny* was, however, exceptional in that it expressed a political stance—as indicated by Brecht's description in a programme note: "The small epic play *Mahagonny* merely comes to the obvious conclusions about the unstoppable disintegration of existing social classes."[52]

Mahagonny was one of four chamber operas performed in a single evening, to an "international and elegant audience, leading lights of the state and city authorities, royal personages, a lot of press and music people."[53] However accustomed these sophisticated spectators may have been to new kinds of opera, it seems that many of them were taken aback by the way even the appearance of *Mahagonny* departed radically from convention. Settings were indicated by projected drawings by Caspar Neher, Brecht's childhood friend who designed many key Brecht productions during and after the Weimar period. According to an account written some years later by Lotte Lenya—Weill's wife, and one of the six performers—the audience "stared in bewilderment when the stagehands began to set up a boxing ring on the stage. The buzz increased as the singers, dressed as the worst hoodlums and frails, climbed through the ropes."[54] The two preceding works—by Ernst Toch and Darius Milhaud—had been produced more or less as if they were traditional operas, and were based on stories from a fairytale and from mythology. *Mahagonny* used the boxing ring as a setting for a series of jazz-influenced songs about life in an imaginary permissive society, culminating in a demonstration, with the performers carrying placards bearing the slogans "For the mortality of the soul," "Against Cyvilis," "For earthly rewards," "For natural sexual acts," and, in Lenya's case, "For Weill." Hans Böhm, reviewing the production for *Das Theater*, described the "amusing and original" way the piece was presented, which consituted one of Brecht's earliest applications of the techniques he was by this point calling Epic Theater: "No curtain, and everything—the primitively constructed scenery, the instructions from director and stage manager, the activity of the lighting operator, etc.—in full view of the audience, so that even the performers who aren't on stage can uninhibitedly watch during their pauses and during set-changes."[55] The expressions of bewilderment Lenya recalls developed into a performance of opposition: "In the stalls it was utter chaos. Some were clapping, others were whistling, people loudly and excitedly expressed their opinions."[56]

Böhm "strongly suspected" that Brecht "had stage-managed the whistling-concert as a precaution, in order to spur on the applause all the more forcefully."[57] While there is no record of Brecht having planted whistlers in the house, Böhm was correct in surmising Brecht's intention to provoke the audience. Reporting on the premiere in a letter to Helene Weigel, Brecht wrote: "A great directorial success! A 15-minute scandal!"[58] His plan to have the two female singers enter in the nude had not been allowed, but Lenya writes that "Brecht had thoughtfully provided us with whistles of our own, little trillerpfeifen, so we stood there whistling defiantly back."[59] Brecht's deliberate incitement of a scandal was not simply provocation for its own sake, nor a publicity stunt. One review, by leading music critic Heinrich Strobel, perceptively describes the ideas emerging through the songs: "A social and political slant gradually penetrates what is at first a purely musical play. A plot of sorts begins to take shape, and in conjunction with that change the music grows imperceptibly from dance music to dramatic music. The final song, a revolt against the inherited world order, presented like a revue, rises in a steep dramatic curve."[60] Brecht reinforced the text's communication of political ideas through his staging. As Lenya suggests in describing the erection of the boxing ring, there was considerable shock value in so directly introducing an element of popular culture into the high-art context of a chamber music festival. Brecht first proposed the idea of using a boxing ring as a set the previous December, for the Frankfurt premiere of his one-act play *The Wedding*, and he often returned to it as a device or an image. Staging his works in a boxing ring was an effective means of encouraging the audience to consider drama in the way they would consider a sporting event, and represents one of the earliest means he devised to foster in the spectators some psychological distance from the action on stage. And by preparing the singers to respond in kind to whistling at the end, Brecht made the production continue to foreground its own performance, and strove to ensure that the uproar did not simply look like one more audience protest. The *Mahagonny Songspiel* production, the first in which Brecht had been extensively involved since developing his interest in economics and Marxism the previous summer, demonstrates the beginnings of a more thoughtful, less dismissive attitude toward the role played by the audience.

Reviewers for the Baden-Baden newspapers did not highlight the political resonance of *Mahagonny* as much as Strobel did—or as much as Brecht would have liked. Their response probably better reflects that of the spectators who booed and whistled. Hans Wilfert and Elsa Bauer both regarded Brecht's purpose as consisting more of unflinching depiction of contemporary social conditions than of communicating any particular position about those conditions. For Wilfert, Brecht's poems "reflect uncannily the spiritual demoralization, the terrible emptiness and unrestrained degradation of the urban atmosphere," and the piece is "resolutely about the times, and only ugly and mean because the times are ugly and mean."[61] Bauer agrees about the contemporary orientation of Brecht's texts, but complains that he "holds a mirror of the times up to people, and says 'This is what you're like . . . one can fake intellect to you people with any old nothing, and one can quite easily abuse your most holy feelings—decadence is celebrating victory!'"[62] In many ways, Bauer's response to *Mahagonny Songspiel* is emblematic of the public attitude toward experimentation during the Weimar era. On the one hand, she accepts the principle of opening such festivals to all kinds of work, and for all her antipathy toward Brecht's poems, she unreservedly praises the music, the performances, and even Brecht's direction. But at the same time, she makes very crude distinctions in writing about the public: she insists that she does not wish to be associated with the minority who consider such work art, and maintains that while *Mahagonny* deserved a single performance, "otherwise it belongs in city cabarets after midnight, where people go to make clever jokes." Bauer also makes very clear just what she believes the public should expect from art: "We are not here to be destroyed, but to be 'elevated'."[63] Brecht's objective was in fact by no means nihilistic, indeed he aimed precisely to elevate the spectators, in part by making their role more active. In 1927 he had barely begun his efforts to accomplish that through the theory and practice of Epic Theater, and for a time was able to benefit from the relatively calm and prosperous phase of the Weimar Republic between 1924 and 1929. In that climate, experimental artistic work flourished, and though some Germans continued periodically to perform their opposition to that work, their antipathy did not for the moment tie in to a political hostility toward those who held different views. The accounts and reviews of the performance of *Mahagonny Songspiel* suggest that the protesting spectators were neither as deeply unsettled by the incomprehensible as the Munich audience for *In the Jungle*, nor as inclined mockingly to reject the work as the audiences for *Baal* had been; instead they expressed in a conventional way their dislike of a work they regarded as one among many experiments.

Although most of Brecht's works produced during the Weimar period proved to be controversial, the most famous one did of course become a huge hit: *The Threepenny Opera*. The years from about the middle of the decade to 1929 constituted the Weimar Republic's most stable and successful period, and this economic climate is probably one of the factors which contributed to the rather surprising runaway success, beginning on 31 August 1928, of Brecht and Weill's adaptation of John Gay's *Beggar's Opera*. It seems that in this period the bourgeois society Brecht targeted was better able to withstand his attacks than it was in earlier and later years. The premiere took place at the Theater am Schiffbauerdamm, which had been leased by the young actor and would-be producer Ernst Josef Aufricht. Having fruitlessly asked several playwrights and publishers for an unproduced play with which to open his theater, Aufricht tried Brecht. One of two works in progress Brecht described to Aufricht was an adaptation of John Gay's *Beggar's Opera*, which soon took Aufricht's fancy. Once Brecht and Weill reached an agreement with Aufricht, they wrote the piece in only a few months, along with Elisabeth Hauptmann, who had in fact written all that Brecht initially showed Aufricht. The few weeks of preparation and rehearsal were so beset with problems that the new work was expected to be a huge flop. As Aufricht wrote later, "In general, people's sense was that the play would not be performed to the end, and would certainly not last beyond the premiere."[64] Instead, it became Brecht's first—and remained his biggest—commercial success. Far from offending the audience, as Brecht had in a sense intended it to, *The Three-penny Opera* delighted crowds throughout Germany and beyond.

In a program note, Brecht tried to draw the spectators' attention to the social significance of the story he had adapted from Gay's *The Beggar's Opera*, pointing out that the two works shared the same "sociological causes," namely "a social order in which people of more or less all classes of the population, albeit in very different ways, take moral principles into account not by living in morality but by living off it."[65] To begin with, it seemed as if the first-night audience was going to perceive and dislike this idea. According to Aufricht, the opening, "The Ballad of Mac the Knife," and the first two scenes elicited only frosty silence. A businessman who takes advantage of other people's pity, a ruthless criminal (Macheath) with the appearance and manners of a respectable businessman, alliances between the underworld and both the clergy and the police: this is what Brecht confronted the spectators with, and it seemed that they recognized and disliked the implications. But then the "Cannon Song," a duet performed by Macheath and his best friend Tiger-Brown, the chief of police, went down so well that they had to give an encore, and the audience loved the rest of the show.

That song does not, however, signal any change in *The Threepenny Opera*'s depiction of society. The plot and themes which are developed in the rest of the text are those outlined in the opening scenes: as Brecht himself later put it, the play "showed the close connection between the emotional life of the bourgeois and that of the street robber."[66] Why, then, did Brecht only manage to touch his audience with this provocative critique for barely two scenes? The course of the spectators' response to the opening scenes at the premiere is perhaps exemplary. The text's capacity to disturb the audience lasted only until it was overridden by the appeal of the music. Brecht and Weill had made the work too enjoyable. The English setting enabled the spectators to deny to themselves any connection between the world of the opera and their own society, and in general Brecht's thesis that respectable bourgeois citizens are as criminal as Macheath was conveyed in too general a fashion to really affect the bourgeois audience. Instead they were absorbed by the story and entertained by the songs.

In addition to earning Brecht a good deal of money, *The Threepenny Opera* also provided him with useful insights into audience response, and contributed to his evolving ideas about how to promote what he summarized in his notes on the opera as "complex seeing." Yet even as he enthusiastically describes and explains techniques for making the experience of watching a play more like that of reading or of watching a sporting event, he permits himself to acknowledge that he is asking a lot: "Unfortunately it is to be feared that titles and permission to smoke do not quite suffice to lead the audience to a more fruitful use of the theater."[67] Brecht's big hit left him wishing for a different audience just as much as the various scandals had done, but also sounding rather less confident about his own capacity to bring about the necessary changes.

In spring 1929, through collaboration with Weill and with Paul Hindemith, another highly regarded young composer, Brecht began to develop the form of theater that he would call the *Lehrstück*—literally "teaching-play," though more often translated as suggested by Brecht himself: "the nearest English equivalent I can find is the 'learning-play'."[68] The works performed at that summer's chamber music festival in Baden-Baden included *Lindbergh's Flight* (*Der Lindberghflug*), with text by Brecht and music mostly by Weill and some by Hindemith, and *Lehrstück*, created by Brecht and Hindemith. In various respects, these pieces represented a continuation of the experiment begun with the *Mahagonny Songspiel*, which had premiered to considerable outcry in Baden-Baden two years earlier. In the meantime, Hindemith and others associated with the "Neue Musik" had further developed their ideas about two original approaches to the composition of new musical work: *Gebrauchsmusik*—functional music—and *Gemeinschaftsmusik*—communal music. *Lindbergh's Flight* was an exercise in *Gebrauchsmusik*, written expressly for broadcast over the radio. *Lehrstück* explored the concept of *Gemeinschaftsmusik*, or *Musik für Liebhaber*—music for amateurs, or enthusiasts, which aimed to involve the audience in the performance by including suitably simple parts for them to sing or play. The set for the premiere of *Lehrstück* included a large poster with the words "Making music is better than listening to music"—a motto which encapsulates the impetus behind this movement. As one reviewer described it, "The composition is simple, the refrain added to it simpler still. As in operetta, it is projected onto a film screen. And now we all sing along."[69] But participation through singing would not remain the audience's only form of active involvement in the premiere of *Lehrstück*, which provoked a scandal similar to that incited by *Mahagonny*, though more intense and revealing.

Accounts of Brecht's work often imply that he contrived the *Lehrstück* as a theatrical form and then wrote pieces according to that model, beginning with the two performed at the 1929 festival. In fact, Brecht did not apply the term *Lehrstück* to *Lindbergh's Flight* until later, and he would probably not have called the other piece simply *Lehrstück* had he regarded it as one instance of a new genre; he subsequently renamed it *The Baden-*

Baden Teaching-Play on Consent (*Das Badener Lehrstück vom Einverständnis*). It was Hindemith who took the initiative in the collaboration on *Lehrstück*: he invited Brecht to contribute the texts to a work whose basic shape and approach he had already conceived. And the direction Hindemith was exploring paralleled Brecht's own thinking at this stage of his career. By 1929, Brecht believed that his efforts to alter the way theater was produced and received, to reach a new audience and engage them in a different kind of experience, had foundered because of the resistance to change of the bourgeois cultural institutions he had been obliged to operate within. The *Lehrstück* initially, and later Brecht's evolving notion of the *Lehrstück* genre, were conceived as a means of circumventing the apparatus of conventional theater by replacing the established pattern of active performers facing passive spectators with a fundamentally different model. Brecht described the form of and motivation for that model in the program for the 1929 festival:

The *Lehrstück*, product of various theories of a musical, dramatic and political nature aiming at the collective practice of the arts, is created for the self-understanding of the authors and of those actively participating, and is not meant to be an experience for some group of people. It has not even been completely finished. So the members of the audience, *inasmuch as they do not contribute to the experiment*, would not play the part of recipients, but merely of those in attendance.[70]

Hindemith set Brecht's texts to music arranged for a chorus, a small orchestra and two male voices, along with the non-musical part of a speaker. The piece examines the situation of an airman whose plane crashes, and who begs the chorus to come to his assistance and save him from death. The chorus asks the crowd whether they should help the airman, even though he never helped them. Through a series of illustrative inquiries and explanations, the Chorus teaches the airman and the crowd that people do not help each other and that this individual should consent to his death, since "No one dies when he dies."[71] The premiere took place in a former gymnasium now used as a municipal hall, which was filled to capacity with an audience that included "the ministers of Baden-Baden, composers, writers, academics and journalists," as well as people visiting either for the festival or the spa.[72] No seating was assigned, which was unusual at this time, as was the simplicity of the chairs themselves. On the left of the podium before them the audience saw the chorus and most of the orchestra—made up largely of amateur musicians—with Brecht (who directed) and Hindemith seated at a table with Gerda Müller, who read the speaker's part; on the right was Josef Witt who sang the part of the crashed airman. There was a small playing space in the middle, and above it a screen used for projections, including displays of the texts

designed to be sung by the spectators. The orchestra's brass section sat
behind the audience.

In Heinrich Strobel's view, the *Lehrstück* realized "modern theories of
art as the expression of collective will. We're not asked to believe in some
beautiful illusion, rather we all *work on* something together. The music
and the play, the performers and the spectators act in concert. The composition of Hindemith's music is so simple that it can be played by amateurs. The crowd sings along with important phrases sung by a small
chorus."[73] But Elsa Bauer—who two years earlier had strongly objected
to *Mahagonny Songspiel*—questioned whether underlining Brecht's ideas
by singing them could legitimately be called "collective practice of art,"
especially when most of the audience members disagreed with those
ideas. Bauer also quotes Brecht's program note and calls his statement
that the piece was not designed as "an experience for some group of people" an "outright disgrace."[74] Echoing her remarks about what the public
for *Mahagonny* expected from art, Bauer protests that those who pay for
the performances at the festival are not just "some group of people," but
people who take an interest in new music and have the right to expect
serious work.

To begin with, the audience "followed with keen interest, and animatedly joined in with the choral parts."[75] The greater part of the *Lehrstück*
consists of exchanges among the speaker, the fallen airman, and the choir.
But the fourth section, entitled "Observe Death," entails a "Dance of
Death," which in the first production took the form of a film made for
Brecht featuring the dancer Valeska Gert. She herself wrote that in the
dance, unaccompanied by music, "I keep going through the same stages,
from a slow march to screaming in mortal fear, until I gradually slide out
of life and its worries, becoming tranquil and fading away. Only I die each
time in a different way, one time fearfully, another time more submissively.
The high point of the dance is agony."[76] It became clear that many in the
audience found the filmed dance disturbing, as some spectators whistled,
and others even shouted demands that the performance be halted. In a
note written in 1937, Brecht described what happened at this point during
the premiere: "when the crowd watched the film showing dead people
with great unrest and aversion, the playwright instructed the announcer
to call out at the end: 'Second observation of the representation of death
which was received with aversion,' and the film was shown again."[77] Only
one of the contemporary accounts records such a repetition, which implies
either that Brecht—who in 1937 describes the film quite inaccurately—
invented this incident later as an example that served his current needs,
or that the demonstration of repugnance by some audience members was
intense enough to distract others from exactly what was happening on
stage.[78] Judging by the reviewers' descriptions, Brecht was justified in presenting the audience response to Gert's film as an especially instinctive,

unself-conscious display of repulsion: the "gruesome death-dance" consisted of "grimaces of such repulsiveness . . . that they can scarcely even be considered tolerable."[79] For Inge Karsten, encountering the film under these particular circumstances was decisive: "Though Valeska Gert's 'Totentanz' in itself made a very strong impression artistically, in this context (on the screen) it was simply unbearable"; Bauer agreed that the context more than the film itself made watching it "a torture."[80] It seems that many spectators were taken aback by the unanticipated incursion of a vivid and highly expressive visual representation, without music, into a performance which up until then had entailed only music and spoken text. Hans Wilfert asked, "The whole piece is stylized, so why suddenly this super-naturalistic film?"[81] Gert's own description makes clear that her dance is not a naturalistic representation of death or of dying—less so than the "film showing dead people" erroneously referred to by Brecht might have been—yet several critics balked at the film's "hideous" or "brutal" realism.[82] Gert's dance of death can only be regarded as relatively naturalistic; but the extent of its realism compared to the previous three sections counted for a great deal. Spectators whose experience of *Lehrstück* had entailed willing participation through singing were abruptly confronted with a categorically, jarringly different spectacle that not only did not invite their participation, but further seemed through the intensity of its expression to compel them into a position of passivity. The whistles and shouts of protest against the film thus constitute at once a reaction against the spectacle the audience was being subjected to and a deliberate effort to regain an active role in the performance.

The sixth section of the *Lehrstück*, the "Second Investigation Into Whether People Help People," caused even more pronounced expressions of aversion than the death dance film had done. Three actors dressed as clowns entered the playing space in the middle of the stage and acted out a short scene in which one giant clown, Herr Schmitt, complains of pain in various parts of his body, which the other two then saw off, according to the principle that, as one of the clowns declares, "If your left foot is hurting you, then there's only one thing for it: get rid of the left foot."[83] The actor playing Schmitt, Theo Lingen, had been dressed in an oversized costume on stilts, with a huge head. As Lingen himself recounts in his memoirs, "Then I also had to spray blood with a pair of bellows: now that was really too much for the audience. And when it went as far as my having my head sawn off, because I was complaining that I had a headache, such a scandal broke out as I have never again experienced in the theater."[84] It seems Lingen may have misremembered or embellished some details, since none of the contemporary accounts describe spurts of fake blood, though Bauer did report that the detached limbs were made to look bloody inside. Many spectators protested against this scene through "howling, stamping and whistling," some shouted "Stop the scandal!," and "People poured out of the hall in droves."[85] According to an account written some years later by the composer Hanns Eisler, some spectators were too overwhelmed by the sawing off of Herr Schmitt's feet to protest: "These feet were stilts made very crudely out of wood. For many spectators this rough bit of fun turned into something horrifying. Some of them fainted, even though it was only wood being sawn and it was certainly by no means a naturalistic representation."[86] Bauer wrote that "Some ladies felt sick, and so did I!"[87] The protests prompted a counter-reaction of applause in support of the performance. Lingen's recollections include one ironic detail of the tumult generated by the clown scene: as he "looked at the raging and yelling spectators, I saw before me in the first row a dignified, white-haired gentleman sitting there completely calm, and appearing to take no part in the scandal. The gentleman was Gerhart Hauptmann."[88] Amidst all the uproar, Lingen and the two other clowns completed the scene, which ended with stretcher-bearers removing the "grotesque mutilated corpse."[89] After the seventh and concluding section of the Lehrstück, a battle broke out between opponents of the piece who renewed their storm of howling, stamping and whistling, and others who with equal if not greater fervor applauded and cheered.

The critics who objected to the clown scene stressed that it was the interlude's style rather than the meaning they discerned in it that put them off. Karsten wrote: "as for this gruesome clowning, the idea behind which was altogether acceptable—'If thine right eye offend thee, pluck it out; if thine left eye offend thee, cast it from thee'—expressed in this unaesthetic way it was simply a scandal."[90] Karl Holl was more favorably disposed toward the impulse behind the Lehrstück, but he too criticized the inclusion of a scene which was "set up in such a revoltingly crude way that it severely harmed the effect of the entire effort."[91] As Eisler remarked, it is puzzling that the circus-like, unmistakably non-naturalistic style of the clown scene should have been perceived by many audience members and critics as disturbingly lifelike. Yet somehow Herr Schmitt's dismemberment struck even Strobel as convincing: in his appreciative review he describes a scene "of stirring realism, inserted with ingenious instinct into the clear tectonic structure of the Lehrstück."[92] What Strobel considered an inspired artistic choice his colleagues regarded as such an extreme assault on the audience that two of them termed it sadistic: for Holl, the clown scene was bound to provoke opposition "because it took a kind of sadistic pleasure in working with what is cruel and disgusting," and Karsten believed that the spectators protested "because the nerves of people who in any case were already irritated were trampled about on with a brutality that had something downright sadistic about it."[93] Brecht's aim was not to unsettle so many audience members for his own sadistic pleasure, but rather to unsettle them into considering human relations in a different and unaccustomed light. Yet the incongruity through which he accomplished this with the clown scene was too stark for many of the spectators—as Strobel put it, "Sensitive souls, who value death only as a tenor-singing savior, took exception to the distressing realism."[94] No doubt those spectators who found the grotesque dismemberment "distressing in the extreme" were too overwhelmed by the scene's visceral impact to consider what Brecht wished them to take from it.[95] Those who did reflect on the implications of Herr Schmitt's ill-treatment might well have reached conflicting conclusions; as Jan Needle and Peter Thomson write: "Whether or not this was intended to be a parable about the danger for the masses of *accepting* piecemeal alleviation for their plight or a warning against the *offering* of such alleviation in the first place is not clear."[96]

How the *Lehrstück* as a whole should be interpreted was a vexed question in 1929 and has remained that way, especially because Brecht and Hindemith held different views about the piece they had collaborated on, and because Brecht soon reworked his version, and over the years represented its meaning in various ways. But the contemporary critics who objected to the *Lehrstück* almost all considered it politically tendentious, and no doubt many other spectators regarded the piece, and felt threatened by it, in the same light. Holl stated quite flatly that Brecht and Hindemith were "preaching a radical socialist world view." He speculated that the reaction to the clown scene resulted from many spectators' discerning this orientation: "It may be that a good number of the protesters only reacted with whistling and shouting because they sensed the 'devil,' and wanted to repulse an alien doctrine."[97] This echoes the comment made thirty years earlier in connection with Hauptmann's *Before Sunrise*, comparing the first audience's "dull feeling" of discomfort to "the fine sense of smell of a hunting-dog." For neither the first nor last time, Brecht's work was labeled bolshevist: Karsten described the *Lehrstück* as "absolute bolshevism in the German theater," and another reviewer called the production a "case of artistic bolshevism."[98] Both critics wrote in daily newspapers, but their invective echoed the increasingly effective polemics of the right wing, for whom "cultural bolshevism" (*Kulturbolschewismus*) represented one of the foremost evils of the Weimar Republic. Regarding any off-putting work as threateningly left-wing recalls the association of anything offensive at the time of *Before Sunrise* with socialism. That connection is of course accentuated by Hauptmann's presence in the audience in Baden-Baden, and one critic even indignantly complained about the playwright's reaction to the *Lehrstück*: "Why did Gerhart Hauptmann remain sitting quietly throughout the entire performance without protesting against this disgraceful work?"[99] To have done so, Hauptmann would have had to respond as the protesters at the Freie Bühne did thirty years earlier—by opposing a spectacle that aroused unpleasant feelings and raised uncomfortable questions, rather than thinking about those feelings and questions.

Presumably Hauptmann wished to remain open to experiments such as the one carried out by Brecht with Hindemith, and saw no grounds for protesting against the *Lehrstück* even if he himself found it flawed or in questionable taste. By 1929, such openness to the views of others was once again dwindling in Weimar Germany, as indicated by some of the more impassioned negative reviews of the *Lehrstück*. The premiere gave rise to ad hominem attacks on both Brecht and those who did not protest against his work. Karsten expressed a contemptuous incomprehension toward the audience members who did not share her response: "what sort of people are these, who not only let themselves be led around like fools by such literary sadists, but even deck them with laurels?"[100] And Bauer, two years after complaining about Brecht's treatment of the Baden-Baden public with *Mahagonny*, this time put her condemnation of the playwright in much stronger terms: "What Herr Brecht really deserves for his sorry effort, unaesthetic, brutal, and sickening in its . . . political tendentiousness, is to be dealt with in a way that can't be described by a journalist."[101] Karsten more explicitly advocates making Brecht pay for his misdeeds, asking how much longer Brecht will be allowed to continue to "spread his artistic revelations among the people," and expressing the wish that the clowns had amputated not Herr Schmitt's limbs, but Brecht's, "in order to render him harmless for good."[102]

Such attacks on an artist would be regarded by most as irresponsible journalism, and the premiere of the *Lehrstück* did in fact lead to an exchange of views about the kind of opinions a critic should and should not voice. Karsten not only expressed her satisfaction over the widespread protests against Brecht and Hindemith's piece, but also wrote that "if Herr Brecht thinks he can abuse the public, then they have the right to rebel against the work."[103] Hans Wilfert sharply criticized this part of her review, regretting "in the name of responsible criticism . . . that a critic should believe herself justified in granting the audience the right to behave poorly."[104] Since she endorsed the audience's protest only after the performance, Karsten interfered far less in this particular instance of reception than did the critics who contributed to the uproar during Brecht's 1926 production of *Baal*. But Karsten's review could do far more damage in the long term. In highlighting her approval of the protest, Wilfert in fact criticized one of the least extreme manifestations of irresponsibility in Karsten's piece. (And many earlier theatergoers who objected to work by Hauptmann, Jarry, and Synge, as well as some judges and magistrates, would have agreed with her statement.) Karsten's journalistic irresponsibility consists far more in her divisive vilification of those members of the public who appreciate work like Brecht's, and her virtual incitement of physical violence against him. In the context of the disintegrating Weimar Republic, reviews like Karsten's took on real political significance. The *Lehrstück* also caused a very definite reaction on the part of the authorities in Baden-Baden, who withdrew their financial support for the festival, which the following year took place in Berlin.

For Klaus-Dieter Krabiel, who has carried out the most detailed examination of the premiere of the *Lehrstück* to date, the scandal it caused was to a considerable degree "calculated," "preprogrammed" by Brecht.[105] By 1929—even more than in 1927—Brecht had no need to cause a sensation. Brecht may well have asserted that the response of spectators who did not take part was unimportant, but clearly through the *Lehrstück* he conducted a dual experiment—first in theater which involves the audience as participants, second in theater which provokes through its stark depiction of death and inhumanity. According to Krabiel, the strategies for altering the relationship of theater and spectators that Brecht was exploring in the late 1920s included aiming to divide the audience, and he certainly accomplished that with the *Lehrstück*. As one of the reviewers who commented on this put it: "this piece provokes an intellectual separation; one is simply forced to take a position toward it, to say Yes or No."[106] It is in the nature of theater scandals that the performance should cause segmentation of the audience into two or more groups, but in various respects the protests generated by the *Lehrstück* and by much of Brecht's work stand out. He contrived affronts to the spectators' sensibilities deliberately and with definite ideas in mind. By devising provocative pieces Brecht functioned not simply as the playwright who provided the material, but also as a director, developing a performance through collaboration; and each scandal, rather than remaining an isolated incident, formed part of an ongoing experiment.

Following the sensational single performance of the *Mahagonny Songspiel* in summer 1927, Brecht and Weill, in collaboration with Neher, developed the six songs into a full-length opera, *The Rise and Fall of the City of Mahagonny (Aufstieg und Fall der Stadt Mahagonny)*. To the material from the *Songspiel* Brecht added new songs based on poems he had previously written or on drafts for other unfinished projects. The *Songspiel* had neither a real plot nor distinct characters; Brecht gave the opera both. The six original songs were integrated into a sequence of twenty scenes which tell the story of Mahagonny, a "web-city" founded near America's gold coast to attract people by offering all the pleasures they might desire. The city faces ruin once its customers become disenchanted, and then faces destruction by a hurricane. As the storm approaches, Jimmy Mahoney (later renamed Johann, Hans, or Paul Ackermann) realizes that there ought not to be any prohibitions, and once the hurricane has passed leaving the city unharmed, Mahagonny is reborn as the place where one may do anything one likes. However, those who enjoy the unlimited pleasures available in Mahagonny must still buy them, and when Jimmy cannot pay for a round of drinks, and no one else will pay for him, he is arrested and subsequently executed—"For lack of money / Which is the greatest crime / That occurs on earth." Jimmy's final realization of the city's failure to bring satisfaction—"The joy I bought was no joy, and the freedom I got for my money was no freedom"[107]—appears to be confirmed in the closing scene, in which several competing groups of demonstrators parade around, with Mahagonny in flames in the background.

The Threepenny Opera was designed to be performed by actors rather than opera singers, as much of its music was accessible, some of it infectious. Brecht and Weill had written it quickly in order to take advantage of Aufricht's offer to inaugurate his theater. *The Rise and Fall of the City of Mahagonny*, which the pair worked on intermittently for three years beginning in spring 1927, better reflects both the preoccupations and aims of the two men and the artistic climate of which they were part. Beginning in the mid-1920s, opera houses throughout Germany produced new work which strove to push opera beyond its well-established boundaries. Alban Berg's *Wozzeck*, premiered in December 1925, is one celebrated example, and Ernst Krenek's *Jonny strikes up* (*Jonny spielt auf*) is another. These were the first of a number of successful *Jazz-* and *Zeitoper*—operas that told stories set in the contemporary world of train stations and factories, often featuring music heavily influenced by American jazz. *Jonny* was first produced in Leipzig in February 1927, directed by Otto Klemperer, who later that year took over the Kroll-Oper in Berlin. The Kroll soon became the outstanding venue for experimentation in opera, through its interpretations of classics as well as through its productions of new work. Opera in general and the Kroll in particular were among the primary beneficiaries of Prussia's and Berlin's generous support of the arts during this, the most prosperous period of the Weimar Republic. Klemperer had liked *Mahagonny Songspiel* and other music by Weill, so Brecht and Weill justifiably imagined that their opera would be produced at the Kroll. But they did not complete *Mahagonny* until April 1929, by which time a new economic crisis had set in, bringing with it diminished audiences and less openness to challenging work, and later that year Klemperer decided against a production, on account of the work's "crassness."[108]

Klemperer's criticism is striking in one of the leading figures in Weimar-era innovation, but also understandable. *Mahagonny Songspiel* had evoked a world of dissipation and immorality; the opera depicted that world at length and in detail. The refrain which states the principles of life in Mahagonny, first sung about halfway through and often reprised, runs:

First, don't forget, comes eating,
Second comes love,
Third we mustn't forget boxing,
Fourth boozing as long as you can.[109]

Such are the activities to which the characters devote their time. And far from merely confronting the spectators with episodes revolving around debauchery and abandon, *Mahagonny* urged them to ponder what they were watching and listening to. Repeatedly the text makes general statements about people and societies, underlining the implied representative quality of this made-up city and its story: "For what all men lust after is / To not suffer and to be able to do anything,"; "Money makes you sensual,"; "Just how terrifying is a typhoon / Compared to a person who wants to enjoy himself?"; and so on. And the introduction to the penultimate scene even more directly exhorts the audience to reflect: "Many of you may not like seeing the following execution of Jimmy Mahoney. But in our opinion you too, sir, would not want to pay for him. So great is the regard for money in our time."[110]

The departure of Otto Klemperer had not ended the Leipzig Opera House's commitment to an adventurous program, and his successor Gustav Brecher boldly agreed to stage *Mahagonny*; but Klemperer's trepidation over a production at the Kroll at a time when he could not afford to alienate his dwindling audience was borne out by a tumultuous scandal. The Austrian critic Alfred Polgar wrote the most detailed and evocative description of that acrimonious evening:

Here, there, above, below in the electrically charged auditorium dissent flared up, dissent woke up more dissent, which for its part awoke dissent to the power of three. . . . War cries, in a few places a little hand-to-hand combat, hissing, clapping which sounded grimly like symbolic slaps in the face for the hissers, enthusiastic rage and enraged enthusiasm mixed up together. At the end: *levée en masse* of the malcontents, smashed down by the hail of applause.[111]

Klaus Pringsheim described the spectators as "terribly worked up, inflamed with anger, in a passionate fury," and noted in particular the protests of the female audience members: "Young and old Saxon women yelled '*Pfui*' and 'Stop it' before the end, some of them even '*Pfui Teufel*'."[112] The protests intensified in the course of the performance. Some accounts report spectators leaving the theater, but it appears that most of those who objected to the performance preferred to remain and express themselves.

It was widely agreed among the reviewers that the scandal over *Mahagonny* was entirely to be expected: as Eberhard Preußner wrote, "Mahagonny is no kind of opera for the subscribing audience; it is impossible for them to like it."[113] Others considered the piece's departure from established norms as more radical still: for Pringsheim, "This opera, which only pretends to be one, is an attempt, not at renovation, but at abolition of the art form of opera."[114] More recently, Weill biographer Ronald Sanders has argued that *Mahagonny* "really *is* opera in every sense of the word: two and a half hours of continuous recitative, arioso, aria, and ensemble."[115] Sanders is correct in underlining *Mahagonny*'s formal and structural resemblance to other opera, but Pringsheim's notion that Brecht and Weill disguised their piece as opera in order to attack the institution of opera from inside was valid also, especially as concerns Brecht's motivation. As

Preußner reasoned, while the new work may technically have constituted an opera, it differed so much from standard fare that it could not appeal even to committed operagoers. Then as now, opera attracts a specialized audience, whose horizon of expectations is particularly well defined. *The Threepenny Opera* debuted in a Berlin theater before spectators who if anything anticipated a less accessible piece than it turned out to be, and were quickly won over by the enjoyable songs. The patrons of the Leipzig Opera House brought with them expectations which, though expanded by the innovations of the 1920s, nonetheless would not easily accommodate *Mahagonny*'s combined challenge of sophisticated music and political content. The reception of the opera thus repeated on a larger scale the response to the *Songspiel* in Baden-Baden, where an elite audience had also found Brecht and Weill's piece off-puttingly extreme even in a festival devoted to innovative work. The significance of audience composition and context to the initial reception of the *Mahagonny* opera was confirmed by its success in Berlin two years later when performed at the same theater that had premiered *The Threepenny Opera*.

If Brecht and Weill had made it too easy for the audience to ignore the ideas communicated in *The Threepenny Opera*, with *Mahagonny* they went so far in the opposite direction that the audience misinterpreted the piece's political thrust as more extreme than it actually was. As with the *Lehrstück* the previous summer, Brecht aimed to compel the audience to react. As Preußner put it, "The audience is asked to do without pleasure, no longer to leave their everyday concerns outside, but to bring them into the opera house with them. *Mahagonny* demands that one take a position, not through its artistic form but through its content."[116] Pringsheim wrote more specifically about what that content suggested to the Leipzig operagoers, characterizing Brecht's intention as "with each word to tear down a piece of bourgeois heaven, with each step so to speak to kick bourgeois society in the facade." He also correctly stresses that *Mahagonny* does not amount to communist propaganda, though he believes that the protesters did regard it that way more and more as the performance proceeded, culminating in the closing demonstration which made it explicit, when, "relieving them like an overdue sneeze, their honest indignation broke out as the impudent Bolshevik finally showed his true colors."[117] To regard the closing moments as a communist demonstration is actually to misunderstand Brecht and Weill's work, though some critics as well as spectators did so. As Weill later wrote later in connection with a production in Cassel, "It is made clear that the final demonstrations are in no wise 'Communistic'—it is simply that Mahagonny, like Sodom and Gomorrah, falls on account of the crimes, the licentiousness and the general confusion of its inhabitants."[118] While the Leipzig production may not have made this point quite so clear, it is undeniably there in the text: far from demanding a change to a communist social system, the demonstrators' banners reflect, as the scene's heading indicates, "increasing confusion, rising prices, and hostility of everyone toward everyone else."[119] Spectators and critics mistakenly read *Mahagonny*'s critique of capitalism as communist propaganda.

The Weimar Republic's deteriorating political climate in 1930 made narrowly political interpretations of art all the more common and likely. After the Wall Street Crash in October 1929 had brought an end to Germany's economic recovery, the political climate in the Weimar Republic had become more polarized than ever. While the parties of the center failed to command respect or votes, tensions increased between radical groups on the right and left. Polgar's account of the scandal includes some description of the mood he discerned in the auditorium before the performance of *Mahagonny* began: "Already at the beginning of what was to become a stormy evening, various feelings hung in the air. A tension, an unease you could sense in advance, the sound of people straightening out their passions. . . . It also smelled strongly of displeasure that had been brought along and was waiting to be triggered."[120] At any time, the patrons of an institution such as the Leipzig Opera House—even more so than the kind of people who would sit in uncomfortable seats to hear experimental music in Baden-Baden—would have approached a work by Brecht with some apprehension, given his reputation. The success of *The Threepenny Opera* had not altered the widespread conception of Brecht as a writer who appeared to court controversy by challenging conventional forms of art, and often doing so with an apparently subversive political agenda. An article in the Nazi-led *Zeitschrift für Musik* celebrated the outcry over *Mahagonny* by contrasting it with the success of *The Threepenny Opera*. The piece acknowledged that the later work was "by no means substantially nastier," but exclaimed with satisfaction—and with a clear allusion to the opera's focus on *dürfen*, what one may or may not do—"But what you were still permitted to do in 1928, you are no longer permitted to do in 1930!" The editorial depicts the evening as a "people's court" whose verdict would lead to "a decisive change in the status of Herr Brecht's filth-poetry." Ordinary Germans had nobly defended themselves against the assaults of contemporary art: "But what exactly is behind this theater battle? The point is that part of the audience—for the moment still the smaller proportion—took matters in its own hands, had to do so, because it saw that the dignity and reputation of art is being betrayed and walked all over, first by a modern and influential metropolitan press which unscrupulously praises even the most appalling works, but second by the art authorities of towns and even of the state."[121] The Nazi periodical's effort to represent the protests against *Mahagonny* as a spontaneous demonstration is, however, contradicted not only by Polgar's perceptions, but more tellingly still by other reports to the effect that the performance led to "organized demonstrations of disapproval by swastika-wearers and hooligans clad in black, white and red, who had been paid as a claque by men behind them with plenty of capital."[122] It is certainly quite plausible that the Nazis might have bought whole blocks of seats in order to ensure sufficient numbers to create a resounding disturbance.[123] And Lenya wrote, "I have been told that the square around the opera house was filled with Nazi Brown Shirts, carrying placards protesting the *Mahagonny* performance."[124] In 1923, the National Socialists had tried to exploit *In the Jungle* in the same way, but their success was limited, and did not last because of the economic upturn. Seven years later they could tell they had the wind behind them once again: the climate was much better suited to the right-wing's efforts to win supporters, and votes, with this kind of attack on cultural institutions.

Critic and satirist Kurt Tucholsky—writing under one of his many pseudonyms—offered some trenchant remarks about protests against Brecht's work. He divided contemporary theater and opera into work which pleased conservative Germans through its reassuring familiarity, and another strain against which they protested: "The other is for them simply anything new, everything they abhor: socialism, Jews, Russia, pacifism, the abolition of paragraph 218 [a law prohibiting abortion], disruption of their morals and disruption of business and of the common folk . . . *Pfui!* Disgraceful! Stop it!" Tucholsky then underlined the role played in such protests by the Nazis: "these throwers of stink-bombs operate against anything that seems strange to them and anything not written by a member of the party." Yet he also maintained that the significance of such conflicts was minimal, that shouting against or cheering for Brecht's work was not "a substitute for political struggle," since "It doesn't make fewer people unemployed."[125] On that point Tucholsky may well have been wrong. The *Zeitschrift für Musik* ended its editorial by saying that it remained to be seen what direct consequences the Leipzig scandal would have; in fact, the immediate consequence was that a nationalist member of the Leipzig city council tried to have *Mahagonny* withdrawn immediately from the opera house's program, and did succeed in delaying the second performance. According to Lenya, that performance "was played with the house lights on and police lining the walls of the theatre."[126] Altogether the Leipzig production received only five performances but a lot of press coverage, and several other German opera houses dropped Brecht and Weill's controversial work from their programs. Only three other cities dared to stage *Mahagonny* in 1930, albeit in a somewhat shortened version, and while the production in Cassel met with no significant opposition, National Socialists disrupted performances in Braunschweig and Frankfurt. The editors of the *Zeitschrift für Musik* could thus gloatingly declare that "March 9 surely represents, in and beyond Leipzig, a Day of Awareness of the first order; the golden age for pimp poets is over!"[127]

The Rise and Fall of the City of Mahagonny was a particularly important work in the development of Brecht's distinctive approach to theater—what since 1926 he had been calling Epic Theater. Because he and Weill wrote the opera over a period of three years, during which they completed, together or separately, several other pieces including *The Three-penny Opera* and *Lindbergh's Flight*, *Mahagonny* represents perhaps the most emblematic Weimar-era realization of Brecht's theoretical ideas. The notes he (along with publisher Peter Suhrkamp) wrote on the opera in 1930 contain some of his best-known programmatic statements about Epic Theater, including the list of "shifts of emphasis" from the dramatic to the epic form of theater. According to that list, whereas the dramatic theater "wears out the spectator's capacity for action," the Epic Theater "awakens his capacity for action"; in Leipzig, most of the audience was aroused to action—but only to action directed against the performance. And in the same essay Brecht wrote eagerly about the new stance which he believed could be promoted in the operagoing public by applying the methods of his Epic Theater: "by allowing the spectator to as it were cast his vote instead of experiencing something, by getting him to look closely at something instead of putting himself into it, a change is launched which goes far beyond formal matters and begins for the first time to affect the actual, social function of theater."[128] Certainly the first-night audience members found they were not able simply to have an experience through the work by getting caught up in it, and they reacted so forcefully against it partly because they felt it was not carrying out opera's customary function. But their response was not thoughtful, as Brecht had intended; if they voted, they simply voted against a performance which contradicted their aesthetic and political expectations. Brecht's Epic Theater techniques had succeeded in preventing the spectators from responding to *Mahagonny* as they would have to a conventional opera, but failed to compel them to adopt the stance he wished to introduce into the theater.

Brecht did offer his own analysis of the reception of *Mahagonny* in relation to the response he aimed to elicit. In a note in the program for the Berlin premiere in December 1931, Brecht focused on what he believed was one of the "primitive misunderstandings" behind the opposition that the opera had by then prompted in several cities: the idea that "the work was thus in favor of excesses being available as widely as possible for nothing, that it was therefore *in favor of* excesses," when its actual aim was "precisely to demonstrate the connection between the purchasability of pleasure (entertainment, relaxation) and its excessive character."[129] In that context, Brecht may have been trying to forestall a further scandal in Berlin; elsewhere he represented the opposition in an almost favorable light. In the notes he wrote shortly after the Leipzig premiere, he maintained:

As for the content of this opera—*its content is enjoyment*. That is, fun not only as form but as subject-matter. Pleasure . . . appears here in its current historical role: as merchandise.

It is undeniable that this content must initially have a provocative effect.

According to Brecht's interpretation of the reaction to his own work, *Mahagonny* was bound to provoke because, unlike most operas, it does not merely provide enjoyment, but analyzes enjoyment from a sociological perspective, and in doing so points to the unequal distribution of pleasure. He discusses the example of "The Guzzler," the glutton who eats himself to death, arguing that "His enjoyment provokes, because it contains so much"[130]—that is, the glutton's death raises the question of why some people die of hunger while others have too much to eat.

Yet Brecht's analysis amounts to wishful thinking. In a footnote he quotes without commentary a few sentences of Polgar's review: "A dignified gentleman with an empurpled face had pulled out a bunch of keys and fought penetratingly against the Epic Theater. His wife didn't desert him in this decisive moment. The lady had stuck two fingers in her mouth, screwed up her eyes and blown out her cheeks. She whistled more loudly than he did with the key of the safe."[131] Brecht implies that this passage corroborates his contention that the glutton's enjoyment "provokes because it contains so much"; but there is no evidence that the couple Polgar described were responding to the multiple meanings they perceived in the events on stage. On the contrary, such a vehement protest suggests an all too simple rather than a complex reaction. Brecht's later reflection on the first-night response probably comes closer to the truth: *Mahagonny* provoked the spectators because they mistakenly believed it was celebrating the distasteful excesses it depicted, and not because they recognized the sociological implications of that behavior. Polgar's own thoughts about the couple were more perceptive than Brecht's seem to have been: he wrote that the man's whistling "had something merciless about it, something which cut into one's stomach," and the passage Brecht quoted goes on, "A dreadful, nasty sight."[132] Polgar portrays the husband and wife as exemplars of those privileged members of society whose resistance to aesthetically and politically challenging art expressed itself in the form of an almost manic hatred—the kind of hatred which, in these fateful years, the Nazis were fostering and exploiting. Decades later, Carl Zuckmayer commented regretfully on the reaction of German intellectuals such as himself and Brecht to the political climate of the early 1930s: "During those last years before the end of the Weimar Republic, most of us lived like farmers who make hay or cut crops while storm clouds gather on the horizon. . . . In the period before the power to act was taken from us, did we do enough to change our destiny? I don't think so."[133] While one cannot of course hold Brecht individually responsible for the Nazis' rise to power, it is difficult not to wish he had given more serious consideration during these critical years to the full significance of protests like that aroused in 1930 by *Mahagonny*.

In December 1931 *The Rise and Fall of the City of Mahagonny* finally reached the stage in Berlin, and far from causing another scandal, became quite a hit. Produced by Aufricht in the Theater am Kurfürstendamm rather than an opera house, and performed by actors instead of singers, the Berlin *Mahagonny* had more in common with *The Threepenny Opera*, the popular theatrical hit of 1928, than with *Mahagonny*, the controversial avant-garde opera of 1930. One critic wrote that "the whole work in its present form gives the impression of a big cabaret-style revue."[134] And by the end of 1931, the Great Depression had plunged Germany into its own crisis of mounting unemployment and inflation, which threw an altogether different light on the story of Brecht's Mahagonny. The critics declared that the work had been overtaken by events; as one of them put it: "Times are much more revolutionary and aggressive than Bert Brecht seems to imagine they are. . . . March 1930—how long ago that is already!"[135]

The last production of a Brecht play to provoke a scandal before he went into exile in early 1933 was a revival of *A Man's a Man* (*Mann ist Mann*) directed by Brecht himself at the Staatstheater in Berlin in February 1931. Although the script was no longer new, many of the techniques Brecht adopted for the staging departed so far from conventional practice and even from his own previous experiments as to make this in some respects a premiere. Ihering began his review by comparing it with the 1926 production of *Baal*, for which Brecht likewise returned to and revised one of his previously staged plays, though the "experiment in direction and acting" that he carried out with *A Man's a Man* was "more thoroughgoing and more radical" than his modified version of *Baal*.[136]

A Man's a Man had first been produced in September 1926, and despite some mild protests during the simultaneous premieres in Darmstadt and Düsseldorf, it went on to become one of Brecht's most successful plays of the period; by 1930 about a dozen German theaters had staged *A Man's a Man*. But the 1931 production caused controversy in the theater even before it opened. Brecht's co-director Ernst Legal withdrew from the project shortly before the premiere, and the program listed no director at all; it did include an article by Emil Burri, who had also collaborated on the production with Brecht, which reported that "A few times during the rehearsals for *A Man's a Man* there were disagreements about matters of principle between the actors and the director."[137] It was with the acting that Brecht experimented most determinedly, encountering considerable resistance from the cast and finally leading Legal to dissociate himself from the strange results.

The subtitle to *A Man's a Man* reads "The transformation of the porter Galy Gay in the military barracks of Kilkoa in the year nineteen hundred and twenty-five."[138] The setting is a Kipling-inspired but fantastical colonial India. Galy Gay is "a man who cannot say no," and who therefore lends himself perfectly to the scheme of three British soldiers he encounters.[139] The fourth man in their squad, Jeraiah Jip, gets trapped inside a temple during their attempt to loot it, and if he is still missing at roll call, they will have to answer to the fearsome Sergeant Fairchild, so they need a substitute. Galy Gay shows himself to be the perfect scapegoat when, at the vague prospect of making some profit from a deal involving an elephant, he insists to his own wife that he is not Galy Gay. With the help of the canteen owner Widow Begbick, the soldiers get the porter to abandon the name and identity of Galy Gay by incriminating him in a fake auction of a fake elephant, leading to a death sentence. They pretend to execute Galy Gay, who on recovering from a faint and finding he is still alive, accepts the identity of Jeraiah Jip and gives the funeral oration for Galy Gay. The army heads off to battle, and Galy Gay eagerly accepts uniform and equipment and joins them. In the original version—the one used in all previous productions—there followed two more scenes among the soldiers, culminating in Galy Gay's single-handed destruction of a fortress. For the 1931 production, Brecht cut those two scenes, so that the play did not end with Galy Gay performing heroics. Brecht had originally designated *A Man's a Man* a comedy; in connection with his Berlin production he called it a parable. The final words in the 1931 version were contained in the last of a series of projected texts: "Deep in remote Tibet lies the mountain fortress of Sir El-Djowr. On behalf of Royal Shell it is captured by the scum, among them the soldier Jeraiah Jip. You have seen that one can use him for whatever one likes. In our time he is used to fight wars."[140]

The most striking visual feature of the 1931 *A Man's a Man* was the grotesque costumes Brecht had used to make the soldiers seem like—in his own words—"especially large and especially broad monsters:"[141] two of the actors walked on stilts in oversized uniforms, the costume of a third was padded, and they wore giant hands, noses, and ears. On a wire across the stage hung a half-curtain, a device Brecht famously employed in many productions, attracted by its capacity to hide some of the stage while keeping the rest of it still visible to the audience; in this instance the wire also provided the actors with something to help them keep their balance. The scenery consisted of only the chairs, tables, poles and sheets necessary to suggest the various settings. One reviewer remarked, "the stage apparatus had been rendered barren by all the machinery, wires and struts, and was enlivened only by Caspar Neher's fantastical pictures."[142] Projections were used both for Neher's drawings and for the texts which preceded most of the scenes. Some parts of the action were accompanied by commentary—

or, according to some accounts, stage directions—read aloud by the stage-manager, and one of the songs was sung from offstage through a megaphone. And the actors had been directed by Brecht to depersonalize their performances by speaking in a monotone: in one reviewer's description, "The actors talk like automata or schoolchildren reciting a poem."[143] The production ended with a striking and memorable image marking Galy Gay's full transformation into the soldier Jeraiah Jip: Peter Lorre as Galy Gay reappeared with a whitened face and covered with weapons. As the Russian writer Sergei Tretiakov described it, "there appears at the footlights—with a knife between his teeth, grenades hanging off his tunic, and in a uniform stinking of the filth of the trenches—the shy and demure middle-class fellow of yesterday, today a murdering machine."[144]

The audience responded to this strange performance with growing impatience. One critic reported that "disruptions, whistling, prattling by talkative spectators, and scoffing laughter" set in from the point where the soldiers shoot Galy Gay.[145] Felix Hollaender gave an example of the spectators' verbal interventions during the play's final scenes:

The actor Lorre gives the cue. At one point he has to say, "I want all this to stop." A lady replies from the circle in a quiet, shy voice: "So do we."
   That's the signal, and now the theater scandal begins, brusquely interrupting the performers in the middle of their dialogue right through until the end.[146]

According to most accounts, this adverse reaction primarily took the form of whistling and mocking laughter, but others suggest that at least some of the spectators displayed real anger. Another critic summarized the tumult as "Vehement disruptions which obviously aren't prepared, but do endanger the end of the evening."[147] And Tretiakov evoked the atmosphere through descriptions of audience members: "Women stamped with their heels, lawyers fled the auditorium snorting with rage, throwing crumpled-up programs at the actors as they left."[148] As in many other instances, Ihering gives more weight than most of his colleagues to any favorable reaction, writing that the audience "whistled in the middle, but at the ending showed their appreciation of the piece's intention by applauding," and he is not the only one to mention significant applause.[149] Still, uproar similar to that during opening-night occurred on subsequent evenings, and after only five performances, *A Man's a Man* was withdrawn from the program of the Staatstheater.

The most significant ways in which the first-night audience performed their opposition to Brecht's new production of *A Man's a Man* were through shouting comments back at the stage and through laughter. Bernhard Diebold, writing in the *Frankfurter Zeitung*, analyzed the quality and content of the laughter:

The audience smiles more and more comfortably, without indignation and without anger . . . They enjoy their utter superiority over so much impotence in this poetic work's second manifestation—and its "epic" direction. . . .

Oh yes they laugh. The bit of whistling and clapping get lost in the gentleness of the laughter.[150]

These remarks apply also to the verbal interruptions, through which the spectators clearly expressed not so much rage or even annoyance as a less impassioned wish to demonstrate that the performance no longer absorbed them. Those audience members, similarly to those at Brecht's production of *Baal* at the Junge Bühne, responded in a manner reminiscent of the theatergoers of earlier centuries, who clearly and quickly expressed their opinion of new plays, and when they did not approve frequently shouted out derisory comments. In both contexts the initial form of recreation, watching a prepared performance as a group, in effect gives way to another, participating in a spontaneous, improvised display designed to mock the performance; in many cases, individuals aim to impress or amuse their fellow spectators through their wit. For Diebold, that shift from taking in to laughing at the performance, from watching it to seeing through it, involves a feeling of superiority, a notion which points to a useful way of conceiving of both this and the more hostile kinds of adverse reaction. When spectators—like those at the first night of *A Man's a Man* in 1931 or at the 1926 *Baal*—find a production poor, without finding its shortcomings or its incomprehensibility threatening, they do in a sense feel superior to it. But when—like the first audiences for, in particular, *In the Jungle* in 1923—they are bewildered and unsettled by a production they do not understand, they feel, if not inferiority as such, a distinct absence of that assured sense of superiority. Tretiakov—in contrast with Diebold and most of the other critics—discerned the latter kind of reaction in the opening-night audience for *A Man's a Man*. In his recollections about his contact with Brecht, written a few years later, he commented on the mind-set of the spectators who demonstrated their displeasure:

The intelligent Berlin bourgeois does not go to the theater in order to be disturbed. . . .

He's always above the action or at least on the same level. He cannot grant that suspicious, enigmatic events should occur on stage, events which might possibly offend his solid being.[151]

Tretiakov uses the same spatial image as Diebold while focusing in particular on the audience's experience of the play's action: storytelling that is not transparent discomforts conservative Berlin theatergoers because they do not understand and therefore feel lower than the play. He also proposes that such theatergoers are all the more resistant to what they don't comprehend because they can't be sure it isn't insulting them. Judging from the consensus of the various accounts, Tretiakov's analysis appears less pertinent to the 1931 response to *A Man's a Man* than to the most fervent among the earlier protests against Brecht's work; laughter, rather than angry shouts of *"Pfui!"* characterized the opening-night reception of *A Man's a Man*. For the most part, the spectators at the Staatstheater performed their opposition without really protesting against the play, but rather by giving increasingly free expression to their belief that the production was amusingly bad. The importance of this scandal lies above all in the relationship between the production's failure to hold the audience's attention and Brecht's aims, which he formulated in some detail in response to the reviews.

The critics' response to Brecht's production echoed that of the first-night audience. Several expressed sympathy for the actors, whom they did not hold responsible—"victims not of the laughing audience, but of the epic director and his blindly knocked-together literary work."[152] Ihering, as ever predisposed to find value in Brecht's work, felt that some of the actors did succeed in delivering the lines as Brecht wished, whereas others were miscast. He praised Helene Weigel, who played Begbick, because she "spoke in a relaxed manner, endearingly, and in a meticulous performance which at the same time conveyed the essence of the text with clarity," but argued that Lorre lacked precisely what the role required—"comprehensibility, clarity, and the capacity to speak in a way that illustrates and explains."[153] The laughter from the auditorium might suggest that some spectators found Lorre's strange rendition of Galy Gay amusing—but clearly most of that laughter was derisive, and more than one critic commented on the absence of humor from Lorre's performance.

Brecht responded unusually directly to the critics' judgment of the acting in his production of *A Man's a Man*. In a letter he wrote to a Berlin newspaper in March 1931, he explained why in his opinion Peter Lorre's lead performance, which had come in for a great deal of criticism, was exemplary. Brecht first mentions that "Presumably the objection to his way of speaking applied less to the first part of the play than to the second, with its long speeches." The timing of the most substantial protests by spectators shows that they as well as the critics found those passages least engaging. Brecht explained that "The content of the speeches consisted of contradictions, and the actor had to try, rather than getting the spectator caught up in contradictions himself by identifying with individual sentences, to *keep him out of them*." To this end, "Certain particularly significant sentences were therefore 'highlighted,' i.e., loudly called out."[154] The examples Brecht gave of such lines include "I want all this to stop!", but clearly the first-night spectator who responded out loud to that line was not expressing her considered opinion of the carefully communicated contradictions. By speaking the lines as Brecht had asked him to, namely in a monotone except for certain key sentences which he declaimed, Lorre had indeed ensured that the spectators did not become caught up in the contradictions of the speeches, but he had gone too far in the other direction: he kept the audience so far out that they took less and less interest in the text.

The second of the two main objections to Lorre's performance discussed by Brecht is "that he only acted episodes." Just as Brecht had Lorre separate out individual sentences, he approached the entire part of Galy Gay according to the principle that "Since everything depends on the development, on the flow, it must be possible to clearly see the individual phases which therefore must be separated." Brecht underlines the contrast between this and the conventional style of acting: "Unlike the dramatic actor, who has his character from the start and then simply exposes it to the trials and tribulations of the world and of tragedy, the epic actor lets his character come into being before the spectator's eyes through the way it behaves." The marked discrepancy between the purpose of and negative response to Lorre's unusual performance revolves around the connections the spectators did or did not perceive and draw among the deliberately separated sentences and phases. In his discussion of Galy Gay's long speeches, Brecht wrote that "The sentences (sayings) were thus not brought home to the spectator, but distanced from him; the spectator was not led but left to make his own discoveries."[155] As Michael Patterson formulates the intention, "the spectator is not to be spoon-fed by the actor's interpretation but to seek out his own meanings from the clues given by the actor."[156] Clearly the majority of the first-night audience considered Lorre's interpretation of Galy Gay poorly conceived and executed, rather than one which stimulated them to make any discoveries of their own.

Brecht's letter combined forthright defense of his approach and of Lorre's performance—referring to the "truly great" way he delivered one of the long speeches—with far less confident-sounding reflections on the obstacles he faced in carrying out such radical experiments. His main argument in the letter was that the criteria for judging acting need to be changed, that spectators need to learn a different way of responding to actors: "It is fundamental to the social transformation of the theater that the spectator cannot be worked on as much as usual. His interest should not be aroused in the theater, but brought there by him and then satisfied." Regarding the "episodic" charge, Brecht proposed that "An attitude is here required of the spectator which roughly corresponds to the reader's turning back to earlier pages in order to make comparisons." His production of A Man's a Man could only have succeeded with an audience who had already learned this new attitude; given that this audience had not, the effect of Lorre's epic acting was to diminish rather than foster engagement with and appreciation of the text. The fact that the spectators did not disrupt the production until about its last third indicates that this was by no means an unreceptive audience. Brecht in effect recognizes this in not—as he might have done in earlier years—holding the spectators responsible for their own failure to appreciate his efforts. Brecht acknowledged with regret that it did not, yet, come easily to the average theatergoer to understand an actor's performance as he wished them to understand Lorre's, and mused that "It is possible that the epic theater, more than other theater, needs an advance loan in order to show itself to full advantage."[157] He no longer dismissed the failure of his innovations with the too simple argument that this was the wrong audience, nor did he reiterate his earlier conviction that new techniques by themselves could alter the way theater spectators engage with a performance.

Some of the critics saw value in the experiment Brecht had conducted. Ihering, not surprisingly, was one of them: "A test which failed, but which contains unusually rich material for discussion."[158] Willy Haas, though far less well disposed toward Brecht than Ihering, also acknowledged that the playwright and director was exploring interesting themes and techniques, but raised the question, in light of the "highly grotesque and eccentric" results, "whether it belongs in the theater at all, that is whether these experiments aren't, for lack of homogeneous means, just built on castles in the air."[159] Both critics in effect endorse Brecht's own contention that the public needed to learn to watch the kind of theater he experimented with more determinedly in this 1931 production than in perhaps any other. But whereas Ihering seems to consider that such an evolution in theatergoers' habits of spectatorship might well come about, especially if this experiment were discussed as widely as he believed it deserved to be, Haas suggests rather that taking too great a leap in progressing toward a new kind of theater is liable to prove fruitless. In a note in his journal a decade later, Brecht himself acknowledged the less than complete success of his 1931 experiment: "The production of *A Man's a Man* at the Staatstheater in Berlin . . . was not fully developed."[160] How Brecht might have further explored the relationship between acting styles and audience response if the Weimar Republic had lasted beyond 1933, we can only guess.

Throughout the final years of the republic, Brecht did remain one of the most active and prominent figures in the arts, continually carrying out bold experiments and causing widely publicized controversies. In May 1930, the organizers of a Berlin festival of New Music—including Hindemith, Brecht's collaborator the previous summer—refused to include a new *Lehrstück* Brecht had written with Eisler and Slatan Dudow entitled *The Measures Taken* (*Die Maßnahme*) unless they could first inspect the text to assure themselves that its political content was not too extreme. The authors refused, and *The Measures Taken* was not produced until December, with a cast including the Berlin Workers' Choir. That choice reflected

Brecht's determination during this period to introduce his work to seg-
ments of the public other than the predominantly middle- and upper-class
regular theatre- and operagoers. And he followed through on his desire
to find out how the spectators reacted to *The Measures Taken* by having
them fill out questionnaires afterwards. Another experiment with the
Lehrstück form also provided him with interesting data about audience
response: when a Berlin school—pupils, their teacher, and an amateur
orchestra—produced the 'school opera' *He Who Says Yes* (*Der Jasager*) in
June 1931, the response was largely positive, to Brecht's consternation. He
had not seen that performance, but believed his piece had been misinterpreted, and asked another school to produce *He Who Says Yes* for a young
audience. Based on that version and the discussions it generated, Brecht
wrote a second play, *He Who Says No* (*Der Neinsager*), and urged that the
two should always be performed together. One of the few films Brecht
ever worked closely on, *Kuhle Wampe*—developed with director Slatan
Dudow and writer Ernst Ottwalt—caused considerable controversy over
the issue of censorship. Large numbers of workers were involved in shoot-
ing the film (the title is the name of a working-class outlying district of
Berlin), which in March 1932 was banned on the grounds that it defamed
the government and the Church and included references to abortion. This
led to outcry from the communist and left-wing press, and to a declaration
of protest by the German League for Human Rights. At the end of May,
Kuhle Wampe was finally shown, in a substantially edited version.

Brecht carried out his most innovative and revelatory experiments of
the early 1930s first with *A Man's a Man* in 1931 then the following year
with *The Mother* (*Die Mutter*), an adaptation of Gorky's 1905 novel. The
original tells the story of Pelageya Vlassova, a poor worker's widow
whose concern for the welfare of her revolutionary son leads her to learn
about and then involve herself in the activities of a revolutionary group,
until she becomes an outstandingly well-educated and effective participant in the class struggle. Brecht—collaborating on this occasion with Slatan Dudow and Günther Weisenborn—preserved the principal contours
in his version, though eliminating Vlassova's faith in Christianity, and
extending the time period to include the First World War and the November Revolution of 1917. The play, "written in the style of the *Lehrstücke*,"
consists of fourteen scenes of crisp dialogue, introduced with one- or two-
sentence headings and interspersed with songs, several of them sung by
a chorus of revolutionary workers.[161] *The Mother* was produced as a joint
venture involving Aufricht, the communist-oriented Group of Young Actors (Gruppe Junger Schauspieler) and the Junge Volksbühne, a supporters' organization founded by the workers' movement, and the cast
included "members of proletarian agit-prop troupes."[162] The premiere
took place at the Komödienhaus am Schiffbauerdamm; but before the
opening night in January 1932, *The Mother* was performed four times be-

fore invited audiences of factory committee members, and representatives of numerous women's and proletarian groups. On the basis of these spectators' comments, Brecht and his collaborators continually changed the text and the production. After more than thirty performances in two commercial theaters in Berlin, this deliberately portable production—Neher had designed a very simple set with canvas stretched over a metal frame, plus a screen for projections (according to Weigel, who played Vlassova, it could all fit in a small car[163])—was taken into the rest of the city and performed with some success in various workers' meeting places. In February the police tried to prohibit one production in the Moabit district on the basis of fire regulations; the cast gave a reading of the play, which reportedly met with an even more enthusiastic response than had the full stagings. Brecht later claimed that "Around 15,000 working-class Berlin women saw a performance of the play."[164] Yet in the prevailing circumstances of frequent and often deadly street battles between Nazis and communists, and given Hitler's increasing political power, it soon became unfeasible to continue the performances.

In defending his poorly received staging of *A Man's a Man*, Brecht had focused his attention on explaining Peter Lorre's experiment in epic acting, without discussing his wife Weigel's, though Ihering was not alone in finding her performance effective. According to Weigel, Brecht did not think highly of her acting until she played the lead in *The Mother*.[165] By performing that role in a production that proved effective with its audiences and thus seemed to endorse Brecht's theatrical ideas, Weigel provided Brecht with a far better model of epic acting than had Lorre's Galy Gay. In the notes Brecht wrote shortly after the production of *The Mother*, he explained that an epic actor will "do all he can to make himself observed standing *between* the spectator and the event," then described how Weigel had accomplished this, most significantly in her manner of introducing the character:

In the first scene, the actress took up a particular characteristic posture in the middle of the stage, and spoke the sentences as if they were actually written in the third person; not only did she not pretend to be Vlassova in reality, or to take herself for her and to speak these sentences in reality, but she even prevented the spectators from imagining themselves, out of thoughtlessness and old habits, to be in a particular room.[166]

For Brecht the composition of *The Mother*—as a full-length application of techniques derived from the *Lehrstücke*—supported by Weigel's exemplary acting, made this production one of the most satisfying of the interwar years. In his writings about it afterwards, he underlined the piece's Marxist underpinnings and its primary interest in reaching a working-class audience, whom it aimed to "teach certain forms of political struggle."[167] His observation of different spectators' reactions made him almost gleeful at the production's apparent confirmation that the right kind of theater could truly speak to a working-class audience:

Where the workers reacted immediately to the subtlest twists in the dialogue and easily embraced the most complicated assumptions, the bourgeois audience had trouble following the course of the story and didn't grasp its essence at all. The worker . . . was not for a moment put off by the extremely terse and dry way in which the various situations were outlined . . . The West-ender sat there with a bored smile whose stupidity looked positively comical.[168]

The Reichstag fire in February 1933 forced Brecht to flee Berlin, and brutally interrupted the theatrical experiments he was conducting with particular commitment and energy during the Weimar Republic's final years. During the fifteen-year exile that ensued, Brecht was never able to work in a sustained way within the theatrical environment of a single city or country. In 1948, shortly before Brecht and Weigel returned to Germany, she suggested that he bring together his theoretical ideas in a single essay, in preparation for the work they hoped to resume in Berlin. The result was the *Short Organon for the Theater* (*Kleines Organon für das Theater*). In the prologue, Brecht refers to "the accumulated innovations from the Nazi period and the war, when practical demonstration was impossible."[169] It was not until the following year when he and Weigel founded the Berliner Ensemble that Brecht could again carry out the kind of "practical demonstration" he had in mind. This was especially unfortunate for someone whose work depended so much on practice: Brecht was never the kind of dramatist who wrote scripts which he then handed over to director and actors, but a man of the theater who took even more interest in how best to perform a scene than he did in how best to word its dialogue. The fact that for fifteen years Brecht seldom had the opportunity to work firsthand and at length on productions also contributed to the widespread perception of Brecht as the advocate of certain theoretical notions about the theater, rather than as a playwright and director. His 1937 piece "A short list of the most popular, common, and banal misconceptions about the Epic Theater" begins

1. It is an ingenious, abstract, intellectualistic theory which has nothing to do with real life.
(In reality it arose from and is associated with many years of practical activity. . . .)[170]

With the Berliner Ensemble Brecht could finally focus on the practical activity, and during the seven years up to his death in 1956, as they mounted the productions which made him and the company internationally admired and influential, Brecht and the actors he worked with seldom mentioned theory in the rehearsal process.

When Brecht wrote about his Weimar-era work during his exile, he implied that the reception of that work had been much more favorable than was in fact the case. In the summary of his prewar activity which follows the passage quoted from "A short list," Brecht mentions no adverse response other than to state that "A few plays were banned by the police."[171] Surely the uproar in the auditorium which led to such prohibition—scandalized spectators yelling "*Pfui!*" or mocking the performance through laughter—is more significant than the bans themselves. Brecht's voluminous writings on the theater, including those unpublished during his lifetime, fill five volumes of his collected works, yet both during and after the Weimar era, he wrote remarkably little on the subject of hostile audience response. It is striking that a theater practitioner as interested as Brecht was in how theater spectators react to performances should have never developed a precise theoretical orientation toward the kind of impassioned demonstrations many of his Weimar-era productions had generated.

Yet there can be no question that his prewar experience contributed to the later evolution of his ideas. Just as practical exploration in relation to each new production interested Brecht more than did the idea of applying previously formulated theoretical propositions, the practical experience he gained from the Weimar years, rather than any theory based on them, provided the basis for his later experiments with audience response. The fact that scandals comparable to those of the Weimar period never occurred after 1933 at least suggests that, whether he said as much or not, the Brecht of the exile and East Berlin years aimed to avoid rather than provoke audience protests. The many and varied productions on which Brecht collaborated in Germany between 1922 and 1932 served as a testing ground, a series of experiments through which he explored the nature and possibilities of audience response in the theater, and which led him gradually to revise his notions about how best to engage the spectators.

In the *Short Organon*, Brecht described the effect that conventional theater has on its audience: "these people seem relieved of all activity and look as if something is being done to them."[172] With his early works, Brecht had certainly often succeeded in making the spectators active, yet the form which their activity took was not always desirable or productive. The young Brecht was not overly concerned about this, and well aware that controversy and scandal helped him to make his name. But once he had established himself, and more importantly once he had begun to see the world through the lens of Marxism, the question of exactly how the audience responds to theater became the primary focus of his work, practical and theoretical. I have traced the gradual refinement of Brecht's position in the course of the various Weimar-era productions: from his dismissal of public resistance to *In the Jungle* and *Baal* to his calculated experiments with provocation in *Mahagonny Songspiel* and later the *Lehrstück*; from his reflections on the disappointing success of *The Threepenny Opera* to his probable awareness that he had not in fact prompted the spectators of *The Rise and Fall of the City of Mahagonny* to cast a vote in the way he intended; from his argument in relation to *A Man's a Man* that new criteria needed to be developed for the judgment of acting to his delighted observation of workers' response to *The Mother*. By 1933 he had first-hand experience of the two extremes of response whereby an audience might fail to perceive and understand his work in the way he wanted them to: *The Threepenny Opera* had proven so entertaining that the spectators had not recognized its social critique, whereas his 1931 production of *A Man's a Man* had made it so difficult for the audience to become engaged by the events on stage that they too had not seen in it what Brecht had hoped they would. In the 1933 notes to *The Mother*, Brecht characterized that play's "anti-metaphysical, materialistic, *non-aristotelian*" type of drama thus: "Endeavoring to teach its spectator a quite distinct practical mode of behavior aimed at changing the world, it must begin by having him adopt a fundamentally different attitude than he is used to."[173] So it was in connection with his last and probably most satisfying prewar production that Brecht best formulated the objective he would spend the rest of his life striving to accomplish. During and after his exile, Brecht weighed the response he wished to prompt in the audience far more carefully against the reaction he could reasonably expect than he had prior to 1933.

Brecht specified in the *Short Organon* that the "productive attitude toward nature and toward society" he wishes the audience to adopt is "a critical one."[174] Generating that critical attitude was Brecht's aim from the very start of his career, as indicated already by the 1922 diary entry about avoiding other theater's "effort to carry people away with it" in his first plays. But as he grew older and accumulated more experience, Brecht realized that spectators cannot be coerced into adopting such an attitude, but must be led toward it by a performance which also takes account of inescapable psychological inclinations. Brecht's suggestion that the premiere production of *Drums in the Night* in 1922 should incorporate placards displaying sentences including "Don't gawp so romantically!" encapsulates his youthful notion of how best to influence the audience's reception of his work. And even ten years later, in the notes to his far more thoughtful production of *The Mother*, Brecht mentions that "In order to combat the 'immersion' of the spectators and 'free' association, small choruses can be placed in the auditorium to demonstrate for them the correct attitude."[175] But that was an exceptionally extreme proposal, echoing to some extent the overly bold experimentation of his staging of *A Man's a Man* a year earlier. For the most part, from that production on, Brecht focused his attention not on how to cajole the audience into the desired attitude, but how to bring that response about through sensitive and detailed employment of the multiple factors which contribute to spectators' reactions. The closing lines of one of Brecht's best-known plays, *The Good Person of Szechwan* (*Der gute Mensch von Sezuan*) probably constitute his most direct appeal to the audience's own judgment: "Honored public: go and find the conclusion yourself: / There must be a good one around, there must, must, must!"[176] Even when he did not make his intentions so explicit, Brecht wanted the spectators to think along those lines at the end of all his plays and productions, to ponder the questions raised and contradictions depicted by the performance. And the older Brecht got, the more honest he was about his degree of success. A blurb he wrote in 1952 for a collection documenting the Berliner Ensemble's first six productions indicates that still in East Germany after the war, just as during the Weimar Republic, Brecht considered that the public had not learned the attitude he wished them to: "Two arts need to be developed: the art of acting and the art of watching."[177]

The premiere production of *The Mother* in 1931 stands out because it was performed before, and by all accounts very well received by, a working-class audience. Especially from the time of Brecht's engagement with Marxism in the mid-1920s, that remained the audience he most wished to reach and to influence. For some years he believed that one way to accomplish this was by dividing the audience. In the notes to *The Mother* he asserted that whereas aristotelian drama makes the audience into a "collective entity," his non-aristotelian drama "splits its audience."[178] And in theory such division occurred along class lines: in a 1939 essay he asserted that in Weimar-era theatrical experiments conducted by himself, Erwin Piscator, and others, "the performances split the audience up into at least two mutually hostile social groups, so that the common experience of art broke down."[179] But here as elsewhere, Brecht depicts as productive reception which was more often counterproductive. Performances of his work which caused scandals certainly divided the audience into antagonistic groups, but even when that separation did reflect class distinctions, the spectators clearly did not experience it as enlightening. *The Mother* gave Brecht the satisfaction of observing the contrasting responses of middle- and working-class spectators; but he himself explained that such observation was possible because the play had been presented either to bourgeois spectators or to workers—he was never able to describe with equal satisfaction a division within a mixed audience. Then under his severely constrained circumstances during the fifteen years he was away from Germany, it was difficult for Brecht to make any theater at all, let alone to target productions to specific audiences.

When Brecht wrote the *Short Organon* in 1948, he did so in the expectation that he would soon once again be able to include in his preparation of new productions consideration of the particular audience he hoped to reach. Laying out his ideas for the theater he felt was appropriate to the post-war period, his "theater of the scientific age," Brecht characterized working-class spectators as "those who are necessarily most impatient to effect great changes" in society, and underlined how important it was for his theater to pursue such an audience, "so that they can be usefully entertained there with their great problems." He admits that ascertaining how to make theater to suit those people's needs, and budgets, may take some time, but insists that "we can be sure of their interest."[180] But his experience during his final years working with the Berliner Ensemble proved him wrong. As John Willett writes, when Brecht resumed his theatrical activity in Germany in the late 1940s, "he found that the workers were not all that scientific and sceptical any more than they had been under Hitler; and the audience which he demanded was slow to come forward. Apart from the occasional factory performances in its early days, his company played in the centre of Berlin"—not in the suburbs as Brecht had urged in 1948.[181] While he generally called the antithesis of his Epic Theater "dramatic" or "aristotelian," sometimes he used the term "bourgeois theater"; yet most of his work before, during, and after his exile was produced in essentially bourgeois theaters to bourgeois spectators. As Jan Needle and Peter Thomson assert, somewhat overemphatically: "Whether he ever admitted to himself, or recognized, the failure of his attempts to speak theatrically to the class he so admired and so completely misunderstood we will never know. . . . All his later, and great, plays were aimed once more at educating the bourgeois, and his audiences were, inevitably (and still are, even at the Berliner Ensemble's East Berlin home) predominantly middle-class."[182] In East Germany, Brecht was operating within a supposedly post–revolutionary society which ought to have made building a working-class audience relatively straightforward. Instead, his further exploration of how best to reach such an audience mostly took the form of repeated debates and clashes with party officials over his work's compliance with their doctrines.

Another work whose composition was largely contemporaneous with that of *The Mother* was *Round Heads and Pointed Heads* (*Die Rundköpfe und die Spitzköpfe*); but Brecht wrote that this work "unlike *The Mother*, is addressed to a 'wider' public and takes more account of purely entertainment requirements."[183] In thus conceiving more broadly of his target audience and showing greater readiness to make his work enjoyable, Brecht anticipated his subsequent development more than he himself realized. Few of his works after *The Mother* would be so deliberately focused on a particular, socio-economically defined audience. And Brecht's gradual recognition of the necessity to entertain the spectators constitutes one of the most important changes in all his work. By 1948 he ironically alluded to his earlier stance—or to the popular conception of that stance—in the Prologue to the *Short Organon:* "Let us therefore, no doubt to general regret, revoke our decision to emigrate from the realm of the pleasing, and announce, to even more general regret, our intention of henceforth settling down in that realm. Let us treat the theater as a place of entertainment, as is only proper in an aesthetics, and investigate which kind of entertainment appeals to us!" Brecht underlines the magnitude of this change in his standpoint by quoting his own notes to *Mahagonny*, which ended with this formulation of his goal in the late 1920s and early 1930s: "to develop a means of enjoyment into a subject of study and to convert certain institutions from places of pleasure into organs of mass communication."[184] Few of the productions Brecht was involved in during the Weimar period succeeded with a popular audience, and when that did happen it afforded him (besides invaluable financial support) less artistic satisfaction than did the more frequent scandals. Between leaving and returning to Germany, Brecht wrote a dozen or so new dramas and adaptations, among them his most highly-regarded plays. In developing those works, Brecht consistently bore in mind the importance of striking a balance between his own aim of prompting the spectators to adopt a critical attitude, and theatergoers' desire for a pleasurable experience.

While in the post–Weimar period Brecht increasingly acknowledged the necessity of sufficiently entertaining the spectators, he did continue to stress the complementary importance of not absorbing them too much. From at least the mid-1920s, Brecht regarded the arousal of empathy as one of the chief shortcomings of the "dramatic" theater to which he opposed his Epic Theater. In those years of youthful ambition his impassioned hostility toward conventional theater led him to depict empathy as something to be avoided at all costs. In 1926, discussing dramatic characters and how actors portray them he said, "Contrary to present custom, they ought to be presented to the spectators quite coldly, objectively, classically. For they are not matter for empathy; they are there to be understood."[185] Brecht first put this view into practice with a play—as opposed to an opera or other musical work—in his 1931 production of *A Man's a Man*, but the reception provided clear indications that a consistently cold and objective portrayal of character thwarts understanding as much as it does empathy. If his subsequent experiment with the same ideas in *The Mother* succeeded far better, that was perhaps due not only to Weigel's central performance, but also to the staging. Brecht wrote that the projections of texts and images onto an upstage screen in *The Mother* "do not set out to help the spectator, but to oppose him: they thwart his total empathy, interrupt his getting mechanically carried away."[186] The scene titles incorporated into his production of *A Man's a Man*, like those in *The Threepenny Opera* three years earlier, had failed to achieve the same effect. In *The Mother*, Brecht employed in a modified fashion techniques he had already tried, and much of his work after 1933 would similarly entail modulation of previously devised ideas.

Only after he fled Germany did Brecht begin to employ the word *Ver-fremdung* (most often translated, regrettably, as "alienation") to describe the desired result of the acting and staging techniques tried out in his Weimar-era productions. In the *Short Organon* Brecht gives the following succinct definition of *Verfremdung:* "A defamiliarizing depiction is one that does allow us to recognize its subject, but at the same time makes it appear unfamiliar."[187] Brecht had wanted his audiences to experience, for instance, *In the Jungle,* or the clown scene in *Lehrstück* in that way, but instead they had resisted any recognition and found the performances unfamiliar to the point of being repellent to them. With *The Threepenny Opera,* conversely, Brecht's efforts to make the spectators mentally stand back from the piece and consider its implications made little or no difference to their uncritical enjoyment of an entertaining musical. During his exile, Brecht developed his ideas about how best to accomplish *Verfremdung,* paying particular attention to the area of acting, where putting the *V-Effekte* into practice was most difficult. In a 1940 essay, he wrote of the actor who employs the technique of the *Verfremdungseffekt:* "When he appears on the stage, besides what he actually is doing he will at all essential points discover, identify, and suggest something else that he isn't doing."[188] It is far easier to understand this notion in theory—aided by concrete examples such as "The Street Scene"—than to imagine it applied to the portrayal of an actual character in a play, by Brecht or any other dramatist.[189] To some extent, the evolution of Brecht's own work bore this out: once his energy was focused primarily on production at the Berliner Ensemble, he wrote and spoke much less often about *Verfremdung.* Instead he spent weeks on end experimenting in collaboration with many others in pursuit of the most effective way to present a given play.

In other respects also, Brecht's positions on certain issues central to his aesthetic changed somewhat during his exile and then more markedly once he returned to Berlin. From about the mid-1930s on, he became more willing to allow for at least some empathy. In the 1940 essay on acting, he wrote that the actor in his kind of theater "need not, however, renounce the means of empathy entirely," though he only approved its use during rehearsals;[190] and in the *Short Organon* in 1948, he still represented empathy as an outcome to be avoided, but less categorically than in earlier writings. Then once he resumed practical work back in Germany, the reaction of actual, not just hypothetical audiences to the plays he had written during his exile caused him to retreat further from his earlier uncompromising view. *Mother Courage and her Children* in particular confronted Brecht with the magnitude of the challenge facing himself and others producing his work once he created complex, fully rounded characters that elicited a strong emotional as well as psychological response. Brecht complicated matters for himself when in the 1920s and 1930s he overstated his opposition to emotion in the theater. The final line of the list in the

1930 notes to *The Rise and Fall of the City of Mahagonny* reads "Feeling" for the dramatic theater, "Reason" for the Epic Theater, and despite Brecht's efforts to stress that the list showed "merely shifts of accent" and not "absolute antitheses," people treated this as evidence that the theater Brecht advocated would banish emotion altogether in favor of cool rationality.[191] In 1938 when he revised the notes, Brecht removed that line from the list, but by then the damage had been done. Repeatedly during the later 1930s and through until the 1950s Brecht found it necessary to explain that "The epic theater isn't against the emotions; it examines them, and is not satisfied just to generate them," and that Epic Theater "by no means renounces emotions."[192] Even the changes Brecht made to the script of *Mother Courage* did little to prevent spectators within Germany and beyond from being profoundly moved by its central character, whose "inability to learn from the fruitlessness of war" he wanted the audience to see critically.[193] In some of his comments on *Mother Courage* one senses Brecht straining almost despairingly to depict as successful his efforts to stimulate one kind of response, even as he admits that spectators repeatedly responded quite differently. In discussing the scene where Courage's mute daughter risks and eventually causes her own death to save many others' lives, Brecht wrote in 1952: "Spectators may identify themselves with mute Kattrin in this scene; they may via empathy find their way into this person and enjoy feeling that such powers exist in them too—yet they will not have experienced empathy throughout the whole play, hardly in the opening scenes, for instance."[194] By the end of his life Brecht had distanced himself from much of his earlier theory, including the label Epic Theater, and seems to have been moving toward the alternative of Dialectical Theater. That shift is reflected in one of his latest statements about empathy, which suggests that theater practitioners should recognize the inevitability of some degree of empathy and aim to incorporate that into a response conceived of as dialectical: "the most likely result is that truly rending contradiction between experience and portrayal, empathy and demonstration, justification and criticism."[195]

Brecht is sometimes considered an inflexible thinker whose work entails the punctilious application of extreme aesthetic and political theories; in fact, he was always far more interested in practice than theory. While one could trace the development of Brecht's ideas via his gradually changing theoretical pronouncements, it makes more sense to focus on the experiments he carried out, from his first efforts in the early 1920s right up until his death. Those experiments included a great variety of approaches to playwriting as well as to production. In the early years of his exile, when he was doing all he could to combat Nazism and alert the rest of the world to Hitler's danger, he wrote plays and adaptations in many different styles, from the naturalism of *Fear and Misery of the Third Reich* (*Furcht und Elend des dritten Reiches*) to the blank verse of *The Resistible Rise of Arturo*

Ui (*Der Aufhaltsame Aufstieg des Arturo Ui*). The discoveries made and lessons learned through each exercise affected the positions he took up in his theoretical writing, but more importantly contributed to his next experiment.

Brecht is without question one of the most important figures in twentieth-century theater, all the more so because from his earliest writing in his twenties until decades after his death his work has aroused great controversy. The extent to which Brecht influenced other playwrights and theater practitioners is one much-debated point. Many critics and scholars followed Alfred Kerr in asserting that Brecht had simply rehashed ideas he took from earlier and contemporary writers and directors, and from different countries' theatrical traditions. And because Brecht's lifelong commitment to collaboration was not accompanied by a commitment to publicly acknowledging his collaborators, he undoubtedly took far too much credit for work actually created in large part by often overlooked associates, many of them women, like Elisabeth Hauptmann and Ruth Berlau. But to claim that none of Brecht's ideas were his own is to misunderstand his work. As Michael Patterson writes, "Any epigone can copy what has gone before; it takes an original mind to transform it into something usable in the present."[196] Like Shakespeare, Brecht took stories invented by earlier writers and, drawing on whatever other sources and approaches inspired him, turned them into theater. That Brecht did so through collective work is part of his originality; as Peter Thomson says, "No other writer of comparable status has attempted so consistently to collaborate."[197] It was above all through the performances by the Berliner Ensemble in London and Paris in the mid-1950s that Brecht gained international recognition as a director and playwright. What those productions showcased was not the work of an individual artist, but rather the outcome of a meticulous collaborative rehearsal process. The practical demonstration provided by his own stagings of *Mother Courage* and *The Caucasian Chalk Circle* certainly made an impression on many other playwrights and theater practitioners, as did Brecht's theoretical writings once they became widely read outside as well as within Germany in the 1960s and 1970s. Since Brecht's most influential work was the product of thirty years of experiments, his contemporaries and successors also learned from his experience; and since the Weimar period provided Brecht with the only stable laboratory before the Berliner Ensemble, the implications of the often fervent reception of his pre-exile productions have fed into others' work too.

In a program note for the December 1931 Berlin premiere of *The Rise and Fall of the City of Mahagonny*, Brecht briefly reflected on the scandals caused by the opera in Leipzig and elsewhere: "There was nothing to object to in these scandals, in as far as they were not based on primitive misunderstandings.... The scandals created by *Mahagonny*—when the opera is understood correctly—simply correspond to the great, deep and comprehensive scandal which itself gave rise to the opera."[198] In other words, Brecht didn't mind scandals when they arose from "correct" interpretation, that is, expressed the same indignation about social injustice that the piece in question aimed to arouse. As with many other such statements about the reception of his Weimar-era work, Brecht was putting a good face on an experiment that had misfired. But even if, for understandable strategic reasons, Brecht repeatedly represented as successful playwriting and staging techniques which had in fact not proven effective, clearly he did draw lessons from the offended shouts of "*Pfui!*" and from the scornful laughter. If he had not, then he would have continued to espouse and practice confrontation of the audience. Instead, he moderated his approach, and sought means to strike the right balance between earning the spectators' attention and encouraging them to think critically. In 1944, Brecht formulated the following standard: "The modern theater mustn't be judged by how far it satisfies the audience's habits, but by how far it changes them."[199] The productions which caused scandals during the Weimar Republic failed just as much to achieve the second aim as the first, but in the long term that dual failure helped Brecht to develop a more realistic and sophisticated theatrical aesthetic.

Afterword

If the scandals of the modern theater resulted from the clash between unprecedentedly confrontational drama and an unprecedentedly passive audience, clearly such a convergence could have only a limited lifespan. Theater's newly acquired capacity, and tendency, to affront a large segment of the public did not endure for more than a few decades; even as individual theatergoers angrily voiced their disapproval, their collective preconceptions and expectations were undergoing profound and lasting changes. The extent to which the public came to associate theater with direct confrontation, and thus grew less susceptible to that confrontation, is neatly exemplified by the reception history of Peter Handke's 1966 play *Publikumsbeschimpfung* (translated as *Offending the Audience*[1]). Not only does the text culminate in a volley of insults addressed directly to the audience—including "snot-lickers" (*Rotzlecker*), "Nazi pigs" (*Nazischweine*) and "arse-lickers" (*Schleimscheißer*; literally "slime-shitters")—but the whole play constitutes a very deliberate rejection of theatrical representation: as the actors tell the audience, "You won't see any spectacle. / Your curiosity won't be satisfied. / You won't see a play."[2] Handke's use of obscene and offensive language recalls Jarry's "*merdre*," while the emphatic assault on conventions of stage representation harks back to Brecht. One newspaper's review of the premiere announced: "Audience insulted: 'You brats, you goggle-eyes!' No German audience has ever experienced anything like it."[3] But when theatergoers did respond negatively to *Offending the Audience*, it was through "ironic clapping, howling, and laughter" rather than passionate expressions of outrage, and the play became one of the most successful of the decade.[4] As if to make this example even more emblematic, within a few years of the premiere Handke became so frustrated at how *Offending the Audience* was being produced and received that he forbade further productions.

The 1930s and Europe's descent into war mark the end of the heyday of the theater scandal. While many post-war plays have caused controversy, few if any have generated protests by spectators in the auditorium. German-language theater in particular has continued periodically to incite audience protests—such as those at the 1988 Vienna premiere of Thomas Bernhard's *Heroes' Square* (*Heldenplatz*)—but for the most part demonstrations of opposition during performances have given way since the war to earnest debates via newspaper op-ed pieces and letters to the editor. In 1926, Mrs. Sheehy-Skeffington and her collaborators literally stormed the stage of the Abbey theater to protest against *The Plough and the Stars;* the 1963 "storm" (in Eric Bentley's phrase) over Rolf Hochhuth's *The Deputy* (*Der Stellvertreter*) consisted largely of written words, along with some demonstrations—*outside* theaters.[5] In 1889, Dr. Kastan performed his opposition to *Before Sunrise* through shouts and gestures and in 1980, Mrs. Whitehouse (well-known in Britain as the spokesperson for such organizations as the "Clean up TV Campaign") expressed her opposition to Howard Brenton's *The Romans in Britain* by bringing a private prosecution against director Michael Bogdanov. And these more recent controversies have generally revolved around the treatment of one particular issue: Hochhuth's critique of the Catholic Church's policies during the war in *The Deputy,* one scene involving homosexual rape in *The Romans in Britain.* By contrast, the intensity and the complexity of the audience protests examined in this study indicate that those spectators perceived a broadly based attack on their values.

The rise of cinema and television during the twentieth century has of course deprived theater of a good deal of its earlier cultural prominence and influence, but that development is only one factor among many contributing to the change in public response to theater. The decline in the capacity of new plays to provoke immediate protest reflects the inevitable process whereby public conceptions of all cultural forms constantly undergo modification in light of the most recent practice. As Susan Bennett puts it, "Cultural assumptions affect performances, and performances rewrite cultural assumptions."[6] Whereas the cultural assumptions of late-nineteenth and early-twentieth-century theatergoers did not yet embrace the notion that theater might serve as a means of boldly challenging received ideas, by 1980, someone like Mrs. Whitehouse probably did accept that new plays tended to call conventional wisdom into question. What she objected to was a particular, extreme instance of that by then common stance. And cultural assumptions about theater include conditioning regarding modes of response, so that post-war theatergoers not only anticipated that the newest drama might well confront them, but also in effect agreed that if they took offense they would express themselves through means other than disruptive behavior in the auditorium.

Do these alterations of assumptions amount to a change in the basic contract between stage and audience? I would contend that the twentieth century saw changes in certain terms of that contract, but not in its fundamental shape. The arrangement which Bennett characterizes as traditional, whereby "With this social contract put into place, usually by the exchange of money for a ticket which promises a seat in which to watch an action unfold, the spectator accepts a passive role and awaits the action which is to be interpreted," did not really become established until the late nineteenth century.[7] To begin with, that "passive role" did not sit comfortably with those audiences who found themselves confronted by challenging new work. Eventually, however, almost all audiences did indeed accept a passive role, and at the same time they came to expect new drama's adversary stance.

A further key shift has taken place, since World War II especially, in the ideological attitude of the predominant audience relative to new theater. As Alan Sinfield summarizes in an essay on post-war English theater, "The most insidious trap for radical theatre in the sixties was a tendency to attract likeminded audiences, who instead of being challenged were able to congratulate themselves on their commitment."[8] In the 1960s as in the 1890s, the audiences for the newest theater in Europe and America constituted an elite, a tiny fraction of the population; but by the 1960s that elite welcomed apparently oppositional drama, whereas many of their counterparts around the turn of the century reacted angrily to perceived attacks on their values. Bennett foregrounds the emergence since the 1960s of a huge, international range of non-traditional theater, but her very characterization of these companies as theaters "which speak for dominated and marginalized peoples" underlines the probability that such work will be produced to like-minded audiences who are unlikely to protest against performances.[9] A related factor, of greater significance in Europe than in the U.S., is state support for theater. Unlike the earliest fringe theaters inspired by Antoine's Théâtre Libre, subsidized theater can never really claim to be free because funding by the establishment of experimental work necessarily compromises any oppositional production.

Further developments in the physical configuration of theater space have also contributed to the relative infrequency of theater scandals in recent decades. The confrontational drama of the late nineteenth century was first produced in a period marked by a new separation, through building design and lighting, of stage and auditorium. That division amplified the scandalizing potential of the performances, since the spectators were subjected to challenging, taboo-breaking work in an environment which granted them no active role. For most of the twentieth century, leading theater architects and designers have aimed to reverse that stark separation of stage and house. Iain Mackintosh characterized this trend as "the post-war cry for escape from the proscenium arch."[10] Keir Elam has also underlined this key shift in theatrical practice from the nineteenth-century model, wherein "Every theatrical element, from the usually static set to the 'imprisoned' spectator, has a more or less immutable place . . . , allowing little scope for variation or violation of the strictly demarcated divisions" to the twentieth century, when "The centre of the theatrical transaction has become . . . less an absolute stage-auditorium divide than a flexible and, occasionally, unpredictable manipulation of body-to-body space (for example in the theatres of Beck and Schechner)."[11] Audience members whose position may justifiably be compared to that of prisoners are more likely to rebel against a performance by which they feel affronted than are those who detect that their role in the event, like the organization of the event as a whole, is open and variable.

The aim of making the spectators' role once again more participatory is fundamental to much twentieth-century theatrical innovation. In his 1913 manifesto, Marinetti claimed that "The Variety Theatre is alone in seeking the audience's collaboration. It doesn't remain static like a stupid *voyeur*, but joins noisily in the action."[12] The primary goal of Brecht's de-termined experimentation with dramatic and operatic form was to make the spectator a more active partner in the stage-audience relationship. And Bennett, focusing on the last three decades, stresses that "Now so much non-traditional theatre restores the participative energies of the theatre spectator."[13] Elam points to the extreme form of this effort in the radical theater experimentation of Beck, Schechner, and others in the 1960s. In reference to such theater, Giorgio Strehler commented in 1977 that "*in-volvement* nowadays often takes on the meaning of a real and individual physical involvement," a development borne of a more widespread in-tention "to overthrow traditional relationships (*all* traditional relation-ships)," about which he concludes that "the lack of alternative proposals, the lack of a new order to formulate new relations leads us to regard these minute attempts as buds of indecision with little future."[14]

One might contend that the wide range of non-traditional theater cele-brated by Bennett has proven Strehler wrong—that the efforts in the 1960s literally and physically to involve the audience have given way to a va-riety of more subtle and more effective strategies to "increase the specta-tor's activity."[15] Yet as Baz Kershaw demonstrates, during the same period "the protocols of audience membership in virtually all forms of Western theatre, but particularly in so-called mainstream theatre, have under-mined participation in performance." He even goes so far as to suggest that the gradual changes in those protocols indicate "Western theatre's increasing capitulation to near-fascistic forces in its socio-political envi-ronment."[16] While Bennett and Kershaw focus their primary attention on different forms of theater, that divergence does not altogether account for the contrast between their overall arguments. Bennett describes her own study as "a testimony to the contemporary emancipation of the spectator" while Kershaw proposes that "the growing importance of applause, as other forms of participation diminished, is an index of audience acquiescence in twentieth-century Western theatre."[17] To some extent, the two critics arrive at such different conclusions because they adopt such different approaches: where Bennett writes about how audiences *in theory* receive the non-traditional theater she celebrates, Kershaw draws conclusions from evidence of *actual* audience response. My own consideration of theater scandals between the 1880s and the 1930s leave me sharing some of Kershaw's nostalgia for a time when theater spectators participated more actively in performance, yet suspecting that the kind of undemonstrative response Bennett describes might be more productive.

I shall end my exploration of the modern theater scandal by considering another form of audience response which is in a sense its opposite: the standing ovation. In a theater scandal, the audience members interrupt the performance to protest against it, marking it as a violation of some preconceived standard; with a standing ovation, the spectators wait until the end to express their approval, marking that performance as surpassing their expectations. Both phenomena claim authenticity but risk appearing contrived. Kershaw presents the standing ovation as one manifestation of the applause whose dominance he decries. He quotes British theater critic Lyn Gardner's recent commentary on first-night audiences' "increasing fondness for the standing ovation."[18] Based on my own experience, this development is by no means confined to premieres, especially in the United States. But does the rise of the standing ovation embody theater audiences' acquiescence in a model of reception that only permits them to respond in a limited number of ways at particular times? Or does it perhaps suggest that theatergoers are eager to recover a more participatory role in the theatrical event? If theater audiences do wish to involve themselves more than merely by applauding at the end, the new means they have adopted up to now (Kershaw also mentions applauding "at the first entrance of the star actor," and "at the sets of modern musicals"[19]) more often entail acclaiming the performance than opposing it. It remains to be seen whether, in the further evolution of theater in the twenty-first century, audiences will begin to reclaim their right to voice dissenting as well as approving reactions in the theater. If not, performing opposition as examined in this book will remain a thing of the past.

Notes

PREFACE

1. Alfred Polgar, "Krach in Leipzig: *Aufstieg und Fall der Stadt Mahagonny,*" *Tage-Buch* 11.12, 22 March 1930, rpt. in Alfred Polgar, *Kleine Schriften,* vol. 6, ed. Marcel Reich-Ranicki and Ulrich Weinzierl (Hamburg: Rowohlt, 1982), 273–74. Unless otherwise indicated all translations—often intentionally literal—are mine.

2. Martin Esslin, *Brecht: the Man and his Work* (New York: Anchor, 1961), 46.

3. Marc Baer, *Theatre and Disorder in Late Georgian London* (Oxford UP, 1992), 60–61.

4. Susan Bennett, *Theatre Audiences: A Theory of Production and Reception* (London & New York: Routledge, 1990), 1–2, 149.

5. Marvin Carlson, "Theatre Audiences and the Reading of Performance," in *Interpreting the Theatrical Past: Essays in the Historiography of Performance,* ed. Thomas Postlewait and Bruce A. McConachie (U of Iowa P, 1989), 82, 85–86, 97.

6. Hans Robert Jauss, *Toward an Aesthetic of Reception,* trans. Timothy Bahti (U of Minnesota P, 1982), 25.

7. Norbert Elias, *The Civilizing Process,* trans. Edmund Jephcott, ed. Eric Dunning, Johan Goudsblom, and Stephen Mennell, rev. ed. (Oxford: Blackwell, 2000), 415.

8. James H. Johnson, *Listening in Paris: A Cultural History* (U of California P, 1995), 1, 3–4.

9. Anaïs Nin, *The Diary of Anaïs Nin 1931–1934* (New York: Swallow, 1966), 229.

10. Antonin Artaud, *The Theater and its Double,* trans. Mary Caroline Richards (New York: Grove, 1958), 81.

INTRODUCTION

This is a revised and expanded version of Neil Blackadder's essay "Modern Theatre Scandals and the Evolution of the Theatrical Event" *Theater History Studies* 20 (2000).

1. Review of *Ubu Roi* (Jarry) at Théâtre de l'OEuvre, Paris, *Le Petit Parisien* 11 Dec. 1896, rpt. in Henri Robillot, "La Presse d'Ubu Roi," *Cahiers du Collège de Pataphysique* 3–4 (1950): 78–9.

2. "Un Spectateur," review of *Ubu Roi* (Jarry) at Théâtre de l'OEuvre, Paris, *La Presse* 12 Dec. 1896, rpt. in Robillot, "La Presse," 78.

3. Baer, *Theatre and Disorder*, 57.

4. Quoted in F. W. J. Hemmings, *The Theatre Industry in Nineteenth-Century France* (Cambridge UP, 1993), 77.

5. Quoted in Andrew Gurr, *Playgoing in Shakespeare's London*, 2nd. ed. (Cambridge UP, 1996), 260.

6. Quoted in George W. Brandt, ed., *German and Dutch Theatre, 1600–1848* (Cambridge UP, 1993), 493.

7. Quoted in A. M. Nagler, *Sources of Theatrical History* (New York: Theatre Annual, 1952), 335.

8. Plato, *The Republic*, trans. Desmond Lee, 2nd. ed. (Harmondsworth: Penguin, 1974), 287.

9. *The Letters of Horace Walpole*, ed. Mrs. Paget Toynbee, vol. 5 (Oxford: Clarendon, 1904), 93.

10. *The Poems of Samuel Johnson*, ed. David Nichol Smith and Edward L. McAdam, 2nd. ed. (Oxford UP, 1974), 109.

11. Quoted in Michael R. Booth, "The theatre and its audience," in Michael R. Booth et al., *The Revels History of Drama in English VI: 1750–1880* (London: Methuen, 1975), 22.

12. Letter from William Smith to David Garrick, June 26, 1774, *The Private Correspondence of David Garrick*, vol. 1 (London: Colburn and Bentley, 1831), 639.

13. Quoted in Montague Summers, *The Restoration Theatre* (London: Kegan Paul, 1934), 31.

14. Washington Irving, *Letters of Jonathan Oldstyle, Gent.; Salmagundi*, ed. Bruce I. Granger and Martha Hartzog (Boston: Twayne, 1977), 13.

15. Molière, *Le Misanthrope* ll. 795–96.

16. *The Complete Works of Henry Fielding, Esq.: Plays and Poems, vol. Five* (London: Frank Cass, 1902, rpt. 1967), 38.

17. Matthew Josephson, *Victor Hugo* (New York: Doubleday, 1942), 141.

18. René Jasinski, "La Bataille d'*Hernani*," *Nouvelle Revue des Jeunes* 2 (10 May 1930): 636.

19. Quoted in Athenaide Dallett, "Protest in the Playhouse: Two Twentieth-Century Audience Riots," *New Theatre Quarterly* 12.48 (November 1996): 323.

20. Booth, "The theatre and its audience," 21.

21. Order issued by Cambridge University authorities, March 1632, quoted in Gurr, *Playgoing*, 47; E. Rodocanachi, quoted Hemmings, *Theatre Industry*, 99–100.

22. Peter Stallybrass and Allon White, *The Politics and Poetics of Transgression* (Cornell UP, 1986), 84, 90, 88.

23. Iain Mackintosh, *Architecture, Actor and Audience* (London & New York: Routledge, 1993), 26.

24. George Saunders, *A Treatise on Theatres* (London, 1790), 36, 37.

25. Richard Cumberland, *Memoirs of Richard Cumberland* [1806] (Philadelphia: Parry and McMillan, 1856), 387.

26. Colley Cibber, *An Apology for the Life of Colley Cibber* [1740], ed. B. R. S. Fone (U of Michigan P, 1968).

27. Faye E. Dudden, *Women in the American Theatre: Actresses and Audiences, 1790–1870* (Yale UP, 1994), 15, 62.

28. William Bodham Donne, *Essays on the Drama and on Popular Amusements,* 2nd. ed. (London: Tinsley and Jones, 1863), 206.

29. Maurice Descotes, *Le Public de Théâtre et son histoire* (Paris: PU de France, 1964), 16.

30. Quoted in Richard Sennett, *The Fall of Public Man* (New York: Norton, 1976), 208.

31. Quoted in Russell Jackson, *Victorian Theatre: the Theatre in its Time* (Franklin, NY: New Amsterdam, 1989), 62.

32. Mackintosh, *Architecture,* 41.

33. Sennett, *Fall,* 207, 209.

34. William B. Worthen, *The Idea of the Actor: Drama and the Ethics of Performance* (Princeton UP), 83, 72.

35. Quoted in Joyce Mekeel, "Social Influences on changing audience behavior in the London theatre 1830–1880," Diss. Boston University 1983, 180.

36. Booth, "The theatre and its audience," 24.

37. Hippolyte Taine, *Notes on England* [1860–70], trans. Edward Hyams (London: Caliban, 1995), 214.

38. W. H. Hudson, quoted in Michael R. Booth, *Theatre in the Victorian Age* (Cambridge UP, 1991), 23.

39. Stallybrass and White, *Politics,* 87.

40. Quoted in Jackson, *Victorian Theatre,* 59.

41. Vladimir Alekseevich Gilyarovsky, quoted in Laurence Senelick, ed., *National Theatre in Northern and Eastern Europe, 1746–1900* (Cambridge UP, 1991), 404.

42. Quoted in Booth, "The theatre and its audience," 25.

43. Descotes, *Public de Théâtre,* 308.

44. Carlson, "Theatre Audiences," 90.

CHAPTER 1

1. Curt Baake, review of *Vor Sonnenaufgang* (Hauptmann) at Freie Bühne, Berlin, *Berliner Volksblatt* 22 Oct. 1889, rpt. in *Berlin—Theater der Jahrhundertwende. Bühnengeschichte der Reichshauptstadt im Spiegel der Kritik (1889–1914),* ed. Norbert Jaron, Renate Möhrmann, and Hedwig Müller (Tübingen: Niemeyer, 1986), 96–97.

2. Cf. Norbert Jaron, Renate Möhrmann, and Hedwig Müller, "Zur Berliner Theatergeschichte," introduction to Jaron, Möhrmann, and Müller, eds., *Berlin,* 12.

3. Theodor Fontane, review of *Das Friedensfest* (Hauptmann) at Freie Bühne, Berlin, *Vossische Zeitung* 2 June 1890, rpt. in *Aufsätze, Kritiken, Erinnerungen,* vol. 2: "Theaterkritiken," ed. Siegmar Gerndt, in *Sämtliche Werke,* ed. Walter Keitel (Munich: Hanser, 1969), 856.

4. Michael Hays, *The Public and Performance: Essays in the History of French and German Theatre, 1871–1900* (Ann Arbor: UMI Research Press, 1981), 29.

5. Heinrich and Julius Hart, "Das »Deutsche Theater« des Herrn L'Arronge," *Kritische Waffengänge* 4 (1882), quoted in Jaron, Möhrmann, and Müller, "Zur Berliner Theatergeschichte," 2.

6. Otto Brahm, "Der Naturalismus und das Theater," in *Kritiken und Essays,* ed. Fritz Martini (Zurich: Artemis, 1964), 411.

7. Quoted in Peter De Mendelssohn, *S. Fischer und sein Verlag* (Frankfurt: Fischer, 1970), 93.

8. Cf. De Mendelssohn, *S. Fischer,* 96.

9. Julius Bab, *Das Theater der Gegenwart. Geschichte der dramatischen Bühne seit 1870* (Leipzig, 1928), 56.

10. Ernst von Wolzogen, "Freie Bühne. Berlins Publikum und Presse über Hauptmanns Drama *Vor Sonnenaufgang,*" *Die Gesellschaft* 5 (1889): 1736.

11. Gerhart Hauptmann, *Vor Sonnenaufgang* (Frankfurt: Ullstein, 1959), 32. Subsequent parenthetical references will be to this edition.

12. Paul Schlenther, *Wozu der Lärm? Genesis der Freien Bühne* (Berlin: S. Fischer, 1889), 22.

13. Bab, *Theater,* 56.

14. Schlenther, *Wozu,* 22.

15. Peter Sprengel, ed., *Otto Brahm—Gerhart Hauptmann. Briefwechsel 1889–1912* (Tübingen: Gunter Narr, 1985), 95, 97. Regrettably, it is not known exactly what cuts were made for the production at the Freie Bühne. Cf. Gernot Schley, *Die Freie Bühne in Berlin* (Berlin: Haude & Spenersche Verlagsbuchhandlung, 1967), 50.

16. Baake, review, 96.

17. Karl Frenzel, review of *Vor Sonnenaufgang* (Hauptmann) at Freie Bühne, Berlin, *National-Zeitung* 21 Oct. 1889, rpt. in Jaron, Möhrmann, and Müller, eds., *Berlin,* 91.

18. Baake, review, 96.

19. Adalbert von Hanstein, *Das jüngste Deutschland. Zwei Jahrzehnte miterlebter Literaturgeschichte* (Leipzig: Voigtländer, 1901), 170.

20. Schlenther, *Wozu,* 23.

21. Otto Brahm, "Gesellschaftsdrama und soziales Drama," in *Kritiken und Essays,* 299.

22. Hanstein, *Jüngste Deutschland,* 170.

23. Wolzogen, "Freie Bühne," 1736.

24. Isidor Landau, review of *Vor Sonnenaufgang* (Hauptmann) at Freie Bühne, Berlin, *Berliner Börsen-Courier,* 20 Oct. 1889, rpt. in Jaron, Möhrmann, and Müller, eds., *Berlin,* 90.

25. Heinrich Hart, review of *Vor Sonnenaufgang* (Hauptmann) at Freie Bühne, Berlin, *Tägliche Rundschau,* 22 Oct. 1889, rpt. in Jaron, Möhrmann, and Müller, eds., *Berlin,* 94.

26. Landau, review, 90.

27. Wolzogen, "Freie Bühne," 1735.

28. Landau, review, 90.

29. Ibid.

30. Schlenther, *Wozu,* 25.

31. Hauptmann, *Vor Sonnenaufgang,* 62.

32. Schlenther, *Wozu,* 25.

33. Landau, review, 90.

34. Schlenther, *Wozu,* 28.

35. Fontane, review of *Vor Sonnenaufgang* (Hauptmann) at Freie Bühne, Berlin, *Vossische Zeitung* 21 Oct. 1889, rpt. in *Aufsätze,* 2: 821.

36. Schlenther, *Wozu*, 28.

37. Landau, review, 90.

38. Ibid.; cf. Schlenther, *Wozu*, 28.

39. Max Osborn, *Der Bunte Spiegel: Erinnerungen aus dem Kunst-, Kultur- und Geistesleben der Jahre 1890 bis 1893* (New York: Friedrich Krause, 1945), 131.

40. Baake, review, 96.

41. Edgar Steiger, *Das Werden des neuen Dramas*, vol. 2: *Von Hauptmann bis Maeterlinck* (Berlin: Egon Fleischel, 1903), 1.

42. Brahm, "Gesellschaftsdrama," 299.

43. Landau, review, 87.

44. Quoted in De Mendelssohn, *S. Fischer*, 109.

45. "Der Naturalismus vor Gericht," *Freie Bühne* 1.5 (5 Mar. 1890), 133–34.

46. Ibid., 134.

47. Ibid.

48. Ibid.

49. Mary Douglas, *Purity and Danger* (London: Routledge, 1966).

50. Landau, review, 90.

51. J. Kastan, *Berlin wie es war*, 2nd. ed. (Berlin: Rudolf Mosse, 1919), 265.

52. Quoted in De Mendelssohn, *S. Fischer*, 109.

53. Schlenther, *Wozu*, 31, 32.

54. Landau, review, 90.

55. Jaron, Möhrmann, and Müller, "Zur Berliner Theatergeschichte," 31.

56. Gustav Freytag, *Die Technik des Dramas*, 10th ed. (Leipzig: S. Hirzel, 1905), 15.

57. Ibid., 59.

58. Richard Dehmel, "Die neue deutsche Alltagstragödie," *Die Gesellschaft* 8 (1892): 485.

59. Hanstein, *Jüngste Deutschland*, 170.

60. Landau, review, 90.

61. Wolzogen, "Freie Bühne," 1742.

62. Bennett, *Theatre Audiences*, 150.

63. Hart, review, 95.

64. Steiger, *Das Werden*, 5.

65. Jaron, Möhrmann, and Müller, "Zur Berliner Theatergeschichte," 35.

66. Fontane, review, 856.

67. Quoted in Albert Soergel, *Dichtung und Dichter der Zeit* (Leipzig: Voigtländer, 1911), 202.

68. Osborn, *Der Bunte Spiegel*, 131.

CHAPTER 2

1. Henri Fouquier, review of *Ubu Roi* (Jarry) at Théâtre de l'Œuvre, Paris, *Le Figaro* 11 Dec., 13 Dec. 1896, rpt. in Robillot, "La Presse," 85.

2. Alfred Jarry, "Réponses à un questionnaire sur l'art dramatique," in Alfred Jarry, *Ubu*, ed. Noël Arnaud and Henri Bordillon (Paris: Gallimard Folio, 1978), 321.

3. Fouquier, review, 85–86.

4. Aurélien Lugné-Poe, *Acrobaties*, vol. 2 of *La Parade* (Paris: Gallimard, 1931–33), 160.

5. Letter from Alfred Jarry to Aurélien Lugné-Poe, 8 Jan. 1896, *Ubu*, ed. Arnaud and Bordillon, 412–13.

6. Letter from Alfred Jarry to Aurélien Lugné-Poe, 1 Aug. 1896, *Ubu*, ed. Arnaud and Bordillon, 417.

7. Alfred Jarry, "De l'inutilité du théâtre au théâtre," *Mercure de France* Sep. 1896, rpt. in *Ubu*, ed. Arnaud and Bordillon, 307, 309.

8. Jarry, "Réponses," 317.

9. Jarry, "De l'inutilité," 309; Jarry, "Réponses," 317.

10. Jarry, "Réponses," 317.

11. René Peter, *Le Théâtre et la vie sous la troisième République* (Paris: Marchot, 1947), 2: 26–27.

12. Lugné-Poe, *Acrobaties*, 174–75.

13. Noël Arnaud, *Alfred Jarry, d'Ubu roi au Docteur Faustroll* (Paris: La Table Ronde, 1974), 253.

14. Géroy, "Mon ami Alfred Jarry (Souvenirs)," *Mercure de France* 1 July 1947: 508.

15. Quoted in Norman L. Kleeblatt, "MERDE! The Caricatural Attack against Emile Zola," *Art Journal* 52.3 (1993): 54.

16. Laurent Tailhade, *Quelques fantômes de jadis* (Paris: Éditions française illustrée, 1920), 216.

17. Henri Béhar, *Jarry Dramaturge* (Paris: Nizet, 1980), 75.

18. Elias, *Civilizing Process*, 114, x-xi.

19. Stallybrass and White, *Politics*, 140.

20. Jacques Lacan, *Écrits* (Paris: Seuil, 1966), 660–61.

21. Rachilde, *Alfred Jarry, ou le Surmâle de lettres* (Paris: B. Grasset, 1928), 89.

22. Alfred Jarry, *Ubu Roi*, in *Ubu*, ed. Arnaud and Bordillon, 31.

23. Quoted in René Druart, "Un témoignage sur la générale d'*Ubu Roi*," *Cahiers du Collège de 'Pataphysique* 20 (1955): 53.

24. Rachilde, review of *Les Jours et les nuits* (Jarry), *Mercure de France* Aug. 1897: 144.

25. Eugen Weber, *France, Fin de Siècle* (Harvard UP, 1986), 38.

26. Rachilde, review, 143–44.

27. Quoted in P. Lié, "Notes sur la seconde représentation d'*Ubu Roi*," *Cahiers du collège de Pataphysique* 20 (1955): 52.

28. Jarry, letter, 8 Jan. 1896, 412.

29. Letter from Alfred Jarry to Aurélien Lugné-Poe, 7 Dec. 1896, *Ubu*, ed. Arnaud and Bordillon, 425; "Répertoire des costumes," *Ubu*, ed. Arnaud and Bordillon, 452.

30. Jarry, letter, 8 Jan. 1896, 413.

31. Jarry, letter, 8 Jan. 1896, 413; Lié, "Notes," 52; "Répertoire des costumes," 451.

32. Jarry, letter, 8 Jan. 1896, 412.

33. Robert Vallier, review of *Ubu Roi* (Jarry) at Théâtre de l'Œuvre, Paris, *République Française* 12 Dec. 1896, rpt. in Robillot, "La Presse," 76.

34. "Un Sarcisque," review of *Ubu Roi* (Jarry) at Théâtre de l'Œuvre, Paris, *L'Evénement* 11 Dec. 1896, rpt. in Robillot, "La Presse," 78.

35. Jarry, letter, 8 Jan. 1896, 413.

36. Lugné-Poe, *Acrobaties*, 176.

37. Arthur Symons, "A Symbolist Farce," *Studies in Seven Arts* (London: Constable, 1906), 372.

38. Alfred Jarry, *Œuvres complètes*, vol. 1, ed. Michel Arrivé (Paris: Gallimard Pléiade, 1972), 1056.

39. "Coquerico," review of *Ubu Roi* (Jarry) at Théâtre de l'Œuvre, Paris, *La Patrie*, 11 [?] Dec. 1896, rpt. in Robillot, "La Presse," 82.

40. Vallier, review, 76.

41. Rachilde, *Alfred Jarry*, 80.

42. Symons, "A Symbolist Farce," 372.

43. Jarry, "Réponses," 320.

44. Review of *Ubu Roi* (Jarry) at Théâtre de l'Œuvre, Paris, *Le Soir* 11 Dec. 1896, rpt. in Robillot, "La Presse," 83.

45. Georges Rémond, "Souvenirs sur Jarry et autres (fin)," *Mercure de France* 1 Apr. 1955: 666.

46. Tailhade, *Quelques fantômes*, 214.

47. Ibid., 214–15.

48. Arnaud, *Alfred Jarry*, 321.

49. Ibid.

50. Georges Vanor, review of *Ubu Roi* (Jarry) at Théâtre de l'Œuvre, Paris, *La Paix* 11 Dec. 1896, rpt. in Robillot, "La Presse," 77.

51. "L.-B.-D.," review of *Ubu Roi* (Jarry) at Théâtre de l'Œuvre, Paris, *Gil Bas* 11 Dec. 1896, rpt. in Robillot, "La Presse," 77.

52. Review of *Ubu Roi* (Jarry) at Théâtre de l'Œuvre, Paris, *La Lanterne* 12 Dec. 1896, rpt. in Robillot, "La Presse," 81.

53. "Coquerico," review, 82.

54. Jules Renard, *Journal (1887–1919)* (Paris: Gallimard Pléiade, 1960), 363.

55. Catulle Mendès, review of *Ubu Roi* (Jarry) at Théâtre de l'Œuvre, Paris, *Le Journal* 11 Dec. 1896.

56. Edouard Noël and Edmond Stoullig, *Les Annales du théâtre et de la musique* vol. 22 (1896) (Paris: Ollendorff, 1897), 423–24.

57. Fouquier, review, 85.

58. Mendès, review.

59. William Butler Yeats, *Autobiographies* (London: Macmillan, 1955), 348.

60. Renard, *Journal*, 363.

61. Rachilde, *Alfred Jarry*, 80.

62. Lié, "Notes," 49; Lugné-Poe, *Acrobaties*, 177.

63. Roger Valbelle, "M. Firmin Gémier nous dit ce que furent la répétition générale et la première d''Ubu-Roi'" *Excelsior* 4 Nov. 1921.

64. Valentin Mandelstamm, *Fantasio* 15 April 1908, rpt. in Lié, "Notes," 52.

65. Valbelle, "M. Firmin Gémier."

66. Mandelstamm, 52.

67. Valbelle, "M. Firmin Gémier."

68. Henri de Régnier, "Alfred Jarry," *De mon temps* (Paris: Mercure de France, 1933), 152.

69. "Coquerico," review, 82.

70. "C de N.," review of *Ubu Roi* (Jarry) at Théâtre de l'Œuvre, Paris, *Paris* 11 [?] Dec. 1896, rpt. in Robillot, "La Presse," 78.

71. Renard, *Journal*, 363.

72. Sigmund Freud, "Dreams in Folklore," *Standard Edition of the Complete Works of Sigmund Freud,* trans. and ed. James Strachey, vol. 12 (London: Hogarth Press, 1958), 187.

73. Dominique Laporte, *History of Shit,* trans. Nadia Benabid and Rodolphe el-Khoury (Cambridge: MIT Press, 2000), 32.

74. Stallybrass and White, *Politics,* 191.

75. Jarry, *Ubu Roi,* 37, 39.

76. Review, *Le Petit Parisien,* 79.

77. Jarry, *Ubu Roi,* 39, 40–41.

78. Review, *Le Petit Parisien,* 79.

79. "L.-B.-D.," review, 77.

80. "Un Sarcisque," review, 78.

81. "Pompier de Service," review of *Ubu Roi* (Jarry) at Théâtre de l'Œuvre, Paris, *La Paix* 11 Dec. 1896, rpt. in Robillot, "La Presse," 76.

82. Quoted in Arnaud, *Alfred Jarry,* 317.

83. Francis Jourdain, *Né en 76* (Paris: Pavillon, 1951), 204.

84. Alfred Jarry, *Ubu enchaîné,* in *Ubu,* ed. Arnaud and Bordillon, 206.

85. "Pompier de Service," review, 76.

86. Francisque Sarcey, review of *Ubu Roi* (Jarry) at Théâtre de l'Œuvre, Paris, *Le Temps* 14 Dec. 1896, rpt. in Robillot, "La Presse," 75.

87. Vallier, review, 76.

88. Sarcey, review, 75.

89. Claveau, review of *Ubu Roi* (Jarry) at Théâtre de l'Œuvre, Paris, *Le Soleil* 11 Dec. 1896, rpt. in Robillot, "La Presse," 76.

90. Henry Céard, review of *Ubu Roi* (Jarry) at Théâtre de l'Œuvre, Paris, *Le Matin* 11 Dec. 1896, rpt. in Robillot, "La Presse," 84.

91. Tailhade, *Quelques fantômes,* 215.

92. Romain Coolus, "Notes dramatiques," *Revue Blanche* 1 Jan. 1897, 39.

93. Jourdain, *Né en 76,* 204.

94. Camille Mauclair, *Revue Encyclopédique* 172.6, rpt. in Robillot, "La Presse," 80.

95. Rachilde, review, 144.

96. Alfred Jarry, "Questions de théâtre," *Ubu,* ed. Arnaud and Bordillon, 344–46.

97. Alfred Jarry, "Les Paralipomènes d'Ubu," *Ubu,* ed. Arnaud and Bordillon, 323.

98. Jarry, "Programme," 337.

99. Jarry, "Questions," 344.

100. Noël and Stoullig, *Annales,* 424.

101. Weber, *France,* 162.

102. Jarry, "Questions," 345–46.

103. Ibid., 347.

CHAPTER 3

1. Quoted in Hugh Hunt, *The Abbey: Ireland's National Theatre, 1904–1979* (Columbia UP, 1979), 18.

2. Quoted in Lady Augusta Gregory, *Our Irish Theatre,* 1913 (Oxford UP, 1977), 237.

3. Quoted in Robert Welch, *The Abbey Theatre, 1899–1999: Form and Pressure* (Oxford UP, 1999), 19.

4. Joseph Holloway, *Joseph Holloway's Abbey Theatre*, ed. Robert Hogan and Michael O'Neill (Southern Illinois UP, 1967), 53, 57.

5. Ibid., 63.

6. Quoted in Mary Trotter, *Ireland's National Theaters: Political Performance and the Origins of the Irish Dramatic Movement* (Syracuse UP, 2001), 117.

7. Holloway, *Joseph Holloway's Abbey Theatre*, 72.

8. W. G. Fay and Catherine Carswell, *The Fays of the Abbey Theatre* (New York: Harcourt, Brace, 1935), 211.

9. Mary Colum, *Life and the Dream* (New York: Doubleday, 1947), 137.

10. Ibid., 101.

11. Trotter, *Ireland's National Theaters*, 126.

12. Donna Gerstenberger, "A Hard Birth," 1964, rpt. in *John Millington Synge's The Playboy of the Western World*, ed. Harold Bloom (New York: Chelsea House, 1988), 52.

13. C. P. Curran, *Under the Receding Wave* (Dublin: Gill and Macmillan, 1970), 106–7.

14. Gregory, *Our Irish Theatre*, 67.

15. "The Abbey Theatre, The Playboy of the Western World," *Freeman's Journal* 28 Jan. 1907, rpt. in James Kilroy, *The 'Playboy' Riots* (Dublin: Dolmen, 1971), 8.

16. Ibid.

17. Maire Nic Shiubhlaigh, *The Splendid Years* (Dublin: James Duffy, 1955), 83.

18. Holloway, *Joseph Holloway's Abbey Theatre*, 81.

19. John Millington Synge, *The Playboy of the Western World*, ed. Malcolm Kelsall, rev. ed. (London: A & C Black, 1994), 78. Subsequent parenthetical references will be to this edition.

20. For an estimation of house sizes based on box office receipts, see Robert Hogan and James Kilroy, *The Abbey Theatre: the Years of Synge, 1905–1909* (Dublin: Dolmen, 1978), 144.

21. Report on *The Playboy of the Western World* (Synge) at Abbey Theatre, Dublin, *Freeman's Journal* 29 Jan. 1907, rpt. in Kilroy, *The 'Playboy' Riots*, 15.

22. Ibid., 16

23. Nic Shiubhlaigh, *The Splendid Years*, 86.

24. "Disturbance at the Abbey Theatre," *Daily Express* 29 Jan. 1907, rpt. in Hogan and Kilroy, *The Abbey Theatre*, 126.

25. Report, *Freeman's Journal* 29 Jan. 1907, 15.

26. Ibid., 16.

27. Fay and Carswell, *The Fays*, 215–16.

28. Cf. Kilroy, *The 'Playboy' Riots*, 17.

29. Report, *Freeman's Journal* 29 Jan. 1907, 16, 17.

30. "Disturbance," *Daily Express* 29 Jan. 1907, 126.

31. Ibid.

32. *Dublin Evening Mail* 29 Jan. 1907, rpt. in Kilroy, *The 'Playboy' Riots*, 18.

33. Quoted in Editorial, *Sinn Fein* 2 Feb. 1907, rpt. in Kilroy, *The 'Playboy' Riots*, 66.

34. Report on *The Playboy of the Western World* (Synge) at Abbey Theatre, Dub-

lin, *Freeman's Journal* 30 Jan. 1907, rpt. in Kilroy, *The 'Playboy' Riots*, 26; Gregory, *Our Irish Theatre*, 68.

35. "The National Theatre," *Irish Independent* 31 Jan. 1907, rpt. in Hogan and Kilroy, *The Abbey Theatre*, 141.

36. Report, *Freeman's Journal* 30 Jan. 1907, 27.

37. Ibid., 28; "The Abbey Theatre," *Daily Express* 30 Jan. 1907, rpt. in Hogan and Kilroy, *The Abbey Theatre*, 128.

38. Report, *Freeman's Journal* 30 Jan. 1907, 28.

39. "The Abbey Theatre," *Daily Express* 30 Jan. 1907, 128.

40. Holloway, *Joseph Holloway's Abbey Theatre*, 84.

41. Report, *Freeman's Journal* 30 Jan. 1907, 31.

42. "The Abbey Theatre," *Daily Express* 30 Jan. 1907, 129.

43. Ibid.

44. Holloway, *Joseph Holloway's Abbey Theatre*, 84.

45. Report on *The Playboy of the Western World* (Synge) at Abbey Theatre, Dublin, *Freeman's Journal* 31 Jan. 1907, rpt. in Kilroy, *The 'Playboy' Riots*, 42, 43.

46. Ibid., 44.

47. F. W. J. Hemmings, *Theatre and State in France, 1760–1905* (Cambridge UP, 1994), 123.

48. Report on *The Playboy of the Western World* (Synge) at Abbey Theatre, Dublin, *Evening Mail* 1 Feb. 1907, rpt. in Kilroy, *The 'Playboy' Riots*, 62.

49. Fay and Carswell, *The Fays*, 216.

50. Report, *Evening Mail* 1 Feb. 1907, 62.

51. "The Abbey Theatre," *Daily Express* 4 Feb. 1907, rpt. in Hogan and Kilroy, *The Abbey Theatre*, 143.

52. Quoted in David H. Greene and Edward M. Stephens, *J. M. Synge, 1871–1909*, rev. ed. (New York UP, 1989), 264.

53. "Last Night's Row at the Abbey," *Evening Mail* 30 Jan. 1907, rpt. in Hogan and Kilroy, *The Abbey Theatre*, 134.

54. Gregory, *Our Irish Theatre*, 67.

55. Fay and Carswell, *The Fays*, 213–14.

56. "The People and the Parricide," *Freeman's Journal* 29 Jan. 1907, rpt. in Kilroy, *The 'Playboy' Riots*, 19.

57. *Irish Independent* 1 Feb. 1907, rpt. in Kilroy, *The 'Playboy' Riots*, 63.

58. "The Abbey Theatre," *Freeman's Journal* 28 Jan. 1907, 9.

59. Gregory, *Our Irish Theatre*, 80.

60. Editorial, *Sinn Fein* 2 Feb. 1907, 66; review of *The Playboy of the Western World* (Synge) at Abbey Theatre, Dublin, *Evening Mail* 28 Jan. 1907, rpt. in Kilroy, *The 'Playboy' Riots*, 13.

61. *Irish Independent* 1 Feb. 1907, 63; Gregory, *Our Irish Theatre*, 194.

62. Gregory, *Our Irish Theatre*, 68.

63. "The National Theatre," *Irish Independent* 31 Jan. 1907, 141.

64. "The Abbey Theatre: Mr. Synge's New Play," *Daily Express* 28 Jan. 1907, rpt. in Kilroy, *The 'Playboy' Riots*, 11.

65. *Irish Independent* 1 Feb. 1907, rpt. in Kilroy, *The 'Playboy' Riots*, 65.

66. "The Abbey Theatre," *Daily Express* 30 Jan. 1907, 129.

67. Fay and Carswell, *The Fays*, 213; report, *Freeman's Journal* 31 Jan. 1907, 43.

68. "A Western Girl," letter to *Freeman's Journal* 28 Jan. 1907, rpt. in Kilroy, *The 'Playboy' Riots*, 10.

69. Holloway, *Joseph Holloway's Abbey Theatre*, 81, 277.

70. "A Western Girl," letter, 10.

71. Padraic Colum, *The Road Round Ireland* (New York: Macmillan, 1926), 368.

72. *Theatre Business: The Correspondence of the First Abbey Theatre Directors: William Butler Yeats, Lady Gregory, and J. M. Synge*, ed. Ann Saddlemyer (Penn State UP, 1982), 73–74.

73. Colum, *The Road*, 368.

74. Quoted in Curran, *Under the Receding Wave*, 108–9.

75. Fay and Carswell, *The Fays*, 212; Curran, *Under the Receding Wave*, 107–8.

76. Report, *Freeman's Journal* 30 Jan. 1907, 30; "The Abbey Theatre," *Daily Express* 30 Jan. 1907, 129.

77. Report on *The Playboy of the Western World* (Synge) at Abbey Theatre, Dublin, *Irish Independent* 29 Jan. 1907, rpt. in Kilroy, *The 'Playboy' Riots*, 17.

78. Report, *Freeman's Journal* 30 Jan. 1907, 31. The quoted line is actually spoken by Old Mahon.

79. *Evening Herald* 1 Feb. 1907, Quoted in *J. M. Synge: Interviews and Recollections*, ed. E. H. Mikhail (London: Macmillan, 1977), 43, 44.

80. Report, *Freeman's Journal* 30 Jan. 1907, 30.

81. "The People and the Parricide," *Freeman's Journal* 29 Jan. 1907, 20.

82. A. E. F. Horniman, letter to *Evening Telegraph* 12 Feb. 1907, rpt. in Hogan and Kilroy, *The Abbey Theatre*, 162.

83. *Irish Times* 29 Jan. 1907, quoted in Richard M. Kain, "The *Playboy* Riots," *Sunshine and the Moon's Delight: A Centenary Tribute to John Millington Synge, 1871–1909*, ed. S. B. Bushrui (Gerrards Cross: Colin Smythe, 1972), 179.

84. Ellen Duncan, letter to the editor, *Irish Times* 31 Jan. 1907, rpt. in Kilroy, *The 'Playboy' Riots*, 57.

85. "The Abbey Theatre," *Daily Express* 30 Jan. 1907, 129.

86. Gregory, *Our Irish Theatre*, 68.

87. Report, *Freeman's Journal* 30 Jan. 1907, 29.

88. "The Scene at the Theatre. By one of the Ejected," *Freeman's Journal* 31 Jan. 1907, rpt. in Kilroy, *The 'Playboy' Riots*, 45, 46.

89. "The Abbey Theatre," *Daily Express* 30 Jan. 1907, 128.

90. Report, *Freeman's Journal* 30 Jan. 1907, 29.

91. Court report, *Freeman's Journal* 31 Jan. 1907, rpt. in Kilroy, *The 'Playboy' Riots*, 47, 48–49.

92. Quoted in Hunt, *The Abbey*, 19.

93. "Last Night's Row at the Abbey," *Evening Mail* 30 Jan. 1907, 134, 135.

94. "The Scenes at the Abbey Theatre," *Daily Express* 1 Feb. 1907, rpt. in Hogan and Kilroy, *The Abbey Theatre*, 135, 137.

95. Court report, *Evening Herald* 31 Jan. 1907, rpt. in Kilroy, *The 'Playboy' Riots*, 51–52.

96. "The Abbey Theatre," *Daily Express* 4 Feb. 1907, 140.

97. Ibid.

98. "The Scenes at the Abbey Theatre," *Daily Express* 1 Feb. 1907, 138–39.

99. "The Abbey Theatre Disturbance," *Daily Express* 2 Feb. 1907, rpt. in Hogan and Kilroy, *The Abbey Theatre*, 139.

100. "The Scenes at the Abbey Theatre," *Daily Express* 1 Feb. 1907, 138.

101. Lady Gregory, letter to J. M. Synge, rpt. in Kilroy, *The 'Playboy' Riots*, 88–89.

102. "The Abbey Theatre Disturbances," *Daily Express* 5 Feb. 1907, rpt. in Hogan and Kilroy, *The Abbey Theatre*, 152.

103. Gregory, letter to Synge, 89.

104. Fay and Carswell, *The Fays*, 219–20.

105. *Evening Standard* 15 June 1907, quoted in Dawson Byrne, *The Story of Ireland's National Theatre*, 1929 (Dublin: Talbot, 1971), 63.

106. Fay and Carswell, *The Fays*, 226.

107. Gregory, *Our Irish Theatre*, 103.

108. Quoted in ibid., 224.

109. John P. Harrington, *The Irish Play on the New York Stage, 1874–1966* (UP of Kentucky, 1997), 62.

110. Nic Shiubhlaigh, *The Splendid Years*, 117.

111. Gregory, *Our Irish Theatre*, 104.

112. Quoted in ibid., 102.

113. Interview in *Evening Sun* (New York), quoted in ibid. 237–38.

114. *Gaelic American* 14 Oct. 1911, quoted in Daniel J. Murphy, "The Reception of Synge's *Playboy* in Ireland and America: 1907–1912," *Bulletin of the New York Library* 64.10 (Oct. 1960): 528.

115. *Gaelic American* 28 Oct. 1911, quoted in Gregory, *Our Irish Theatre*, 223.

116. Nic Shiubhlaigh, *The Splendid Years*, 118.

117. Gregory, *Our Irish Theatre*, 102, 133.

118. Ibid., 111.

119. *New York Times* 28 Nov. 1911, quoted in ibid., 224.

120. Gregory, *Our Irish Theatre*, 113.

121. Ibid., 119.

122. *North American* (Philadelphia) 17 Jan. 1912, quoted in ibid., 229–30.

123. Nic Shiubhlaigh, *The Splendid Years*, 133.

124. *North American* (Philadelphia) 20 Jan. 1912, quoted in Gregory, *Our Irish Theatre*, 232.

125. Nic Shiubhlaigh, *The Splendid Years*, 135.

126. Gregory, *Our Irish Theatre*, 234.

CHAPTER 4

1. Robert Hogan and Richard Burnham, *The Years of O'Casey, 1921–1926: a Documentary History* (U of Delaware P, 1992), 281.

2. Holloway, *Joseph Holloway's Abbey Theatre*, 236.

3. Letter from Michael J. Dolan to Lady Gregory, 1 Sep. 1925, quoted in Hogan and Burnham, *The Years of O'Casey*, 281–82; letter from George O'Brien to W. B. Yeats, 5 Sep. 1925, quoted in ibid., 282–83.

4. Dolan, letter, 281.

5. Letter from George O'Brien to W. B. Yeats, 13 Sep. 1925, quoted in Hogan and Burnham, *The Years of O'Casey*, 283–84.

6. Letter from W. B. Yeats to George O'Brien, 10 Sep. 1925, quoted in Hogan and Burnham, *The Years of O'Casey*, 283; Lady Augusta Gregory, *Lady Gregory's Journals, 1916–1930*, ed. Lennox Robinson (New York: Macmillan, 1947), 87.

7. Gregory, *Lady Gregory's Journals*, 88.

8. Gabriel Fallon, *Sean O'Casey, the Man I Knew* (Boston: Little, Brown, 1965), 89.

9. Sean O'Casey, *Three Plays* (New York: St. Martin's, 1957), 170–71. Subsequent parenthetical references will be to this edition.

10. Letter from Sean O'Casey to Lennox Robinson, 10 Jan. 1926, rpt. in *The Letters of Sean O'Casey, 1910–1941*, vol. 1, ed. David Krause (New York: Macmillan, 1975), 165.

11. Ibid.

12. Ibid., 166

13. Sean O'Casey, *Inishfallen, Fare Thee Well*, vol. 2 of *Mirror in My House* [1949] (New York: Macmillan, 1956), 235.

14. Ria Mooney, *Players and the Painted Stage*, ed. Val Mulkerns, in *George Spelvin's Theatre Book* 1 (Summer 1978), 43, 45.

15. Fallon, *Sean O'Casey*, 88.

16. "New Sean O'Casey Play at the Abbey," *Evening Mail* 9 Feb. 1926, rpt. in Hogan and Burnham, *The Years of O'Casey*, 287.

17. Holloway, *Joseph Holloway's Abbey Theatre*, 251.

18. "New Sean O'Casey Play," *Evening Mail* 9 Feb. 1926, 287.

19. Letter from Lennox Robinson to Lady Gregory, 1 Feb. 1926, quoted in Hogan and Burnham, *The Years of O'Casey*, 294.

20. "Abbey Theatre Scene," *Irish Times* 12 Feb. 1926, rpt. in Hogan and Burnham, *The Years of O'Casey*, 295.

21. Holloway, *Joseph Holloway's Abbey Theatre*, 253.

22. "Abbey Theatre Scene," *Irish Times* 12 Feb. 1926, 295.

23. "Riotous Scenes," *Irish Independent* 12 Feb. 1926, rpt. in Hogan and Burnham, *The Years of O'Casey*, 300.

24. "Abbey Theatre Scene," *Irish Times* 12 Feb. 1926, 295.

25. Mooney, *Players*, 45.

26. "Riotous Scenes," *Irish Independent* 12 Feb. 1926, 300.

27. Shelah Richards, unpublished memoir quoted in Hogan and Burnham, *The Years of O'Casey*, 298.

28. "Riotous Scenes," *Irish Independent* 12 Feb. 1926, 300.

29. "Abbey Theatre Scene," *Irish Times* 12 Feb. 1926, 295.

30. Gregory, *Lady Gregory's Journals*, 97.

31. Richards, unpublished memoir, 298.

32. "Riotous Scenes," *Irish Independent* 12 Feb. 1926, 300–1.

33. Richards, unpublished memoir, 298.

34. Gabriel Fallon, "The First Production of *The Plough and the Stars*," *Sean O'Casey Review* Spring 1976, 169.

35. "Riotous Scenes," *Irish Independent* 12 Feb. 1926, 301; Stephen Gwynn, *Observer* (London) 14 Feb. 1926, rpt. in Robert G. Lowery, *A Whirlwind in Dublin: The Plough and the Stars Riots* (Westport, CT: Greenwood, 1984), 39.

36. O'Casey, *Inishfallen*, 238.

37. "Riotous Scenes," *Irish Independent* 12 Feb. 1926, 301.

38. *Guardian* (Manchester), quoted in Lowery, *A Whirlwind*, 31; "Abbey Theatre Scene," *Irish Times* 12 Feb. 1926, 296.

39. O'Casey, *Inishfallen*, 239.

40. Baz Kershaw, "Oh for Unruly Audiences! Or, Patterns of Audience Participation in Twentieth-Century Theatre," *Modern Drama* 42 (2001), 138–39, 135.

41. "Abbey Theatre Scene," *Irish Times* 12 Feb. 1926, 296.

42. "Riotous Scenes," *Irish Independent* 12 Feb. 1926, 301.

43. O'Casey, *Inishfallen*, 238.

44. Fallon, *Sean O'Casey*, 92.

45. "Abbey Theatre Scene," *Irish Times* 12 Feb. 1926, 296.

46. "Riotous Scenes," *Irish Independent* 12 Feb. 1926, 301–2.

47. Gregory, *Lady Gregory's Journals*, 97

48. "Abbey Kidnapping Plot Fails," *Irish Times* 15 Feb. 1926, quoted in Hogan and Burnham, *The Years of O'Casey*, 308.

49. Ibid., 309.

50. Maureen Malone, *The Plays of Sean O'Casey* (Southern Illinois UP, 1969), 6.

51. David Krause, "Some Truths and Jokes about the Easter Rising," *Sean O'Casey Review* Fall 1976, 13.

52. Letter from Sean O'Casey to Sara Allgood, 23 Feb. 1926, rpt. in O'Casey, *Letters*, 174.

53. Quoted in Krause, "Some Truths," 15.

54. Hanna Sheehy-Skeffington, letter to the editor, *Irish Independent* 15 Feb. 1926, rpt. in O'Casey, *Letters*, 168.

55. Sean O'Casey, letter to the editor, *Irish Independent* 20 Feb. 1926, rpt. in O'Casey, *Letters*, 169.

56. Sheehy-Skeffington, letter, 168.

57. O'Casey, letter to the editor, 171.

58. "*The Plough and the Stars* Author Replies," *Irish Independent* 2 Mar. 1926, 177, 178.

59. Holloway, *Joseph Holloway's Abbey Theatre*, 266.

60. *Irish Times* 12 Feb. 1926, rpt. in Lowery, *A Whirlwind*, 35; Tommy Irwin, *Voice of Labour* 20 Feb. 1926, rpt. in ibid., 75.

61. Welch, *The Abbey Theatre*, 95–96.

62. Sean O'Shea, letter to the editor, *Irish Independent* 15 Feb. 1926, rpt. in Lowery, *A Whirlwind*, 62.

63. *Voice of Labour* 13 Feb. 1926, rpt. in Lowery, *A Whirlwind*, 52.

64. "*The Plough and the Stars* Author Replies to Republican's Charges. A Piquant Debate," *Irish Independent* 2 Mar. 1926, rpt. in O'Casey, *Letters*, 178.

65. "Riotous Scenes," *Irish Independent* 12 Feb. 1926, 300.

66. *Irish Times* 12 Feb. 1926, 35.

67. "These People Will Never Learn Sense," *Evening Mail* 12 Feb. 1926, rpt. in Hogan and Burnham, *The Years of O'Casey*, 305.

68. Sheehy-Skeffington, letter, 168.

69. Johnson, *Listening in Paris*, 3.

70. Gwynn, *Observer* 14 Feb. 1926, 39.

71. Sheehy-Skeffington, letter, 167–68.

72. Holloway, *Joseph Holloway's Abbey Theatre*, 254.

73. "Riotous Scenes," *Irish Independent* 12 Feb. 1926, 300.

74. Quoted in Lowery, *A Whirlwind*, 106.

75. Holloway, *Joseph Holloway's Abbey Theatre*, 268.

76. O'Casey, *Inishfallen*, 245.

CHAPTER 5

1. Klaus P. Fischer, *Nazi Germany: A New History* (New York: Continuum, 1995), 185.

2. Emil Faktor, review of *Vatermord* (Bronnen) at Deutsches Theater, Berlin, *Berliner Börser-Courier* 15 May 1922, rpt. in Günther Rühle, *Theater für die Republik, 1917–1933, im Spiegel der Kritik* (Frankfurt: Fischer, 1967), 377.

3. Walter Panofsky, *Protest in der Oper: Das provokative Musiktheater der zwanziger Jahre* (Munich: Laokoon, 1966), 171.

4. Carl Zuckmayer, *Als wär's ein Stück von mir* (Frankfurt: Fischer, 1966), 265.

5. Walter Hinck, "Brecht und sein Publikum," *Frankfurter Hefte* 9 (1954): 940.

6. John Willett, *The Theatre of the Weimar Republic* (New York/London: Holmes & Meier, 1988), 96.

7. Fritz Kortner, *Aller Tage Abend* (Munich: Kindler, 1959), 358.

8. Bertolt Brecht, diary entry 10 Feb. 1922, *Werke: Große kommentierte Berliner und Frankfurter Ausgabe,* ed. Werner Hecht, Jan Knopf, Werner Mittenzwei, and Klaus-Detlef Müller (Berlin & Weimar: Aufbau; Frankfurt: Suhrkamp, 1988–2000), 26: 271. Cf. John Willett, *Brecht on Theatre* (New York: Hill and Wang, 1964), 9. Where applicable, I give page references to Willett's translations in his widely used collection of Brecht texts.

9. Richard Rieß, review of *Trommeln in der Nacht* (Brecht) at Kammerspiele, Munich, *Magdeburgische Zeitung* 5 Oct. 1922, rpt. in *Trommeln in der Nacht,* ed. Wolfgang M. Schwiedrzik (Frankfurt: Suhrkamp, 1990), 277.

10. Bertolt Brecht, "Programmzettel," *Werke* 24: 25.

11. Bertolt Brecht, *Im Dickicht der Städte. Erstfassung und Materialien,* ed. Gisela E. Bahr (Frankfurt: Suhrkamp, 1968), 92.

12. Horst Wolfram Geißler, review of *Im Dickicht* (Brecht) at Residenztheater, Munich, *München-Augsburger Abendzeitung* 11 May 1923, rpt. in Rühle, *Theater,* 451.

13. Geißler, review, 451–52.

14. Karl Bauer, review of *Im Dickicht* (Brecht) at Residenztheater, Munich, *Augsburger Neueste Nachrichten* 11 May 1923, rpt. in Rüdiger Steinlein, "Expressionismusüberwindung: Restitution bürgerlicher Dramaturgie oder Beginn eines neuen Dramas?" *Brechtdiskussion* (Kronberg: Scriptor, 1974), 46; Georg Jacob Wolf, review of *Im Dickicht* (Brecht) at Residenztheater, Munich, *Münchner Zeitung* 11 May 1923, rpt. in Rühle, *Theater,* 449.

15. Herbert Ihering, review of *Im Dickicht* (Brecht) at Residenztheater, Munich, *Berliner Börsen-Courier* 12 May 1923, rpt. in Rühle, *Theater,* 448.

16. Wolf, review, 449; Karl Bauer, review, 45.

17. Letter from Bertolt Brecht to Julius Berstl, 22 Sep. 1922, *Werke* 28: 174.

18. Thomas Mann, "German Letter" *The Dial* Oct. 1923, 375.

19. Josef Stolzing, review of *Im Dickicht* (Brecht) at Residenztheater, Munich, *Völkischer Beobachter* 12 May 1923, rpt. in Rühle, *Theater,* 453.

20. Mann, "German Letter," 374.

21. Bertolt Brecht, "Vorspruch," *Werke* 24: 10.

22. Hanns Johst, *Der Einsame* [1917] (Berlin: Albert Langen/Georg Müller, 1938), 8, 11.

23. Bertolt Brecht, *Frühe Stücke* (Frankfurt: Suhrkamp, 1967), 26, 56–57, 81.

24. Alfred Kerr, review of *Baal* (Brecht) at Altes Theater, Leipzig, *Berliner Tag-*

eblatt 11 Dec. 1923, rpt. in *Baal. Der böse Baal der asoziale,* ed. Dieter Schmidt (Frankfurt: Suhrkamp, 1968), 176.

25. Egbert Delpy, review of *Baal* (Brecht) at Altes Theater, Leipzig, *Leipziger Neueste Nachrichten* 10 Dec. 1923, rpt. in *Baal,* ed. Schmidt, 171–72.

26. Hans Georg Richter, review of *Baal* (Brecht) at Altes Theater, Leipzig, *Leipziger Tageblatt* 11 Dec. 1923, rpt. in *Baal,* ed. Schmidt, 182.

27. Herbert Ihering, review of *Baal* (Brecht) at Altes Theater, Leipzig, *Berliner Börsen-Courier* 9 Dec. 1923, rpt. in *Brecht in der Kritik,* ed. Monika Wyss (Munich: Kindler, 1977), 33, 34.

28. Hans Natonek, review of *Baal* (Brecht) at Altes Theater, Leipzig, *Neue Leipziger Zeitung,* 10 Dec. 1923, rpt. in *Baal,* ed. Schmidt, 175.

29. Ibid., 173.

30. Richter, review, 181, 182.

31. Natonek, review, 173, 174.

32. Ihering, review of *Baal* 1923, 37.

33. hgr, *Leipziger Tageblatt* 14 Dec. 1923, rpt. in *Baal,* ed. Schmidt, 185.

34. Bertolt Brecht, "Vorspruch," 10.

35. Bertolt Brecht, *Lebenslauf des Mannes Baal, Werke* 1: 157.

36. Paul Fechter, review of *Baal* (Brecht) at Junge Bühne, Berlin, *Deutsche Allgemeine Zeitung* 16 Feb. 1926, rpt. in *Baal,* ed. Schmidt, 190.

37. Alfred Kerr, review of *Baal* (Brecht) at Junge Bühne, Berlin, *Berliner Tageblatt* 15 Feb. 1926, rpt. in *Baal,* ed. Schmidt, 188.

38. Julius Hart, review of *Baal* (Brecht) at Junge Bühne, Berlin, *Der Tag* 16 Feb. 1926, rpt. in *Baal,* ed. Schmidt, 194.

39. Monty Jacobs, review of *Baal* (Brecht) at Junge Bühne, Berlin, *Vossische Zeitung* 16 Feb. 1926, rpt. in *Baal,* ed. Schmidt, 197.

40. Ernst Heilborn, review of *Baal* (Brecht) at Junge Bühne, Berlin, *Frankfurter Zeitung* 17 Feb. 1926, rpt. in *Baal,* ed. Schmidt, 200.

41. Jacobs, review, 197.

42. Hart, review, 194, 195.

43. Heilborn, review, 201.

44. Ihering, review of *Baal* (Brecht) at Junge Bühne, Berlin, *Berliner Börsen-Courier* 15 Feb. 1926, rpt. in *Baal,* ed. Schmidt, 185–86.

45. Herbert Ihering, "Klärung," in Ihering, *Bertolt Brecht hat das dichterische Antlitz Deutschlands verändert,* ed. Klaus Völker (Munich: Kindler, 1980), 30–31.

46. Kortner, *Aller Tage,* 385.

47. Johannes W. Harnisch, review of *Baal* (Brecht) at Junge Bühne, Berlin, *Der Montag* 15 Feb. 1926, rpt. in Rühle, *Theater,* 689–90.

48. Zuckmayer, *Als wär's ein Stück,* 357.

49. Kortner, *Aller Tage,* 411–12, 384.

50. Bertolt Brecht, "Junge Bühne—Sozialrevolutionäre," *Werke* 21: 286–7.

51. Willett, *The Theatre of the Weimar Republic,* 207.

52. Quoted in Brecht, *Werke* 2:454.

53. Elsa Bauer, review of *Mahagonny Songspiel* (Brecht/Weill) at Deutsche Kammermusik Baden-Baden, *Morgenzeitung und Handelsblatt Baden-Baden* 19 July 1927. (Author unnamed, but review attributed to Bauer by Wyss, *Brecht in der Kritik,* 73.)

54. Lotte Lenya, "I remember *Mahagonny*," *Philips Music Herald* 4.1 (Spring 1959), 7.

55. Hans Böhm, review of *Mahagonny Songspiel* (Brecht/Weill) at Deutsche Kammermusik Baden-Baden, *Das Theater* 1 Aug. 1927, 350.

56. Elsa Bauer, review.

57. Böhm, review, 350.

58. Letter from Bertolt Brecht to Helene Weigel, 18 July 1927, *Werke* 28: 289.

59. Lenya, "I remember," 7.

60. Heinrich Strobel, review of *Mahagonny Songspiel* (Brecht/Weill) at Deutsche Kammermusik Baden-Baden, *Berliner Börsen-Courier* 19 July 1927, quoted in Brecht, *Werke* 2:454.

61. Hans Wilfert, review of *Mahagonny Songspiel* (Brecht/Weill) at Deutsche Kammermusik Baden-Baden, rpt. in *Brecht in der Kritik*, ed. Wyss, 69.

62. Elsa Bauer, review.

63. Ibid.

64. Ernst Josef Aufricht, *Erzähle damit Du Dein Recht erweist* (Berlin: Propyläen, 1966), 73.

65. Bertolt Brecht, "Einführung:»Die Dreigroschenoper«" *Werke* 24: 57.

66. Bertolt Brecht, "Über die Verwendung von Musik für ein episches Theater" *Werke* 22: 156–57, cf. Willett, *Brecht on Theatre*, 85.

67. Bertolt Brecht, "Anmerkungen zur»Dreigroschenoper«" *Werke* 24: 59, cf. Willett, *Brecht on Theatre*, 44.

68. Bertolt Brecht, "The German Drama: pre-Hitler," *Werke* 22: 941, cf. Willett, *Brecht on Theatre*, 79.

69. Karl Laux, "Skandal in B-B" *Hindemith Jahrbuch* 2 (1972), 171.

70. Bertolt Brecht, "Zum *Lehrstück*," *Werke* 24: 90.

71. Bertolt Brecht and Paul Hindemith, *Lehrstück* [vocal score] (Mainz: Schott, 1929), 46.

72. Laux, "Skandal," 171.

73. Heinrich Strobel, review of *Lehrstück* (Brecht/Hindemith) at Deutsche Kammermusik Baden-Baden, *Der deutsche Rundfunk* 3 (1929), rpt. in *Brecht in der Kritik*, ed. Wyss, 95.

74. Elsa Bauer, "Deutsche Kammermusik B.-Baden," *Morgenzeitung und Handelsblatt Baden-Baden* 30 July 1929.

75. Hans Wilfert, review of *Lehrstück* (Brecht/Hindemith) at Deutsche Kammermusik Baden-Baden, *Badeblatt der Stadt Baden-Baden* 31 July 1929, quoted in Klaus-Dieter Krabiel, *Brechts Lehrstücke* (Stuttgart: Metzler, 1993), 344n13.

76. Quoted in Krabiel, *Brechts Lehrstücke*, 345n16.

77. Bertolt Brecht, "Zur Theorie des Lehrstücks" *Werke* 22: 352.

78. Cf. Krabiel, *Brechts Lehrstücke*, 345.

79. M. Unger, "Musikfest in Baden-Baden," *Berliner Börsen-Zeitung* 1 Aug. 1929, quoted in Krabiel, *Brechts Lehrstücke*, 70; E.S., "Das Musikfest der Linken," *Neues Wiener Journal* 4 Aug. 1929, quoted in Krabiel, *Brechts Lehrstücke*, 348.

80. Inge Karsten, "Deutsche Kammermusik 1929," *Badische Volkszeitung* 30 July 1929. (Author unnamed but Karsten listed as arts correspondent, and review attributed to Karsten by Krabiel, *Brechts Lehrstücke*, 339 [and incorrectly to Elsa Bauer by Wyss, *Brecht in der Kritik*, 97.]); Bauer, "Deutsche Kammermusik B.-Baden."

81. Wilfert, review of *Lehrstück*, quoted in Krabiel, *Brechts Lehrstücke*, 70.

82. A. Einstein, "'Gemeinschafts-Musik' in Baden-Baden," *Berliner Tageblatt* 31 July 1929, quoted in Krabiel, *Brechts Lehrstücke*, 70; M. Marschalk, "Skandal um Brecht und Hindemith," *Vossische Zeitung* 30 July 1929, quoted in Krabiel, *Brechts Lehrstücke*, 70.

83. Brecht and Hindemith, *Lehrstück*, 35.

84. Theo Lingen, *Ich über mich* (Velber bei Hanover: Friedrich, 1963), 43.

85. Karsten, "Deutsche Kammermusik 1929"; Bauer, "Deutsche Kammermusik B.-Baden."

86. Hanns Eisler, "Bertolt Brecht und die Musik," *Sinn und Form* Sonderheft 9 (1957): 439.

87. Bauer, "Deutsche Kammermusik B.-Baden."

88. Lingen, *Ich*, 43.

89. Marschalk, "Skandal," quoted in Krabiel, *Brechts Lehrstücke*, 66.

90. Karsten, "Deutsche Kammermusik 1929."

91. Karl Holl, review of *Lehrstück* (Brecht/Hindemith) at Deutsche Kammermusik Baden-Baden, *Frankfurter Zeitung* 2 Aug. 1929, rpt. in *Brecht in der Kritik*, ed. Wyss, 92.

92. Heinrich Strobel, review of *Lehrstück* (Brecht/Hindemith) at Deutsche Kammermusik Baden-Baden, *Der deutsche Rundfunk* 3 (1929), quoted in Krabiel, *Brechts Lehrstücke*, 70.

93. Holl, review, 92; Karsten, "Deutsche Kammermusik 1929."

94. Strobel, review, 95.

95. H. Boettcher, review of *Lehrstück* (Brecht/Hindemith) at Deutsche Kammermusik Baden-Baden, *Deutsche Tonkünstler-Zeitung* 27 (1929), quoted in Krabiel, *Brechts Lehrstücke*, 70.

96. Jan Needle and Peter Thomson, *Brecht* (U of Chicago P, 1981), 65.

97. Holl, review, 92.

98. Karsten, "Deutsche Kammermusik 1929"; F. W. Herzog, "Bilanz der deutschen Kammermusik Baden-Baden 1929," *Rheinisch-Westfälische Zeitung* 1 Aug. 1929, quoted in Krabiel, *Brechts Lehrstücke*, 67.

99. F. W. Herzog, "Bilanz," quoted in Krabiel, *Brechts Lehrstücke*, 67.

100. Karsten, "Deutsche Kammermusik 1929."

101. Bauer, "Deutsche Kammermusik B.-Baden."

102. Karsten, "Deutsche Kammermusik 1929."

103. Ibid.

104. Hans Wilfert, *Badeblatt der Stadt Baden-Baden* 1 Aug. 1929, quoted in Wyss 98.

105. Krabiel, *Brechts Lehrstücke*, 66.

106. E. Preußner, "Gemeinschaftsmusik 1929 in Baden-Baden," *Die Musik* 21 (1928/29), quoted in Krabiel, *Brechts Lehrstücke*, 345n26.

107. Bertolt Brecht, *Aufstieg und Fall der Stadt Mahagonny* (Frankfurt: Suhrkamp, 1955), 70, 76.

108. Quoted in Brecht, *Werke* 2:464.

109. These are the lines used in the premiere, as revised by Brecht in response to objections about the script's sexual content (with *Liebesakt*, meaning the sex act, changed to just *Liebe*), quoted in anon., review of *Aufstieg und Fall der Stadt Mahagonny* (Brecht/Weill) at Opernhaus, Leipzig, *Zeitschrift für Musik* 4 (1930): 292.

110. Brecht, *Aufstieg*, 8, 24, 36, 71.

111. Polgar, "Krach in Leipzig," 275.

112. Klaus Pringsheim, review of *Aufstieg und Fall der Stadt Mahagonny* (Brecht/ Weill) at Opernhaus, Leipzig, *Weltbühne* 26.12 (18 Mar. 1930): 433.

113. Eberhard Preußner, review of *Aufstieg und Fall der Stadt Mahagonny* (Brecht/Weill) at Opernhaus, Leipzig, *Musik und Gesellschaft* 1930/31: 33.

114. Pringsheim, review, 434.

115. Ronald Sanders, *The Days Grow Short: The Life and Music of Kurt Weill* (New York: Holt, Rinehart and Winston, 1980), 151.

116. Preußner, review, 33.

117. Pringsheim, review, 434, 433.

118. Quoted in David Drew, "The History of Mahagonny," *Musical Times* Jan. 1963, 20.

119. Brecht, *Aufstieg*, 77.

120. Polgar, "Krach in Leipzig," 274–75.

121. Anon., review, *Zeitschrift für Musik*, 292.

122. *Sächsische Arbeiter-Zeitung* quoted in Brecht, *Werke* 2: 465.

123. Cf. Sanders, *The Days*, 149.

124. Lenya, "I remember," 8.

125. Peter Panter [Kurt Tucholsky], "Proteste gegen die Dreigroschenoper," *Weltbühne* 8 April 1930: 557–58.

126. Lenya, "I remember," 8.

127. Anon., review, *Zeitschrift für Musik*, 292.

128. Bertolt Brecht, "Anmerkungen zur Oper *Aufstieg und Fall der Stadt Mahagonny*," *Werke* 24: 78, 81, cf. Willett, *Brecht on Theatre*, 37, 39.

129. Bertolt Brecht, "Erklärung," *Werke* 24: 86.

130. Brecht, "Anmerkungen zur Oper," 77–78, cf. Willett, *Brecht on Theatre*, 36.

131. Ibid., 78, cf. Willett, *Brecht on Theatre*, 36.

132. Polgar, "Krach in Leipzig," 276.

133. Zuckmayer, *Als wär's ein Stück*, 380.

134. Franz Köppen, review of *Aufstieg und Fall der Stadt Mahagonny* (Brecht/ Weill), at Theater am Kurfürstendamm, Berlin, *Berliner Börsen-Zeitung* 22 Dec. 1931, rpt. in Wyss, *Brecht in der Kritik*, 117.

135. Alfred Einstein, review of *Aufstieg und Fall der Stadt Mahagonny* (Brecht/ Weill), at Theater am Kurfürstendamm, Berlin, *Berliner Tageblatt* 22 Dec. 1931.

136. Herbert Ihering, review of *Mann ist Mann* (Brecht) at Staatliches Schauspielhaus, Berlin, *Berliner Börsen-Courier* 7 Feb. 1931, rpt. in Rühle, *Theater*, 1072.

137. Emil Burri, "Anmerkungen zu den Proben von *Mann ist Mann*,"quoted in Brecht, *Werke*, 2: 418.

138. Bertolt Brecht, *Mann ist Mann* (Frankfurt: Suhrkamp, 1953).

139. Brecht, *Mann ist Mann*, 16.

140. Brecht, *Werke* 2: 412.

141. Bertolt Brecht, "Anmerkungen zum Lustspiel *Mann ist Mann*," *Werke* 24: 45.

142. B. W., review of *Mann ist Mann* (Brecht) at Staatliches Schauspielhaus, Berlin, newspaper unidentified, 7 Feb. 1931, rpt. in Rühle, *Theater*, 1072.

143. Anon., "Berliner Theaterwinter 1930/31," *Literarische Welt* 24 (1931), quoted in Michael Patterson, *The Revolution in German Theatre, 1900–1933* (London: Routledge & Kegan Paul, 1981), 180.

144. Sergej Tretjakow, "Bert Brecht," *Erinnerungen an Brecht*, ed. Hubert Witt (Leipzig: Reclam, 1964), 76.

145. B. W., review, 1072.

146. Felix Hollaender, "Skandal um Brechts *Mann ist Mann*," rpt. in *Lebendiges Theater* (Berlin, 1932), 314.

147. B. W., review, 1072.

148. Tretjakow, "Bert Brecht," 77.

149. Ihering, review of *Mann*, 1073.

150. Bernhard Diebold, review of *Mann ist Mann* (Brecht), at Staatliches Schauspielhaus, Berlin, *Frankfurter Zeitung* 11 Feb. 1931.

151. Tretjakow, "Bert Brecht," 76–77.

152. Diebold, review.

153. Ihering, review of *Mann*, 1074.

154. Brecht, "Anmerkungen zum Lustspiel," 47–48, cf. Willett, *Brecht on Theatre*, 54.

155. Ibid., 47–50, cf. Willett, *Brecht on Theatre*, 54–56.

156. Patterson, *The Revolution*, 181.

157. Brecht, "Anmerkungen zum Lustspiel," 48, 49, 51, cf. Willett, *Brecht on Theatre*, 55, 56.

158. Ihering, review of *Mann*, 1074.

159. Willy Haas, "Der Fall Brecht. Zum Theaterskandal bei »Mann ist Mann«" *Literarische Welt* 8 (20 Feb. 1931).

160. Quoted in Bertolt Brecht, *Werke* 2: 419.

161. Bertolt Brecht, "Anmerkungen [1933]," *Werke* 24: 115.

162. Bertolt Brecht, "[Das Stück *Die Mutter*]," *Werke* 24: 110.

163. Helene Weigel, "Erinnerungen an die erste Aufführung der *Mutter*," *Materialien zu Bertolt Brechts* Die Mutter, ed. Werner Hecht (Frankfurt: Suhrkamp, 1969), 29.

164. Brecht, "[Das Stück *Die Mutter*]," 110.

165. Weigel, "Erinnerungen," 33.

166. Brecht, "Anmerkungen [1933]," 119, cf. Willett, *Brecht on Theatre*, 58–59.

167. Brecht, "[Das Stück *Die Mutter*]," 110.

168. Bertolt Brecht, "Was ist primitiv?" *Werke* 24: 114–15, cf. Willett, *Brecht on Theatre*, 62.

169. Bertolt Brecht, "Kleines Organon für das Theater," *Werke* 23: 66, cf. Willett, *Brecht on Theatre*, 179–80.

170. Bertolt Brecht, "Kleine Liste der beliebtesten, landläufigsten und banalsten Irrtümer über das Epische Theater," *Werke* 22: 315, cf. Willett, *Brecht on Theatre*, 162.

171. Ibid.

172. Brecht, "Kleines Organon," 75–76, cf. Willett, *Brecht on Theatre*, 187.

173. Brecht, "Anmerkungen [1933]," 115, cf. Willett, *Brecht on Theatre*, 57.

174. Brecht, "Kleines Organon," 73, cf. Willett, *Brecht on Theatre*, 185.

175. Brecht, "Anmerkungen [1933]," 122.

176. Bertolt Brecht, *Der gute Mensch von Sezuan*, *Werke* 6: 279.

177. Brecht, *Werke* 23: 191.

178. Brecht, "Anmerkungen [1933]," 128, cf. Willett, *Brecht on Theatre*, 60.

179. Bertolt Brecht, "Über experimentelles Theater," *Werke* 22: 547, cf. Willett, *Brecht on Theatre*, 132.

180. Brecht, "Kleines Organon," 74, cf. Willett, *Brecht on Theatre*, 186.

181. John Willett, *The Theatre of Bertolt Brecht*, revised ed. (New York: New Directions, 1968), 182–83.

182. Needle and Thomson, *Brecht*, 78.

183. Brecht, "Über die Verwendung von Musik," 162, cf. Willett, *Brecht on Theatre*, 89.

184. Brecht, "Kleines Organon," 66, 65, cf. Willett, *Brecht on Theatre*, 180, 179.

185. Bernard Guillemin, "Was arbeiten Sie? / Gespräch mit Bert Brecht," *Die Literarische Welt* 30 July 1926, 234, cf. Willett, *Brecht on Theatre*, 15.

186. Brecht, "Anmerkungen [1933]," 116, cf. Willett, *Brecht on Theatre*, 58.

187. Brecht, "Kleines Organon," 81, cf. Willett, *Brecht on Theatre*, 192.

188. Bertolt Brecht, "Kurze Beschreibung einer neuen Technik der Schauspielkunst, die einen Verfremdungseffekt hervorbringt," *Werke* 22: 643, cf. Willett, *Brecht on Theatre*, 137.

189. See Bertolt Brecht, "Die Strassenszene. Grundmodell einer Szene des epischen Theaters," *Werke* 22: 370–81, cf. Willett, *Brecht on Theatre*, 121–28.

190. Brecht, "Kurze Beschreibung," 642, cf. Willett, *Brecht on Theatre*, 136.

191. Brecht, "Anmerkungen zur Oper," 78, cf. Willett, *Brecht on Theatre*, 37.

192. Brecht, "Kleine Liste," 315, cf. Willett, *Brecht on Theatre*, 162; Bertolt Brecht, "Formprobleme des Theaters aus neuem Inhalt," *Werke* 23: 110, cf. *Brecht on Theatre*, 227.

193. Bertolt Brecht, "Mutter Courage lernt nichts," *Werke* 25: 241, cf. Willett, *Brecht on Theatre*, 221.

194. Bertolt Brecht, "»Die dramatische Szene«," *Werke* 25: 231, cf. Willett, *Brecht on Theatre*, 221.

195. Brecht, "[Nachträge zum *Kleinen Organon*]," *Werke* 23: 290, cf. Willett, *Brecht on Theatre*, 277.

196. Michael Patterson, "Brecht's legacy," in *The Cambridge Companion to Brecht*, ed. Peter Thomson and Glendyr Sacks (Cambridge UP, 1994), 278.

197. Peter Thomson, "Brecht's lives," in *The Cambridge Companion*, 31.

198. Bertolt Brecht, "[Erklärung]," *Werke* 24: 86.

199. Bertolt Brecht, "Kleines Privatissimum für meinen Freund Max Gorelik," *Werke* 23: 39, cf. Willett, *Brecht on Theatre*, 161.

AFTERWORD

1. Peter Handke, *Offending the Audience* in Peter Handke, *Kaspar and Other Plays*, trans. Michael Roloff (New York: Farrar, Straus and Giroux, 1969). Handke's title *Publikumsbeschimpfung* would be more accurately rendered as "insulting the audience," or "calling the audience names."

2. Peter Handke, *Stücke 1* (Frankfurt: Suhrkamp, 1972), 44, 45, 46, 19.

3. Quoted in Dieter E. Zimmer, "Beat-Drama," *Die Zeit* 21 June 1966, 8.

4. FR, "Experimenta endete mit Theaterskandalen," *Frankfurter Rundschau* 11 June 1966, 13.

5. Eric Bentley, ed., *The Storm over The Deputy* (New York: Grove, 1964).

6. Bennett, *Theatre Audiences*, 2.

7. Ibid., 177.

8. Alan Sinfield, "The theatre and its audiences," in *Society and Literature 1945–1970*, ed. Alan Sinfield (London: Holmes & Meier, 1983), 181.

9. Bennett, *Theatre Audiences*, 1.

10. Mackintosh, *Architecture*, 47.

11. Keir Elam, *The Semiotics of Theatre and Drama* (London and New York: Methuen, 1980), 63.

12. Quoted in Michael Kirby, *Futurist Performance* [1971] (New York: PAJ, 1986), 181.

13. Bennett, *Theatre Audiences*, 182.

14. Giorgio Strehler, "On the Relations between Stage and Stalls: the Background and Modalities of Involvement," in *Theatre Space*, ed. James F. Arnott et al. (Munich, Prestel, 1977), 148.

15. Bennett, *Theatre Audiences*, 185.

16. Kershaw, "Oh for Unruly Audiences!" 136, 141.

17. Bennett, *Theatre Audiences*, 186; Kershaw, "Oh for Unruly Audiences!" 136.

18. Lyn Gardner, quoted in Kershaw, "Oh for Unruly Audiences!" 133.

19. Kershaw, "Oh for Unruly Audiences!" 133.

Selected Bibliography

Abercrombie, Nicholas, and Brian Longhurst. *Audiences: A Sociological Theory of Performance and Imagination.* London: Sage, 1998.

Arnaud, Noël. *Alfred Jarry, d'Ubu roi au Docteur Faustroll.* Paris: La Table Ronde, 1974.

Arrivé, Michel. *Les Langages de Jarry: Essai de sémiotique littéraire.* Paris: Klincksieck, 1972.

Artaud, Antonin. *The Theater and its Double.* Trans. Mary Caroline Richards. New York: Grove Weidenfeld, 1958.

Baer, Marc. *Theatre and Disorder in Late Georgian London.* Oxford UP, 1992.

Barish, Jonas. *The Antitheatrical Prejudice.* U of California P, 1981.

Bartram, Graham, and Anthony Waine, eds. *Brecht in Perspective.* London and New York: Longman, 1982.

Bauland, Peter. *Gerhart Hauptmann's* Before Daybreak: *A Translation and an Introduction.* U of North Carolina P, 1978.

Beaumont, Keith. *Alfred Jarry: a critical and biographical study.* New York: St. Martin's, 1984.

Béhar, Henri. *Jarry Dramaturge.* Paris: Nizet, 1980.

Benjamin, Walter. *Versuche über Brecht.* Frankfurt: Suhrkamp, 1966.

Bennett, Susan. *Theatre Audiences: A Theory of Production and Reception.* London & New York: Routledge, 1990.

Blau, Herbert. *The Audience.* Johns Hopkins UP, 1990.

Bloom, Harold, ed. *John Millington Synge's* The Playboy of the Western World. New York: Chelsea House, 1988.

Booth, Michael R., et al. *The Revels History of Drama in English VI: 1750–1880.* London: Methuen, 1975.

Booth, Michael R. *Theatre in the Victorian Age.* Cambridge UP, 1991.

Braun, Edward. *The Director and the Stage: From Naturalism to Grotowski*. London: Methuen, 1982.

Brauneck, Manfred, and Christine Müller, eds. *Naturalismus. Manifeste und Dokumente zur deutschen Literatur 1880–1900*. Stuttgart: Metzler, 1987.

Brecht, Bertolt. *Baal. Der böse Baal der asoziale. Texte, Varianten, Materialien*. Ed. Dieter Schmidt. Frankfurt: Suhrkamp, 1968.

——. *Im Dickicht der Städte. Erstfassung und Materialien*. Ed. Gisela E. Bahr. Frankfurt: Suhrkamp, 1968.

——. *Werke. Große kommentierte Berliner und Frankfurter Ausgabe*. Ed. Werner Hecht, Jan Knopf, Werner Mittenzwei, and Klaus-Detlef Müller. 30 vols. Berlin & Weimar: Aufbau; Frankfurt: Suhrkamp, 1988–2000.

Brockett, Oscar G., and Robert F. Findlay. *A Century of Innovation: A History of European and American Theatre and Drama since 1870*. Englewood Cliffs: Prentice-Hall, 1973.

Carlson, Marvin. *The French Stage in the Nineteenth Century*. Metuchen, NJ: Scarecrow Press, 1972.

——. *The German Stage in the Nineteenth Century*. Metuchen, NJ: Scarecrow Press, 1972.

Claus, Horst. *The Theatre Director Otto Brahm*. Ann Arbor: UMI Research Press, 1981.

Cowen, Roy C. *Der Naturalismus. Kommentar zu einer Epoche*. Munich: Winkler, 1973.

Damerval, Gérard. *Ubu Roi: la bombe comique de 1896*. Paris: Nizet, 1984.

Deak, Frantisek. *Symbolist Theater: The Formation of an Avant-Garde*. Johns Hopkins UP, 1993.

Descotes, Maurice. *Le Public de théâtre et son histoire*. Paris: PUF, 1964.

Dickson, Keith A. *Towards Utopia: A Study of Brecht*. Oxford: Clarendon, 1978.

Dumur, Guy, ed. *Histoire des spectacles*. Paris: Gallimard, 1965.

Eksteins, Modris. *The Rites of Spring: the Great War and the Birth of the Modern Age*. Boston: Houghton Mifflin, 1989.

Elias, Norbert. *The Civilizing Process*. Trans. Edmund Jephcott, ed. Eric Dunning, Johan Goudsblom, and Stephen Mennell. Rev. ed. Oxford: Blackwell, 2000.

Ellis-Fermor, Una. *The Irish Dramatic Movement*. London: Methuen, 1954.

Esslin, Martin. *Brecht: the Man and his Work*. New York: Anchor, 1961

Ewen, Frederic. *Bertolt Brecht, His Life, His Art and His Times*. New York: Citadel, 1967.

Fischer, Matthias-Johannes. *Brechts Theatertheorie. Forschungsgeschichte—Forschungsstand—Perspektiven*. Frankfurt: Lang, 1988.

Flannery, James W. *W. B. Yeats and the Idea of a Theatre*. Yale UP, 1976.

Foster, R. F. *Modern Ireland, 1600–1972*. New York: Viking Penguin, 1988.

Frazier, Adrian. *Behind the Scenes: Yeats, Horniman, and the Struggle for the Abbey Theatre*. U of California P, 1990.

Fuegi, John. *Bertolt Brecht: Chaos, According to Plan*. Cambridge UP, 1987.

Gilliam, Bryan, ed. *Music and Performance during the Weimar Republic*. Cambridge UP, 1994.

Gourdon, Anne-Marie. *Théâtre, public, perception*. Paris: CNRS, 1982.

Gregory, Lady Augusta. *Lady Gregory's Journals, 1916–1930*, ed. Lennox Robinson New York: Macmillan, 1947.

———. *Our Irish Theatre*. 1913. Oxford UP, 1977.

Grene, David H., and Edward M. Stephens. *J. M. Synge, 1871–1909*. Rev. ed. New York UP, 1989.

Grimm, Jürgen. *Das avantgardistische Theater Frankreichs, 1895–1930*. Munich: Beck, 1982.

Gurr, Andrew. *Playgoing in Shakespeare's London*. 2nd ed. Cambridge UP, 1996.

Handke, Peter. *Kaspar and Other Plays*. Trans. Michael Roloff. New York: Farrar, Straus and Giroux, 1969.

———. *Stücke 1*. Frankfurt: Suhrkamp, 1972.

Harrington, John P. *The Irish Play on the New York Stage, 1874–1966*. UP of Kentucky, 1997.

Hauptmann, Gerhart. *Notiz-Kalender 1889 bis 1891*. Ed. Martin Machatzke. Frankfurt: Propyläen, 1982.

———. *Vor Sonnenaufgang. Soziales Drama*. Frankfurt: Ullstein, 1959.

Hays, Michael. *The Public and Performance: Essays in the History of French and German Theatre, 1871–1900*. Ann Arbor: UMI Research Press, 1981.

Hecht, Werner, ed. *Brechts Theorie des Theaters*. Frankfurt: Suhrkamp, 1986.

———. *Brechts Weg zum epischen Theater*. Berlin: Henschel, 1962.

Hemmings, F. W. J. *Theatre and State in France, 1760–1905*. Cambridge UP, 1994.

———. *The Theatre Industry in Nineteenth-Century France*. Cambridge UP, 1993.

Hermand, Jost, and Frank Trommler. *Die Kultur der Weimarer Republik*. Munich: Fischer, 1978.

Hern, Nicholas. *Peter Handke: Theatre and Anti-Theatre*. New York: Ungar, 1972.

Hilscher, Eberhard. *Gerhart Hauptmann: Leben und Werk*. Frankfurt: Athenäum, 1988.

Hogan, Robert, and Richard Burnham. *The Years of O'Casey, 1921–1926: a Documentary History*. U of Delaware P, 1992.

Hogan, Robert, and James Kilroy. *The Abbey Theatre: the Years of Synge, 1905–1909*. Dublin: Dolmen, 1978.

———. *The Irish Literary Theatre: 1899–1901*. Dublin: Dolmen, 1975.

Holloway, Joseph. *Joseph Holloway's Abbey Theatre*. Ed. Robert Hogan and Michael O'Neill. Southern Illinois UP, 1967.

Hughes, Leo. *The Drama's Patrons: A Study of the Eighteenth-Century London Audience*. U of Texas P, 1971.

Hugo, Victor. *Hernani*. Ed. Pierre Richard and Gérard Sablayrolles. Paris: Classiques Larousse, 1971.

Hunt, Hugh. *The Abbey: Ireland's National Theatre, 1904–1979*. Columbia UP, 1979.

Ihering, Herbert. *Bertolt Brecht hat das dichterische Antlitz Deutschlands verändert*. Ed. Klaus Völker. Munich: Kindler, 1980.

Innes, Christopher. *Avant Garde Theatre 1892–1992*. London & New York: Routledge, 1993.

Jackson, Russell. *Victorian Theatre: the Theatre in its Time*. Franklin, NY: New Amsterdam, 1989.

Jaron, Norbert, Renate Möhrmann, and Hedwig Müller, eds. *Berlin—Theater der Jahrhundertwende. Bühnengeschichte der Reichshauptstadt im Spiegel der Kritik (1889–1914)*. Tübingen: Niemeyer, 1986.

Jarry, Alfred. *Ubu*. Ed. Noël Arnaud and Henri Bordillon. Paris: Gallimard Folio, 1978.

————. *Ubu Roi.* Trans. Barbara Wright. New York: New Directions, 1961.

Jasper, Gertrude. *Adventure in the Theatre: Lugné-Poë and the Théâtre de l'Oeuvre to 1899.* Rutgers UP, 1947.

Jauss, Hans Robert. *Toward an Aesthetic of Reception.* Trans. Timothy Bahti. U of Minnesota P, 1982.

Johnson, James H. *Listening in Paris: A Cultural History.* U of California P, 1995.

Joost, Jörg-Wilhelm, Klaus-Detlef Müller, and Michael Voges. *Bertolt Brecht: Epoche— Werk—Wirkung.* Munich: Beck, 1985.

Kavanagh, Peter. *The Story of the Abbey Theatre.* New York: Devin-Adair, 1950.

Kershaw, Baz. *The Radical in Performance: Between Brecht and Baudrillard.* London: Routledge, 1999.

Kiberd, Declan. *Synge and the Irish language.* Totowa, NJ: Roman and Littlefield, 1979.

Kilroy, James. *The 'Playboy' Riots.* Dublin: Dolmen, 1971.

Klotz, Volker. *Dramaturgie des Publikums.* Munich: Hanser, 1976.

Knopf, Jan. *Brecht-Handbuch. Theater. Eine Ästhetik der Widersprüche.* Stuttgart: Metzler, 1980.

Krabiel, Klaus-Dieter. *Brechts Lehrstücke.* Stuttgart: Metzler, 1993.

Krause, David. *Sean O'Casey: the Man and his Work.* 2nd ed. New York: Macmillan, 1975.

Krause, David, and Ronald Ayling, eds. *Sean O'Casey: Centenary Essays.* Totowa, NJ: Barnes & Noble, 1980.

Leppmann, Wolfgang. *Gerhart Hauptmann: Leben, Werk und Zeit.* Bern: Scherz, 1986.

Londré, Felicia Hardison. *The History of World Theater: from the English Restoration to the Present.* New York: Continuum, 1991.

Lough, John. *Paris Theatre Audiences in the Seventeenth and Eighteenth Centuries.* Oxford UP, 1957.

Lowery, Robert G. *A Whirlwind in Dublin: The Plough and the Stars Riots.* Westport, CT: Greenwood, 1984.

Lugné-Poe, Aurélien. *Acrobaties.* Vol. 2 of *La Parade.* 4 vols. Paris: Gallimard, 1931– 33.

Lynch, James J. *Box, Pit and Gallery: Stage and Society in Johnson's London.* U of California P, 1953.

Lyons, F. S. L. *Culture and Anarchy in Ireland.* Oxford UP, 1979.

Mackintosh, Iain. *Architecture, Actor and Audience.* London & New York: Routledge, 1992.

Mahal, Günther. *Der Naturalismus.* Munich: Fink, 1975.

Malone, Maureen. *The Plays of Sean O'Casey.* Southern Illinois UP, 1969.

Marshall, Alan. *The German Naturalists and Gerhart Hauptmann: Reception and Influence.* Frankfurt: Lang, 1982.

Mikhail, E. H., ed. *J. M. Synge: Interviews and Recollections.* London: Macmillan, 1977.

Milfull, John. *From Baal to Keuner. The 'Second Optimism' of Bertolt Brecht.* Bern/ Frankfurt: Lang, 1974.

Miller, Anna Irene. *The Independent Theatre in Europe: 1887 to the Present.* New York: Long & Smith, 1931.

Mittman, Barbara G. *Spectators on the Stage in the Seventeenth and Eighteenth Centuries.* Ann Arbor: UMI Research P, 1984.

Mullin, Daniel C. *The Development of the Playhouse: A Survey of Architecture from the Renaissance to the Present*. U of California P, 1970.

Nagler, Alois M. *Sources of Theatrical History*. New York: Theatre Annual, 1952.

Needle, Jan, and Peter Thomson. *Brecht*. U of Chicago P, 1981.

Nicoll, Allardyce. *The Garrick Stage: Theatres and Audience in the Eighteenth Century*. U of Georgia P, 1980.

Niessen, Carl. *Brecht auf der Bühne*. Cologne: Institut für Theaterwissenschaft, 1959.

O'Brien, Joseph. *'Dear, Dirty Dublin'*. U of California P, 1982.

O'Casey, Sean. *Inishfallen, Fare Thee Well*. Vol. 2 of *Mirror in My House* [1949]. New York: Macmillan, 1956.

———. *Three Plays*. New York: St. Martin's, 1957.

O'Driscoll, Robert, ed. *Theatre and Nationalism in Twentieth-Century Ireland*. U of Toronto P, 1971.

O'hAodha, Micheál. *Theatre in Ireland*. Totowa, NJ: Roman and Littlefield, 1974.

Osborne, John. *The Naturalist Drama in Germany*. Manchester UP, 1971.

Panofsky, Walter. *Protest in der Oper: Das provokative Musiktheater der zwanziger Jahre*. Munich: Laokoon, 1966.

Patterson, Michael. *The Revolution in German Theatre, 1900–1933*. London: Routledge & Kegan Paul, 1981.

Pedicord, Harry W. *The Theatrical Public in the Time of Garrick*. New York: King's Crown Press, 1954.

Peter, René. *Le Théâtre et la vie sous la troisième république*. 2 vols. Paris: Marchot, 1945.

Pick, John. *The West End: Mismanagement and Snobbery*. Eastbourne, UK: John Offord, 1983.

Postlewait, Thomas, and Bruce A. McConachie, eds. *Interpreting the Theatrical Past: Essays in the Historiography of Performance*. U of Iowa P, 1989.

Rachilde. *Alfred Jarry, ou le Surmâle de lettres*. Paris: B. Grasset, 1928.

Rebellato, Dan. *1956 And All That: The Making of Modern British Drama*. London: Routledge, 1999.

Robichez, Jacques. *Le Symbolisme au théâtre: Lugné-Poe et les débuts de l'Oeuvre*. Paris: L'Arche, 1957.

Roose-Evans, James. *Experimental Theater: From Stanislavsky to Peter Brook*. New York: Universe, 1984.

Rühle, Günther. *Theater für die Republik, 1917–1933, im Spiegel der Kritik*. Frankfurt: S. Fischer, 1967.

Saddlemyer, Ann, ed. *Theatre Business: the Correspondence of the first Abbey Theatre Directors: W. B. Yeats, Lady Gregory and J. M. Synge*. Penn State UP, 1982.

Sanders, Ronald. *The Days Grow Short: The Life and Music of Kurt Weill*. New York: Holt, Rinehart and Winston, 1980.

Scharang, Michael, ed. *Über Peter Handke*. Frankfurt: Suhrkamp, 1972.

Schechter, Joel. *Durov's Pig: Clowns, Politics and Theatre*. New York: Theatre Communications Group, 1985.

Schlenther, Paul. *Wozu der Lärm? Genesis der Freien Bühne*. Berlin: S. Fischer, 1889.

Schley, Gernot. *Die Freie Bühne in Berlin*. Berlin: Haude & Spenersche Verlagsbuchhandlung, 1967.

Schlueter, June. *The Plays and Novels of Peter Handke*. U of Pittsburgh P, 1981.

Schumacher, Claude. *Alfred Jarry and Guillaume Apollinaire*. Basingstoke: Macmillan, 1984.

Schumacher, Ernst. *Die dramatischen Versuche Bertolt Brechts 1919–1933*. Berlin: Rütten & Loening, 1955.

Sennett, Richard. *The Fall of Public Man*. New York: Norton, 1976.

Shattuck, Roger. *The Banquet Years: The Arts in France, 1885–1918*. Rev. ed. New York: Random House, 1967.

Speirs, Ronald. *Brecht's Early Plays*. London: Macmillan, 1982.

Sprengel, Peter. *Gerhart Hauptmann: Epoche—Werk—Wirkung*. Munich: Beck, 1984.

Stallybrass, Peter, and Allon White. *The Politics and Poetics of Transgression*. Cornell UP, 1986.

Steinweg, Reiner. *Das Lehrstück. Brechts Theorie einer politisch-ästhetischen Erziehung*. Stuttgart: Metzler, 1972.

Styan, J. L. *Drama, Stage and Audience*. Cambridge UP, 1975.

———. *Modern Drama in Theory and Practice*. 3 vols. Cambridge UP, 1981.

Suvin, Darko. *To Brecht and Beyond: Soundings in Modern Dramaturgy*. Brighton: Harvester, 1984.

Synge, John Millington. *The Playboy of the Western World*. Ed. Malcolm Kelsall. Rev. ed. London: A & C Black, 1994.

Szondi, Peter. *Die Theorie des modernen Dramas*. Rev. ed. Frankfurt: Suhrkamp, 1963.

Taylor, George. *Players and performances in the Victorian theatre*. Manchester UP, 1989.

Taylor, Ronald. *Literature and Society in Germany 1918–1945*. Brighton: Harverster, 1980.

Theater in der Weimarer Republik. Berlin: Kunstamt Kreuzberg & Institut für Theaterwissenschaft der Universität Köln, 1977.

Das Theater und sein Publikum. Vienna: Institut für Publikumsforschung, 1977.

Thomson, Peter, and Glendyr Sacks, eds. *The Cambridge Companion to Brecht*. Cambridge UP, 1994.

Trotter, Mary. *Ireland's National Theaters: Political Performance and the Origins of the Irish Dramatic Movement*. Syracuse UP, 2001.

Voigts, Manfred. *Brechts Theaterkonzeptionen. Entstehung und Entfaltung bis 1931*. Munich: Fink, 1977.

Völker, Klaus. *Bertolt Brecht: Eine Biographie*. Munich: Hanser, 1976.

———. *Brecht-Chronik: Daten zu Leben und Werk*. Munich: Hanser, 1971.

Wagner, Gottfried. *Weill und Brecht: Das musikalische Zeittheater*. Munich: Kindler, 1977.

Watt, Stephen. *Joyce, O'Casey, and the Irish Popular Theatre*. Syracuse UP, 1991.

Weber, Eugen. *France, Fin de Siècle*. Cambridge: Belknap Press of Harvard UP, 1986.

Weill, Kurt. *Ausgewählte Schriften*. Ed. David Drew. Frankfurt: Suhrkamp, 1976.

Welch, Robert. *The Abbey Theatre, 1899–1999: Form and Pressure*. Oxford UP, 1999.

Wickham, Glynne. *A History of the Theatre*. Cambridge UP, 1992.

Wiles, Timothy J. *The Theater Event: Modern Theories of Performance*. U of Chicago P, 1980.

Willett, John. *Brecht in Context*. London: Methuen, 1984.

———, ed. *Brecht on Theatre: The Development of an Aesthetic*. New York: Hill and Wang, 1964.

———. *The New Sobriety: Art & Politics in the Weimar Period*. New York: Pantheon, 1978.

———. *The Theatre of Bertolt Brecht*. Rev. ed. New York: New Directions, 1968.

————. *The Theatre of the Weimar Republic*. New York/London: Holmes & Meier, 1988.

Williams, Raymond. *Drama from Ibsen to Brecht*. New York: Oxford UP, 1968.

Witt, Hubert, ed. *Erinnerungen an Brecht*, Leipzig: Reclam, 1964.

Worthen, William B. *The Idea of the Actor: Drama and the Ethics of Performance*. Princeton UP, 1992.

Wyss, Monika, ed. *Brecht in der Kritik*. Munich: Kindler, 1977.

Yeats, William Butler. *Autobiographies*. London: Macmillan, 1955.

Index

About the Author

NEIL BLACKADDER is Assistant Professor of Theatre at Knox College, where he teaches dramatic literature, theatre history, and dramaturgy. His work has appeared in *New Theatre Quarterly*, *Theatre History Studies*, and *American Theatre*.